GOING DARK

A GABRIEL JETS NOVEL

GOING
DARK

JOLENE GRACE

bhc
press™

Livonia, Michigan

Editor: Chelsea Cambeis

Epigraph taken from *The Prince* by Niccolò Machiavelli. Public Domain.

GOING DARK

Copyright © 2019 Jolene Grace

Published by BHC Press

Library of Congress Control Number: 2019947296

ISBN: 978-1-64397-048-6 (Hardcover)
ISBN: 978-1-64397-049-3 (Softcover)
ISBN: 978-1-64397-050-9 (Ebook)

For information, write:
BHC Press
885 Penniman #5505
Plymouth, MI 48170

Visit the publisher:
www.bhcpress.com

To my husband, Branden,
for his support and encouragement
and our daughters.

Never attempt to win by force, what can be won by deception.
— Machiavelli, *The Prince* —

GOING DARK

1

Amelia Sinclair was running late for work. She drove through the nearly empty streets of Manhattan, stomping on the brakes at the red lights. She neared East Forty-Second Street and prepared to turn right. The traffic light changed from yellow to red, and she came to a sudden halt, testing the limits of her 2010 minivan.

Come on. Turn to green. She wheezed under her breath. The dashboard clock read 3:15 a.m. Amelia considered running the light, but a group of rowdy men, liquored up, stumbled on the road, pushing and shoving one another. Following their movements with her eyes, her mind caught her by surprise as it replayed Frank Sinatra's "New York, New York." The city that never sleeps was a far cry from its glory days. Overcrowded, noisy, and dirty, she bet Sinatra would sing a different tune if alive.

A honk blared behind her. She stepped on the gas, and the minivan's engine roared. *Did the light change to green?* She hoped.

Going through the motions of daily life, Amelia parked the minivan in the underground garage, a preferred parking spot of the United Nations employees. She squeezed the car between a Mercedes and a BMW, a rarity, because the foreign dignitaries were chauffeured in unmarked cars, stashed in parking lots with security guards around the clock.

She checked her watch. *Pushing 3:30. I'm late.* And of all days, today she couldn't afford that. Armed with her press credentials, laptop bag, and umbrella, Amelia locked the car and sped up toward the employee entrance.

The lot felt cold and windy. Even with cars packed in rows, not a soul in sight. Amelia squeezed her bag as if bracing herself as to what laid ahead. She reached the entrance and stepped in, the air chilled from the powerful AC. She shivered. Four years working at the UN and she wasn't fully acclimated to the morgue-like temperatures of the building.

Mike, the security guy at the desk, lifted his head to find out who was walking in. Recognizing the familiar face, he took off his reading glasses and tossed aside the morning edition of *The New York Times*.

"Hi Mike." Amelia rummaged through her bag, searching.

"Miss Sinclair. Good to see you. Is it still raining out?"

"It stopped. Thank God." Amelia was losing the battle with her bag. "I had it. I swear I had my badge. Mike, I'm going crazy."

Mike tilted his head to one side, gave a crooked smile, and pointed to her pocket. "I think you better check your left pocket."

Amelia returned a doubtful look as her left hand went for the pocket. Relieved, she retrieved her picture credentials. It read "CWG Chief Foreign Liaison."

Mike scanned it through the system and motioned her to move forward through the metal detector.

"The building's quiet today?" Amelia gathered her belongings from the belt after the machine was done scanning them, making sure she wasn't bringing a gun inside.

"Not a peep."

With that, their conversation reached its limit. She racked her brain to come up with something warm and friendly to say. She'd known Mike since her first day on the job, but had said no more than two words to him. *Why do it today?* She was elbow-deep in work: phone calls to make, B-rolls to cut—no time for small talk. His puppy-like eyes giddily waited for her to prolong the chit-chat. Bag across her shoulder, ready to leave, Amelia saw a photo of a teenager, no older than sixteen, proudly perched up on his beat-up desk.

"Is that your boy?" she heard herself say.

The security guard's face lit up, and his lips stretched in a wide smile. "Mike Junior. He's a few years older than when we took this photo. Headed to SUNY, freshman in the spring."

Amelia nodded approvingly. "I better get going." With that, she headed to the "fishbowl."

Being a reporter, representing one of the top four networks, meant nothing to the UN bigwigs. The journalists were pushed to the bottom floor, below the security guards and custodian locker rooms. The old steam room at the east corner of the building was fashioned in the 70s as the media quarters. The UN's attempt to keep these pesky journo types away from the action, away from getting their scoop.

In summer, the fishbowl was hot, unbearable. In winter, same. Bodies pressed tightly together, fighting for elbow room; the few lucky enough to have a permanent desk grew the envy of the rest. More time was spent discussing the seating arrangements than an ongoing crisis in a foreign country.

Amelia hit the light switch. The ceiling fluorescent lights came on, drowning the fishbowl in harsh brightness. She squinted to adjust her sight. At her computer desk, she wiggled the mouse to wake up the computer screen. The best-case scenario, she'd see no urgent messages, but Murphy's Law could tip the scales the other way. The computer came to life. The breaking news ticker scrolled at the top, showing that the rest of the world was relatively peaceful at the moment. Checking her email could wait a moment. First, coffee.

In a corner, tucked away next to an exposed steam pipe, was the coffee station. More news tips and gossip happened here than in any other room in the UN. She discarded the coffee filter, changed the water, and pressed the ON button. Coffee started to drip, filling the canister, teasing Amelia's soul. Her wanting eyes pulled away from the drip and zoomed in on the working TV monitors above. The voices of ABC, CBS, her own network, and NBC were in a shouting match for her attention. Each was reporting on the latest White House scandal, a story bound to dominate the news cycle, a story Amelia had no stake in. The coffeemaker beeped and Amelia hungrily poured the bitter mixture in a mug. After a long inhale, she found herself at her desk, fingers blazing on the keyboard. She recalled the employee email page when the desk phone blinked.

"Amelia." She picked up on the first ring.

"Darling." A female with a heavy British accent sounded off in the receiver.

"Sybil? Finally back at work? You got tired of the sunshine in the Bahamas?"

"Don't be ridiculous. Give me a fruity drink with an umbrella, foreign men in speedos, and the beach—baby, I'm never coming back."

"But here you are—what happened?"

"Vacation got cut short. Those bastards on the foreign desk can't wipe their twats without me." Sybil meant what she said.

"You're irreplaceable."

"I'm a workhorse. They'll work me till I drop dead, right here at this desk."

Amelia made no point to argue. "That much is true."

"Child, take it from me. Get out of this hell, before it's too late. No rainbows in this biz."

"You're feeling grim." Amelia minimized the email page and opened the CWG employee portal, looking for internal notes from Sybil, figuring out the purpose of the call, without having to ask. She found none.

"Your boss, Harold, wants video of the rape story. The girl in India, gang-raped on the bus. We got our hands on cell phone footage. Not of the actual..." She didn't finish. She didn't have to. Amelia understood that if such video existed, it would be shared on social media, but completely unacceptable to broadcast over Western channels.

"I'm queuing the coordinates. Satellite channel AB is open. Read me the numbers when you have them."

"Hold on. I got them—75.03.78.111.000."

Amelia inputted the numbers Sybil gave her in the system, and her monitor connected to the overseas foreign desk. It turned from black to the test color pattern, then the footage was transmitted and recorded by Amelia's equipment.

While it played out, Sybil resumed the conversation. "You're doing a story on the press conference?"

"I'm planning on it. I doubt management cares about a delegation returning from Russia. Much ado about nothing."

The two laughed. "Yeah, much ado about nothing," Sybil repeated.

Amelia returned her attention to her email page. The video would take several more minutes to play over the satellites. She muted Sybil, who was silent at the moment.

The internet connected and displayed her inbox. She briefly took her eyes off the computer and shifted them to the TV monitor; the system was still going on. From the corner of her eyes, she spotted the top email. It was different from the rest; she didn't like the look of it. The subject line was in Arabic and translated to Amelia Sinclair.

Hesitant, Amelia hovered over it with the cursor. *Should she open it?*

"Kid, did you get the last transmission?" Sybil's voice echoed, startling Amelia.

She gasped, taking her hands off the computer, and wheeled her chair away from the desk.

She collected herself, cutting the connection to the satellite and returning to the line. "Yep. Got it." She ended the call without another word.

Alarmed by the unopened email, Amelia stood and poked her surroundings with probing eyes. Her breath slowed down, and she put a lid on her jilted nerves.

She went ahead and pressed on the subject line. A link in the body paragraph prompted her to take further actions. She clicked again and a new window booted. A grainy, shaky video began to play in a loop. She squinted. A concerned gut feeling intensified in the pit of her stomach as she watched the images replay. By the fourth play, familiar faces flashed in front of her. Amelia's face grew pale, long. Her biggest nightmare was unfolding in thirty seconds of footage. Separated by thousands of miles, her hands were tied behind her back. Amelia shook like a tree branch in January.

Four journalists—Bo Breeks, Tom Seed, Dustin Mark, and Joseph Alexander, whom she knew personally—were pushed, shoved, and roughed up by masked assailants. She pressed on the stop button countless times, but it was of no use. The system didn't respond. It kept playing.

Amelia buried her head in her hands, eyes locked to the ground, and repeated, "No one knew they were in Syria. No one knew." Evidently, by the video, someone had found out and was preparing to expose their secret.

2

Panic washed over her. Eyes on the screen, Amelia picked up the phone and dialed a number. Then waited. *"The number you're trying to reach has been disconnected,"* a female voice announced in both Farsi and English.

She slammed the phone. Her source in Damascus couldn't be reached. Without his help, she didn't have a way to verify the authenticity of the vid. Amelia exited out of the web portal. She probed the AP Breaking News tracker for a sign that the damaging material was leaked to the media. Encouraged by the lack of evidence to support that, Amelia nervously tapped her fingers on the desk as she considered her next move. The face of Bo, her friend and mentor, flashed in front of her eyes. Seeing him helpless and defenseless in the images unnerved her to the core. The lives of three others and Bo hung on by a thread.

Contingencies were put in place to safeguard the journalists, if the plan failed. For starters, her source in Damascus should have made contact with the team when they landed. She glanced at the clock to verify her timeline—eighteen hours had passed since their commercial flight landed.

The source was to meet them at the airport, brief them on the situation on the ground, then send a message to Amelia if danger was lurking. *Did the meeting happen?* No message meant the plan was a go. Without being able to tell the time of the day, or where the four were ambushed, Amelia was stuck and could only go on those thirty seconds of low-quality video.

Exasperated, Amelia walked over to the flat screens and flipped through the channels, searching for a story coming from Syria. She could think of a million ways the lives of the four could play out—kidnapped, tortured, held for ransom. The one option Amelia didn't dare to think was they could be dead by now.

ABC showed an ongoing police car chase in Mississippi, CBS replayed the newscast from the night before, and CWG opened the early morning show with a Miss Universe interview. Syria was not on their radar. Four Western journalists missing was not on their radar either. She hated to admit it, but by the look of it, the video was meant for her eyes only. With that revelation, Amelia returned to her desk, and her body dropped in the chair. She reached for the phone a second time. Another man, however, picked up.

3

A voice came over the line, sounding exhausted. "Yep?" The man sounded off.

"Harold, it's Amelia. We've got a situation."

A brief silence followed. "I'm listening."

"It's the four. Someone knows about them. They've been ambushed." She added, "I think."

Speaking rapidly, the voice gave instruction. "Amelia, here's what I want you to do. Get off the phone and meet me at CWG. How fast can you get here?"

"Twenty minutes, tops."

She heard static on the line, muffled sounds. "That should work. Make sure you don't talk to anyone else. Okay?" He fired off, "It's imperative that you don't say a word before we've got the chance to meet. Okay?"

Amelia was listening, but her thoughts ran wild.

"You with me?"

"I...they...how could this happen?"

He grunted in the receiver. "What difference does it make? Get to CWG." The line went dead.

Paralyzed by fear, Amelia stared at the phone. The conversation with her executive producer sunk in.

She told herself to hurry, but her hand on the mouse hit play once again. It started back on. Same pixelated quality, no sound, hard to distinguish shapes and faces. Amelia pressed pause before the image faded to black, slowly dragged it back a frame, then another frame. Her face grimaced, and her burrow hiked at the image frozen on the screen. She spotted a window. *Okay.* Using a bit of deduction, that meant the four were jumped inside. *Maybe in their hotel room?* The tidbit opened the door to more questions. *Why ambush a group of Western journalists in a hotel?*

Amelia reserved their rooms, personally, at the Hilton International Hotel. Her laptop bag lay on the floor. She picked it up and pulled out a planner and scanned through the pages. Between paid bills, bills to pay, and doctor appointments, she found what she was looking for—a telephone number, beginning with +96311, Damascus's area code. She went ahead and dialed Hilton International, rehearsing what to say to the receptionist. Her lips quivered at the prerecorded message: "The number you're trying to reach is no longer in service." She hung up before the message finished playing in English.

Damascus was under a siege. For months, a steady stream of reports painted a picture to the rest of the world of a country in deep civil conflict. A political power threatened by a sect using religion as a false pretext to attack, kill, and destroy. The Syrian president was not an ally to the US but not a foe either. Amelia couldn't find the rationale on why he would give the orders to attack the journalists. There must be another explanation.

Keeping the still image on the screen, Amelia called up a web browser and navigated to a page in Farsi. Underground bloggers, armed with cell phones and weak internet connection, were filing witness accounts of military movements on the ground in Syria as a warning to their countrymen. She should have checked their latest updates first, and not relied on the Western media.

The blog on the top of the page was uploaded at 01:23 a.m. local time—a series of Instagram videos of refugees lugging kids, bags, and food provisions, crossing the border between Syria and Turkey, searching for a safe haven, a shield from the gunfights and violence. She scrolled through the photos of hallow faces, stained in muck, vacant eyes, and terrified expressions. Mothers dragging children twisted in sobs, fathers bent under the weight of sacks with belongings packed in the heat of fleeing a war zone. Her heart cracked for them. Yesterday, they were living a life in a country they'd known since birth; today, that home feeling was ripped from underneath them. Tomorrow, they'd be nomads without a land to call their own.

Her gaze drifted away from the post and to the framed photos on her desk. She held onto her daughter, barely two years old in the picture, with the same intensity as these women. Her daughter, Ava, was born out of wedlock, the fruit of passion and lust, an adventure short-lived in a period of Amelia's life plagued by uncertainties. Before Ava came along, Amelia didn't consider having children. Her work and career were her life's purpose. But children, they change everything. Guilt beamed on her face from feeling relieved that she could go home at the end of the day. Ava had a mother. But the whereabouts of the four—they were sons, brothers, husbands, friends—were a mystery, like that video.

Since 2009, after the murders of two high-profile American journalists in Iraq, the four networks came to a conclusion that it was too risky to send in their own. Footage of the frontlines was badly needed, so they resorted to hire freelancers to go in the war zones, chasing the stories and a payoff. Amelia, Frost, and the rest couldn't trust a hired hand with this project. A lot rode on it. Precisely why they opted to keep it under a tight lid.

CWG. Amelia gasped. The upper management had to be notified of the missing four. The shit storm was about to snowball, with catastrophic consequences.

She peeled herself off the chair. She better get on with it and not make Frost wait. Amelia forced a shut-off of the computer system and picked up her laptop bag, but left the umbrella behind. On her way out, she paused and looked at the empty desks on either side of hers. On the left, Jack Sullivan filed reports for NPR; on her right was Ivan, reporting for the *Guardian.* She could write a note to either. Then Frost's voice sounded in her ears: *speak to no one.* The note, the explanation, would have to wait. Amelia headed for the door and cut the lights off. The fishbowl returned to darkness.

Outside the United Nations, under the heavy flags that adorned the main entrance, Amelia checked the time on her smartphone—4:15. CWG was twenty blocks away from East Forty-Second. Even with light traffic, if she drove, a car accident or a road closure could delay her. The subway was her best and safest option, Amelia concluded.

At Grand Central, she bought a one-way ticket and hopped on train seven. The car was halfway full with early-bird commuters. A man in rags had stretched out across several seats, sleeping, undisturbed by the rest of the passengers. Amelia picked a seat on the other side of the car and sat across from a frail woman with headphones and a Walkman in her lap. Amelia did a double take at the Walkman, surprised to see the working CD player. The old lady studied Amelia with brown beady eyes, refusing to break eye contact. The train doors closed. The woman stubbornly stared at Amelia, who settled in to take the longest subway ride of her life. By Fifty-First, the old shrew had dozed off, leaving Amelia alone to sort through her thoughts and put them in order.

The train moved again. Amelia took her cell phone from her coat jacket and let it rest in her lap. She debated whether to watch the video again, to keep it fresh in her memory, though she doubted she'd ever be able to forget it. In the midst of indecision, her fingers were a step ahead of her. She swiped the screen and went straight to the email app. At the top of her inbox was the email; no other new messages. Against her better judgment, Amelia pressed on the link. The vid began to play.

By the shakiness of it, Amelia believed it was recorded with a hand-held cell phone. A light shined in Tom Seed's face for a mere second, before his captors pushed the camera away. The light was brighter, more yellow and orange than natural light. Maybe a flashlight, or something similar; it came from an object and not the sun. She calculated the time difference. Syria was seven hours ahead. Amelia knew that their Lufthansa commercial flight arrived without delays. She'd verified that the night before she left work, expecting not to hear from the team for twenty-four to forty-eight hours, depending on the situation on the ground. Following that train of thought, the team put boots on the ground in Damascus a little after 6:30 p.m., give or take forty minutes to go through customs.

Her subway ride made a stop, breaking her concentration. She turned to the window to see what stop she was on. 66th, a sign read. Her stop. *Damn it.* Amelia hissed.

"Hold it! Hold the door, please," she yelled at a group of passengers, who ignored her.

As the doors began to close, she threw her arm in between, triggering the automatic motion detector. The doors slowly returned to their original position, allowing Amelia to get off.

As she rushed out of the underground station, the timeline circled back in her mind. The kidnappers could have snatched the four at any point after 6:30. The window of opportunity was too wide, and Amelia lacked leads to bridge the gap.

There was one more possibility that Amelia thought about, a possibility that was out there. The video showed the four taken against their wills. The video didn't show whether the kidnappers recognized their targets. *Were the four at the wrong place, at the wrong time? Was it mistaken identity?* Her gut feeling told her there was more to the video than met the eye.

4

The four unmarked Ford Explorers, with dark windows, zipped through the treacherous traffic of Washington, DC, leaving behind flustered commuters blaring their horns. In the backseat of the second Ford, Secretary of State Conrad Burks chased away a headache. He massaged the temples of his head, overworked by the demands of the job and the young administration of President Delay. A hundred days in, the White House spent its time putting fires on two fronts—domestic and international.

His hands relaxed to the side of his body when the convoy came to an abrupt stop on C Street. He threw on his suit jacket, then waited. Behind the tinted windows, he saw his Secret Service detail jump out on to the street, a formation of six agents. Two spread out to have a better view of the incoming traffic, and one stayed to the front of the second Ford; the rest split to clear the entrance to the Truman Building. When they determined the coast was secured, an agent gave a verbal command: "Go ahead."

Burks stepped on the wet pavement and surveyed his surroundings. The frequent trips abroad kept him away for prolonged periods. His body ached to stretch his legs. He lifted his head. Thick, thunderous clouds blocked the sunlight, predicting an imminent rainstorm. He was a man of impressive stature: tall, slender, muscular. His presence commanded respect.

Gone away to an international summit for the better part of last week, it felt good to be back. When he returned his eyes to the building, an agent stretched out a hand and handed Burks a briefcase. The politician nodded as a thank-you and headed for the entrance, marked Employees Only.

He'd brought news with him, certain to cause waves in Delay's White House. The international community was clear: they were watching, waiting for America to pull the trigger on an execution plan for Syria.

Blood was spilled, innocent lives lost in a senseless conflict. Refugees were scaling the European borders, demanding safe passage. World leaders looked to POTUS to lead the pack.

With the briefcase in hand, Burks rode the elevator, remembering where he'd stashed the aspirin. On the seventh floor, Missy Hobbs, his executive assistant, welcomed him back with a beaming face.

"Good morning, sir. Welcome back." The redhead flashed white teeth.

"Thank you. It's good to be back." Expecting an avalanche of messages, he inquired, "Urgent messages? White House first priority; the rest will wait."

Hobbs opened her mouth to speak.

The chirp of Burks's phone cut her short. "Hang on." He reached for the phone attached to his belt. Burks glanced at it, then realized he was checking the wrong phone. The other phone was in his inner coat pocket.

While he retrieved it, Hobbs said, "The White House called as you were pulling up."

Eyes locked on the screen, lower jaw tensed, Burks said, "I'm wanted in the Situation Room."

"I'll call down to your detail and have the car turn around."

Hobbs left his side while Burks walked in his office to steal a moment of privacy and find the aspirin. The massive oak desk was covered in paperwork, files, and random notes. Despite Hobbs's pleas to allow her to tidy up the space, Burks dismissed that idea.

"Missy, I exist in the uncertainty between chaos and order," he would proclaim, victorious, and stubbornly add more chaos to the pile of paper.

The leather chair absorbed the weight of his body and squeaked when Burks swirled from side to side, searching the drawers for headache pills.

Defeated, he yelled for Hobbs to come in. "Missy, I can't find anything in this damn mess."

"That seems unlikely."

Burks scowled. "You got something for a headache? My head is throbbing and is driving me nuts."

Hobbs maneuvered behind his desk, picked up a stack of papers, and pointed to the aspirin bottle. "The car's waiting. The CIA DCI called and asked to speak with you."

"Post called? What does he want?" Burks asked, more to himself than Hobbs. He popped two baby aspirins and chewed them.

The White House-encrypted cell phone beeped, a reminder that he was summoned to the Sit Room. With a last grunt, Burks cocked his head back and stood. "I'm out of here, Missy. Hold the fort while I'm gone."

Hobbs followed behind, notepad and pen in hand. "If DCI Post calls, what should I tell him?"

The mention of Post left a bitter taste in Burks's mouth, but his face bore no expression. "Yeah, right, Eugene. Call the CIA and get a hold of him. Transfer the call to the Ford."

The cell buzzed again. Burks hit the mute button without looking at the message. "Hold the nonessential calls. I've got a feeling it's going to be a long day at the White House. Call them, too, and tell them I'm on my way, before they send the generals to escort me personally." He flashed a smile, then he left the same way he came in.

5

At 4:28 a.m., the White House placed its first call of the day to POTUS's chief of staff, Robert McKaine, who picked up the phone and listened intently to the Sit Room watchman's urgent report. He gave precise instructions and hung up. An hour later, he was at his office, working at a fever speed, occasionally glancing at the clock on the wall, allowing the president an extra minute of shut-eye before he was looped in on the developing situation.

McKaine's smartphone rattled on, a blocked number. *The NSA.* He answered it. "Yeah, what's going on?"

The voice on the other end didn't hesitate. "It's time, Mr. McKaine. We must bring the president in. The Sit Room is ready to brief."

"Give me the latest," McKaine ordered.

"From the information coming in—we're most likely dealing with a hostage situation. Journalists in Syria. Our own."

"Shitheads." McKaine ended the call.

McKaine's blue eyes shifted around the room, his pulse pumping blood at a high rate. The Delay administration needed a win, a breeze under its wings to weather the ongoing slaughter on Capitol Hill. With Congress divided, POTUS's agenda was stale and crippled. Adding to the toxic mix, the disappearance of journalists in a country the US had no pull or allies to lobby on its behalf would give the appearance that Delay was a weak leader.

Cursing the journalists under his breath, McKaine waited for the line to connect him to the East Wing.

The president eventually answered. "This better be good," he barked in the receiver.

"Mr. President, I'm sorry to wake you, but the Sit Room needs you."

The mention of the Sit Room sobered the POTUS. "Twenty minutes, I'll be there." Then the phone went dead.

Next, McKaine called down to the kitchen staff, ordered coffee—black, one sugar—and sent it to the Oval Office. He thought about it for a moment and ordered a cup for himself, too. By the end of the day, he would consume enough coffee to give his own doctor a heart attack.

As Delay strolled in through the East doors of the Oval Office, an aide brought in the two cups of hot coffee. Its aroma scented the room. McKaine stood at the edge of the desk, feet planted on the plush carpet embroidered with a bald eagle, its head facing olive branches. Below the eagle, arched in wheat and cream color, a quote by FDR summarized this administration's attitude: "The only thing we have to fear is fear itself."

"Good morning, sir," McKaine said first.

Delay nodded and sipped the coffee. "Did we get everyone in the Sit Room?"

"Everyone but Burks. The secretary's on his way."

POTUS licked his lips, salivating over the first cup of the day. He looked over McKaine, locking eyes on the view outside the floor-to-ceiling windows. The Lincoln Memorial, built in direct view of the Oval Office, looked back at Delay.

"It's shaping up to be a gray morning," Delay predicted.

Distracted by his phone, McKaine missed the last part. He said, instead, "Conrad's in too. They're ready for us."

The president returned his attention to the chief of staff. "Let's not make them wait. A crisis awaits us."

6

Delay and McKaine finished off the coffees when they reached the Sit Room. McKaine keyed in the security code; the passcode was accepted, and the door automatically unlocked. POTUS surveyed the crowd. The room was packed; he recognized a few faces.

McKaine took his assigned seat, on the right of Delay. The president remained standing, as if he prepared to address the crowd. His eyes glided around the room, stopping at General Abbs's stone-cold face. The general wore his Navy Dress Blues. Medals adorned the front of the suit. They made eye contact.

With a nod, Delay allowed Abbs to do his thing. "Abbs—why don't you start. Give us the cut-and-dry."

"Certainly." Abbs cleared his throat, and an associate recalled stills on flat screens.

Bodies shuffled in chairs. Some averted their eyes away, the severity of the photos too much, too fast.

The general pointed with a laser pen to the screens and carried on. "This is the latest from the drone, sir. The eyewitness reports we collected have been contradicting, at best."

POTUS examined the intel at his disposal. Charcoaled buildings, demolished by a blast, held his interest. Next to him, McKaine had devoured the situation report and absorbed the hourly updates since the early call. POTUS was playing catch-up with the unfolding crisis. Asking the questions fell on his right-hand man.

"General, let's rewind. What are we looking at?"

"At approximately 6:40 local time, a bomb exploded in the Damascus Central Square." Abbs paused. No one asked for clarification, so he continued. "The bomb blast came from the southwest corner of the square. Judging by its magnitude—a VBIED, packed with C-4."

The photos changed. A new set showed a man cradling an infant's limp body, survivors scouting the debris, a slow fire finishing off a stroller.

Delay's hand clinched in a fist. "How many?" he asked in an even tone.

"Currently twenty-five. The phone lines went down. So did electricity in some parts of Damascus." Abbs shifted and shot a look at McKaine.

"There is more, Mr. President." McKaine took over, leaning forward. "Twenty minutes after the bomb, four US journalists were kidnapped from their hotel."

The general passed a map to Delay, who studied it.

"Hilton International was in the middle of the blast." McKaine pointed to a spot marked with a red dot.

"What's your working theory? A coincidence?" Delay split his attention between Abbs and McKaine.

"Unlikely," the general said.

"We believe the journalists were the intended target. The bomb—" McKaine stopped, choked up by words. "The bomb was the diversion. To get our attention. Taking four of our own is not good, showing us that *they're* willing to kill twenty-five of their own for four of ours."

POTUS dropped the map on the table, lower jaw tensed. He snapped his spine straight. "Which guerilla group is behind this?"

"I'm afraid we don't know, sir. Intel is slowly dripping." A voice cut in from behind Delay.

He didn't move from his seat. Delay recognized the voice belonging to DCI Eugene Post.

"The CIA's working on speeding up the process. It's worth noting, they, whoever they are, haven't released a video taking credit for the square blast."

"If such a video surfaces, I want it yanked off the net. The families of the four should be notified first. Not learn it from YouTube," Delay fired off to the room. "What's our next step? We must be doing more than collecting intelligence." The last part was meant as a vailed insult to Post.

"If I may add, Mr. President," Post slithered, "until we know for sure who kidnapped the Americans, I think the only thing left for us is to sit tight and wait. In my experience, sir, terrorists want—no, crave—attention. In the next few hours, we'll know for sure who's behind this."

Signaling the end to the Sit Room briefing, Delay stood and buttoned his suit. "McKaine, figure out which network the journalists belonged to and loop them in on the situation. Make sure Post's at that meeting too." He addressed the group. "I'm not about to face an angry group of journalists and tell them that the only thing we're doing is waiting for the terrorists to raise their hand."

To Abbs, Delay instructed, "Keep up the hourly updates." Then his eyes searched for a face—Burks's. "Burks, walk with me."

POTUS left the secured room, appalled by the barbarity. *Twenty-five of theirs for four of ours* played on in his mind.

• • • •

The CWG building was an impressive structure. It rose thirty-six floors off the ground, dwarfing its surroundings. Amelia rushed to reach the entrance, feeling sluggish. The adrenaline started to normalize in her system as the caffeine wore off. She would have to fuel up again. The phone in her back jean pocket buzzed. She saw Frost's name and answered, semi-irritated by the executive producer.

"How far are you?" Frost never gave her a chance to speak first.

"I'm walking in."

"Are you sure no one has seen the vid but you?"

Amelia rolled her eyes, glad he couldn't see her. "I'm sure. Or at least I haven't shared it with anyone. No way to tell what the sender intended to do with it," Amelia explained the obvious.

"Right. Right. Come straight to my office. I'm waiting." Harold got off as Amelia swiped her employee pass and took the elevator to the fourteenth floor.

Frost came from behind his desk, pulling Amelia in by the arm when she stepped in. The door slammed behind her, and she felt boxed in. A quick scan of the office. Same as the last time she was here. Four years ago, handing her resignation in. A pregnant chief foreign correspondent complicated the gig. Frost refused to let her go, releasing her from her contract, but persuading her to stay and work at the UN instead. She stopped her eyes on the glass case, awards and trophies neatly stacked. Two golden Emmy statues glistened under the spotlights. A bolt of regret stabbed her in the ribs—an Emmy she wouldn't receive as a UN story chaser.

"Good. You're here. Who saw you coming in?" Frost's voice snapped her back to reality.

"The security guard and the guy on domestic, browsing his Fantasy Football team."

"Is the vid on your laptop?"

"Uh-huh." Amelia dropped her bag and pulled her computer out.

"The sender sent it to your personal or professional email account?"

"Personal." The laptop was coming to life.

"That's odd. Why send it to that account? If the sender wanted you to go live with the vid..."

Amelia listened to his rationale, but her mind worked on a separate theory of the sender's motives. She had given the four her personal account as a backup. They could reach her day and night on it. Under the right pressure—*torture*, she scowled at that thought—any one of them could have given up her email address.

Staring back at the email page, she slung it around and shared it with Frost. He pointed to the words in Arabic. "This one?"

"Amelia Sinclair," she translated as she clicked to open the email.

"One mystery solved. He knows your name."

"That's one theory." What she wanted to say was, *Or someone gave it to him.*

Frost didn't wait for Amelia. He went ahead and double-clicked the link. The familiar page opened up, the vid playing on repeat.

"What's that?" Frost pointed to the header of the page. Bold letters in Farsi scrolled on the top.

Had it been there? Amelia couldn't recall seeing the banner before.

"Muslim Brotherhood," she translated.

They exchanged uneasy looks.

Frost watched the montage, then a second time, before he spoke. "Shame it's in poor quality. Can't tell what's what. Forget about looking for unique markers to give you a lead to go on." He'd reached the same conclusion as Amelia.

The first frame of the video showed a group of men dressed in black grabbing at a person. The smoke made it impossible to see a face. In a flash, Frost and Amelia saw Bo's bloodied face in the next frame, before the video cut back to the kidnappers shoving and pushing the other three journalists. The footage ended abruptly.

Amelia and Frost fell into silence. Frost clicked a command on the keyboard, zooming in on the footage. The closer he got, the more pixilated the video became, rendering it useless. Amelia stopped looking over his shoulder, attention focused on the news recap broadcasting on a TV screen in his office. A story played of a possible bomb explosion in Damascus Square.

"A toddler operates a cell phone camera better than that," Frost exclaimed, defeated.

"What do we do now, Harold?" Amelia stopped watching.

Eyes fastened on hers. "I've called help. A guy I met awhile back. We did a story on...he consulted."

"On?"

"Excuse me?"

"Consulted on what? You didn't finish?"

"The Central Intelligence Agency."

Amelia drew in a breath and held it in. "Jesus, Harold. You've lost the plot. The CIA—what's he gonna do?"

"You got a better idea? Call 911? 'Operator, I smuggled four journalists with fake papers into Syria. Did I mention they're kidnapped—can you help me?'"

"Not in those words. But, yeah, something along those lines." Amelia had to agree that her plan was flawed.

"Don't be naïve. Not long ago, you were a foreign correspondent. Remember Iraq?" His words moved at high speed. "Who pulled you out of a burning building in Baghdad? Who smuggled you to safety when the mujahideen started raining bullets in Jalalabad?"

Amelia knew the name; she knew it well. She saw his face in her memory, swimming to the surface. "Stop, please."

"Say his name, Amelia."

"Bo. His name is Bo."

Frost retreated. Amelia did the same.

"All I'm asking from you is to meet with the agent. Listen to his idea. If we don't like it, we'll go with your plan." Frost spoke, finger pointing to the paused vid. "So help us God, we must bring the four home."

7

Delay dropped in the chair behind his desk. Burks and McKaine sat on a sofa. The three were quiet, not discussing the elephant in the room. McKaine was the first to check his smartphone. Burks followed his lead. Delay rearranged a stack of paper, with no particular purpose. He skimmed through pollster data, showing his approval rating had dropped by a point overnight. A hundred days in his presidency, his popularity was riding on the coattail of right below fifty percent.

"We build this country so our people can be free," Delay managed to say. Burks squared his shoulders, listening. McKaine continued to fidget with his phone, having heard the speech before. "We fight wars, poverty, crimes. Americans die daily of the very things we fight. I have to ask, gentlemen, what are we doing to save their lives?"

With the corner of his eyes, Burks probed McKaine, who wasn't looking up. Pressured, Burks rattled off, "Sir, the State Department issued public warnings about traveling to Syria. We've explained to the public that if they chose to travel, we'll offer them limited help. I don't think this administration could have done anything else to prevent the four from traveling." His words, however, didn't reach POTUS. Delay was trashing the drawers, searching. The lack of nicotine was making him craw the walls. *One hundred and fucking fifty-five days without a cigarette.*

Unable to find a smoke, Delay massaged a stress-relief ball in the palms of his hands. He looked like a Rottweiler pacifying an urge.

"Bob, did you hear Eugene in the Sit Room? The nerve of this guy. I should fire him."

"You can't fire the DCI of the CIA, Mr. President. We've been over the reasons why." McKaine killed the smartphone and dropped it in a side pocket.

"No? I thought he, like you two, serve at the pleasure of the president."

"Both Republicans and Democrats love Post. He's the longest serving DCI in the CIA history. You fire him, we better pack our bags and board the White House." McKaine was the voice of reason. He leaned in. "Why kick that hornet's nest? We've got pressing issues, an agenda, a country to run. If the spooks want Post, then let them have him."

Burks wedged in a word. "Mr. President, I think while we're waiting for the CIA's initial threat assessment report, we should start working with our international allies. Find out if more journalists were abducted."

"Good idea. Keep Bob posted."

They prepared to wrap the meeting up, when Patricia Clark, the president's secretary, knocked on the door and popped her head in. "I'm sorry to interrupt. Director Post's on line two. He says it's urgent."

Delay held his attention on Burks. "Stick around to hear what he has to say." Facing Patricia, Delay instructed, "Send the call through."

Momentarily, the line on the desk phone blinked. McKaine and Burks stood up, next to the desk.

"You're on, Post. I'm with McKaine and Burks. We've got a minute. Make it count."

"I think we've hit a breakthrough. An executive producer placed a call to one of my own. He requested the two meet. The producer was elusive of the topic, but strongly hinted that he was in possession of a video depicting the kidnapping of Americans." Post slowed down, waited for a reaction; none followed, so he resumed. "My agent has agreed to a meet with the producer. In fact, he's en route."

Delay threw glances split between Burks and McKaine, waiting for the perfect opportunity to jump in and cut off Post. "That's excellent. McKaine has the lead on the journalists' fiasco. Report to him."

With Post off the phone, POTUS expressed his wishes. First to Burks: "Work our allies, see what they can come up with." Then, McKaine: "Keep an eye on Post. I don't trust the old son-of-you-know-what as far as I can throw him."

• • • •

In the back of his motorcade, Burks was relieved to be pulling away from 1600 Pennsylvania Avenue. He checked his phone with a stricken expression. The screen lit up with ten missed calls and eight voice mails, five of which were from Post's private number. He ran a hand over his silver hair, contemplating. The right thing to do was to return Post's calls, work together with him on sorting through the kidnappings. But Delay's treatment of Post had drawn a red line in the sand, and Burks didn't want to deal with their turf war. He slid the phone in his jacket, leaving the call back for a later time.

On the seventh floor of the Truman Building, the secretary of state summoned his staff in his office to fill them in. As the last person joined the rest, Burks began to explain, "In the Sit Room, the NSC briefed the president and me on a developing hostage situation. Four American journalists were kidnapped in Damascus last night." Burks's eyes moved from face to face. "The president has tasked me—us—with the responsibility of bringing in a tight circle of allies in the fold to help us. Needless to say, this is a nightmare from every angle. We must move with care and be delicate. Since the civil war in Syria is in full swing, I suspect we'll receive a push back from a number of countries. That should not deter us from serving the president and providing help to the White House."

No staffer attempted to speak but one, Deputy Assistant Matthew Parks.

"What about Saudi Arabia? The royal family has pull with the Syrian president. They can intervene on our behalf."

Burks considered the suggestion for a moment.

Missy Hobbs chimed in. "The Saudi king would be a problem. He's condemning the US military for failing to stop the female suicide bomber last month. She took out a significant number of Saudi Royal Guards."

"The Pentagon." Burks's face hardened.

Parks offered a back-door solution. "Prince Abdul Ahram Alammani. He'd help rally support for our military base in Kuwait."

"That won't be cheap. He's greedy. But might be our only way in." Burks warmed up to the idea of bringing the Saudis on board. "What options do we have on the table to pass a message to the prince, without tripping wires, wagging the tongues?"

An unexpected visitor brought the meeting to a halt. Post strolled in Burks's domain, confident, without his security detail.

Burks's backside was casually resting on his desk. The sight of Post in the State Department whipped him up. "DCI Post?"

"Mr. Secretary, I hope you won't object to my intrusion." Post maneuvered through the bodies, directly facing Burks.

"Everyone, the DCI and I have to go over things. Thanks for the great ideas. Make something happen by the end of the day."

The staffers whispered among one another as they headed out of the office. Burks and Post didn't move, eyes rigid with spite.

Burks motioned to the couch. "What brings you here, Eugene? Don't remember you recently visiting the State Department?"

"It's not like you to dodge phone calls," Post shot back, tie loose, ready to talk shop. "I won't take it personally, not yet at least." He held his gaze on Burks. "Listen, I'm a friend, and I've a vested interest to see this mess sorted out. I know what you're planning. I can't blame you. The

State Department is in a jam. A hostile country with a hostage situation—you're practically blindfolded."

"Go on."

"It's natural to reach out to the Saudis. I gotta warn you, Delay will be looking for blood when this house of cards falls apart. Kidnappings of this kind tend to drag on. Months. Think Iran, Afghanistan, Iraq—the CIA still has men rotting away in their hellholes, and we can't get them out." Post wet his lips. "Don't do it, Burks. The Saudis don't hold a key that's going to unlock that cell."

With a finger on his lips and legs crossed one over the other, Burks said, "We do nothing?"

Post swatted the air with his hand. "We do everything possible, of course. The CIA will get to the bottom of this. We aren't allowed time to work. Gathering intelligence is a form of art. Can't rush it."

"The president's expecting results, fast." Burks shook his head.

"The president's drafting his victory speech. His people are figuring out how to turn this into a victory to sell to the American people for his second term."

Burks didn't object. "I don't know how in the world, with the technology at our disposal, we don't know who took the damn word worms."

The DCI flicked a threatening look. "Cool it. The CIA isn't an almighty protector. We work in backwaters. Some places don't have running water, electricity—forget about wireless. Don't start me on Delay's proposed budget cuts. It's going to cripple the CIA for generations to come."

Burks had seen the budgetary proposal. Post had a right to be worried. "The Saudis are the safest bet." Burks changed topics.

"The prince? You can't be serious! He's a weasel. Won't do a fucking thing for us. Plus, you're racking your brains of how to pass a message to him."

"How can you possibly know that?"

"Come on. It's my job to know it. I'm a reasonable man and a patriot. So, I've brought you a gift."

"A gift?"

"A name that can help you."

"Why aren't you using that gift, then?"

"The CIA has plenty on its plate. And Delay asked you and McKaine to be the lead."

Burks waited to receive Post's offering.

"Khalib Osmani."

The name didn't sound familiar; a shadow of doubt ran across Burks's face. "Who's he?"

"The prince's first cousin, a general in the Royal Army. We've used him in the past."

"You trust him?"

Post fixed his tie. "No one can be trusted, Conrad, but he's the best fucking option right now." Post was on his feet. "The next time you decide to run your own covert ops, maybe you should consider looping me in, too. I can be a friend from time to time."

Burks slumped to one side in the chair, defeated by the conversation. *Had he misjudged Post's character?* Post was pressing on the doorknob. "Post?" Burks called out. "How do we get in touch with Osmani?"

Without looking back, Post returned, "Don't bother. The CIA's going to arrange that. When it's safe to pass your message, we'll let you know." One foot out the door, Post had the last word. "Keep in touch, Conrad."

8

The walls of the office began to close on Amelia. Frost pacing back and forth gave her motion sickness, too. She was going out of her mind, ready to snap.

"Did he say when he's gonna call back?" Amelia's question broke the monotony of Frost's rhythm.

"No. He said he'd call me when he secured a safe house for us to meet."
Amelia's stomach curled in a ball. She swallowed hard. "The wait is
killing me." She woke up the computer, preparing to watch the video.

"Don't do it."

"Why not?" Amelia ignored him and went ahead.

"Look behind you." Frost pointed to the glass framing his office,
overlooking the main news floor. Not an empty seat in sight.

"When did…" Amelia didn't finish.

"We need to get out of CWG."

"And go where?"

Frost thought about it for a beat. "A loft in Brooklyn. I own the
building. We're going to be safe there." Not giving Amelia an opportunity
to protest, he ordered, "Grab your bag and the laptop."

The breeze outside CWG felt good on Amelia's face. She breathed
in and held her breath. Frost took her by the elbow, and the two stepped
in unison.

"Traffic will be a nightmare, but we're going against it. If we're lucky,
forty minutes to Brooklyn. What do you think?"

Amelia wasn't thinking about the drive; he was squeezing too hard
with his grip.

In the car, Amelia rubbed her sore elbow as Frost navigated out of
the parking lot. He cut lanes, swerving in and out of traffic, coming too
close to bumpers. When they exited the highway, he adopted a safer distance; the speed dropped down too. Amelia blinked back tears, searching
for words, but they died in her throat.

Frost's phone chirped with an incoming call. Before picking it up, he
said, "It's him. Agent Jets."

Amelia was pale. The motion sickness had returned.

"Harold Frost speaking," Frost said, followed by silence. The man on
the other end was talking, but Amelia couldn't hear a word.

"Like I said—it's a video. I can't be sure. Judge for yourself when you
see it." More pausing. "I left CWG. I couldn't stick around any longer." Frost
glanced over to Amelia. He hesitated, before answering. "Am I alone?"

Amelia shook her head, her eyes screaming, *Don't involve me!*

"I'm with the UN foreign correspondent liaison."

Amelia's shoulders slumped forward, and she buried her face in her hands.

"We're headed to a building I own in Brooklyn. If you have a pen and paper, I'll give you the address."

Off the phone, Frost had one hand on the wheel. Manhattan was in the rearview mirror.

Amelia cleared her throat. "It's impossible to shake this feeling off."

"What do you mean?"

"Feeling of lightness—that it wasn't me in Damascus. Harold, if something happens to me..."

"Nothing is going to happen; Ava is always going to have a mom."

Amelia didn't reply.

Frost stuck his foot in the mouth. "Ava's father, Khalib, Khalid—is he around?"

"Khalib Osmani. He's never been around. Last I heard, his parents married him off." Her voice was cold and detached. "She's never going to know about the so-called father who abandoned her before she was born." She meant it.

Frost let the silence grow between them. The sound of the tires skidding the pavement filled the gaps of unspoken words.

Brooklyn was a jungle of ultra-modern buildings and scarce parking spots. Amelia watched Frost painfully circle over and over the same two-block radius, unsuccessfully. He moved a block over—same situation. Another block—at last, a spot behind a dump truck.

The loft building owned by Frost was the first on the street corner, in a recently gentrified neighborhood, Frost pointed out. He offered details: from the balconies, you had a direct view of the Brooklyn Bridge and the river. The building was divided in four lofts—three occupied at the moment, one vacant, the top floor with a penthouse scenery. He wasn't exaggerating. When the elevator doors opened, Amelia walked in the airy space, with white marble floors and curved windows framed with crown molding.

"Wow."

"Nice, right?" Frost motioned her to come closer. "Make yourself at home."

"Pays to be an executive, huh?"

"I'm afraid not. Family inheritance. My dad owned it; before that, his dad and his brother. When I got it, thought about selling it."

"It's a cozy place to come to after a day at the network."

Frost laughed. "No Brooklyn for me—long drive. I'm in Midtown." He tossed his jacket on a metal barstool. The car keys he placed on a wood table.

Amelia headed for the windows, eyes cast on the sweeping panoramic view. Her back facing Frost, she asked, "How much have you told him?" Arms crossed in front, she turned.

"Not a whole lot. I mean, when I called him, I hadn't seen the video." Frost was grabbing a frying pan out of a cupboard.

"You really think he'll help us?"

"We should wait and see from which direction the winds are gonna blow. I don't see what motive he could have to hurt us. Soon enough, we're going to find out."

Amelia retreated, wrestling inside with the notion of trusting a spook.

9

Amelia scarfed down her scrambled eggs and toast and chased the food with the last of her OJ. Frost, she noticed, hadn't touched his plate.

"How long has it been?" Amelia picked up her phone to check the time.

"Over an hour."

"Should we call him again?"

"No point in doing so. I don't have a cell number for him, just a general 212. A secretary passed a message to him the first time around when I called."

"It's the CIA—why make it easier on the rest of us?"

Frost stood, searching the main room of the loft.

"You need help?"

"I got it," Frost said from behind the kitchen bar. He returned to his seat, with a pen and a notepad in hand. "I was thinking, we should make a list of things that we know for certain and speculations. You know, to be prepared in case we're asked to—"

"In case what?" Amelia said, puzzled.

"In case we're asked to give statements."

It was Amelia's turn to stand, taking her dirty plate and glass to the sink. She smacked her lips, then bit her lower lip, as if afraid of what she might say.

"You're up to watching the vid again?"

If it meant not talking about statements and investigations where she was a suspect, then yes, she was prepared to watch the video again. She moved to the couch and picked up her computer, but the machine showed no sign of life. She pressed the ON key. Nothing happened.

"Shit. It's dead."

"Tell me you brought your charger."

Amelia wasn't listening. She dumped the contents of her bag on the marble floor; her belongings spilled out. She probed the mess, checking off items in her mental list: ChapStick, check; two blue and red notebooks, check; pens and pencils, check; a clear baggie with elastics, check; hairbrush, check too. *Where's the charger?*

Frost interrupted her thoughts. "Think—where could the charger be?"

Frustrated, she blurted out, "The car. I think it's in your car. I'll go down and look for it." She stood, leaving the mess on the floor.

"You stay in the loft. I know the area better." He pointed to his cell on the table, by the car keys. "If Jets calls while I'm gone, we're in apartment twenty-three, and the code to the door is 8791. Can you remember that?"

"Wait, you want me to talk to the CIA? I don't know what to say to him."

"I'll be back before he shows up. Just in case, though. It'll be all right," Frost promised and then left her alone in the unfamiliar loft.

To keep herself distracted, Amelia tapped on a news app on her phone and read the headlines. If the competition had the scoop on CWG journalists going missing in Damascus, they would be on the story, without mercy. A newsroom operated under the premise of *first and wrong rather than last and right*. No mention of CWG, journalists, or Damascus in the same sentence. Amelia relaxed. Then a voice, coming from outside, made her heart drop. She heard it clear, yelling, "Allahu Akbar! Allahu Akbar!" followed by a female scream.

Searching for a scoop of her own, Amelia rushed to the window, where an hour earlier she'd fallen in love with the view. From this angle, she saw a group of people surrounding something. A package, maybe— she couldn't tell. No police sirens. That was a good sign.

Her pulse kicked a notch when she heard rushing footsteps coming closer. Panicked, she grabbed the laptop, and another item—she didn't know what, but small enough to shove it in her back pocket—then searched for a hiding spot. No walls, no rooms, but windows and sunlight—she was exposed. *The window—she could climb down.* Amelia gave it a push, but it didn't budge. She was running out of time. The steps were outside the front door. Desperate, she ran in the bathroom—a locked door keeping her alive. She crumbled on the floor, laptop close to her chest, and thought what a cliché it would be if she died in Frost's loft.

Her breathing grew heavy. Her body trembled, but she wasn't in control to make it stop. The adrenaline had hijacked her nervous system, which was now operating on autopilot. She listened for the steps and swore she heard a person walking on the marble floor. She pushed herself to rely on her senses—one set of footsteps. But she didn't trust her judgment in this situation. With her cell in her hand, she dialed 911 and then froze. If she was going to get killed, she should call Ava's nanny and speak with her child. Her heart nearly jumped out of her chest when she felt a vibration come from her back pocket. *What is this?* She reached in and took out Frost's cell. Then it hit her—Jets, the CIA agent.

She pressed on the green icon, and the lines connected. The receiver pressed to her ear, Amelia waited.

"Is someone there?" A male voice came over the wire.

"Who is this?" Amelia dared to say.

"I'm a friend. I won't hurt you."

She shook her head, as if the voice could see her. The footsteps were canvasing the loft; Amelia could hear them well.

"What is your name?"

"Amelia. Amelia Sinclair."

"Amelia. My name is Gabriel Jets. I'm a friend of Frost. You have to listen carefully. We're running out of time."

"I can't... I can't." Fear choked her.

"You have to trust me, Amelia. I need to know your location."

Before she could answer, a kick came through the door. The lock popped out of its socket, and the line disconnected.

10

The existence of the vid took DCI Post by surprise. It wasn't part of the plan. *His* plan. Behind the closed door of his office at the CIA HQ, Post worked on ironing out that kink.

Sitting at his desk, he picked up the phone and dialed a number.

A female came on the line. "Director?"

"Any word from Jets?"

"No, sir. At 11:42, he disconnected his phone. He hasn't turned it back on or reached the safe house yet. Jets needs to make contact with us again in twenty-five minutes."

Post thought, then replied, "Keep me posted." He hung up and sat back in his chair. Jets was an exceptional agent, who didn't miss a target when given a case. His involvement was troublesome, but not unworkable. Post decided to let Jets follow through with meeting Frost and read the agent's assessment report before making his final decision on how to proceed.

In the meantime, Post reached for the phone again.

"This is Webb." A man spoke in the receiver.

"Webb, I need you to pull a report on one Harold Frost, an executive producer at CWG."

"I'm on it. How do I classify the brief? Is it assigned to a particular operation?"

"Restricted handling. My eyes only."

"I'll send the report to your office as soon as I'm done pulling the data."

"It's a rush job," Post added.

Off the phone, the DCI ran the facts of the op in his mind. There was nothing to be done for the four. They sealed their fate—wrong place, wrong time type of situation—when they got themselves in the crossfire of the black op. The executive producer was a potential threat, but Post placed an early message to his associates, who were working on neutralizing him. How they chose to do it was beyond his reach. A call came through on his private line, and Post wasted no time answering it.

"Yeah."

"Sir, we received a report that a man was killed in front of a building in Brooklyn." Brief hesitation followed before the voice carried on. "The suspect appeared to be a Muslim, shouting 'Allahu Akbar' before he stabbed his victim."

"And this is of interest to the agency how?" Post scanned the walls of his office. His eyes stopped at a discolored spot. A missing frame—Delay's official portrait. He flicked a look of satisfaction, having removed it himself after a night of drunken stupor and rage.

"Sir...the address where the murder occurred matched the address for Agent Jets's mission."

The corners of Post's mouth softened and relaxed in almost a smile. His fear evaporated. Frost had been removed, gone out of the picture. A sloppy kill and not in Post's style, who preferred to dispose of his enemies convolutedly, without a fuss, and certainly without making it a spectacle.

Post returned to the conversation. "Have we established contact with Jets?"

"No notes in the system to suggest that, sir. Local police responded to the crime scene. Metro is investigating."

"Tap the precinct's system and pull their crime report. We must be prepared to extract Jets at a minute's notice."

The flash indicator on his computer alerted him that he'd received a high-priority report. He turned his attention, reading Frost's FBI file. At first glance, Frost lived an unremarkable life.

Male, forty-seven years of age, unmarried, address in Midtown. Owned his home. Steadily employed at CWG for twenty-eight years. Bachelor's degree from NYC, master's from Columbia. Slightly bored, Post flipped back and forth in the fifty-page report, stopping to read parts in Frost's background that he could manipulate and turn Frost into a suspect on a dime. After browsing the file, Post clicked off the system and moved on.

He opened the lower left drawer of his desk, revealing a security lockbox that used fingerprints to unlock. Pressing his right thumb on the top of the safe, he waited for the sophisticated locking device to identify the finger markers. A green light blinked, granting access to Post. A maroon manila folder rested inside. Post picked it up with care, shadows moving in his eyes. It contained six colored photos, filed in random order, that held Post's interest. The first one belonged to Harold Frost. Post tossed it aside. Next was Bo Breeks, Tom Seed, Dustin Mark, Joseph Alexander. The last image, Post brought closer to him. The only female of the group—Amelia Sinclair. A mole was operating inside Post's team. Sinclair receiving the video was not by mistake; it was planned and calculated. The sender wanted to protect the female. *But why?* Figuring out that connection would lead him to the traitor. Post escalated Amelia to a high-value target.

11

The phone slipped out of Amelia's hand on impact. She curled in a fetal position, waiting for the inevitable. A set of hands lifted her off the floor, shaking her upper body to come back to it.

"Amelia? Amelia Sinclair? Are you hurt?"

Her eyes were slow to focus. She saw a square male face. The details were murky.

"I'm Gabriel Jets." He was so close to her, she could feel his breath on her face. "Were you with Harold?"

She moved her head in a yes signal. She was trembling, and her breathing was labored; putting thoughts in a chronological order was out of the question.

"You're the CIA?" she heard herself ask.

The man nudged her toward the living room. She saw what was left of the door after he broke it.

"Did you..." Amelia didn't finish. Her vision had normalized. She stared into his deep-brown eyes, noted his jet-black hair, cut short.

"Are you okay?" Agent Jets put a hand on her shoulder and held it there. "For a moment, it looked like you wouldn't be able to control your panic attack."

"I'm fine." Amelia brushed off his concerns. "Where's Harold? Did you run into him coming up?"

Agent Jets ignored her question. "We don't have time. You've got to ditch the loft." He hurried to the same window that jammed on Amelia.

Eyes on the street, he looked right then left. "Do you have your stuff ready to go? Forget about it, if you don't. Take your laptop."

Amelia protested, not willing to take orders from Jets. "I'm not going anywhere with you. Besides, Frost will be back any minute."

Then she saw the flashing lights of an ambulance. A fire truck arrived in front of the loft entrance. Police sirens blared.

"Did someone get hurt?"

Jets held her gaze steady, holding back, not giving an indicator of what was to come. "Too late. We can't use the main entrance." He shortened the distance between the two. Amelia took a step back, feeling threatened. "I won't hurt you, miss. But if I have to drag you out of this loft, I'm prepared to do it."

"I have rights."

Reaching his limits, Jets squeezed his lips, turning white. "I get you're frightened. If you want to help the four, I'm your only bet."

Amelia didn't move, but returned back his concerned look. Footsteps were making their way up; voices boomed over the stairs. They heard the knocking on doors. The police had started to canvass the area for witnesses and suspects. She thought of screaming for help, but Jets had thought of that too. His hand pressed against her mouth, and no sound could come out. His arm was wrapped around her waist, pressing her arms together. No point in struggling.

"I don't want to do this, Amelia. Don't you see what's at stake? The lives of four people trapped in Syria depend on you." She was listening, tears wedged in the corner of her eyes. "If you promise not to scream, I'll let you go. Okay?"

Amelia moaned in agreement.

Free from his grip, Amelia gathered her bag and laptop. She was ready to follow him.

Jets put pressure on the window with his shoulder. It loosened up, and he was able to lift the latch. "We're going to use the fire escape. It connects to the side streets." He swept the streets a last time. "You first."

She grabbed the window frame with her hands and prepared to step outside onto the fire escape when a bullet whizzed by them, hitting the wall. With one fluid motion, Jets pinned Amelia to the floor. Another gunshot. A sniper on a rooftop was aiming for her head, wanting her dead.

Jets cursed under his breath. He'd miscalculated the situation.

Jets, still on top of her, waited for two beats, then drew his weapon. Amelia felt the cold metal of his Glock brush across her skin, sending a jolt of disbelief down her spine.

"On my count, I want you to run for the fire escape. Climb down as fast as you can," he whispered in her ear. "My SUV's parked on the east corner. Okay?"

The police were at the door, knocking, asking for access to the loft. On the count of three, Jets vaulted to his feet and started shooting rapid cover fire in the direction of the sniper. Amelia did as she was told and ran for the fire escape, racing down the steps without looking back. She jumped from the fire escape, falling and twisting her left ankle when she hit the asphalt. Sharp pain bolted through her body as she tried to stand, but Jets was right behind her. He scooped her into his arms and sprinted toward the street corner.

Jets floored the SUV; the tires skid, leaving black marks on the concrete. Amelia glimpsed behind her, the loft no longer visible. She returned her eyes on the road in front and, lips trembling, said, "Was that a sniper?"

"Yep."

"After me?"

"It seems so."

Jets twisted the wheel. The SUV veered to the right. He brought it down to thirty-five.

"Why are you slowing down, Agent? Aren't we supposed to be running away?"

"It won't do us any good if a traffic cop busts us for speeding." He left it at that.

Her chin retreated in, chasing away emotions.

After looping in and out of residential neighborhoods, Jets rejoined the overcrowded traffic lanes on the highway, headed away from New York. Within the hour, it was thinned out, and the SUV glided at a nice speed.

Amelia picked up where they'd left off. "Where are you taking us?"

Jets ignored her and her questions, which sunk her mood to the lowest point of the day. She sulked in the seat, defeated.

• • • •

Welcome to Philadelphia was the first road sign she'd seen in a while. She looked over to Jets, but his face gave away nothing.

"Agent, Philadelphia?" Amelia was at her wit's end. She groaned when Jets didn't reply. "I've got to go home to my child. Please."

"Ma'am—" Jets started to say.

"Drop the ma'am. It's Amelia."

"Amelia, when we get to the safe house, I promise you can ask me your questions. I'll answer them."

Amelia showed signs of becoming combative, same as in the loft. Jets had to keep her calm, exerting his power to control the situation. The mission had failed. Plan A laid on the streets of Brooklyn, bludgeoned to death. The sniper—Jets had no explanation for that. Plan B was in motion, but for it to work, Amelia had to cooperate.

"New York isn't safe. It'll blow over. When the heat goes to a simmer, I'll drive you personally to your home," Jets promised.

• • • •

The afternoon grew into an early evening, when Jets parked the SUV in the driveway of a house, outside Philly, according to the GPS coordinates preloaded in the car. He eased out of the SUV. Amelia didn't move. Her ankle was angry at her, swollen with a ring around it in purple hues. He carried her to the front door, wishing he could help her with the pain.

He punched in an eight-number code into the keypad hanging on the door. The inside of the house looked like a showroom to Amelia. The furniture was arranged with taste, too much taste for the average person.

Jets let her rest on the couch. For a moment, their eyes met, then the contact dissolved rapidly.

"You've banged up your ankle pretty good." Jets handed her a throw pillow to elevate the injured foot.

"Broken, you think?"

"Fracture maybe, but I'm thinking more likely you twisted it seriously," Jets said. "Hang on." He left the room.

He did a perimeter check. No sign of a threat in the remaining rooms. A scan outside through the curtains revealed no unwelcomed company. Staying in the safe house should buy them extra time, Jets determined.

With a frozen bag of peas in hand, he walked back in and placed it on her ankle.

Amelia winced. "Can you hand me my cell phone? It's in the bag. I don't want the nanny to worry."

"Rest for a minute, then you can call. You need to recuperate."

Amelia didn't have it in her to argue. She relaxed on the couch and closed her eyes. "A minute," she muttered, quickly drifting asleep.

He was relieved to see her doze off. Her stubbornness would complicate things for him down the road. The next leg of the mission was to get in touch with the CIA. In the bathroom, he went through the linen closet. Nothing but towels. In the drawers: toothpaste, toothbrushes, toiletries, unopened—all good—but not what he needed. *It was in this room. Every stash house had them; he was just not looking in the right place.* The large oval mirror hanging on the wall was the last place he hadn't checked. With the tips of his fingers, Jets traced the edges of the mirror until he felt an object attached to the back. *Jackpot!*

The satellite phone vibrated when the power booted up. Under the home button, Jets dialed the one saved number. As he waited for the other end to answer, he cracked the bathroom door a sliver, listening for Amelia.

"Gabriel, what took you so long?" The familiar voice of his handler boomed in his ear.

"It was complicated. Far from straightforward." He thought he heard noises and stopped talking.

"The satellite phone's pinging your location in Philly."

"I have my hands full."

"You mean a dead body in Brooklyn, who happened to be Harold Frost, your intended target? You're referring to that situation?"

"There's more, Polina."

The wire grew quiet as Polina waited for an explanation.

"The woman Frost was with—she's...with me."

"Gabriel, how could you? That's against protocol." Polina gathered speed. "It's not CIA jurisdiction. This isn't the FBI or the five-o. You're a clandestine operative."

She was right, of course, but what was he supposed to do? *Stay out of the sniper's way and let him have a clear shot at Amelia's head?* Not his style, not on his watch. You hire a sniper when you had no other options of getting rid of a target. Midday in Brooklyn, while a dead body lay on the pavement, with cops circling the block—it ran deeper in Jets's mind than a kidnapping in Syria, if there was even a connection to that.

"A sniper tried to take her out." He cut Polina off.

"A sniper? Where? At the loft building?" She was clacking on a keyboard, he heard.

"The sniper fiasco is bothering me. I've been racking my brain to find an explanation."

"You sure he was aiming for her?"

"He could've taken me out first, but he didn't. The sniper waited till I moved out of the way so she could climb down the fire escape."

"I'm adding this to the brief. When we get off the phone, I'm sending it over to the DCI, who personally called to inquire about your status."

Jets brushed the DCI comment aside, though it was unusual.

"Add in there that the video is secured."

"You've watched it? A hacking team was assigned to extract it from her email account."

"By the sound of your voice—they're running into a roadblock."

"Precisely. How did you know?"

"A hunch. This case smells."

"Sit tight. I'm putting the finishing touches on an extraction plan for you. Her...there's not much I can do for her, I'm afraid."

"P.? I gotta ask for a favor."

"Shoot."

The clacking ceased, and he pushed forward. "I wanna know details about the sniper."

"You want me to break in the Metro internal servers and snoop around?"

"Can you do that for me?"

Polina sighed. "For you—I'll do it."

Jets suspected the sniper had unfinished business with Amelia and would be back to finish the job. Jets wanted to be prepared. He killed the power to the satellite and returned it behind the mirror.

In the living room, Amelia was waking up, moaning from the pain that sent sharp stabs up and down her leg. She narrowed her eyes on Jets, demanding, "How long have I been out?"

"Not long. Fifteen minutes, maybe." He handed her a bottle of water. "You should get fluids in. It'll help with your ankle."

He patted her leg and sat on the edge of the sofa. "Still not looking good."

"Forget about that. You said I can use a phone."

Reluctantly, he stuck a hand in his pocket and tossed her his work phone. "It's encrypted. Won't be able to track the call."

Amelia dialed her home. "Hey, Marga, it's me. How are things at home?" She frowned. "I see. I'm tied up at work. Might be home late."

Jets motioned to his wristwatch, making a circular motion.

She understood. "Maybe at the UN for the remainder of the night."

He nodded approvingly.

"I'll call you again, when Ava wakes up from her nap, to hear her voice." She finished off with a, "You take care too."

The phone was in her lap, her face full of sorrow. "Is my family in danger, Agent?"

"Call me Gabriel. I don't think so. To be on the cautious side, can they stay the night elsewhere?"

Amelia's mouth curved downward. "I suppose Marga can take Ava to her house."

"That would be best. We'll figure this out." He patted her leg gently.

12

The strains of the day were showing on Burks, who was drowning his failures with a dry martini, two olives. His sleeves were rolled at the elbow, the tie was on the ground, and the jacket a crumbled mess on the couch. A prelude by Claude Debussy played a soulful melody on the record player. His thoughts of the conversation with Post didn't improve his mood.

Outside his office doors, staffers were racking their brains, hammering a plan their boss could present to the White House in the morning.

When the clock stroked 12:30, Burks called Hobbs through the intercom on his desk phone. She arrived momentarily, standing by his desk, like a faithful soldier, waiting for orders.

"Missy, tell the team to call it a day." He took a generous sip of the martini.

She quietly filled him in on the progress they'd made. "We're hitting a dead end. The team can go home, but I'm prepared to stay the rest of the night."

"That won't be necessary. Go home and sleep. We'll tackle this in the morning."

Hobbs hesitated, then headed for the door. "Do you want me to close the door?"

"Nah. Leave it be. I won't be much longer."

Burks lifted the glass and examined the clear color of the gin reflecting the light on his desk. A phone rang on Hobbs's desk and she answered. "If that's my wife, tell her I'm coming home," he ordered. "I bet she'd be happy to see me." Burks cracked a smile at the ironic comment.

Shortly, Hobbs walked back in while Burks tilted the tall glass back to swallow the last gulp. The taste of the hard liquor lingered in his mouth, gently burning the tip of his lips.

"Mr. Secretary?" she said, concerned.

"What's with the official title?" Burks rose to his feet and began to gather himself.

"The phone call—it was DCI Post."

The mention of Post gave Burks a pause. His eyebrows hiked like hills.

She resumed, "He said to give you this note." Hobbs handed him a note folded in two, ripped from a yellow legal pad.

He glanced at it. "That asshole."

Despite Hobbs's protests and assurances that she could stay for longer, Burks sent her on her way. She'd done plenty for today; he saw no reason to keep her around. It was between him and Post.

Burks notified the secret detail and his driver that he wouldn't be going straight home. They were headed across town, to a neighborhood Burks was familiar with. Twenty years and some change ago, his young wife at the time and the then-lawyer had purchased their first home. The streets of Rose Commons held a bouquet of sweet memories, but tonight's visit wasn't shaping to be a drive through the reel of the past.

The Ford skidded on the highway at a hellish speed. Burks dreaded the rendezvous. The SUV pulled in the driveway of a colonial home with tall white pillars. A figure waited on the steps. Burks told the driver to keep the engine running; he wouldn't be in for long.

The tobacco smell choked Burks as he inched forward. Post's eyes darted in Burks's direction, like a thief in the night, when he heard the squeaking of shoes. The porch light was killed—for what purpose, Burks didn't dare think.

"Smoking's gonna kill you." Burks climb the first step and stopped.

"Conrad, a lovely surprise."

"I doubt that," Burks murmured. "I received the summons—do you mind if we step in?"

"Go right ahead." Post flicked the cigarette into the night.

In a living room, Burks chose to sit in an armchair, leaving the sofa to Post.

"Thanks for coming on short notice." Post lit a match to start a fire in the fireplace. He rubbed his hands together as he faced Burks.

"Your note was very explicit. I'm afraid I didn't have a choice in the matter."

Post's lips twitched. "We always have a choice. You made the right one tonight." Taking the conversation in a new direction, he asked, "Are you drinking?"

"I can go for a martini," Burks said coolly.

Post disappeared behind a liquor bar, returning with two Bud Light cans. "Sorry, pal. I'm afraid at the CIA, we aren't fancy. Beer okay?"

Burks reluctantly accepted the can, gripping it in his palms.

"What do you think of the hostage situation?"

Post's question poked a sore spot with Burks. Instinctively, his defense mechanism kicked in high gear. "The best-case scenario—the four men are still alive and we can bring them home."

"And the worst scenario?" Post was on a fishing expedition.

"The loss of life is tragic."

"Spoken like a true politician. Giving a non-answer answer."

Burks left the can on the table, his face hardened. "What is your take on the hostage situation?" His voice was cold as ice.

Post drank his beer. "This is not going to end well for Delay and the current administration." His eyes circled around the room, coming back to Burks. "I want to know, are you with me or not?"

"And if I say I'm not?"

"The State Department is at the epicenter of this. Who knows? A network might get lucky and get its hand on the kidnapping vid."

Burks's eyes were wide, wild with hate. "You wouldn't dare."

Post shook his head. What he would or wouldn't do was far beyond Burks's reach. Beyond the White House's reach. He was a free agent, operating on his own.

13

In the espionage business, the greatest liars were the agency's best assets. If they were willing to sell their governments' top secrets to make a profit, the CIA gladly filled their pockets, turning a blind eye on their transgressions. Traitors, too, operated in the US, collecting secrets and selling them to the highest bidder. *Could Amelia be one of them or at least a willing participant? Possibly. Most likely.* Jets was in the early stages of the assessing process. At first glance, the facts stacked against her favor. Facts could be manipulated; a gut feeling could not. His gut wasn't saying much.

"Shouldn't you be trying to reach Harold, Agent? I mean, Gabriel. Maybe someone in your office?" Amelia said quietly.

He hadn't told her. She didn't know. *How could she?* Frost was killed in front of the building; they escaped through the side street.

Jets, still sitting on the edge, leaned in. "Frost—he's no longer with us."

Her face was white like a sheet of paper; Jets thought she was going to be sick.

"Like, murdered? Is that what you mean?"

"The cops were canvassing the area when I got to the loft."

"Do you think the same man who shot at me killed Harold too?"

"Hard to say. I don't think so. Harold was stabbed. It's not likely that it was the same man." His lips didn't finish the rest.

She picked up on his reluctance. "What are you not telling me?" Her eyes were pleading.

"The sniper and Harold's killer could be a team."

Shaken, Amelia fought the tears. "Poor Harold. Why would anyone want to hurt him?"

"Did you hear a scream? A car driving fast? Maybe you saw something."

She shook her head. "Nothing." Her lips trembled. Then Amelia remembered. "A man yelled 'Allahu Akbar.' A woman screamed immediately after that."

Jets was thrown off by the "Allahu Akbar" detail and was sort of troubled by it. It didn't add up—four Americans were kidnapped in Syria; less than twenty-four hours later, on American soil, their executive gets hacked to death.

"Amelia, Frost said on the phone that he had a video of the kidnapping. Do you know why he would receive it?"

His question seemed to startled her. She looked puzzled. He did too. An awkward silence followed, before Amelia carried on. "Harold is dead. He really is dead."

Her avoidance of the question was not a good sign, Jets admitted. *What was she hiding and why?*

"It doesn't add up, Ms. Sinclair," Jets prompted. "Harold sounded worried on the phone when he called me first thing this morning. Then, when I got to the building, he was killed and well...we had the sniper situation. I simply don't know." He laid out the facts in front of her. "What bothers me the most is why send a video with such sensitive information and then try to kill the only person who has seen it?"

Amelia didn't offer an explanation.

"Unless..." He waited.

"Unless, what?"

"What I'm trying to say is that maybe no one sent the video to Frost in the first place. Maybe he died today, in Brooklyn, trying to protect someone."

The revelation of Frost's death was the last drop in the bucket. Amelia crumbled, came undone, broken and ready to talk.

"No one sent a video of the kidnapping to Harold. I received the video around 4:30 a.m. this morning." She sobbed. "After I watched it, I tried to call the team. Their plane landed in Damascus at 6:30 p.m. local time. I wasn't able to get in touch with them, so I called Harold and briefed him."

The sensitive thing would have been for Jets to back off, give her water and space until she regained her composure. It wasn't his style. He dug in. "What happened after you got off the phone with Harold?"

"Well, you know most of it, actually. Harold asked me to meet him at his office. He told me not to speak with anyone—to just grab my work bag and go. So that's what I did." She was a mess.

"Did you show him the video?"

"Uh-huh." She sniffled. "In his office, in Midtown. A couple of times. Then, he got spooked. Worried. Asked me to leave and go with him to the loft in Brooklyn."

From what Amelia was able to tell him, Jets constructed a timeline, theirs and his, cross-referencing overlapping points. Then it hit him. *Odd,* he thought; *DCI Post had asked about the kidnapping video before Jets's secretary gave him Frost's missed call message and request for a meet-up.* He pushed to remember. Jets wasn't wrong. Post did say "obtaining the video" as the primary objective.

"Amelia, where is the video?"

"It was sent to me in a form of a link. My email. The sender had spelled out my name in Farsi."

"What did it say?"

"It prompted me to click on a link that took me to a new web page, where the video played on a loop."

"I need to see the video immediately."

Amelia eyed the bag by the front door. "It died when Harold and I got to Brooklyn. That's why he left. To see if my charger was in his car. But then...oh God." She was no longer able to contain her tears. Her voice was inaudible.

Jets gave up on her for the time being and let her cry. He crossed the room and stood by the window. It could have been the wind blowing the tree branches in a stormy night, but he drew back the curtains slightly as his eyes narrowed on the two shadows moving aggressively toward the house entrance, taking cover. They were not his extraction backup, not in the least. Their movement formation was tactical, military—guns for hire. In a fluid motion, Jets killed the lights in the living room. Amelia ceased to cry. He moved back to the couch and pointed for her to lie on the ground. She obeyed without an argument. He set aside questioning who sent the killers after them and how they'd found about the CIA stash house. His priority was to control the situation by dropping the two. If not them, it would be him and Amelia in body bags.

Squatting by the front door, gun gripped in hand, Jets waited for the boots' sound. When he was no longer able to hear their steps, Jets squeezed the muzzle. A bullet hissed in the night.

14

The shooting was over in a flash for Amelia, who laid flat under a table, eyes shut and hands covering her ears. Her breathing was shallow, and her thoughts refused to cooperate. Jets braced her shoulder and whispered it was time to make a run for it. She went ahead first, her body halfway out, Jets following closely behind.

She heard him say from behind her, "I put three in the guy storming the front. The second split; he's out back."

Jets pressed an object in her back and continued, "You know how to use one of these?"

Amelia desperately wanted to say, *NO, forget about it. I don't do guns.* She pressed her heels backward, a baffled expression locked on her face.

Jets retreated the spare gun to its holster, understanding she would be of no help to him. His hand slid past her and forced the doorknob.

"Run as fast as you can. Don't look back and try to keep your head down as low as you can." His words were flying. "Hope that ankle is feeling better."

Following his instructions, Amelia ran down the driveway, when the next wave of gunfire erupted. A man yelled, "Shit!" which startled Amelia. Against her better judgment, she looked back in the direction of the voice. *Bad mistake.* She tripped, tumbled, rolled down, and landed on top of a dead body. When she came back to it after the initial shock, she felt warm, thick liquid smeared on her forehead her hands drenched.

She rose to her knees, arms extended wide in front of her, as she examined the wetness. *Blood.* It was blood. Panic washed over her. Before she could scream, a hand gripped her mouth, robbing her of the ability to yelp.

"Get in the car." Jets tossed her limp body across his shoulder.

Hunched over, head between her legs, Amelia was choking on her vomit. Their SUV rumbled. Jets gunned it and whipped the wheel to the left. From the corner of her eyes, she saw his right arm out the window, gun flashing, sending a spray of bullets toward the stash house. Mortified, Amelia closed her eyes to prevent them from capturing the rest in a memory file.

They must have been driving for a while, though she could only speculate. Amelia lost track of the time and gave up on reasoning with reality. The sniper and the assassins at the house were out of her realm of expertise, she reckoned.

"You feeling all right?" His attention was on the road ahead, not her.

"I tripped over a dead body." She sighed, plagued by flashbacks.

"Check the glovebox for napkins."

With a stack of napkins in her lap, she wiped her face but regretted it immediately. The blood had dried up, caked on her; blood splotches formed circles. She examined herself in the mirror of the sun visor. Words died in her throat but then bubbled up in panic.

"It won't come off. Gabriel, it's not coming off." She was scrubbing hard. The napkin tore from the pressure, leaving red marks to add to her battered looks.

He threw a glance at her and had to agree. She was a mess: specks of puke on her blouse, jeans with blood stains on them, as well as her fingertips. The napkins wouldn't do.

"We can't stop at a gas station. Video cameras," Jets rationalized out loud.

"What about a hotel?"

"Too risky. Video surveillance, too. Front desk receptionist, guests. They'll pick up our scent in no time." He said, "We need a private place. Off the beaten path, where they won't know to look."

Amelia stared out the window into the darkness. It was hard to think.

"I know just the right place."

She gazed at him evenly. "And where is that?"

Jets didn't reply. He swerved and exited the highway, fishtailing on the road. Pedal to the metal, they were flying at a reckless speed. He prayed for Polina to be home. She was his last hope to figure out this whole mess.

15

Burks, in a heap, and Burks's convoy left the meeting with Post. From the back, the secretary of state instructed that he was not going home yet. H Street would be the next stop. With the windows rolled down, Burks watched the streetlights twinkle against the starry night, seething in despair by Post's proposition.

The cell phone chirped. McKaine's private number beamed on the screen.

Burks accepted the call. "Robert."

"Do you have an update?"

Burks had that and more. A decision was made without his input or willingness. "My office's back channeling to the Saudis through a mediator."

"A mediator? Who?"

"The prince's first cousin—Khalib Osmani."

McKaine was quiet, but Burks heard the jolting of notes. He moved on. "We're passing a message to General Osmani, who happens to be traveling to Syria to address the cabinet members."

"Interesting. You think he'll go for it?" McKaine prompted.

"We'll have to play it by ear, I'm afraid."

"The kidnappers haven't come forward. No ransom demands, no prisoner exchanges, no video proclaiming their prize possession. The NSC's prognosis is grim." McKaine's voice was clearer. "If the State Department fails this administration, I won't be able to help you. The White House wants a win. And if we don't bag it, you'll have to shoulder it. Are we on the same page?"

Post's prediction echoed in Burks's ears. The White House had chosen its fall guy, like Post had said would happen.

"I'm personally overseeing the Osmani connection," Burks weakly replied.

With no other words left to say, the two hung up. Burks sunk deeper in the seat. He stuck a hand in his coat pocket, his fingers feeling the note inside. If he made the call, he sealed his fate—no telling how it would end for him. If he didn't make the call, the White House would crucify him, let him hang to dry.

With a grunt, Burks punched in the number scribbled on the note, dreading the outcome. He winced when the call was picked up.

"That didn't take long," Post said.

"McKaine threatened me, like you said. The NSC is advising the president that there's no chance of bringing the Americans home alive." He stopped to inhale and held his breath in. "As you asked, I told Robert about Osmani."

"Good boy, Conrad. You're playing for the right team, for once."

The line went dead. Burks eased out of the car and told his Secret Service agents to stay back. Etching a lonely figure in the night, Burks wrestled with the notion that he'd betrayed his countrymen and the homeland.

• • • •

In the West Wing, McKaine stared at the silent phone. A flame of suspicion in Burks's capabilities started to blaze, wreaking havoc. An agent in a dark suit and a wire in his ear stood by McKaine's desk, waiting for directions on how to proceed.

McKaine double-checked Khalib Osmani's name jotted in an illegible handwriting. He flicked a look to the agent, then extended his hand, the note wedged between his fingers.

"Get me a copy of the latest sitrep and an intel report on this character. I wanna know what we're up against."

The agent nodded. "Disseminate the report to the four?" By *the four*, he meant NSA, CIA, FBI, and State.

With a hardened face, McKaine shot back, "We're keeping this tight to the vest." He pointed a finger to himself.

Lips pursed together, McKaine's mind put two and two together, but the numbers didn't add up. Burks was in charge of America's allies, Post in charge of stealing their secrets, McKaine in charge of safeguarding the president. His ability to predict their enemies' chess moves in the political arena had won them the White House.

The agent hadn't left the room, when McKaine asked, "Time frame on my request?"

"The sitrep should be within the hour. The file on Osmani—it depends. How far do we cast the net?"

"Per your discretion. I want to get a good picture of who he is." McKaine added, "Dax—if the secretary is still at her desk, ask her to bring an erase board in."

The board was brought in to a boardroom on the ground floor of the White House, along with a box of markers. Another agent had joined McKaine and Dax to sift through the neat stack of files organized on a desk. Armed with a red marker, McKaine wrote in bold letters: "What

We Know/What We Don't Know." He stepped back and marveled at his ingenuity.

Dax notified McKaine, "The sitrep is ready for you, sir."

"Drop the formality, Dax. In this room, we're three knuckleheads plowing through this cluster fuck."

"Fair enough. It's uploaded on the drive."

McKaine blinked surprise and confusion at the mention of the "drive."

Dax picked up on that and asked to see McKaine's smartphone. "It's the internal encrypted drive." He pointed to an app on McKaine's screen. "Tap on it and log in with your credentials."

A cloud drive crunched zeroes and ones, momentarily displaying a digital copy of the requested report.

"Who do we have to thank for this creation?" McKaine let slip.

"The IT guys." Lance threw in a word.

McKaine wasn't listening; he was reading the NSC's outlined and detailed take on the situation in Syria. A sentence caught his attention. He re-read it. *"It's the National Security Council's understanding that the Muslim Brotherhood had taken under their control the north, south, and west outskirts of Damascus."* His eyes glided on the paragraph below. *"The Syrian president's military forces received air support from Russian fighter jets."* The statement continued, *"The military maneuver took place at 1200 local time, lasting an hour."*

McKaine found that portion of particular interest. "Guys, do we know if air control suspended inbound and outbound flights that day?"

Dax and Lance exchanged looks. Dax took the lead. "The air space was cleared at 14:40—flights after that were allowed to land."

"How wide of a terrain did the Russians cover during that strike?"

Lance was up. "Isolated pockets."

"I want specifics."

"Tadamon and Al-Midan," Lance said.

"These are the two neighborhoods where the insurgents have a heavy control. Or am I mistaken?"

"You're correct. Sir, if I may ask—what are you trying to find?" Dax was treading lightly.

McKaine left the smartphone on the desk and resumed writing on the board under the "what we know" column. When he was done, he underlined it and pointed with the marker. "The Russians and the Syrian president were in the midst of trying to gain control of two neighborhoods that were crawling with heavily armed militia. They weren't trying to protect safe neighborhoods—why not?" McKaine leaned on the desk like a professor posing a question to the class, with an answer only he knew.

"They were pushing them out?" Dax gave it a shot.

"Someone's paying attention." McKaine flashed a rare smile. "It's this way—the Russians came in to retake a territory, not to defend it. Pay attention, here's where it gets slippery. The Damascus Square is on the opposite side of town. The Russians dropped their bombs. Then, less than four hours later, the militia regrouped and detonated a bomb? Unlikely."

"Maybe it was payback."

"Or maybe this is deception." McKaine liked the word and wrote it with a blue marker on the board. "Deception," he repeated.

16

The highway between Maryland and Alexandria, Virginia, was a straight shot, with little scenery to see along the way. The speedometer marked down another mile. Amelia was in Jets's custody, even if she didn't know it. He planned to eventually turn her over to the FBI because it was the bureau's jurisdiction, but not before he figured out what part she played in the kidnapping and the murder of Harold Frost.

Amelia woke up in a stupor, plagued by her nightmares. Her eyes blinked, accepting that it had happened.

"Where are we?" Amelia asked, disoriented by the darkness and sleep deprivation.

"I-95, headed to Alexandria."

"Virginia? What's there?"

"My handler lives in town. We're going to pay her a visit."

"She can help us?" Amelia wasn't giving up on extracting information from Jets.

"Polina knows computers, technology. If anyone can trace where the link originated from—it would be her." Jets meant it.

Jets had planned to interrogate her at the stash house, but since the assassins showed up, the car ride was now his best bet. He saw a way in when Amelia ceased with the questions. She fidgeted with her fingers, while Jets stepped in the well-familiar role to him of an interrogator.

"How well do you know the four missing?"

"Pretty well. One is actually my mentor. I owe Bo my life." She sighed.

"What did he do?"

She didn't answer immediately; instead, her memories brought her back to Baghdad in 2003, mere months after then President George W. Bush declared war on Iraq.

"Bo, he's the cameraman and photographer," Amelia began. "We were with the first wave of foreign correspondents to arrive in the country when the American-Iraq war started. Our station was in the green zone, controlled by the military. Information was controlled by the military, too, who were spoon-feeding us what they wanted us to report back home."

"I remember 2003 well. Maybe you and I have crossed paths."

She shrugged. "For a few months, we played by their rules, until we developed a rapport with locals. One night, an Iraqi driver smuggled us deep in Al Qaeda territory. Before long, a group of mujahideen drove us off the road." Her voice grew rigid with regret. "One thing led to another. They had us kneeled, Kalashnikovs pointed to our heads. I've never been more scared in my life. Bo talked them out of it. He told them that I was his daughter. We were traveling to see family. He bribed them with money. He was prepared to take a bullet for me." She stopped, grief welling in her chest.

"You have a habit of not following rules?" Jets's question was meant to get a rise out of her, and it worked.

"Don't ask me private questions if you're going to make snap judgments," she hissed. "May I remind you—the CIA's weapons of mass distraction torrent of supposed evidence in Iraq? You boys did what you did, and we did what we had to do to uncover the truth." Amelia made a valid point.

"What's the truth, Amelia? What really happened to the four?"

"I don't know. I have no idea." Amelia tensed up.

"You can save Bo by being honest with me. Put an end to the charade."

She shot him a fierce look. "That's what I want to do. That's what Harold wanted to do. He called you for advice yesterday. We were doing all right before you showed up, Agent."

Eyes locked on Amelia, Jets had reached the limits of his patience. Before he could name her a suspect in his investigation, she screamed, "Watch out!"

He cut the wheel, miscalculating. The SUV lost its balance. Jets regained control of the car, moments too late. The ditch had partly damaged the hood; a busted taillight fluttered like a disco ball. The deer on the road left, unscathed. Amelia's seat belt absorbed the hit, but by the look of it, Jets didn't buckle up. His head was limp on the wheel, and a film of blood trickled on the dashboard.

Amelia reached over and tapped his shoulder. No sound, no movement. "Agent? Agent Jets, are you all right?" she whispered.

She shook him a little harder, but he remained the same. She shook harder, repeating, "Wake up. Please wake up." Again, nothing happened. Amelia lit the overhead light, searching for the source of the blood. No cuts on his face, an abrasion under his left eye, but that was about it. Pressing with the tips of her fingers, she touched the back of his neck, feeling the vertebrae, fearing he'd broken his neck. It looked normal to her. Amelia ran a hand in his hair; she felt moistness. Her palm was bloody. He had a nasty gash toward the middle of his skull and was losing blood.

She clicked off her buckle and pushed her door open. From the back of the SUV, Amelia brought out a small first aid kit, packed with Band-Aids, a gauze pad, and tape. Not much she could do with that. She improvised. A bottle of water served as a disinfectant. The gauze pad, she pressed to the wound, slowing down the bleeding. The Band-Aids were too small, so she threw them aside.

She continued to talk to him. "Please, Agent Jets, wake up. I can't do this on my own. If you hear me, please wake up."

The set of headlights came to the back of her, without notice or warning. They blinded her, and she thought the worst.

"Lady, you okay?" A shadow stepped out of a car, flashlight in hand.

"The driver. He's hurt."

A deputy dressed in a beige uniform, with a Maryland State Trooper patch pinned on his chest, approached the car accident. "Did you hit a deer?" he asked.

He came around the SUV, inspecting the collision. Seeing no deer, he walked the other way around, flashing in the window. "Jesus!" he yelled, realizing that Amelia wasn't the driver. "How long has he been out?"

"Maybe ten minutes, fifteen minutes."

"I'm going to radio in for an ambulance."

Jets moaned, starting to regain consciousness.

"Buddy, you all right?" The trooper and Amelia had exchanged places. "You with me?"

"My head kills," Jets muttered.

"You took a pretty good knock to the head. Hold tight, all right? I told your lady friend, I'm calling for an ambulance."

"No ambulance. I'm fine. A nasty headache, that's all."

"Gabriel, you should let a doctor check you."

Jets was alert and clutched the ignition. The SUV wouldn't start.

"No use in trying. Your vehicle's totaled. A tow truck has to come and move it." The trooper spoke while taking the plate number down. "I'll be back."

The trooper walked back to his cruiser, paying attention to his computer.

"Amelia, listen to me. The plates, the insurance, will check out. As far as he knows, we simply had a car accident."

"What should I tell him if he asks for my ID?"

"You don't have it. He doesn't have probable cause to search the car. Follow my lead."

The trooper was speaking in his radio, giving the location of the accident. A dispatcher told him help was on the way; the ambulance was diverted because the driver refused medical help.

"How long before the tow truck?" Jets asked.

"About twenty minutes. Where were you guys headed?"

"Alexandria."

"The tow's gonna drop the car off in Springfield. You can catch a ride with him." The trooper prepared to leave. "You sure you don't wanna see a doctor?"

"No, Officer. Thank you, I'll handle it."

"If I got a nickel for every time someone on the side of the road said that to me." He whistled and left the two to wait for the tow truck to show up.

17

In Springfield, the tow truck driver sorted paper in two separate piles: the pink slips he'd file for his records, the yellow ones for the customer, Jets. Slouched in a roughed-up leather office chair, the driver copied the insurance card and the driver's license, briefly pausing to gesture to Jets that the bathroom was at the end of the corridor.

Jets splashed cold water on his face, avoiding the nasty cut on his head. It stung, and he thought six or seven stitches were in order to close the gash. Back at the front desk, Jets pushed the boundaries of the driver's hospitality when he asked to use the phone.

"Local calls only," the driver warned.

With the receiver in hand, Jets had no idea who to call. His eyes stopped on a taxi service flyer hanging from a message board above the desk.

"Do you know if they're a twenty-four-hour cab company?"

The driver pretended not to hear the question. Jets dialed, guessing he would have to find out for himself.

"White Top, Yellow Cab Company, what can I do for you?"

"I'm at Rocky's Tow Truck on Main Street, Springfield. I have to get to Alexandria—do you go that far?"

"That would be fifteen miles. Do you have an address in Alexandria? I can give you the exact fare amount."

"Westover."

"My computer is slow, sorry."

"When's the next available cab?" Jets was antsy.

"Hmmm, my next one should be able to pick up in, uhh...five to ten minutes. Would that work?"

"Perfect."

"Do you still want the trip mileage and fare?"

"That's okay."

The truck driver finished up about the same time the cab showed up. With his yellow slips underarm and Amelia right behind him, they jumped in the cab and left Springfield in a hurry. He gave a generic location; he didn't know Polina's exact home address.

The ride was tense; Amelia didn't dare ask how he was feeling. From the corner of her eye, she could tell he was fuming. When they reached Westover, the cabbie wanted a house number.

"It's been years since I've been to her house," Jets announced. Both the cabbie and Amelia had a similar thought. "There was a CVS on the corner, then a block up the street. A house, smaller than the rest. Red shutters." He was throwing out information the cabbie didn't care for.

"Westover has a new CVS. It's four blocks east."

That couldn't be the right direction. The CVS Jets remembered was in an older building, before the company started to build their own.

"You mean, the CVS on Franklin Street?"

"That must be it."

"I got a tell ya, I get all sorts of strange birds, especially at night time, and hope I don't lose my tip, but you two are pretty strange."

The sight of CVS on Franklin Street caused a memory chain reaction in Jets. He'd been here. From a pocket, he pulled out a fifty and thanked the driver.

With the dawn climbing over rooftops, Jets spotted Polina's home on the corner of the street. A Cape Cod cottage, red shutters, the smallest on the block—he'd given a precise description to the cabbie.

"Wait for me by the mailbox." Jets left Amelia alone.

• • • •

Amelia scanned her surroundings. Mostly colonial style homes, a quiet street, trimmed lawns. A lilac tree in full bloom blocked her view, but she could see Jets's arms stretch out.

Jets knocked on the door with the lion head knocker.

Polina slightly cracked it, then wider until the door was open all the way. She stared at him, half-surprised, half-furious. "You've seen better days." She offered a lopsided smile.

"Good seeing you, too, P."

"Coming in?"

"I'm not alone."

That wiped the smile off her face. She poked her head farther out, not seeing the second visitor. "The woman? You're crazy, bringing her to my house!"

"I got ambushed at the stash house. There is no other place I can take her."

"What do you mean, ambushed?" She raised her hand. "Tell me inside. God knows who's watching."

Jets revealed himself to Amelia and waved her in.

Amelia had reservations since Springfield about Jets's idea to pay a visit to his handler. She went along with it, telling herself, *last stop, then I'm going home.* The house door slammed behind her. She didn't want to stay.

A blonde-haired woman, with a pixie haircut and stunning blue eyes, greeted her lukewarmly. "Amelia Sinclair, I presume?" She said, "I'm Polina."

"Nice to meet you."

"The two of you look like hell. Your ankle, his head—I'm afraid I can't help with that. But can I offer you a cup of coffee?" Polina headed for the kitchen.

Jets helped Amelia to the couch.

"Look at you taking care of me, when your head needs stitches."

"It's a cut, not a big deal."

Polina studied their body language and interaction, despising Amelia because of Jets. She cut their moment short by storming the living room with two cups of coffee, one for Amelia and one for herself.

"Gabriel, we should talk." She held her gaze on him, but spoke to Amelia next. "Amelia, rest up."

In her office, she let it rip. "Have you lost your mind? You've brought a suspect to my home. We're CIA."

"The stash house was made—" Jets started to explain.

"So you've told me. But look." She pointed to her computer, various portals opened on the screens. "An extraction team arrived to the house, found it empty. Like you've never been there, which is crazy, because I personally pinged the phone signal from the satellite you used."

"A cleaning crew must have swooped in and disposed of the bodies."

A jolt of disbelief crossed her face like a shadow. "Bodies? What bodies?"

"That's what I've been trying to explain. Two roughnecks, armed with Glocks, wired. Three bullets to the first one, and at least as many to the second guy."

Polina's lips slightly shivered. "You think they're after her or protecting her?"

"After. If they're willing to ambush a CIA house and sent a sniper to Brooklyn, they want her six feet under, cold to the touch."

"Fuck. I pulled the trigger and called the FBI."

"Why would you do that?"

"You didn't call. I was worried." Polina swiveled her chair and input a command in the computer, recalling a server window. She typed in a series of codes. Jets glanced occasionally over her shoulder.

"The good news is I called a buddy of mine at the FBI to give me their report on the suspect."

"Did you read it?"

"I did, and you should too. They had quite a bit on her—surveillance, photos, telephone logs."

"That's odd. Is she under investigation?"

"Not a full-blown investigation, but they're keeping tabs on her. She's apparently connected to Khalib Osmani. Wait till you hear about him. A nasty piece of work." She was laying it thick on Jets, feeding the suspicious monster inside.

"I take it you have your hands on Osmani's file too."

"That was the easy part. The CIA has a file on him. Mostly highly classified, but I pulled a few unredacted pages." Polina leaned in. "General in the Royal Army, Saudi Arabia. He's been linked to a number of terrorist attacks." She left it at that.

A message popped on her screen that a flash drive was safe to disconnect from the computer. "This is for you. Read as little or as much."

Jets cocked his head back, arms crossed across his chest, believing Polina's research but disappointed in the outcome. Amelia had a chance to leave when the car rolled in the ditch. She could have asked for help from the trooper. She stopped the bleeding from the cut. *Why?*

"P—her laptop's dead, or so she claims. The video's on her email address."

"Bring me the machine."

Jets carried Amelia's bag and left it by Polina. He took a step back, watching her sleep on the couch. Polina's voice brought him back to her. "As long as we give this baby some juice..." The computer returned to life, a power cord connecting Polina and Amelia's devices.

Polina obtained authorization, penetrated the firewall, and snooped freely.

"I found the video player in the deleted history. I'm restoring it." Polina was doing her thing, blazing on the board.

A video player automatically started. Thirty seconds on a loop.

"No sound, huh?"

"I hate when they make it without sound, don't you?" She typed in sets of codes. "I'm preparing to use a sound recognition system. In theory, the system would use the voice portal on my computer to scan the video for sounds, voices, speech—you get the point."

Jets shook his head no, but Polina didn't care. She was giddy to see whether it'd cracked the challenge. The video played again from the beginning. Sound came from the speakers. Jets and Polina exchanged flustered looks. They could hear people speaking in the video, but they were speaking Farsi. They were back at square one.

"Does your system translate too?" Jets partially joked. "Subtitles?"

"I might not be a linguist like Sleeping Beauty on my couch, but I got a few tricks up my sleeves."

"They're yelling 'Death to America.'" Amelia's groggy voice echoed by the doorframe.

"Amelia, how long have you been..." Jets cleared his throat. "Standing by the door?"

"Long enough, Agent. I see that you hacked my laptop."

Jets paused, not sure how to respond.

"He's just trying to help you, okay? Let's remember that he and I are both trying to help you," Polina interrupted.

"Help me? I didn't think I needed that. My whole life has been turned upside down, all because I received this thirty-second clip."

"But why you, Ms. Sinclair? Of all the media channels, government agencies—hell, even the White House—these so-called terrorists are sending the video to you. How do you explain that?" Polina became the judge and jury, handing down a guilty verdict.

"Thank you for your hospitality. I'm not planning to explain myself to a couple of spooks, because I have nothing to explain." Then, she said, "Now, if you'll excuse me, I'm leaving." Amelia stormed out of the office.

Jets wasn't about to let her leave. He told Polina, "See what else you can find on that video."

"And where do you think you're going?"

"After her. She's the link to figuring out this kidnapping and connected people want her dead."

As he prepared to walk after Amelia, Polina reached over and grabbed his hand. "A phone call to the FBI will have her picked up before she reaches the end of the block. Don't be stupid. You've done everything for this woman."

Jets understood Polina's concern. She probably was right. But Amelia was important, and whether she wanted to admit it or not, her life was in grave danger.

"Keep working. I'll be in touch soon."

"I can't do that, Gabriel. I can buy you a few hours, maybe four. I doubt it. DCI Post's breathing down my neck."

"What do you mean?"

"His office. The suits on the seventh have been calling, hourly, asking for updates on your whereabouts."

Jets frowned. "Did you tell the DCI that you'd spoken with me, when I rung you from the house in Maryland?"

"Of course. Sent a transcript of the convo plus your GPS coordinates. He insisted. Why?"

"A few hours?"

"A few. Better cut your losses with that one and be at Foggy Bottom by eight a.m. or be prepared for recon."

He leaned in and kissed the top of her head. Their friendship, bond... she was important to him.

"Jets?" Polina called out to him. He turned around, and she tossed car keys to him. "Take my spare ride."

In the living room, Amelia threw the bag on her shoulder, prepared to catch a bus, train—a cab if she had to—as long as it took her away from Polina's house, far from Jets.

"Where will you go?" Jets eased into it.

"Home. Do you have one?"

"Do I have a home? Yeah, I have a condo in the city. Rarely get to spend any time there."

She reached the door, but he pressed his back against it. "Agent, move away."

"Twice, I fought off people who want to see you dead. Be rational."

"Am I under arrest?" Her voice went up an octave.

"I'll drive you home, okay? Then I'll leave you alone. I got what I wanted anyways. The video."

Reluctantly, Amelia accepted his offer for a lift.

• • • •

The convertible was compact and fast. It zipped out of downtown. They were headed back north.

"We weren't snooping around your laptop," Jets said.

"Sure you weren't."

"I'm after finding the truth. Bring Bo and the other three home."

"I don't know anything! As I've told you, yesterday morning, I received the video and contacted Harold. That's it." She bit her lower lip. "No one knew they were in Syria, that they were journalists. Not even that they were Americans."

"Well, someone knew. And that someone has unfinished business with you." The last sentence, he dangled over her head.

18

Polina resumed her forensic examination of Amelia's laptop while keeping a watchful eye on a map with a moving red dot. She failed to mention to Jets that the car had a GPS with a tracking device. For his own safety, she convinced herself. A penetrating hacking program was webbing the IP address of the link in the email. If she tracked the IP successfully, a location could lead them to the kidnappers, she speculated. Her investigation wasn't panning out. Never one to give up too easily on things, Polina dived into investigating the video.

The frames were stretched out in an editing program. Using her curser, she split each frame to milliseconds. With a surgical precision, she added an identification marker on each one to determine whether the video was shot in one motion or the frames were altered and then merged together.

She didn't find edits that suggested the video had been tempered with, but Polina managed to calculate how many time frames the camera captured per second—240 fps. The editing software put the resolution of the images at 720p. So, she came up with 720p@240fps. Good resolution, poor quality, but she attributed that to other factors. Lack of light, zooming in or out too fast—she thought of a million reasons the video could be grainy. That didn't interest her a bit.

Definitely a cell phone camera, she concluded.

Polina lost an hour figuring out cell phone camera specs. She was amazed at how rapidly technology was developing. The cameras changed just as quickly. Her luck struck when she ran across an article comparing cell phone camera equipment. Inconclusively, the camera used to shoot the kidnapping was an iPhone 6. A popular phone—nothing odd with that. Her eyes dragged from one monitor to another. Polina watched Jets move up I-95, crossing from Virginia into Washington.

"Crossing a territory," she yelled, fuming for not coming up with that idea sooner.

Inside the CIA's OTS equipment database, Polina identified the top three cell phone models issued to agents undercover in the Middle East. These agents were tasked to blend in; minor details such as the make and model of their cell phones could expose them and risk blowing their cover. The system showed Motorola Nexus as a top choice preferred by the Middle East; second was Samsung, and third, LG. Not an iPhone—not even close.

She raised hands in the air and did a happy dance, when an incoming call snapped her to the present moment. The name on the caller ID starched her soul.

"DCI Post?" Polina answered.

"Where's he?" His voice sounded callous, sober.

"Agent Jets had trouble at the stash house, and he had to leave. He secured the video, and I'm in the process of examining it."

"Is he still with the woman?"

Polina's eyes fluttered, and her lips trembled. "Yes. He believes that she hasn't been completely truthful. And she doesn't know she's a suspect, or she's playing clueless—one or the other," she finished, followed by a nervous laugh.

"You told him I expect to see him tomorrow?"

"I did, sir. He said he would be there."

"If he calls again, I'm your next call. That's an order."

Catching him before he cut the line off, Polina asked, "Sir, if I may ask—what happens to the woman since the video's ours?"

"Do your damn job and quit worrying about what's not for you to worry."

Polina stayed with the phone to her ear long after Post had slammed the receiver down.

• • • •

Post wasn't upset with Jets. He was furious. Twice the same man had blocked Post from killing Amelia; twice she slipped through his fingers. Sitting at his desk, a fine Cuban cigar in front of him, Post was talking himself out of ordering a hit on Jets too. He hated to see a good agent go down, but he'd been planning for too long, leading to this moment, ready to watch Delay's administration crumble down, humiliated and desperate.

His ego sustained a new blow to its cracking façade when the encrypted phone received a message telling Post that Delay had summoned him. Post brought the cigar to his nose and inhaled it in measured breaths.

The phone beeped, with the same message from the White House. The DCI dialed his driver and told him to get ready, they were taking a trip. He rolled the cigar between his fingers, feeling the fine tobacco soften.

• • • •

An aide escorted Post to the president's private study area. The space where he preferred to work from until he was ready to go to work at the Oval Office. A portion of the library in the East Wing was converted into a work space, outfitted with a maple wood desk and chairs. It looked wonky to Post—homey, more like it—not presidential.

"Mr. President." Post was polite, but reserved.

POTUS offered an anemic smile and waved him in. McKaine and Burks, both blurry-eyed, consumed coffee from Styrofoam cups. Post sat between the two of them. A high voltage of disharmony circled the room.

McKaine cleared his throat. "Well, we're all in the room and in the spirit of communication and sharing." He shot a glare at the other two on the couch with him. "There has been a new development."

Delay hadn't heard the news yet personally, so he stared at him evenly.

"A woman—a journalist, to be exact—contacted me via email." McKaine dug into his pocket for a scrap of paper. "Her name is Amelia Sinclair."

The other three missed it. It happened that quick. Post's predominant hand, his left, flinched, clenched in a fist. That would be his only reaction to the mention of Amelia in this room.

"An email, Bob?" Post coolly said. "Emails could be forged."

"That's right. That's why I had the FBI check it, and they concluded it came from a real account associated with the journalist's name. The bureau's putting together a profile for her." He sipped some coffee. "She knows the four missing in Syria, plus she's got a video to prove it."

Burks shifted in his seat. "I thought no one knew about the journalists being kidnapped? And now, suddenly, we have a journalist who knows everything and even has a video clip? Did we miss the mark on this?"

"She identified the journalists. I've emailed her back, asking her to come in to tell us more. Waiting for her reply."

"What guarantee do we have to go on that she isn't looking for a scoop?"

"We don't have a guarantee, but we don't have any leads either. We don't know where they are, who took them, or what they want from us. Besides," he stood, tossing the paper cup in the trash, "she sounds like she's afraid, maybe looking for protection."

"Or maybe she wants to get close, so she can get an exclusive on a critical situation." Post spoke to POTUS. "Sir, let a few of my agents track her down. They're trained in that sort of thing."

Delay carefully listened to the three sides. "I'm going to agree with Bob on this. I'm familiar with her work. She was a foreign correspondent. Several years ago, I'm not sure how long ago, she stepped away from the job." Delay stretched his arms behind his head and held them there.

"What would you like us to do?" Burks asked.

"Invite her to the White House. If she cooperates and helps us— great. And if she's after the 'scoop,' then we have to drink the poison with the medicine," Delay mused. "I don't want to see them in body bags. Nor, do I imagine, does she."

All four men fell silent again before Delay started back on.

"Eugene, go ahead."

For a moment, Post was vulnerable. Amelia and that video had thrown a monkey wrench in the bag. Delay's buck eyes studied Post, probing.

"The middle man, who's negotiating on our behalf, Khalib Osmani, will be contacting Burks this morning to go over details, numbers."

Post's announcement didn't trigger any questions from the rest. Delay dropped his head, reading a memo. Burks finished off his coffee. McKaine gripped the window frame, back turned against the others, watching the iron gates.

19

There was no better feeling than the feeling of coming home. The familiar streets, corners, the trees, reminded Amelia of a safe harbor. Her safe harbor.

When Jets parked the car in front of her garage, she rolled the window down and breathed. *Did the air always smell this crisp?*

The paper man had dropped off the morning newspaper. The lawn guy had mowed the grass the morning before. Nothing had changed in her absence. And she was grateful for that. No shootings or dead bodies when she crossed her front door. She was home.

Jets stuck around outside, with the door wide open. He was deciding whether he should go or stay. He had no evidence tying Amelia to conspiring against her country—suspicions maybe, but it didn't amount to enough.

"You comin' or what?" She made it easy for him to make up his mind.

"For a minute or two. Then I have to hit the road."

"Mhmm. Coffee?"

"Sure. Black."

He could tell she was happy. She had a gentle smile on her face, a lightness in her step.

"So this is home?"

"There was a moment last night when I thought I would never walk through this door, never see these walls."

Jets had similar thoughts too, but he chose not to share them with Amelia.

"What's next for you?" Amelia asked, preparing the coffee.

"Headed back to DC."

"Are you in trouble with your boss?"

It was hard to say. The DCI was unpredictable man, whom Jets had never met one on one. Ordinarily, his bosses at the CS would be calling the shots on an operation. This was where the situation grew sticky. He technically wasn't assigned to an op. As a clandestine agent, Jets was bound by law, or precisely EO 12333, preventing him from spying on US citizens on American soil. The EO had exceptions, but that was for the 176 lawyers employed by the agency to debate.

"I have the video—should be good to go."

She handed him a cup of coffee and showed him to a seat in the living room. "Am I okay to turn on my cell phone?" She clutched the device in one hand like a first-time shooter with a trigger-happy finger.

"Amelia," he began, "the assassins, whoever they are, tracked you to Brooklyn. They knew that you and Harold were headed that way. They, I don't know yet how, tracked us to the safe house in Philly. It might look like you're safe inside your home, but in reality, this house would be the first place they would come looking for you."

The giddiness of being home faded off her face. With a hardened expression, she pressed the power button on her phone in an act of defiance. "I don't want to run. I haven't done anything illegal."

"How did the four enter Syria? What part did you play in that?"

Amelia was about to respond. Her phone rattled repeatedly, receiving voice mails and missed calls. Her eyes watched the screen lighting up, dreading her confession to Jets.

"What's wrong?" Jets read the trouble spelled on her.

"I might have done something stupid last night." She didn't dare to look at him.

"How stupid?"

"Really stupid."

The two stopped talking, hearing car tires spin on the road in front of the house.

Frozen, Amelia whimpered, "Agent?"

Jets had left the armchair and taken cover by the living room window, facing the front lawn. His hand was under his coat jacket, touching the steel handle of his Glock. "Do you have a basement?"

"The stairs are on the other side of the kitchen."

"Get there now."

"Is it them?"

Jets's back was pressed against the wall. The gun was out of the holster, pointed to the ground.

Amelia read his face and knew he wouldn't be explaining himself. If she heard gunfire, she would know the truth. With the basement door locked, she dragged herself to the ground, wrapping hands around her knees, listening. But she heard shoes coming down the stairs. A rap on the door followed.

"It's all clear," Jets said.

She twisted the doorknob, coming face-to-face with Jets.

"They're hunting me, aren't they?"

He nodded. "It appears that way, Ms. Sinclair. How about we go back to you telling me about the really stupid thing you did at Polina's?"

"First, let me show you what I spotted in the video—then we can talk about the other stuff."

The basement was converted to work as Amelia's work space. The pictures hanging on the walls showed her jetting to exotic locations, snapped with foreign dignitaries and ordinary people. Behind her desk, Amelia typed with confidence. He walked around her chair, taking in with a concerned look what she wanted to show him.

The frames quickly played out in thirty seconds, giving no new leads to go on.

"You see it too?" she asked, hopeful.

"I'm afraid without a state-of-the-art forensic lab cleaning the video for me, I don't see much to work with."

"Play it again."

The video reached the thirty second mark and stopped.

"I can tell you the type of guns used by the kidnappers. Berettas or something similar, most likely Berettas. Is that what you saw?"

"Not in the least. But are Berettas readily available in Syria?"

"Syria—" He paused and sighed. "It's classified."

"Secrets."

"To be in power, a country needs secrets."

They agreed to disagree; it certainly didn't help them with the video.

"Let me paraphrase then, Agent Jets." She re-asked her original question. "In your opinion, based on your professional experience—are Berettas often use in international kidnapping cases?"

"No, Berettas are handguns. For kidnapping, you want to pack power, so you would use assault rifles."

Amelia felt satisfied by prying the information out of Jets.

"Stop gloating. Show me what you see."

Instead of letting the footage play out, she dragged the marker and dropped it. She hit pause and shot him a look. "Pay close attention to the right corner of the screen, otherwise you'll miss it."

She hit play, eyes on Jets and not the screen.

His jaw retreated inward. "How could this be?" Jets murmured.

"The human eye's trained to pay attention to the action in the middle. Often, what's going on outside of that narrow window gets missed. A human flaw."

"I'll be damned."

Amelia's cell vibrated. The White House was calling.

20

The instructions directed Khalib Osmani where to be, at what time and date to wait for a CIA messenger. That morning, Riyadh was hot, sticky, and Osmani woke up well before believers rose for adhan. He had no reason to suspect that the meet-up with the CIA would be different than the routine check-ins. Why then did he feel anxious?

The feeling of impending doom had stayed with him for the better part of the morning and intensified when he arrived at Imam Turki Bin Abdullah Mosque. In the parking lot, he popped the clutch, killing the engine of the flashy, expensive car. This month was a Maserati, courtesy of Uncle Sam. He eased from the driver seat and headed in, joining the cluster of the visitors.

He scanned the washroom with wondering eyes, the anticipation building up. Osmani found a spot by a sink and began to prepare his body for Wudu—the traditional washing before prayer. He washed his hands up to the wrist, three times, then rinsed out his mouth—again three times—and washed his face. A voice from behind him greeted him, but was gone by the time he dried his face and turned around. *Not the CIA.*

The muezzin started the call for prayer. The washroom freed up spaces and mats. People moved to a large prayer hall, and Osmani followed.

Cramped on a mat, packed tightly, he focused his eyes on a dead center on the ground. He had to pray if he wanted to blend in. But he had nothing to say to God. God had nothing to say to him. The muezzin opened with Takbir, followed by Shahada. Osmani went through the motions, bending forward, kissing the ground, opening his arms, ready to be embraced by God. He'd sinned. He'd killed. He'd betrayed his country. Or was it the other way around? It didn't matter. God didn't want him. But Osmani prayed that God would want his child. With the other sins, Osmani could wrestle on his own.

The salat, final prayer, ended. Osmani's feet itched to stretch, but he stayed seated on the mat, waiting.

A man with graying hair and white beard broke from a group of devotees and approached the general. "Prayer's over."

Osmani stood. The movements aggravated an injury in his back. "*As-salamu alaykum.*" He rolled the mat and left it on top of a pile of mats by the exit.

The white-bearded guy walked with him. "And peace be upon you."

"New to the mosque? And our city?"

"I'm afraid I'm guilty. Visiting family."

"When did you arrive?"

They moved the conversation outside, where Osmani hungrily lit a cigarette, sucking in a long, nervous drag.

"Several nights ago. There was a mix-up with our bags. We're staying at the Sheraton Hotel while it's being sorted. Then we're moving on to Jeddah."

"The Red Sea."

The CIA informant had played his part, successfully passing on the next location of the meet-up to the asset. Osmani gunned the Maserati out of the lot, navigating to the western neighborhood of Riyadh. The Sheraton Hotel was a skyscraper, with polished flower beds and opulent waterfalls—and a favorite spot for the influential. A lover of all things lavish, the general was *in* with this crowd. His blood lineage secured the respect of others, and the money earned from the CIA gained their admiration.

Getting the keys to the hotel suite was fairly uneventful. He offered a phony name to the receptionist, an alias the CIA fabricated for him. She, in return, handed him the keys to 0710.

The room was on one of the top floors, spacious and outfitted with the latest designer furniture. He'd stepped in similar rooms around the globe, working as an informant. The frivolity with which the CIA threw money at him never had bothered him. He had accepted it.

Osmani grabbed a cigarette from his pack of Dunhill Blue. He lit it and walked out to the balcony. He barely recognized the city from his childhood. Western money had flooded the streets. Expensive stores—the likes of Versace, Fendi, Prada—were snatching prime real estate, luring rich Saudi women in to spend obscene amounts of money on clothes.

He used the phone by the bed to dial room service.

"What would you like?" a female answered in a pleasant voice, with heavily accented English.

"The breakfast special."

Osmani had given the signal; the CIA would pick it up on their end.

Five cigarettes later, a hotel employee wheeled in his breakfast order. Osmani shoved a stack of bills in his hand and ushered him out the door. He lifted the silver lids, searching for the item. The pita bread was burned to a crisp. He crushed it in his hands; a white note was all that was left of it.

He observed random letters scrambled under a barcode, so he reached for the notepad on the nightstand. He sat at the table and wrote down the letters he saw under the barcode.

GENIRY GB ONGNE. ZRRG JVGU Q.

On a separate piece of paper, he neatly wrote out the first thirteen letters of the English alphabet.

A B C D E F G H I J K L M

Underneath the letters, he wrote the rest of the alphabet.

N O P Q R S T U V W X Y Z

He connected the letters in the message to the letters on the notepad.

GENIRY GB ONGNE. ZRRG JVGU Q translated into TRAVEL TO QATAR. MEET WITH D.

Osmani sat back in the chair and crumbled the two notes. He took a lighter and burned them, watching for a moment as the paper blackened, before it turned to ash.

The day had started without a suspicion, but it had flipped with Post ordering a meet-up.

21

McKaine received the FBI report on Amelia Sinclair and frowned. The bureau had kept tabs on her as a foreign correspondent, but the trail went cold when she transferred to the UN. The last four years of her life were unexciting. The money accounts in her name checked out too—no excessive deposits, no shell companies, no random, spur-of-the-moment trips abroad. If she'd been a double agent, McKaine rationalized that she'd been part of a sleeper cell that hadn't been activated until recently.

He dropped her life on his desk and bit on the end of his glasses, fuming that his own mother lived a more jolly life than his suspect.

Dax popped his head in the office and informed McKaine that Amelia wasn't picking up her phone despite continued efforts to reach her.

"We should escalate this," Dax advised.

"I'm afraid we don't have an option. Start a car her way. In the meantime, try her again. Try her office."

To clear his head, he picked up a notepad and wrote questions weighing on his mind: *What's Sinclair's role in the kidnapping? Mastermind or follower? End game?* His mind circled back to the word "deception." Instead of writing *deception* under the questions, he wrote *terrorist* and underlined it. Evading him, toying with the house was an indication of behavior aligning with the anti-government types like the groups chanting, picketing outside the gates of the White House.

He took a peek out the window, curious how that was going. A nice-sized gathering, he noted. Today was Save the Planet's turn to come down to 1600 Pennsylvania and exercise their First Amendment. McKaine zoomed on a sign they held, large enough to see from his office. It read: "Leaders don't make the country awesome," followed by the punch line: "Dolphins do."

What does that even mean? He returned to his chair while Delay crossed the double door that connected their offices.

"No word from the woman, huh?" He paced. McKaine didn't object.

"Dax and Lance will start a car her way. Watch the place if they have to. She will have to go home sooner or later."

"Later?"

"It's not a perfect plan. If we're wrong about her and she's innocent... with damn journalists, we've got to step easy. We want to control the story, sir."

A phone call for McKaine cut the meeting short.

"Yeah?" He was listening. "Would that be all?"

He put the receiver down. "The FBI thinks they got a solid hit on Sinclair. Maybe big enough to give us the upper hand."

Delay ceased pacing. "I won't give the go-ahead to attack a foreign country. She must be questioned immediately. I want the facts."

He stormed out of the office.

● ● ● ●

Dax and Lance brought a brown box, packed with files, to the Cabinet Room. McKaine walked shortly after them, focused, ready to listen to the latest theory. He wanted to avoid advising POTUS to use military force in Syria, but if the FBI presented a strong case that merited such a reaction from this administration, he would pull the trigger.

They laid out on the table a series of black-and-white stills. Dax pointed to the photos and went ahead first.

"We've compiled a timeline."

"How's it lookin'?"

"Not good," Lance chimed in.

A shadow of dismay crossed McKaine's face. "What's the assessed threat level?"

"We'll get to that," Dax said. "We know that the kidnappers haven't presented us with their demands. In fact, they haven't come forward. That hasn't changed."

"Uh-huh."

"It's our understanding that Sinclair has been radicalized, a member of a sleeper cell, operating out of New York, planning coordinated attacks on US soil. One of the theories that we're exploring right now is that the four journalists were kidnapped as a diversion."

Lance said, "We think that while we're developing a strategy to rescue them, we get hit at home. Causing chaos on two fronts will destabilize the country, topple the current government."

"Show me your evidence."

The FBI pointed to the photos capturing Amelia's moves. McKaine put on his reading glasses and examined each photo individually. Dax and Lance began to flesh out the theory with details.

"We knew that Sinclair took the subway on Forty-Second Street at about 5:11 a.m., and twenty minutes later, she got off in Midtown. Our task force was able to locate a camera that captured Amelia walking down Sixty-Seventh Street, north." Dax pointed to the first photo. "Then Sinclair was caught on video entering CWG. The employee log shows she used her employee ID to enter the building."

Lance handed over a CWG employee log printout, her identification number highlighted in yellow.

"Forty minutes later, Sinclair and a possible accomplice, Harold Frost, also a CWG employee, are seen exiting the employee parking lot in the same car. We lost their trail for fifteen minutes, until a toll camera captured Frost's plate number. It seems they left Manhattan and drove to Brooklyn. It's getting confusing, sir."

"Harold Frost and Amelia Sinclair matched the description of two individuals seen entering a loft in Brooklyn. Property records indicate that Frost's the owner of the building in Brooklyn," Dax concluded.

"Have you been able to locate this guy and bring him in for questioning?"

The Feds exchanged glances, saying, *You tell him.*

As senior officer, Dax sighed. "Frost's dead. His body was discovered by Metro Homicide. Witness reports say a masked guy, screaming '*Allahu*

Akbar' stabbed the exec multiple times. Then fled. Homicide hasn't been able to find him."

McKaine ran his hand through his hair and shook his head. The photos presented a picture pointing to domestic involvement in a terrorist act.

"Do you know what happened to Sinclair *afterward?*"

"No sir. The cameras on that street in Brooklyn were down for maintenance for the better part of the day. We don't have much to go on—for now, at least."

"How does Frost play into this?"

Lance looked squarely at McKaine. "He probably had a minor role. He did his part, then Sinclair offed him and fled the scene undetected."

McKaine didn't like that. "The FBI's giving her a lot of credit." He let that hang. "Dax, the first order stands. Search Amelia's place. Get Justice to draft a search warrant if you have to. I believe that's it for the moment."

Dax and Lance gathered the photos and files. Lance asked, "What's the president going to do?"

"Agent Lance, this is a tough call."

The Feds were leaving the White House, escorted by the Secret Service. Lance said he needed to take a leak before the drive back. In the east corridor, in the men's bathroom, third stall, in the ceiling overhead, he discovered the encrypted phone. He checked the rest of the stalls, then dialed a memorized number.

A person picked up. Lance reported, "It's done. McKaine believes Sinclair masterminded the murder and the kidnapping. A threat to national security."

22

Amelia hurriedly shoved clothes in an overnight bag: socks, a pair of jeans, a digital camera, a spare laptop, her passport, and all the cash on hand she found in the house. At the door, she looked back on the silent home, memories of happier times dancing in front of her eyes.

"You ready to go?" Jets asked from behind.

"No. I'm never ready to leave my home. Not under these circumstances."

"They're coming. It's a matter of time." As they faced each other, he said, "If what you showed me on that video is true, this is bigger than a snatching-for-money kidnapping."

"If they kill me, Ava..."

Jets tapped her shoulder. "Let's make sure that doesn't happen."

He pulled away, preparing to leave. Amelia reached and grabbed him. "What is it?" Jets asked, seeing worry on her.

Without a word, she pushed a black, handheld, box-like device in his hand. He recognized it, an older model of Pro-10G Bug Detector.

"I haven't used it in years." She organized her thoughts. "But it looks like the right thing to do. It tracks—"

"It detects GPS bugs and cell phone bugs. Yeah, I know." Jets cut her off. "You're full of surprises, Ms. Sinclair."

His flattery didn't work on her, or at least she didn't show it. "My cell is clean. I would have suggested to take my car, but it's at the UN."

"I doubt Polina's would be either. I'll check for you."

The bug detector changed colors from yellow to green to red, and back, beeped when he turned it on. The back of the car, under the trunk, back tires, side doors, were clear. He moved to the seat on the driver side: no sound. Jets lifted his head, preparing to tell Amelia the good news, when the device went crazy. The lights were switching at a rapid speed; the beeping grew louder.

Amelia rushed to the driver side. Jets bent down, hand stuck under the front tire.

"The car's bugged," she said.

Jets pulled a GPS tracker not much bigger than a dot, laid it on the palm of his hand, and brought it closer to their eyes.

"I'll be damned."

"Polina let you take this car, right? She's the only one who could have done it."

Jets threw the GPS in a street gutter, hating to admit that Polina looked guilty.

He raised his hands, wanting to calm Amelia. "We're jumping to conclusions. It doesn't automatically mean that Polina placed it there."

"How convenient, don't you think? The car she lends us is GPS'd. She's CIA, you're CIA—both trained at the same academy. Haven't you done the same to others?"

He saw no point in arguing with her. Amelia was right to be mad, and she had a point about Polina and Jets being cut from the same cloth. He rejected the notion that Polina was tracking them for nefarious reasons.

"I spoke with P this morning. She had tracked the sender's IP address. She was headed in, so we didn't have a chance to dive into it. Would you feel better if we jump in another ride?"

Amelia's eyes were round and big. "Yes. And did you tell her about what I showed you?"

"No." He pointed to the street. "Standing in the open and yelling will cause a scene. We gotta move."

"Promise me, you won't take me back to her place?"

"I promise. I get that you think P is out to hurt you. She's my handler. Saved my ass countless times. Why would she do that?"

Amelia had an answer for him, but she didn't want to get in the middle of Jets and Polina's complicated relationship.

Jets grimaced, hiding disappointment, his feet planted on the sidewalk. He, too, chose to drop the conversation for the sake of peace between them. But their truce was cut short prematurely as Amelia's cell chirped. He glanced behind and saw her guilty expression.

"Remember I told you I did something stupid?"

Jets remembered. "Yeah?"

"That decision is calling me."

Jets didn't get it; he shrugged.

"Last night at Polina's, when I caught you going through my laptop, I emailed the White House chief of staff."

He heard the words, and now it was his turn to be outraged. "You did what? Your recklessness could tank my career—Polina's too. And that's after the Feds are done slinging mud on you."

The phone continued to ring. "What do I do?"

"The White House calls, you answer it. It's a miracle the DOJ hasn't filed federal charges against you."

She froze.

Jets snapped the phone out of her hand and hit the Answer button.

Amelia took it from him and said, "Hello?"

• • • •

McKaine picked up the phone in the Cabinet Room after the Feds left and personally punched in her digits.

"Hello?" she had said.

He managed his surprise. "May I speak with Amelia Sinclair, please?"

"Speaking."

"Ms. Sinclair, my name is Robert McKaine. I'm the president's chief of staff. Where are you at the moment?"

When she didn't respond, McKaine prompted, "Ms. Sinclair, you emailed me last night. I would like to meet with you. If you tell me your location, I can send a car to pick you up."

Again, Amelia didn't reply. McKaine waited.

"I don't think that's necessary. The car. I mean, sending a car to get me."

"Okay. The video you mentioned in your email. The White House wants it. It's of national security. You understand that, right?"

She said yes, and McKaine relaxed his posture.

"I'll meet you. A public place."

"How's noon?"

"Not good. I can't make it."

The phone was static, then she returned. "We can meet at the Lincoln Memorial, this afternoon."

"Ms. Sinclair, I'm the White House chief of staff. Strolling through Washington without being mobbed by journalists and protesters is an indulgence I can't offer."

"Amy's Diner, tonight at eleven. Do you know the address?"

McKaine thought about it. "Kind of late for a meeting, don't you think? A full day's gonna slip between our fingers without a rescue plan in place to bring back the four in Damascus."

"Do you want the address?"

"I'm familiar with the place."

She disconnected the line.

• • • •

Inches separated them, but it felt as wide as the Grand Canyon. She held her phone in one hand, a crumbled note with Jets's writing—*"Amy's Diner at 11 p.m."*—in the other. Her head hung low, avoiding his eyes narrowed on her.

"What are we going to do, Gabriel?"

"We meet the fucking chief of staff."

23

Post stomped in the Cyber Surveillance Center (CSC), watching, taking in the organized chaos absorbing the six thousand square feet of space. Every inch of wall was covered in a flat-screen monitor displaying geographic areas around the globe. It had taken him fifteen years to get the project off the ground, succeeding by arm-wrestling Capitol Hill politicians. A few backed him up willingly; the majority he threatened to release their dirty secrets in the open.

The CSC had grown into the technology heart of the Central Intelligence Agency. Drones, hacking, eavesdropping: his faithful agents protected the homeland, safeguarding its superpower status. The Delay administration, with its proposed budget cuts and outcry for transparency, wanted to diminish the CSC and topple Post, tarnishing his legacy.

He approached the agent assigned to track Amelia's electronics.

"Do we have eyes and ears on Amelia?"

"The GPS tracker is still pinging them at her house, Director."

Post's nose wrinkled, and his eyes glided to the first screen. It showed a close-up of her home address; the next screen, a bird's-eye view of the neighborhood. The third caught his attention. A car parked on a side street. He recognized the make and the model.

"Zoom in more." As the view enlarged, filling the empty space on the screen, Post smirked. "The brown-nosers are finally joining the party. About time. Cell phone statuses?"

The agent tapped the tablet in front of him, extracting tower data.

"The signal is pinging two working cell phones and a laptop from that location."

"Amelia's or the bureau's?"

"The woman had her phone on, last call lasting two minutes and forty-six seconds. Then she shut it off."

"She's in the wind then?"

"Not at all. I'm tracking Agent Jets's encrypted phone. They were on foot. Last known location's a bus stop. The connection is fuzzy at the moment. Too much cell phone concentration in one place. The radar is picking up their movements, but it's spotty. If they get to an area with less people, that would be better for us."

"Stellar work."

Last night, Post had a soft spot for one of his own. By not showing up for work, Jets had chosen the woman. Post was fine with that. He'd figure out down the road a play to explain the CIA agent's loss of life.

· · · ·

The email from Post bothered Polina, preventing her from focusing at her desk. He called her to the seventh floor for a chat. That's how he'd worded it. *A chat.* More like interrogation. She briefly spoke with Jets on the phone, driving in the main campus. With no option to transfer the conversation to a secure line, they kept it to a minimum. She filled him in on the IP breakthrough, saving the phone camera discovery for later. He'd told her that he had new information about the video to share with her. Later, then, they'd agreed.

When the clock on the wall signaled near time for the meeting with Post, Polina rose from her seat and slipped inside an elevator to the seventh floor.

Post's receptionist greeted her and told her to take a seat. Post was running behind. She probed the waiting area, concluding that it reminded her of a sterile, unfriendly place, where a person came to receive the worst news in his life.

"You can go in now." The receptionist sounded off behind a computer.

Polina found Post with a file in hands, hunched over field reports, with eyes telling her to inch closer, a vague grin on his face.

"You've been with us for six years, right—six?"

She bobbed her head yes.

"In that period, your only partner has been Gabriel Jets."

Another bob.

"That's a bit unusual. We ask that agents and handlers rotate. The reason we do that's to avoid employees fraternizing with each other and prevent a bond of attachment."

"I...I didn't know, Director. Agents and handlers get assigned individually to a mission."

"No, no, Polina. You aren't in trouble. It's an oversight by the HR department. Management is never perfect." He shoved aside the field report he'd been reading. "In this case, that can be helpful. You and Jets know each other very well, from what I've been told. Is that true?"

She saw no reason to lie; either tell him the truth or he'd box her. "On a professional level, we do. I've never been romantically involved with Jets."

"That's good to hear. I was afraid that if you were, the HR suits' heads would explode." He drew in a breath. "I guess our boy, a fine agent at that, isn't coming home to the Farm?"

"I haven't heard from Jets."

"You do know what that means, right?"

Post handed her a photograph of a woman: long brown hair, rich dark eyes, skin darkened by the sun. The same woman had been lying on Polina's sofa the night before—Amelia Sinclair. Polina handed back the photo to Post, not wanting to give herself away.

"Pretty journalist. Real beauty. Shame, though—the Feds have her dead to rights she's behind the kidnapping." He shook his head.

"If I've learned one thing about Jets, it's that he's always after the truth."

"Bet the truth hasn't looked that good in a long time." The sound of his phone receiving a text distracted him. "Polina, if Jets calls, shows up, reaches out, your first call is to my office."

"Would that be all?"

"Yes. Please tell the girl at the desk to hold my calls."

He didn't notice her leave; he paid attention to the text from Burks. It read: *Sinclair located. McKaine to meet with her today.* Her photo was back in his hands. He pocked it with a finger, slightly amused by her ballsiness to email Robert McKaine. He mused that he might even like her, if her expiration date wasn't approaching.

24

Jets and Amelia exited the bus at a random stop. Morning commuters cramped the narrow street, hanging onto their phones, headphones blocking the outside world, providing a relief from their daily existence. Amelia carried her backpack over her shoulders, blending in with faded jeans, gray tee, and baseball cap. Jets, on the other hand, wore a dark suit from the night before, with a visible shiner under his eye, a parting gift from the near accident with the deer.

Shoving their way, going against the mass of people entering a bus, Jets instructed, "For the street cameras, keep your head low."

She wanted to walk with the same speed as him, but the people blocked their path. Maybe by coincidence or not, she didn't care. Jets stretched his arm backward and offered his hand. She gladly accepted. Hand-in-hand, they marched forward. At the crosswalk, Jets spotted what he was looking for, with the view unobstructed. He pointed a finger to it.

"The rental place across the street. It's a best bet to get a reliable vehicle. Even if they run the plates, it won't lead to us." Jets dropped her hand, creating space between them. "Better if you wait at the coffee shop. I'll take care of this on my own."

He read the doubt in her eyes and encouraged her. "Hey, are you okay?" He put his hand under her chin and lifted her face. They stared at each other. "Don't be afraid. I won't let anything happen to you."

"Tired. That's all."

"Grab us coffee. Black for me." He reached in his pocket and handed her a few ones.

She stared at his back as he crossed the street and disappeared inside the rental place, wishing he hadn't left and mad at herself for growing attached to the CIA spook.

At the register, a peppy associate flashed a greeting at Jets. "Hello, my name is Jerry. How may we help you today?"

"I want a car."

"Certainly. What type of vehicle?"

"An SUV, preferably."

"Let me check our system." Jerry tapped on the keys and drew a long breath. "I'm sorry, sir, but it seems that we're all out of SUVs at this location. Can I interest you in a hybrid car? We have a Prius that's ready to go."

According to the quick search he did on Amelia's phone during the bus ride, this rental location was the closest to Jets. A hybrid would have to do; later, he would look for more horsepower.

"I'll take it."

Jerry returned his attention to the computer screen, assisting the customer. "You'll have to fill out a few forms. Pretty standard for walk-ins."

Jets scanned the forms with a pen in hand, prepared to lie about the purpose of the trip and his identity. Then they heard a loud bang coming from the back of the building, which erased the casual smile off Jerry's face.

"That didn't sound good. Do you mind waiting a minute? Actually, you go ahead and fill in the highlighted areas on the forms, and when I get back, I can finish the rest."

Jets nodded.

Jerry stomped through a metal door that connected the front store to the back shop.

Alone in the visitors' lobby, the bang offered Jets a moment of privacy, an opportunity to use the desk phone, without interruption or objection from the employee. The noises sounded serious, but Jets couldn't be sure how long before Jerry returned. He better be brief.

He reached behind the monitor and grabbed the receiver. He punched in the numbers, then waited for Polina. When she came on the line, Jets wasted no time.

"I've got a minute, less than that maybe. Amelia found something on the video I wanted you to check out."

She wasn't having it, with him bossing her around. "No. You listen to me. I left a meeting with our very PO'd DCI. You have to come in. No more games, Gabriel."

He murmured "fuck" under his breath. "I can't, P. I can't let her die."

"You might die."

"Not if I have my guardian angel on my side." He chuckled as he visualized Polina frowning.

She hesitated. "All right. What did she see?"

• • • •

The UH-60L Black Hawk was flying at high altitude. Desert and dunes made up the vista below. The Army tactical transport chopper carried only one passenger—CIA Director Post with requested final destination of Army base in Arifjan, Kuwait. The order was pushed through in a drop of a pin notice, chunks of the report blacked out, including the name of the high-ranking guest, the pilot had noticed.

Arifjan Army Base—or as the employees called it gallantly "Camp Cupcake"—handled special ops in the Middle East and parts of Africa. The base boasted malls, swimming pools, fast-food restaurants, and a state-of-the-art gym. Post wasn't flying to check on the CIA's ongoing missions run from the base; in fact, a handful of selected agents knew of the trip. Typical of Post to hide behind a smoke screen of deception.

With time on his hands while in the air, Post had altered the initial plan, shifting gears and accelerating the speed on the finishing touches. Act three would be his masterpiece, cementing him in power. Amelia and Jets were still a problem, and his trip to Kuwait was partly connected to their existence. The discovery hit him sitting in his office, figuring out what to do with the woman. A footnote in the FBI report, easily missed by the greedy politicians, steered Post to look elsewhere for solutions. The leaked video bothered him since he learned about it. His men were captured on tape, kidnapping their countrymen. At first Post mused one of them sent the video to the journalist. He quickly discarded that idea, because why would they? Neither he nor his men had dealings in the past with Amelia. It made no practical sense. Back to the FBI report: it alleged Amelia had possible terrorist ties. The Feds at some point suspected her of bedding Khalib Osmani. Their investigation dried up, leading to nothing other than speculations.

He repeated the name—Khalib Osmani. The CIA-paid informant and errand boy favored by Post. The DCI utilized the Royal Army general to detonate bombs in squalor-infested neighborhoods, driving international sympathy for causes beneficial to Post.

Pulling—more like, wrangling—strings, Post convinced a cash-strapped FBI agent to turn over to him photos of Amelia's desk and belongings as they were uncovered at the UN. Flipping through the evidence photobook, Post stumbled on pictures of a little girl, framed by Amelia. He didn't have proof with him that Osmani fathered Amelia's kid; he planned to bullshit his way through that conversation.

"Descending in twenty minutes, sir," the pilot updated in a microphone attached to a headset.

"Roger."

Even a thousand miles above ground, the heat in this part of the world was suffocating. The military uniform Post wore was drenched in sweat. He loathed the desert, but was driven by revenge. The game had become personal.

• • • •

Jets wiped a wet brow. The AC window unit looked like a relic, too old to cool off the room. Skipping non-important details, Jets blurted out to Polina, "She noticed that Tom Seed looks up at the camera. His face is twisted in a smirk. Not afraid. Is it possible to clean up that portion of the video?"

"You're drinking her Kool-Aid, huh? Staged kidnapping? That's pushing it even by the CIA's definition, and I'm not sure we have such definition." Polina wasn't budging.

A door slammed in the distance, and a set of footsteps grew closer. Jets propelled himself to beg. "For me, P. Please."

He clicked off before she finished. Jets heard her say, "I'll do anything for—"

Jerry was back behind the computer, his jaw tensed, paying little attention to the desk phone.

"Okay. Thank you and I mean *thank you* for your patience." Jerry skimmed rapidly through the paperwork, lastly asking for IDs. He spent awhile with Jets's perfectly forged driver license.

"Is something wrong?" Jets was sure the ID was perfect; he'd used it to enter Russia. And if it was good enough for comrades, then it should pacify Jerry.

"Nothing wrong. Have you ever been told that you resemble a young Clark Gable, Mr. Samuel?" He read the last name printed on the ID.

"I don't think so."

"Movie buff."

Jets signed the rental lease in four places under the alias Mathew Samuel, an active legend in the CIA network. If the agency came across a hit with that name and he wasn't using it during undercover, it would raise red flags, serious flags. With the limited resources at his disposal, Jets took a gamble.

Behind the wheel of a gold metallic Prius, Jets drove up to the curb where he'd split with Amelia. She clutched two cups of coffee, cringing at the passing cars.

He honked to get her attention. "Jump in."

"Wow!" She reacted at the sight of their ride. "An assassin by profession, an environmentalist at heart."

"Don't be reading my dating profile."

They were laughing when she slid next to him on the passenger seat.

• • • •

The helo wobbled in the air, preparing to land, hurling sand, choking Post. The dry heat of the unforgivable region made the DCI queasy as he jumped off the plane, glad to be on American soil, albeit in the middle of a hostile region. The military base sprung the size of three football fields—vast, concrete, guarded with wire and electric fence.

"The registration center is to the right of the main gate." The pilot uncapped a pen and checked off boxes from a list. "They'll take it from there."

Post slipped inside a large hall, where glass tables and electric-colored chairs were bolted to the floor. It didn't look like a military base past the doors, more like a swanky office building in Manhattan.

A young uniformed man—buzzed hair, green eyes—flipped his head for Post to approach the desk. "ID and paperwork." The soldier extended his hand toward Post.

The forged letter and ID were masterfully falsified by the CIA's OTS forgers. It would pass muster of trained spy eyes, let alone the military.

The soldier's curiosity stiffened his shoulders.

"What's the purpose of the short visit?" The soldier lifted his face, watching Post. "It says in the paperwork that you'll be with us for twenty-four hours. We don't get many one-nighters."

"Washington won't pay for a longer stay, I'm afraid."

The answer sounded reasonable, satisfying the uniform, who rubber-stamped the letter and returned it to Post.

"In this package, you'll find information about Arifjan's conduct and expectations. The US military leases sections of the base to our international allies, and we're respectful of their customs. It's useful to read, if you happened to run into them." He continued, but Post wished he'd shut up. "A map with designated areas—the mall, McDonald's, and the newly opened Starbucks. A taste of home. I suggest you catch the mini-buses connecting the zones. The heat at this time of day kills. I mean that literally. Questions?"

Post had none for him, however, he had plenty for Osmani. He accepted with gratitude the welcome package, tossing it, a short moment after, in the recycle bin outside the center.

Zone four and six belonged to the international tents. Of course, the CIA had penetrated their quarters, planting bugs, spying on America's "friends." Post had prepared for that inconvenience. The miniature jammer, hiding in a fake compartment in the sole of his shoe, would block their frequency, allowing him to interrogate Osmani without the Clandestine Service joining in.

Post heard the song of a group of men—muscled, broad shoulders, tan bodies jogging in unison. He followed them with his eyes, itching for a cigar.

The mini-bus was a pleasant ride, he had to admit. The AC was ablaze, a cold stream blowing in his face—an improvement from the helo. Reluctant to be exposed to the scorching sun, he lumbered off when the bus arrived in Zone six.

There was nothing remarkable about the military barracks, despite its elite location. They were built to withstand gunfire and bomb explosions. Painted in military green with sporadic beige thrown in the mix, the structures were packed closely next to each other, like sardines. On the inside, the interior looked like the Salvation Army was hired to decorate. Metal bunk beds pushed against creamy gray walls, wood tables spaced at random. The open floor plan basked in harsh fluorescent lights.

From time to time, Americans under the influence stumbled into Zone six, looking for their own bunks. The members of the Royal Army chased them out, but the visitor who walked through their door today, feet planted firmly on the ground, was confident in the location.

"You lost?" A voice from a bunk bed close to the door wanted to know.

"Not in the least."

From a corner, General Osmani strutted toward Post, exuding the same level of confidence as the Westerner.

Speaking equal to equal, Osmani addressed the DCI. "Welcome to Arifjan."

"It's been awhile. Time to catch up." A veiled threat was detectable in his voice.

The eyes of the rest watched the unfolding match between the East and West. Osmani and Post took seats on beds across from each other, tucked away to the disappointment of others. Post pressed on the heel of his shoe to activate the jammer. Osmani was his to ravage.

A final interruption came in the form of a telephone call. Osmani retrieved the satellite phone from the hand of a Royal Army guard who said the caller wished to speak with him.

"It's imperative that I speak with the man who's sitting with you," a woman with an American accent demanded.

Osmani smirked and gestured to Post. "It's for you, actually."

He rarely was surprised or didn't foresee a move by his opponents. The phone call was definitely one of those rare moments.

"Hello?"

"It's Polina, Director."

His eyebrows curved like a volcano near eruption.

Polina explained herself. "Jets checked in with me. I'm afraid the news he shared couldn't have waited."

"Go on."

"Sinclair is working on a theory that the kidnapping was staged. Jets asked me to clean up the video."

"Do as he asked you."

Once Post was off the phone, Osmani didn't skip a beat, sticking it to him. "Is everything okay?"

"Forget about this, Khalib. I've brought with me a photo album; I'd like you to look at it."

25

In the Sit Room, the NSC presented POTUS with the latest batch of evidence. He didn't like what he saw and expressed it vehemently to the group. McKaine was absent for the beginning of the briefing.

"You said the Pakistani Secret Service intercepted the call first?" Delay prompted the secretary of defense.

"That's right, sir."

"And the sitrep in front of me was sent to us, when, again?"

"Two days ago. It was held up through the chain of command, checking its validity. Once it cleared the appropriate channels, we were informed of its existence."

Delay sulked deeper in his chair, considering the factors. The one-pager painted a basic parameter of what the Pakistani did after they detected the call.

"Not much to go on."

"A major setback for us, the call wasn't time-stamped." The secretary of defense threw on the table a kernel of truth. "The call could have happened two days ago—frankly, it could be two years ago. They've been sitting on it, waiting for an opportunity to hit us with it."

"No doubt the subject of the said call was an American?"

"The phone number checked out. No doubt."

McKaine swung the door wide, out of breath, playing catch-up with the others. "What have I missed?"

POTUS shared the page with McKaine, who skimmed it over and let it drop on the table, without conviction of its authenticity.

"Robert, you've met with the FBI. What's their take on the woman?" Delay irritably pushed for an explanation.

Before the chief of staff could get a word, the secretary of defense blurted, "Her name's Amelia Sinclair, a reporter. The Pakistani have this intel too."

McKaine reversed gears. "How do they know her name?"

"ISI raided the building. Syria signed off on it." The defense secretary read from an intelligence report. "There was a shootout with the suspect terrorist. In the raid, he was shot by ISI. On his body, the Pakistani discovered a note with a number and a name. Amelia Sinclair, spelled in Farsi."

"They provided us with that detail but not the time of the call?" Delay curled up his lip, pissed the entire group knew that name too.

"Where's the jacket file with the terrorist's bio?" McKaine swept the room, outraged.

"The Pakistani aren't releasing that either."

Delay wasn't having it. His finger twitched to pull the trigger on a plan. The waiting game could cost him to lose points with Congress, the country.

"The FBI has till the end of the day to bring her in. If they can't catch her, place the journalist on the Most Wanted list. She refuses to cooperate—throw the book at her. We'll find a space for her in Gitmo." With that, Delay stormed off, chased by McKaine in the hall.

"Why would a journalist sell her own people to the enemy? Was there an indication of criminal inclination in the FBI profile of her?" Delay held his anger at bay.

McKaine thought about the posed questions, but he couldn't come up with a definite answer. "They kept tabs on her while she traveled abroad. The rest is speculation."

"You aren't buying the ISI's account of events, then?"

"Mr. President, I can't have you close to this. If I'm wrong, I should be the one to answer to the intel probe by Congress."

Delay said nothing more. He stepped in the Oval Office and shut the door behind him, leaving McKaine to figure it out.

• • • •

The past had crawled from under a rock, in the form of a photograph, haunting Osmani. The fruit of his transgressions fell heavy in his hands. She was two in the picture, her mother's dark eyes, his chin and cheekbone structure, same wavy hair as Amelia. He scanned the locked memories in the far corners of his mind for her name. He should know. *Ava.* Her name was Ava, meaning "new life," in a typical Amelia fashion.

Post's eyes weren't leaving his face, taking in and processing each muscle twitch, each blink. A human lie detector.

Osmani slipped the photo beside him. "So you've finally knocked up a poor soul. She's come after you, collecting child support, and you want her gone. I won't do it. I don't kill women and children." Osmani threw in the wind his best bluff.

"She's not mine. And you've killed women and children. I've got plenty of material to support that. The FBI does too. In the States, we have a little document called the Cyber Intelligence Sharing and Protection Act. To put it in terms you would understand, when the Feds come knocking on my door, I can't withhold the material. I don't see a reason to do so."

"What do you want?"

"To tell you a story—the story begins," Post unbuttoned the top of the US uniform, finding a more comfortable position, "with an American journalist reporting from Baghdad. She had a cameraman with her. The two crossed the Green Line, into hostile territory."

As the story moved along, so did Osmani's memories of the initial months in Baghdad during the American-Iraq war. He'd worked as an informant, collecting intel for the Saudi government and selling it to the CIA.

"One night, she was ambushed, trapped by AQ underlings. They dragged her out of the car, threw her on the dirt road, their AK-47s pointed to her head. Death would've been easy, sweet, merciful. None of which is AQ. Torturing her would've been too long. Raping her, now that's more like their MO. Wait for it—our hero's entering the stage."

Osmani remembered the night. Amelia lay on the narrow stretch of unpaved sliver of land, begging them not to shoot her. The cameraman was lying through his teeth to save her life.

"The hero, embedded with AQ by two governments, traveled with that group of thugs. As the first savage laid on top of her, salivating to get a piece of the white woman, a shot echoed in the night. A body went limp, but the journalist survived. It was you who saved her. How am I doing so far? You like it?"

"I've been told I've got a spot-on aim."

"He tracked her months after the fact, abroad, and introduced himself to her. Smitten with gratitude, love at first sight even, the two embarked on an international affair. Short-lived, I'm afraid. His family won't accept her, so he ended it. She was left with a chipped heart and a pregnant belly."

Osmani forced a smirk, disinterested in the ending.

"She gave birth, sacrificing a stellar career for motherhood. A baby girl, Ava. You're looking at it. You're looking at your child. Only child, matter of fact."

"Amelia has nothing to do with our arrangements. The girl in the photo is innocent."

"They all are, Osmani. That hasn't stopped you before."

Post reached in his uniform, taking out a DVD he wanted Osmani to watch. "It's unfortunate that Amelia has met with high-ranking guerilla militia, conspiring against the US. She'd be tried without a jury, locked in solitary for the remainder of her life. Poor Ava will live knowing her mother was a terrorist. A heavy burden for a kid to carry with her."

A subordinate brought a laptop and set it up. The DVD in the internal player booted up. Osmani scoffed at the footage, but his face drained of color and the knot in his gut tightened.

Cleverly juxtaposed footage, shot from various angles, showed Amelia exchanging bags with wanted terrorists and tossing a suspicious-looking item out of a moving car. The video was overlaid with her voice speaking on a phone, at times in Farsi, other parts in English. Osmani jammed the space bar on the keyboard, pausing the extortion.

"It's staged. A fake."

"An excellent forgery. The FBI forensic team won't dig into its validity. She's good for it, in their book. I have to thank you for this gift. I won't deny I was angry with you for tipping her off, pissed off as hell that you captured the kidnapping of the four on tape. Then, resourceful guy that I am, I got to thinking. The US will fry with riots, crying outrage that an American was behind the bomb in Damascus, the kidnapping, the dead bodies."

"Why?"

"Why do all jihadists strap a bomb to themselves?"

"They're believers, promised a life in paradise," Osmani mumbled, burning in rage.

"Is that right?! Well, I guess I'm a believer, too. A believer that not all men deserve to live and be remembered by history."

"I'll do it."

"I haven't told you what I want yet." Post salivated at this part, when a subject resigned from fighting, accepting their destiny.

"Whatever it is—I'll do it. Leave Amelia and Ava out of this."

"It's too late for Amelia. Ava—with some favors—she could be relocated, set up with a nice family. It'll cost you."

"It already has."

26

Placing the call to Post was a mistake, especially considering he warned her in his office. She didn't have leverage against the DCI to level the playing field, and she might have burned the last inch of good grace that man possessed. Was it worth it? Probably not, but it was too late to twist and turn in the wind. A second man, like a shadow lurking in the dark, slammed to the forefront of her imagination—Jets. As her fingers clacked on the keys, Polina sighed, annoyed at the clandestine agent's underestimation of Post's bag of tricks. She had him to blame for dragging her neck-deep in this fucked-up pissing match. The better man wasn't going to win.

The kidnapping video started. She'd seen it countless times, never spotting Tom Seed's facial expression. With cutting-edge technology under her fingertips, Polina deployed a beta facial recognition software as a last-ditch effort. Designed to cull through millions of faces in bustling airports or streets, the system had never been tried before on a fragment of bad quality video.

Inside a drawer, she retrieved her secret weapon—a bag of Sour Patch, a family value size. It was that type of day where coffee would hype her up, but the energy would fizzle fast. The body broke down sugar slowly, while its chemical composition stimulated her frontal lobe. Polina unwrapped the sticky candy and tasted its sour, sugary flavor, feeling instant gratification.

On a notepad next to the computer, she'd jotted reminders, adding a box next to each item to cross off with a check mark. She'd written: *a freeze shot of Seed's face, clean up that shot/enlarge if possible, match all faces in the database.* At the bottom, the last task, she'd highlighted to underline its importance—*save Jets.* Polina hadn't been able to check off a single item of the damn list, and she was bonkers. She shoved a second Sour Patch in her mouth.

Jets and Amelia, from what Polina could tell, operated under the premise that the Seed guy looked calm, not frightened. She pushed back on their baseless insinuations. Her approach had been in line with the CIA—bomb explosion correlating with the kidnapping, leading to provocation, then retaliation by the US government. That made sense. She had tangible evidence to support the CIA's POV, not Jets's. Here was the issue with facts, especially in the espionage business: they could be manipulated, skewed, re-written. Who's to say that an enemy government didn't meddle in the kidnapping, showing the CIA a distortion of true facts, sending Americans to chase their own tail? She could think of three countries in the world powerful enough, with mega resources dedicated to the unbalancing of the homeland: Russia, Pakistan, and Iran.

It would take a significant amount of time and a substantial group of trained analysts to sift through facts from known facts. She had to come up with a new game plan. The beta software worked in the background—scan after scan, no hits. With a command, she shut it down, building the courage to break one of the CIA's cardinal rules. The agency plucked Polina out of a jail cell when the FBI charged her with hacking government servers. It had given her a good life, an exciting one at that, paying her a truckload of cash, asking in return to use her skills to defend the country, not to hack it, downloading its secrets on a flash drive.

Today, she wouldn't think of that promise. Jets—*her* Jets—was in danger. She brought out her personal laptop and positioned it next to the desk computer, connecting the two with a cord. The computers began to communicate with each other, the desk monitor mirroring the laptop's hard drive. She opened a terminal and typed in */pwd/*, leading her into a directory, followed by *<ls>*, the directory listing. From there, she extracted an untested version of a hacking tool she was working on.

The tool worked like a virus, infecting a computer, penetrating corrupt files and extracting bites of data the user wished to hide by masking. She'd fine-tuned it to heal itself and re-write main algorithms if it came in contact with other viruses, rendering the tool undetectable.

The black screen waited for further commands; she obeyed, inputting: *startx/51403618*—permitting the tool to infect her CIA computer. As she worked, the system constantly uploaded files, bundling them in a nest on her personal computer's hard drive. It went on for the second half of the day. Polina kept an eye on the tool doing its thing. Toward the end of the afternoon, the floor had nearly emptied. She recalibrated the tool to focus on the video. The candy wrappers were in a pile on the side of her desk, her teeth in pain from the ridiculous dose of sugar. Waiting for the last data to transfer, Polina gazed at the silent phone on her desk. Jets hadn't called. Worries cascaded in her thoughts, and she didn't stop them.

The system rebooted on its own when it completed the tasks. Command *<shutdown – r – now>* prompted Polina to deny the request, and she disconnected the cable between her laptop and the desktop. Her work screen returned to its normal functions. She transferred her attention to the laptop, going over the latest files of corrupt, deleted information. She already knew that the video had been shot in a continuous motion, no edits or cuts. Polina didn't expect contradiction to that fact. Her eyes caught a short in bandwidth file, extracted from the video. She assumed it was dead static recorded by the camera when it was turned off. Wrong. She double-clicked, her eyes glowing with confusion.

The face on her screen belonged to a no-neck, full-beard, wild black eyes Caucasian male. The camera had caught him on video during the stop command. It wasn't visible on the original video because of the dead static. If it wasn't for the hacking tool, his face would have never been discovered. Back to the beta recognition system—if this face was in a web of databases, she would discover his identity. The image of the man was the same quality as the rest of the video, but he had looked straight into the camera as it shut down, so maybe the beta would shed a light on the mysterious guy.

It notified her when the system retrieved a 68 percent match. 65 percent and above was deemed acceptable, and given how grainy the image was, she'd take it. His name was Thomas Monroe—an American. It didn't display a DOB, SSN, place of employment, or other pertinent biometric information. It was as if someone had gone to great lengths to delete Thomas Monroe, leaving a crumb behind to offset red flags. At first she thought he was in witness protection, but not finding a reasonable answer—why would he be in Damascus with the kidnappers?—she rejected that idea. Military sounded better, so Polina scouted the VA's files for a match. Nope, Thomas Monroe wasn't a veteran. She did the same with Army, Marines, then Navy. The Pentagon kept their files under a strict lock and key, and she had to maneuver carefully. In the Navy roster of active servicemen, she pinged a Thomas Monroe. His data was blocked off. That could be due to two things: one, he was a Navy SEAL; two, he could belong to an elite squad within the SEAL brotherhood. She wasn't ready to give up yet.

The Pentagon was obligated to turn over its personnel file to the DOJ. The DOJ servers, Polina knew from experience, were easier to penetrate. The FBI caught her once, but she wouldn't allow a screw-up this time. Polina weakened the DOJ firewall with fake bots, sending a million requests a minute to overload the system. With finesse, she surpassed the first hurdle, leaving no identifying markers behind. Inside the protected-by-encryption database, Polina tricked it with a dummy key, unlocking the castle without having to break a window.

Once she'd stripped the DOJ files of their security, she started to download files containing the search terms: *Thomas Monroe, Navy, SEAL.* Her work was cut short; the DOJ cyber defense team joined the party, hunting the perpetrator. She'd better leave while still ahead. File number one was quick and short to download; file number two was taking its time, exposing her. To stall for time, she upped the bots' attack, doubting that it would hold off the defense team. The file was downloading painfully slow: 74, 77, 80 percent. Judging by its massive size, this file had a lot of secrets. She wanted it.

The warning message on her end said a third party was forcing its way in the CIA's network.

"Shit. Shit. Shit." Polina cursed under her breath. The CIA wouldn't tolerate the DOJ's attempts. Cyber barbs would be exchanged, reports fired off to supervisors. Heads would roll after internal investigations were concluded. Eight percent to go. In desperation, Polina rerouted the signals from her computer, falsely leaving a signature similar to Russian hackers. The DOJ would get bogged down with the Russian trail before it came back looking for her; by then she'd be *sayonara.*

It worked. The DOJ backed off; the CIA firewalls were intact, and the file had downloaded till the end. In the shorter file, Polina discovered the basics about Monroe. DOB 03/18/1978, Kansas City, MO. Special Forces, Navy SEAL, awarded Medal of Honor. Four tours in Iraq, Afghanistan. He was a lethal weapon, the real deal. In the larger file, she stumbled on a torrent of highly sensitive documents. Of what she could tell, most were redacted. It was too risky to clean them up under the nose of the CIA, a task suitable for home. A classified document, crossed off in black bold lines, had left a few words here and there. She read *"Monroe"* and stopped short from finishing the sentence. The second name on that line caused her to panic.

What have I done?

27

Jets selected Amy's Diner for a reason. It was an old brick building, a lonely structure on a corner street, surrounded by parking lots. By eleven p.m., it would be an empty scene. The recon mission would be an easier task to handle in case McKaine didn't come by himself.

I-95 etched a straight shot to DC, with the occasional set of headlights driving the opposite direction of the rental. To say that Jets was pissed at Amelia would be putting it mildly. He was livid. With a target on her back, she had thrust them both into a dangerous trap.

The Farm drilled in young cadets to avoid running ops on US land at all costs. The agency's oldest adversary—the FBI—operated freely, under a cloud of power and protection by the DOJ at home. Jets could guarantee that McKaine had unleashed the G-men after Amelia. The Justice Department, too, waited in the sidelines to jump on the bandwagon after a successful apprehension.

His cell phone in the cup holder buzzed—a text from Polina instructing him to call her on a secured line. They had things to discuss.

"Who is it?" Amelia spoke for the first time since they left the East Coast.

"Polina."

"Did she find something we can take to McKaine?"

There she went again, name-dropping McKaine, when they should be adding miles away from the Capitol Hill. Jets snapped his head to one side, eyes locked ahead.

"To call her on a secured line. She has sensitive information—didn't specify."

"Do you have access to a secured line?"

"The CIA has black sites scattered in DC. They are monitored, of course, but penetrable. After your rendezvous with the chief of staff, I'll give it a try."

Amelia wrinkled her nose, unflappable. "Would a burner phone do the job?"

"Last resort, Amelia. You buy them at gas stations, pharmacies, or grocery stores—locations with closed-circuit cameras, digital prints traceable to the purchaser."

She got it at last—if the meeting with McKaine went south, Jets would have to explain his actions, be deposed, or worse—testify in court.

"I didn't mean to involve you," she murmured.

"I involved myself by rescuing you from the sniper."

"Was there ever a moment that you doubted if my life was worth saving?"

His eyes fixed on hers. "There is always a moment, no matter who the person is."

The next five exits would lead them to DC. If he took the first one, it would take the longest, leaving Jets with no wiggle room to scope out the area. The last exit would be his safest choice. Calculating the traffic at this time of night, he was looking at twenty to thirty minutes ETA. Before eleven. It would be sufficient to beat McKaine's welcoming committee. He veered the car off the highway, into downtown, pressured to devise an on-the-fly plan. In the field, that never ended well for an agent.

"What were they doing in Syria?"

Amelia offered an ambiguous answer. "Reporting on the war."

"My neck is on the line. Be specific."

"I've got a source on the ground in Damascus. Word got around that President al-Azizi was willing to sit down with a Western journalist. One-time deal. The catch—we had to go to him. He won't travel out of the country." She steeled herself and continued. "The network won't allow foreign correspondents to get so close to a war zone, after losing several in military conflicts. Harold suggested a blackout."

"A blackout?"

"Off the books, forged paperwork, fake names—our own clandestine operation."

"And you trusted your source?"

"Absolutely. A solid guy. I've worked with him in Afghanistan and Iraq."

"Never occurred to you that the 'source' might be bribed?"

"In your world—maybe. Everyone has a price."

"It's your world too, Amelia."

The front light beamed with weak brightness at Amy's Diner. If you blinked, you would miss the makeshift cardboard sign, scribbled with a black marker: "Home Cooking—Come in." Despite its run-down façade, Amy's had been in operation since the '30s. The original owner, close to ninety, still flipped burgers on the grill, with a side of charcoal bacon. The daytime clientele consisted of bankers, lawyers, and their associates. At night, the occasional bum or a poor college student stopped by for a cheap greasy burger and home fries.

Jets circled the block, memorizing license plates, makes and models of cars. He ditched the rental, wedged between a dumpster and a car garage, with the engine on, hidden from the main road. Amelia, seated on the front seat, watched as Jets slid his spare Glock 42 from the inside of his jacket. She shook her head, a firm no to his gesture to take the gun.

Jets ignored her. "You know how to use it?"

Another head shake.

"A lefty or righty?"

"A lefty."

"That's your dominant hand. Grip the bottom. The index finger and the thumb should form a *V*. Helps with the aim. A bullet's been sealed in the firing chamber." He showed her the parts of the Glock. "To reload, pull the slide back. You'll hear a bullet move forward. To hit the target, focus it between the two ends of the viewfinder on top of the weapon. When you've locked it, squeeze the trigger. Careful not to pull it, otherwise you'll slant the bullet, missing."

He eased out of the driver's seat, moving as quickly as he could, and headed into Amy's Diner. She watched him through the back window, losing his silhouette in the dimly lit side street, gun loaded in her hands. *Shoot. Reload. Shoot again,* Amelia repeated, unaware that a sniper, a mile away, perched on the roof of First National Bank of DC, calibrated the SARS, or Special Applications Scoped Rifle, the US military's preferred rifle. An order of "take her out" would sound off in the wire connected to his ear when the terrain below was clear, with the CIA spook to be captured, dead or alive.

28

Osmani was on board with the minor changes to the original plan. Post ended their meeting with the promise to stay in touch with further instructions. He liked it when his enemies were under his thumb, full control, when he left them with no option but to submit to him. Osmani was no different to Post in that regard.

In the helo hangar, Post glanced curiously at his watch, regretting not being home in time to catch the unfolding action in DC. A spec team had been deployed to clean up the mess started by the general. The agreement with Osmani to leave Amelia and Ava alive was already out of his mind. Shame, really. Post disliked the idea of losing a good agent. But he disliked more a disobedient one.

A guy at the desk called out to Post, holding up a phone connected to a cord. Post shuffled his feet, contemplating whether he should take it. Polina had nearly cost him the meeting with Osmani.

He accepted the receiver from the guy tending the desk. Post's pointed glare told him to leave immediately. Alone, he proceeded to speak. "Yeah?"

The voice on the other end called with a new set of troubling news. "The internal network was breached."

"By?"

"The DOJ."

Post's brows connected in the middle. "What were they looking for?"

"Not looking, hunting."

"Go on."

"We're working through the cyber preliminary identity markers. The hacker used a masking key to gain access to the DOJ confidential system. They caught on, not fast enough to catch the perp."

"What led them to our doorsteps?"

"Files were downloaded without permission. Two files in particular. The cyber system tracked the hacker utilizing Russian signatures to throw them off. It worked. Then our team sensed an imminent threat, raised the level, and deployed secured firewalls for extra protection."

"Is the attack ongoing?"

"Negative, sir. The team's in the works of complying a report, and then we stumble on something curious. The reason why I'm calling."

Alarm bells went off in Post's head. "Give me the short and dry."

"One of our own was snooping in the DOJ system, probably the culprit of the illegally downloaded files."

"I assume you ran that by the bureau chiefs?"

"That's right. I'm staring at their denials. None signed off on such actions."

"Were you able to track the hacker's location within Langley?"

"Her name is..."

Post didn't have to hear her name; he knew the one woman under his command who would be daring enough to take on the risk.

The caller finished his sentence. "Polina Kuchek. The DOJ's pissing mad."

"Which files did she gain access to? Anything in particular?"

"Hmm. I'm checking." The caller returned to the line. "Highly classified data. It won't let me see. The name Thomas Monroe's coming up on reverse search. The DOJ's firewalls are back to operational. I'll trip their alarm system if I move further."

"Here's what I want you to do: The Russian bureau chief should commission a field report stating explicitly that the SVR was preparing to test a virus on US government networks. Modify test versions of a virus and include it in the report. Offer the DOJ a copy of it. They'll go away."

"Understood. And what do you want us to do about Kuchek?"

"I'll handle that on my end. Focus on the DOJ."

Polina with the Thomas Monroe files was a deadly combo, even if she didn't know the importance of the trove she'd unearthed. His pursed lips formed a thin line, and in haste, he dialed digits.

When the line opened, Post said, "Is Mary home?"

"No, she's not." The line died after that.

Monroe had been warned to take cover, staying put until Post returned to the States. He turned away from the desk and looked out the window, seeing the moving propellers of the helo, preparing for his departure. The sun drifted behind transparent clouds, clear night skies. Not one, but two of his agents would pay with their lives tonight.

• • • •

Panic washed over her, the depth of her actions not fully sinking in. The DOJ was tracking a Russian breach, though her own would soon join them. She rose from her chair, shoving a wallet, cell phone, and the thumb drive in a purse and packing her desk to leave for the night. The sound of a door opening caused her to lift her head and freeze in place like a statue. Two guys, bodybuilder bodies, in black suits, had entered the access-restricted work area. She noticed they didn't wear CIA badges and there were no wires plugged in their ears. *Not CIA. Definitely not. Who then? Who let them in? Had the CIA figured out it was her in a short span of time? Unlikely.* She wouldn't be sticking around to ask them.

They were focused solely on her, with hunger in their eyes. As she glided her hand under the desk, index finger on the panic button, one of the two flipped back his coat jacket, hand on a holstered gun.

The panic button wouldn't do her any good, considering the two were allowed to march in, obeying commands of higher-ups. She retrieved her finger, squeezing the straps of her purse. The exit door was closest to her desk. It stayed unlocked in case of a terrorist attack—security improvements after 9/11. From there, she could make a run for it down the stairs, banking that the two bulldogs wouldn't shoot to kill.

"Miss Kuchek—don't do anything stupid. We only want to talk." The guy with a hand on the holster played an angle.

His backup stepped forward; part of his wide shoulder fell in his partner's line of shooting. *Did he mean to do that or was it a mistake?* Polina's self-preservation didn't want her to stay in this room with them. She ducked under her desk, head low, as her feet spun toward the exit. A bullet sounded off, hitting the wall above her head. The plaster crumbled on the floor like fine powder. Keeping her wits about her, she shouldered the emergency exit. Another bullet rattled behind her. The staircase was in stark light, not a dark corner to protect her. With her back pressed against the wall, she took several stairs at a time. The liquidators stormed the hallway, closing in. They had the advantage of higher ground. It would be easier to fire off aiming down.

Her thoughts tangled each other. She lost her footing and tripped on a stair, her body laying prone. She dragged herself to the staircase, lifting herself up, wanting to go on, but feelings of doom betrayed her confidence. They were only a floor above, shortening the distance. The ledge on a side door unlocked, and man in beige khakis, square glasses, and a checkered shirt hogged over her.

"Are you hurt?" The badge on his shirt pocket identified him as a graphic designer, a fancy title for a forger in OTS. He used his upper body to lift Polina to her feet. She listened for the shooters, but they had ceased their movements.

"Can't tell you how many times I've tripped on these damn stairs. Going down? Me too. I'll walk ya out."

He led the way with Polina throwing a cautionary glance over her shoulder, suspecting the two would resume.

The graphic designer walked Polina to her car, asking repeatedly whether she was hurt. She thought he might even ask for her number. Polina reassured him that the lack of sleep and workload caused her to get distracted, so she tripped. When he finally left, in the CIA lot, Polina's fears rushed back with vengeance. Tears rolled down her face, holding on to the edge of her chin, before dropping to a splash on the steering wheel.

29

The first drink took the edge off. The second relaxed him. The third and fourth were for good measure. Within the hour, the bottle of vodka had been emptied. On nights like this, the monster inside Burks craved satisfaction. The type of satisfaction he couldn't offer, unless he was out of the country, under the false pretext of a missionary trip. The last, he counted six years and eight days ago. Another wasn't on the books for a while. The job of secretary of state elevated his status, but no precaution was safe enough. He would rely on his stash of porn material.

Sitting at his desk in the Truman Building, with the last sips lingering at the bottom of his glass, Burks stood, his feet not cooperating. Staggering, he held onto the library columns for support. He removed from a shelf a frail copy of the Constitution, a volume of essays by Thomas Jefferson, and a law book on civil rights. The books tumbled to the ground like useless props. The empty spot revealed a built-in safe. He turned the lock four spaces to the right, one space to the left, finishing the combination with seven turns to the right. The lock mechanism of the bulletproof door clicked and cracked slightly. Burks brought out to the glowing light of his desk lamp a stack of DVDs labeled by date on the case with a Sharpie. His feet bucked underneath him. In a haze, his athletic body dropped back in the chair. He tilted the glass toward his mouth and in one gulp, consumed the leftover vodka. With moist eyes, not with remorse but with something sinister, Burks glared at the stack of DVDs on the desk. Reason and logic ceased to connect. The coldhearted bastard desired to relive the evidence of his conquests.

The DVD on top he set aside, remembering the victim's sobs; the next he would enjoy better. He stuck it in the computer. The player booted the system, with seconds of lag time. The pictures of his two daughters, Jennie and Ottie, fell in his view. He couldn't let them see their father as an animal. Burks turned away their rosy faces.

The footage started to broadcast a video feed of a dingy room, no window, no furniture but a stained twin-size mattress. A little boy, around three or four, barely a kid, clutched a stuffed toy, pressed against his naked torso. The child laid on the mattress, curled in a ball, fearful of his fate. With fingers, Burks caressed the image of the boy's body. Memories of his soft, new skin, woke up his urges inside. When did he know little boys excited him? *Always?* As a kid, himself, showering with his brothers, he watched the water drip from them, drops carving their path from their navel, past the pelvis and downward. Their laughs tickled his ears; his hands would grab onto them, pressing, pulling. They would scream for help from their parents, the nanny, an adult for rescue. Mom and Dad wrote it off as a phase, not to be paid attention to or discussed, ever. Raised a strict Catholic, Burks spent his teens devoted to the church, wishing to pursue priesthood to serve not God, but the Devil.

A figure, tall, with a muscle-chiseled back, walked into the boy's prison cell. Burks's favorite part was coming up. With giddiness, he relived the next moments, changing a child's life permanently, in exchange for Burks's gains. In a low mumble—*"shhh...shhh"*—he pacified the kid on the other end of the camera lens. As the younger version of himself pressed against his innocent playmate, Burks couldn't contain it.

The unexpected rap on the door scared the monster away as suddenly as it appeared, snapping Burks to reality. The secretary of state, in a state of paranoia of being caught, with a pounding heart in his chest, powered off the computer and cut short the culmination of the home video. The DVDs he dumped in a random drawer, before he responded to the person outside the door.

"Who is it?" He cleared his throat.

"It's Missy, sir. There's a call for you. The caller won't identify himself and insists to speak with you."

"I'll take it."

Missy switched the lines and sent the call to her boss.

Burks answered—respectable, polite, back to his politician persona. "Secretary Burks."

"It's late, Mr. Secretary. You don't go home?"

"Who's this?"

"I'm a friend of a friend. You've got a favor to ask of me?"

"Are you calling from a confidential line?"

The other side laughed. "Americans. Lies and secrets. Put your worries at rest. I'm following security protocols."

"Our government has obtained information that American journalists were taken in Damascus. We don't have a word by whom or for what purpose."

"Has your information being confirmed?"

"In part, yes, by ISI."

"Pakistan? If you trust them, I've got a couch to sell you."

"I'm afraid we don't have much to go on. The journalists have disappeared into thin air."

"No need for theatrics, Mr. Burks. So what do you want from me?"

"My president has authorized me to ask that you lobby the al-Azizi regime on our behalf." It hurt him to say it, stooping so low to beg for help from a Saudi who despised America and its existence.

"That won't be easy. President al-Azizi is a highly functioning sociopath. He won't let anyone get close to him, not his own generals, advisers. He trusts only the Russians at the moment. Have you tried them yet?"

"The Russians shouldn't come near this." Burks gripped the phone a little harder, his voice up an octave.

"If that's how you want to play it. I'll try but no promises or guarantees."

"On behalf of the US government, I would like to thank you..." Burks began to recite a memorized speech when dealing with foreign dignitaries who had drawn out a conversation.

"Not so fast. I've got something for you too."

Burks listened.

"Our mutual friend asked me to give you the name Luciano, in case you had any doubts."

"How do you know this name?"

"I don't. I made a favor for a friend, remember? I'll be in touch."

The blood in Burks's veins turned ice-cold. The phone still pressed to his ear, he uttered, "*Luciano.*"

30

It started to rain lightly, a drizzle, as Jets came around the corner, setting course to the diner. Amy's was a greasy spoon establishment, a leftover from a generation that didn't care about counting calories and carbs. The only "greens" were the dying pot plants. The first sign of trouble was the empty seats; the servers were gone too. At this hour, the occasional junior associate dropped by for a fat plate of sausage and biscuits and gravy, hitting on an attractive first-year female law student, doing a meager job at impressing her.

Jets stepped in, announced by a bell attached to the front door. A punch in the gut told him to get the hell out of here and take Amelia with him. An elderly man speaking from behind the kitchen grill thwarted the exit strategy.

"You alone?" the cook, in a grease-stained apron, hollered over to the customer.

Jets nodded approvingly.

"Take a seat anywhere you want. Slow tonight. What can I start for you?"

Jets wasn't fully convinced by the cook's sincerity. He'd seen people less convincing take down a good agent who was disarmed by their homely looks.

"Where are the servers?"

"Had a masked hoodlum rob the place a few weeks back, scared the girls working the night shift." The cook approached with a coffeepot and a mug. "You sitting or what?"

He should have swiveled on his heels, leaving the place in a heat and running toward the car in the dark alley, but he was tired and a cup of coffee sounded too good to pass up. Still not taking a seat, he stood by the bar, mug in hand, making small talk.

"Have you seen cars drive by, dark windows, lots of horsepower?"

"The diner's on a main road. All I see every day's cars up, down. Something in particular?"

"Never mind."

"You need another minute to think about your order? The grill's nice and warm. I can throw a burger on."

Jets planned to leave.

"Suit yourself. I'm out back, catching a drag. Call for Hank when you're done."

Jets squatted down fast. Glock in hands, he heard the sound of a shattered window. Hank must have heard it too.

"Hey, hey you—are you a cop?"

He didn't answer, running out the door, back down the street he came from. A woman's silhouette ran toward him. He squinted to make her out. *Amelia.* Amelia was running as fast as her legs would allow her, also holding a gun in her hands, though she held it awkwardly, tilted sideways, ready to shoot it without aiming.

The SUV Jets described to Hank rolled onto the sidewalk and slammed on the brakes. The improvised roadblock created an effective divider between Amelia and Jets. By habit, Jets's eyes darted to the front of the vehicle, where the driver would be. Amelia screamed, her words inaudible. Jets traversed to approach the car from behind, when a meaty guy pushed the side door open. He looked as if he could crush Jets's skull with his bare hands. And if that didn't work, the Ruger pointed between his eyes would do the job.

"Be a fool. Give me a reason to pop you." The Ruger-wielding maniac, in a heavy Eastern European accent, threatened Jets.

Amelia was giving her captors hell on the other side of the car. Jets could hear her struggles and grunts. An opportunity for Jets to strike back presented itself in the form of bright light resembling a flashlight that temporarily blinded his tormentor. Jets wasted no momentum, centered himself in front of him, and delivered a blow to his gut, followed by a right cut to the jaw. The human rock lost his balance, and the gun loosened from his grip, tangled in his feet. Jets liked his odds. He prepared to topple him over, when a bullet slashed the back of his left thigh. Jets slouched on the pavement, losing too much blood, too fast. He was hit, perhaps a nicked artery. Light-headed from his injury, head swaying, he watched the perp lift his arm, helpless to defend himself. Amelia had been subdued in the SUV. She banged on the back window, calling out to Jets. Her pleas fell on deaf ears, when the steel back of the Ruger was introduced to Jets's temple. The impact knocked him to a total blackout.

• • • •

The sniper missed Amelia's head by a one third of an inch. He had her locked and loaded when a gust of wind altered the bullet trajectory. If she'd run away from the street, the recon team would have never been able to catch her. But the shot spooked her, paranoia hijacking her senses and sending her in the direction of her protector. The sniper would get another shot at redemption.

He tracked her movements through the viewfinder, calculating the wind speed and distance. Shooting down a moving target was a form of art that couldn't be rushed.

She stopped abruptly when the SUV, his people, jumped the sidewalk. *Jackpot.* The wire in his ear crackled as an order came in.

"Stand down. Repeat. Stand down. We want the woman alive."

The sniper backed his finger off the trigger, cussing. He pressed a button on his bulletproof vest, transmitting. "And the guy?"

"Kill him."

At least he would get to kill someone tonight. He turned the rifle to face Jets, who was gaining the upper hand over Milo. He had to take the shot, despite the off numbers. The bullet left the chamber, cascading toward Jets. Observing the fruit of his labor through binoculars, the sniper let out a whistle when Jets plopped down. He packed the rifle in a carry-on and vanished in the night. No one would ever know he was even here.

● ● ● ●

Down on the street, the SUV burned rubber on the asphalt, lengthening the distance between themselves and Amy's Diner. They had left a mess behind, but a cleaning crew was on the way to dispose of the body. Jets's body.

Hank didn't know what a cleaning crew meant. He didn't know Jets before he walked in his restaurant, and if he hadn't seen the fight, probably wouldn't remember his face well enough to ID him from a lineup.

But Hank saw it all unfold, laying low behind a dumpster. The pretty woman being roughed up. Jets catching a bullet, Milo's freaky face, the sequence of events embedded in his memory. The owner of Amy's Diner stood over Jets's limp body, checking for a pulse like they did in the movies. Hank rested his hand on the man's shoulder, squeezing. He bent closer to Jets's ear and whispered, "I'm sorry, son. They promised no one would be hurt."

31

Jets moaned from the slaps across his face. Slow to open his eyes, he felt bony fingers probing the lower half of his numb body.

A voice spoke to him. "The bullet grazed the back of your leg, took a good size chunk of meat. I've seen similar wounds in the fucking Korean jungle." Hank expertly examined Jets for more damages. "I'm calling 911. Hang on."

Jets stretched his hand, grabbing on to Hank's. "No. No 911. Help me up."

"Son. You don't understand. You've lost a ton of blood. Plus, a nasty gash on your head."

At least the gash on his head explained Jets's splitting headache. He sat up, too weak to stand on his own, head resting in his hands. The earth spun, and he felt like throwing up. "I'll be fine. What time is it?"

The question sounded odd to Hank, given the circumstances of the night. "10:48 p.m. You gotta be somewhere?"

"They were early."

"Who? The FBI?"

"They didn't look like G-men," Jets mumbled to himself.

Hank chuckled. "A set of different guys dropped by my diner, let's see, dinner time—seven, eight p.m.—flashing badges. Showing me photos of you and that pretty lady. They called you two 'domestic terrorists'—said you two planned on blowing up a building on Capitol Hill. I reckoned to help out. Sent my girls home for the night, tending the shop alone," Hank fessed up with remorse.

"You sure they showed you my photo?"

"Uh-huh. Gave me color copies too."

"You still have them?"

"Behind the bar, under my revolver."

"Mind if I see them?"

Jets's determination had returned. He bent his left leg under the right, crossing them together, gaining strength to stand up. Hank pulled his arm over his neck, so Jets could use him as a crutch. He limped to the diner in pain, leaving droplets of red film behind. Back at the restaurant, Jets plopped down in a corner booth seat, facing the front door. Hank had been right about the photos—one was of Amelia and the other one of him. He looked at his face, remembering the time and place where it was taken—the Farm graduation day. It was the same photograph the CIA kept in his personnel file. *How could the FBI be in possession of it, considering the CIA never disclosed the identity of their agents, especially active agents?*

"It doesn't take a genius to guess these weren't the good guys who came in. Am I right or am I right?"

Jets was preparing to respond when a car rolled to the curb. Three clean-shaved men stepped out. His eyes darted to the Coca-Cola clock on the wall. Eleven p.m. on the dot. Jets coolly turned the photos over, his hands resting on top of them. They both heard the familiar ring of the bell announcing company.

"Can I help you gentlemen?"

One of the three stepped forward, slightly pulling back his coat jacket to reveal the outline of his FBI badge. "Have you seen a woman, brown hair, same color eyes, about five five? Should've come alone."

Hank flicked his head to a side, chin in hand, rubbing it, convincingly selling a lie. "That description matches many of my customers. I can't say for sure. None stand out in memory."

"It's only eleven—maybe she's running behind?" one of the other two pointed out.

"Mind if we stick around for a few?"

"I'm closing for the night."

A Fed motioned to the sign "Open 24/7."

"Roach problem. Was gonna spray—it's been real slow. You folks and that drunk in the back I've been trying to get rid of."

The suits studied Jets sitting in the booth. "Want us to walk him out for you?"

"That would be so nice of you boys. Hope you don't mind that he shit his pants."

They did mind. They didn't want anything to do with him. One said, "Better call a squad car to pick him up. They're better suited for that than us."

Hanks threw his hands in the air and returned behind the bar, offering them free coffee for their trouble. They politely declined and left in a hurry. Jets watched them drive away from the window, arriving to the conclusion that if it walks like a duck and quacks like a duck, then it's a duck. They were the real deal. His scrambled mind agreed approvingly that the men in the SUV and the sniper must be a part of mercenaries, which begged the question—hired by whom?

Hank approached the table and edged his body in the seat across from Jets. "Who are you? Hell of a lot bad people are after you and that lady."

"A cleaning crew will show up shortly. You can't be here when they storm the place. Close it for the night and go home." Jets mustered the energy to stand, hand lying flat on the table. "If they see you, they'll consider you part of the job. No witnesses, no trail leading to them."

Outside the diner, Jets spotted the blood drops. Flashes of Amelia's cries slashed him inside. *He couldn't protect her. He couldn't save her. He'd let her down.* If they didn't kill her on the spot, it meant the mercenaries wanted something from her. She hadn't completed her purpose. Jets altered his mission. Getting to what they were after first gave him a fighting chance of bringing her back alive.

His hand hung in the air, hailing a cab. The driver welcomed the late-night customer, expecting a substantial tip. His enthusiasm evaporated the moment he looked at the miserable-looking dude.

"Out. No. You out." The driver protested in an Indian accent.

Jets drew his gun out of its holster, the barrel pointed at the driver. He was done with Mr. Nice Guy. "Drive."

Exasperated, the cabbie shifted into drive, and the tires started to move. "Where you go?"

A good question—excellent, in fact. Jets hadn't a clue, just far away from Amy's.

• • • •

With a sack over her head, Amelia relied on her other senses to guide her. The SUV drove in a tangled web of turns before it came to a full stop. They dragged her out, hands bound with a zip tie. She didn't dare speak. A door screeched, then slammed behind her. She was brought inside, feeling the breeze of circulating air from overhead fans. Her captor on the left fumbled with a key and unlocked a new door. She didn't move, but with a weapon pressed to her spine, she quickly obeyed.

"Sit," a man ordered her.

Feeling her way, she touched the frame of a metal chair—hard, not made to relax the occupant. A blade slid between her wrists, cutting the ties and freeing them. The bag on her head was removed too. Amelia blinked, adjusting her vision from darkness back to light. She was in a room with beige walls, a bolted-to-the-ground steel table, and two chairs. She'd seen a similar space—in Gitmo, working on a story.

"What's this place?" Air left her mouth. This room was much colder than the hallway. She rubbed her arms to warm up with the friction.

Their non-answer added to the already thick fog of fears clouding her mind. She sat at that table, without an explanation, a chance to make a call, speak to a lawyer—basic liberties guaranteed to every American, taken away from her.

A man, who wasn't part of the ambush, finally joined her. His slender frame, dressed in an expensive, tailored suit, took the second seat in the room.

His sharp eyes met hers. He spoke in an even tone. "Mrs. Sinclair, my name is Special Agent Monroe. And it's not a pleasure to meet you." The square jaw of his face clinched as he introduced himself.

"Where am I?"

Monroe flipped the front page of a folder he brought with him. He relaxed in the chair, reading the content of it without sharing it with Amelia. "We'll get to that part. Right now, I expect your full cooperation with our investigation."

"What investigation?"

His fingers holding the folder eased. He passed it slowly to Amelia. Harold Frost's body lay on an examination table.

Amelia averted her eyes. Seeing the image of him dead made it all seem too real. "Why are you showing me this?" she asked numbly.

"Witnesses spotted Frost going in the loft building, accompanied by a woman. That woman matches your description. You were nowhere to be found when detectives searched his loft. The place was ransacked, a broken-down bathroom door."

Monroe didn't care who killed Frost; he knew. He didn't care about Amelia; she was dead, even if she didn't know it yet. Monroe, however, needed to know Jets's location—his hiding spot. His men snafued by not disposing of the rogue CIA that night. Post made it abundantly clear the longer Jets remained at large, the greater threat he posed to their business.

"I...I really don't know who killed him or why. You've got to believe me."

"And I want to. But things aren't looking good for you, Ms. Sinclair. How did you leave the apartment undetected by the police?"

"I ran down the fire escape."

"How did you know that Frost was the victim?"

"I didn't."

"What were you doing at the loft then?"

"Frost had agreed to meet with someone. He never gave me a name."

"You expect me to believe that? I'm losing my patience. Again, how did you get away?"

"On foot. I ran on foot." The vein on her neck bulged. She lied. "I hid in public places till nightfall."

"If you didn't do anything wrong, why hide? Why run? You could have walked in the nearest police precinct."

Amelia shook her head. "I don't have a good answer to explain my actions."

The line of hard questioning fired back at Monroe. Amelia refused to turn over information on Jets. The interrogation was counterproductive, so Monroe let her stew alone.

Several doors down, in the observation room, a feed connected to a bank of monitors displayed Amelia in different angles, split in a grid.

"What do you think?" Monroe asked one of his own.

"Still generating numbers. The system showed genuine empathy when you showed her the dead guy. Things changed when you asked if she escaped alone. With eighty percent accuracy, the system says she's lying to you." He handed Monroe a message. "The DCI called for you while you were in there with her."

"She's covering for him." Monroe eyed the monitors. "Patch the director through."

When Post came on the line, Monroe still hadn't decided whether he should tell him or not that Amelia wasn't worth their time.

"Is she talking?"

"She's talking. Not telling us what we want, though."

"Not surprising. She'll have to wait. Polina Kuchek, another connected to Jets, stole your files from the DOJ. They're redacted, but she's good. Find her and take care of her."

"And the one in our custody?"

"We're keeping her alive till Burks calls; after, we decide our best course of action."

Monroe hung up and turned his attention to the agents in the room, examining the note once more. "Is the address up to date?"

"Yeah. The subject's in her residence."

In his car, under the driver's seat, Monroe discovered a yellow manila envelope, containing a colored image of Polina and a small chip. He plugged the chip in his smartphone and downloaded her dossier. Monroe studied it briefly, memorizing the street number, and then he punched it in his GPS. He gunned the car out of the black site, his mood significantly improved by the prospect of a fresh kill.

32

"**I** can't find a disturbance call or any 911 calls in the vicinity of the diner." Polina scrolled through the 911 call center's dump server for something useful. "It looks like the cleaning crew arrived soon after you left. A moment too late getting in that taxi and you could have died."

"Do you know where they could've taken Amelia?" Jets's voice sounded off in the receiver as if he hadn't heard a word of what Polina said.

"I'm not explaining myself to you—she's gone, you nearly died. End of story. Leave the country till this blows over. A currier can deliver repo papers. You tell me where you want to go. A sunny place? Maybe trekking in Siberia?"

"They'll kill her if they think she has incriminating information on their organization. They'll kill her either way."

Polina drew in a breath and held it in. "Amelia! Amelia! All roads don't lead to her."

"If the mercenaries are working for an organization that plans to attack this country, think of the lives that hang in the balance. The fact that they've pursued her aggressively means—"

"Stop it! Just stop talking for once. You've got variables of things that could happen. Too many variables, Jets. Not a single solid piece of evidence you can give that she's not one of them. I stole this evening from the DOJ system. Freaks chased me out of the CIA. The fucking CIA—that's a fortress." Her heart pounded.

"Did you get a good look at the 'freaks'?"

"I think so." She dug in her memories. "Two guys, dark two-piece suits. Wired. The taller one was massive, like a slab of granite."

"That's good. Really good. What else, P?"

"I dunno. It sounded like he had an accent."

"An Eastern European accent?"

"Maybe. Yes. How would you know that, Gabriel?"

"What time did you leave?"

"I got home around nine, so eight or eight fifteen."

"Plenty of time, then."

"Anytime you want to fill me in—I'll be right here."

"I walked into the diner, checking the scene. I'm chitchatting with Hank, the owner. I didn't hear the bullet, the sniper used a silencer, but I heard a window shattering. I'm out on the street, running toward Amelia and the car. This SUV then jumps the curb. I'm thinking the same heavy hitters who chased you came after me too."

They fell into a short silence. Jets prompted, "What'd you steal from the DOJ?"

"Two documents, I'm thinking now, are connected to this, whatever this is." Polina switched the phone from ear to ear, eyes piercing her computer monitors with intensity. At her home office, doors bolted and lights off, she dreaded the daunting task of unredacting the DOJ files. It wasn't the files, but what they hid under the black marked-off lines that sent chills down her spine.

"Where did you go after the diner?"

Jets scanned the motel room, disgusted. The Washington Inn was right off the highway, with a neon sign advertising available rooms, free HBO, and Wi-Fi to the guests. No mentions of ID, no requests for a credit card—thirty dollars cash bought him the night in a one-bedroom on the ground floor.

He sighed. "It's a dump."

"That bad, huh?"

"I've seen worse, but, yeah, pretty bad." He winced from applying pressure with a gauze pad on his head gash. His shirt was soaked in blood.

He hadn't examined the leg wound where the bullet grazed him. He expected the matters to look worse there and require medical intervention. "You said that you've lifted two archived files from Justice?"

"Couldn't help myself. They're heavily redacted—commas and periods are the only thing they've left to see."

"Why them, P?"

She thought about her answer, considering the factors. For one, they were on a traceable line; two, name-dropping Post could lead to the worst imaginable scenario. She shifted gears on the conversation. "Check this out. Every video has dead space in the beginning and the end. It captures frames that aren't included in the video, but with the right technology, you can obtain that data."

"The video of the four—you got a hit?"

"I sure did. A face that belongs to an American."

"Amelia said that only four traveled to Damascus."

"She didn't lie about that. I've cross-referenced her account with incoming international flights, three flights to be exact, and a group of four Canadians did land in Syria that day."

"You believe that she's innocent, then?" Jets sounded hopeful.

"Whether I believe her or not, I'm afraid it's not that important. You do and I trust you. Back to the American. My handy beta face recognition software found a match—Thomas Monroe. Just a name, no DOB, no SSN. You get the point?"

"Mmhm. Looks like a military move to avoid tripping wires."

"That was my first impression, but it runs deeper than that. I deployed—never mind how I stole the files. I won't bore you with the technical mumbo-jumbo. Turns out Monroe is a Navy SEAL, decorated soldier, expert in weapons and the caviar-hostage situations."

"What do you mean, 'hostage'?"

"Like this SEAL wrote the playbook on how to make enemies of the state disappear. I'm afraid that's not the worst."

Jets forgot about nursing his injuries. Polina had her foot on a landmine with unpredictable ramifications. "P?"

"When I'm finished rendering the larger file, you could read it for yourself."

"Your home isn't safe. Leave, right now."

"There's nowhere else I can go to do my work."

"Your life's more precious than those files. I want you to leave."

"I'm almost done. Then I'll leave."

It was a bad plan. Polina had never been in the field like Jets. She worked the specs, connected him with sources on the ground, provided him with a lifeline. She couldn't do his job, and he couldn't do hers— that's why they were a good team, balanced.

"By staying inside, you're boxed in. The bad guys have the advantage. If you're on the streets, in a crowd, you can outsmart the enemy."

The line died suddenly, like an invisible hand snipped the wires, not wanting Jets to say another word. He waited to see whether she'd call back. When she didn't, he dialed her. But by that time it was too late.

33

The GPS beeped, pointing Monroe to take a sharp right turn on the Beltway. Within a mile, he would reach Alexandria. From there, another six miles till his next location. He drove at a reckless speed, unbothered by the possibility of a traffic stop. A police chase would only add to the adrenaline of tonight's job.

The streets of Alexandria were quiet without its choking traffic. He pulled into a Hertz rental lot to switch vehicles. The red Chevy Volt awaited its driver. Monroe kneeled by the rear back tire, sticking a hand under the metal and locating with his fingertips the key box. He clicked on the remote control, and the trunk popped up. From there, he removed the only item—a duffel bag Monroe brought with him to the front. After a quick change, applying a minimal disguise, he was transformed into a middle-aged man with graying sideburns. He nodded approvingly in the rearview mirror after the mustache was glued to his upper lip.

The Chevy engine sparked to life, roaring as he floored the gas pedal. He navigated through a labyrinth of one-way streets, making a final stop at a neighborhood CVS. Polina's place was a short walk from there. Given the time of night, well past two in the morning, he spotted three other cars parked, probably owned by store employees.

His wallet, keys, and pocket change, Monroe locked in the glovebox, a safety precaution. A spy of his caliber—and a lethal killer, at that—if captured, Monroe couldn't risk his true identity exposed. With the duffel bag on his back, the dead of the night safeguarded his cover. The homes on the street were nice, large, their front lawns well kept. He wasn't impressed by their tranquility. He looked at it as a waste of emotion.

The streetlight at the end of the street spotlit Polina's front door. Monroe cut through a neighbor's lawn to check the situation out back. He frowned, discovering the four motion detector lights mounted under the gutters and the multi-purpose camera placed at the highest point on the roof, monitoring and changing positions every forty to fifty seconds. He retreated behind a wall of evergreen shrubs, calculating the idle approach of how to tackle the task. A team of three would gain access to the house in less than five; alone, it would be intricate work. The homes were densely built; in all likelihood neighbors on both sides could hear commotions. Then, there was the question of a neighborhood watch—did they have one? *See something, say something* could complicate things for him.

Monroe slid the duffel bag off his shoulders and unzipped it. His hand rummaged around the gear till he found the item. He had only one shot at this. The device resembled a cylinder connected to a switch box with three wires—red, yellow, and blue. He'd seen it in its testing stages in a control environment, with scientists guiding him step by step. Tonight, he'd test its promised powers.

He secured the electromagnetic pulse generator to the base of the streetlight, then dashed back to the dark corners of the grass. The detonation would cause a nuclear electromagnetic pulse, strong enough to kill the source of electricity, along with the power grid of each home in a two-mile radius. Monroe breathed in, stalling. A failure was not in the cards. His thumb moved on top of the red button and flipped it downward. The EMP made a boom sound like a ruptured car tire. It didn't spark, and the streetlight kept on glowing. He didn't know how long it would take. His first indication that it worked was the CVS sign flickered. Then it died. In a domino effect, the porch lights died too, including the light in front of Polina's.

He had to execute the rest of the mission quickly. Surely, the CVS employees would be calling the electric company to send out an emergency vehicle.

Out back on Polina's deck, the camera had stopped switching directions, and the motion lights didn't respond. From a pant side pocket, he pulled a leather pouch containing his jimmy tools. He twisted and turned the lock mechanism; the door let him in. Monroe stood in Polina's kitchen. A short corridor led to the living room. With the curtains drawn, the home was pitch black; he donned the night vision goggles, allowing him to see on the other side of walls as he hunted for his prey.

The body heat indicators picked up on something sprinting up the stairs to the second floor. He spun after her.

● ● ● ●

Polina paused her work, hearing a firework going off in front of her main door. Her first thought was punk kids, followed by Alexandria had voted strict laws against fireworks. *So if not fireworks, then what?*

Her computer distracted her with a notification that it partly decoded the larger of the two files. She squinted and scanned the paragraphs, while Jets probed with an avalanche of questions of where Amelia could be. *How should she know?*

A chunk of text sandwiched randomly between two paragraphs discussing a budgetary proposal to contra the White House prematurely overjoyed her. The short snip mentioned a site in Baltimore. In CIA fashion, it omitted the names of black sites from official docs, only referring to them by their assigned number. B133—a coded location.

Her hand tensed up from squeezing the phone too hard. "Hello? Jets, you still with me?" Polina double-checked the phone screen. The connection had dropped.

The firework didn't feel right. The random disconnected call didn't feel right. Polina began typing like a mad virtuoso on the keys, sending a Mayday call. The lights in her home went off; so did the internet. And she lost cell phone power all at once. She couldn't tell whether the message was successfully transmitted. Her heart dropped. She swallowed hard against emotions. Under her desk, she punched her own panic button, operating on a backup generator. She reached for her gun, not finding it by her side. It was in her purse in the kitchen, where currently an intruder was feeling his way around the new surroundings.

The spare gun was on the second floor by a secured room, with a vault door, she had built. From experience, Polina knew the local 911 center would dispatch a squad car to her address in under nine minutes. If she locked herself behind the steel door, then maybe she had a fighting chance of surviving.

In a rush to go upstairs, she knocked down a lamp off her desk. It tumbled to the ground with a thud. *So much for being incognito.* Polina darted up the stairs, taking two at a time. Like a rabid dog, a bullet bit her on the left side of her torso, lodging inside and breaking a bone. She moaned and fell down, applying pressure with her palms. Beats of sweat covered her forehead as she stood. The second bullet tore the flesh in her shoulder, a through and through shot.

She dragged herself on the second floor, fighting to breathe. Her punctured lung had given up. It was pointless to pick up a gun and shoot. Death was in her room, coming to get her. She reached for the satellite phone charging on her nightstand, pulling together what little time she had left to record her last moments alive as a warning.

• • • •

Monroe came around the corner, spotting the bloody drag marks on the stairs. He side-stepped them to avoid leaving footprints. Upstairs, Polina lay supine, speaking incoherently. The silencer of his gun sent a third and last bullet, hitting the target between the eyes. Her lights went out for good.

Idly, he searched the body and the house to dispose of anything linking him to the crime scene. A car parking outside cut his visit short this time. Through the second-floor windows, he glanced down at the five-o with a flashlight beginning to canvass the area surrounding the place. The cop's backup was on the way, Monroe suspected.

He scurried to the first floor, then back down the corridor and found himself in the backyard. His route was blocked by the officer, who was banging for Polina to come to the door. Monroe switched to an alternate plan. A map of the neighborhood flashed in his memory. His next best option would be the crooked alley that connected the streets behind her home. A second squad car was rolling in. He better hurry. Two streets over and a left turn led Monroe to the CVS, where a Virginia Grid company truck was inspecting wires, surrounded by onlookers, too distracted to notice one less car in their lot.

Monroe, hell-bent, drove directly out of town, and before long, Alexandria was absorbed by the distance. A hand was on the wheel, while the other ripped out the sideburns and the mustache that had left a temporary red rash under his nose. He rolled down his window and watched the wind slap the fake facial pieces right out of his hand. Polina's murder presented a series of minor challenges he would usually relish. *Then why didn't he?* Disappointed in his work, Monroe fumed at the sloppy kill. With a microscopic precision, he retraced his decisions, concluding that if given the chance, he would make the same choices. It was done; he should move on. Amelia Sinclair waited for his return.

At least he could take his time killing her.

34

Jets glanced periodically at his cell, expecting a clarification from Polina on the status of their conversation. The dropped call between the two was permanently erased from his brain.

Standing at the broken bathroom mirror, Jets soaked a gauze pad with vodka to disinfect the gash on his face. The sucker burned, but it stopped the bleeding. The fluttering of the bathroom lights drove him crazy, so he unscrewed them, welcoming the gloominess. This dump appeared more inviting when void of light. Limping, Jets swayed to the bed and eased onto it. His last distinguishable thought was about bed bugs. When he woke up, the sky had wiped out any reminiscence of the night. His hand touched the wound on his head. *Still there.* As he rubbed his stiff-as-a-board neck, he gradually recalled the events from last night, a reminder of his failure to secure his protectee—Amelia.

He looked through the untouched bedcovers for his phone, but discovered it by the sink, buried under the ghastly pads. In a way, he felt grateful that his mind had blocked off that portion from his subconscious. In the hours after he slept, Polina had messaged him once. He pressed on the app, surprised to see a video recording from her.

His knees trembled, and he fell to the ground, coughing spit. It was impossible to breathe. Polina mumbled repeatedly into the camera: *"1500 Connecticut Avenue."* She said a name at the end, or at least it sounded like it, before a bullet in the head shut her up. Jets sobbed in the motel room for the loss of his friend and his moral compass. She warned him that the mission was more than he could chew. *He should be the dead one, not her.* Between remorse and guilt, Jets threw his jacket on and slammed the door behind him. He'd save a silver bullet for Polina's killer. An eye for an eye.

• • • •

The jacket and pants reeked of urine, but at least Jets blended in with the morning walkers along 1500 Connecticut Ave. The address Polina gave him matched the central location for the US Postal Service, though he was at a loss of what to look for: a person, a package, a code? In less than fifteen minutes, he planned to find out. How? He hadn't figured that out yet. He pushed an empty cart in front of him, up and down the street, whispering to himself, eyes on the target.

Staking out took time and patience, both of which Jets was running low on. The clock on the Cathedral of Holy Hearts finally announced the arrival of eight o'clock, a sound Jets had been expecting. He crossed the street and went out back to the USPS building, prepared. A corner lot with a link fence was cramped next to a run-down park, overtaken by the growing DC homeless population. It was littered with trash, beer bottles, the occasional hypodermic needle stuck in the grass. Unfazed, Jets picked a bench with a clear view of the lot, noticing four late arrivals, dressed in the company's signature blue uniforms, headed in.

Jets contemplated what to do with the cart. He couldn't bring it in with him, and he might need it again after he left. The guy on the bench closest to him looked kind of harmless, chugging a beer.

Why not? He figured he wouldn't find a better candidate for the job, and by the way he'd stretched out on the seat, the guy'd probably spend the rest of the day at the same spot.

"Pssst. Pssst. You. Hey, you," Jets called out to him.

The dude moaned in acknowledgment, the best Jets would get out of him.

"Mind looking after my cart? Be back shortly."

More moaning and a nod Jets accepted as an agreement. He parked the cart by the bum and left it there.

The hot and humid lobby elevated Jets's stench. He felt queasy and slightly embarrassed. Without a formed next step, he hung in the main vicinity, contemplating. A massive woman, with long black dreadlocks, asked whether he needed help. He approached her window with caution, gaze fixed on her manicured nails, painted in red, shaped like cat claws.

She wrinkled her nose, hit with a whiff of his BO. "Here to cash your SSI check?"

"No."

At least he didn't think so. *Was he supposed to bring a forged check? Was she passing a code to him? How do you ask a complete stranger whether she kept a package from a CIA agent, or ask for a name of a CIA operative who was passing information?* No training in this world could prepare him for all possible scenarios.

"Stay here," she instructed and left.

She returned with a man, bony, with white hair and wrinkled face.

He glanced at Jets. "Son, you want me to call someone for you?" The quick scan of Jets's face deepened. His furry brow relaxed in recognition. "Shanaia, take five. I got this."

Shanaia gladly allowed the two privacy.

"What's your name, son?"

Seeing no point in lying, Jets introduced himself. "Jets. Gabriel Jets."

"I'm Mr. Rogers. Branch manager. I didn't know if you would show up."

Mr. Rogers brought out from his shirt pocket a ring with keys. "Come with me." He pointed to the wall with mailboxes.

A key matched to a box, numbered 0789. Mr. Rogers took a step aside, allowing Jets to see what was inside. A manila envelope with no name or address. Addressed from no one to no one.

"We received Polina's Mayday too late," Mr. Rogers said with detectable regret in his voice. "She thought you could use this too." The postal worker handed Jets a second, much smaller envelope.

"What's in them?"

Looking over his shoulders, Mr. Rogers bent closer to Jets. "My advice to you—find a safe place, and if you run into trouble, go to the Sour Cherry Bar and ask for Vito."

"Vito?"

Mr. Rogers's lips cracked in a thin smile. His eyes remained serious. "You aren't a good listener, Gabriel. Vito is a friend."

35

Carved in the rocks of the Catoctin Mountain, Camp David awaited the arrival of its most powerful guest—the president of the United States. Under the pretext of a weekend getaway, McKaine had convened a tight group of selected few to join POTUS in the mountains for a crisis summit with a hotly debated topic—what could be done for the kidnapped Americans? The inner circle was vastly divided. McKaine was losing patience and so was Delay. Each had their reasons.

The presidential motorcade formed a warped S like a snake, driving in a smooth union over the hilly paths. Four HMX-1 helos guarded the skies above, adding an extra layer of protection.

Around Camp David, a high security fence stretched out for over one hundred acres of treacherous terrain, while beyond it, an impressive number of Marines, all members of the elite MSC-CD, kept the camp impenetrable. Tonight, the Secret Service had upped the level of security, McKaine witnessed from the back of his limo. A team of two Marines, as opposed to the usual one, was perched up on the observation towers, visible from the road, before entering the conclave.

He whistled under breath and spoke to POTUS. "By the way, the Secret Service has packed this place. It looks like they're ticked off."

"Not surprised in the least." Delay showed no interest in the surrounding visage. "Can't blame them."

McKaine had nothing else to say, sensing Delay's reservations.

"The FBI really thinks she did it?" Delay started back on.

"They've been wrong in the past."

"My predecessors have been wrong in the past."

"She'll turn up. The globe isn't big enough to hide from our forces, sir." McKaine was doing a poor job reassuring the president. "Our main goal for the remaining days is to figure out Syria. Let's leave the criminal chasing to the professionals."

Delay mulled McKaine's words, before he said, "They'll crucify me for this."

"I won't let that happen, Mr. President."

• • • •

Post was spread out in his home study with a lit Cuban cigar slowly burning in the ashtray. Delay's handlers didn't extend a Camp David invitation to him, but Post couldn't care less. He had his own fires to put out, so no invitation equaled quality time spent on perfecting the Trojan horse that would take down the current administration.

A parcel laid flat on a coffee table, "International Delivery, Eugene Post" neatly written across the shipping label in cursive. Till this point, he ignored it, distracted by Monroe's clumsy job in Alexandria and the mercenaries' botched attempt at eradicating Jets. One down, two more to go, and that was just in the States. Four more would die by the end of Post's political revolution. *How many after that?* He preferred to shrug it off.

He slashed the parcel flap open and removed a DVD. He'd been expecting it. After finding out about Osmani's little film montage he sent to Amelia, Post started to think—he could use the media for his benefit. If they knew four Americans were missing, the "fourth branch" of the government would demand action.

His eyes casted straight on the computer monitor and examined the quality of the video, undaunted by the human suffering that plagued the elderly man made to kneel with a sack over his head. A black banner with white letters announced "Muslim Brotherhood" in Farsi. Post eased his back, content with Osmani's work. He spent another minute marveling at the realistic-looking video, then dialed the man who orchestrated it.

"I'm not easily impressed, but you've made yourself useful once again," Post declared arrogantly.

"You've received my gift, then?" Osmani replied.

"Bo Breeks looks like your men have pounded him for days."

"He's cooperating. Kind of lost the will to live. I'm sure you know the feeling I'm talking about. You've made enough men feel the same way."

"Flattery doesn't work on me."

Osmani thought before he answered, "You'll spare their lives?"

"We're long ways before you can make demands. The kid lives. Amelia won't. End of discussion."

Off the phone, Post wasted no time uploading Breeks's video to the dark web, a sure bet digitally savvy journalists would pick it up and blasted on their airwaves. Delay wouldn't be able to hide from their wrath in Camp David for long. Elated by his ingenuity, Post sucked on his Cuban cigar.

• • • •

The tip of a possible location for where the four might have been held came in too late for Burks. The secretary of state, behind the closed doors of his office, drank himself to oblivion, for which he was remorseful. When his convoy drove to Camp David, he was a hurricane of sobs, talking to imaginary people in the backseat with him. A guard, riding with him, phoned ahead to McKaine, but the situation had gone from bad to worse since the call was placed.

McKaine ordered the Marines guarding the south exit of the compound to open it. He also ordered the driver to go ahead south and not go through the main gates. The president couldn't see Burks in this condition. White House aides couldn't see Burks in this condition. McKaine could stomach it for the night, but Burks had explaining to do in the morning.

The headlights of the convoy grew brighter as it approached the assigned log cabin. McKaine perched at the front door, waiting for the last guest to arrive. He left the agents to open the limo door. Burks stumbled out, puking his guts on the ground. McKaine covered his mouth, disgusted. It took two good-sized agents to prompt Burks to stand. His mind was drenched in booze and his feet muddled, so he gave up on using them completely, relying solely on his bodyguards for support.

They carried him in this condition up the stairs, where McKaine approached nervously.

"What in God's name?" Repulsed, McKaine let it slip out.

"L-u-c-i-a-w-n-o." Burks dragged his tongue, spelling out sounds that made sense only to him.

Bewildered, McKaine didn't comprehend. "Conrad, why would you do this? In the middle of a crisis? The president—I—depend on you."

Burks's head hung forward, shoulders lopsided.

"Take him in to sober up." McKaine allowed the agents to get closer to the front door. "What an embarrassment."

He stayed out, watching as the Secret Service left Burks to lie on his side in the bed, worried that he could puke again and choke on his vomit. They decided that a second man should stay in the room with him and watch him.

Burks's driver returned outside, gazing at McKaine evenly.

"Was this the first time?" McKaine demanded.

"I'm not at liberty to say, sir."

"Bullshit. Bull-fucking-shit." McKaine tensed up. "Unless you wanna end up driving Miss Daisy—start talking."

Cornered by the threat of reassignment to a less prestigious role, the driver filled the chief of staff in on Burks meeting with Post, the hush-hush calls, and the late-night binge drinking.

McKaine let the driver off the hook. The raw mountain wind bit his face as he stood alone on the porch, feeling sorry for Burks. He stammered, "I'll be damned."

36

Burks woke in a dark, unfamiliar room, fully clothed with a hammering headache. He felt as though a train had dragged him for miles, frail and worthless. He swung his feet to sit up. Not a single recollection of last night's events entered his brain.

"Mr. Burks?" A voice outside the door called out to him, followed by a series of knocks on the door.

"Yeah?" Burks sounded groggy, his mouth dry.

The doorknob twisted. A government agent entered his room, letting the daylight in too. Burks raised his arm, protecting his eyesight.

"Who are you?"

"FBI. Agent Lance." The agent casually stuck a hand in his pocket. "Mr. McKaine needs a word with you."

"Sure. Where's he?"

"In the main residence."

Burks didn't know what "the main residence" meant. He wasn't at the White House; he wasn't at home. *Then where the hell was he?* He didn't want to ask the cocky agent; he wouldn't be the laughingstock of the administration. He staggered to the post of the bedframe and stood. He walked in a zigzag pattern, but at least he was walking on his own.

Soberly, Lance asked, "You want me to call you help?"

"I want you to get the F out."

In the bathroom, he held on to the sink, building up the courage to look at himself in the mirror. *When did he fall from grace so fast? Allowing a subordinate to get under his skin?* He lifted eyes to the mirror, and he saw not his outlines, but the ones of his victim—Luciano. That hurt. It hurt, and it burned.

Lance was still in the bedroom. Burks heard him say, "The president has left for his morning run. Mr. McKaine would like a word before POTUS returns."

"That's fine."

"He also said he's coming here."

Burks was under the water in the shower, paying scant attention to the FBI stooge. Fragments of his memory had begun to manifest. There was an early evening conversation with Osmani. The purpose of the call was a mystery for now. Missy Hobbs handed him a suitcase, not the one he carried paperwork in—bigger, for clothes. He was in a car...going where? His mind was exhausted, fractured.

Thankfully, Lance had left when Burks finished with the shower. On an armchair, a clean suit and a tie waited for him. Someone had brought in his suitcase. The blinds were lifted up; he could see the snowcaps of the mountains. His room, no longer a black hole, appeared to be a log cabin. The wheel of his brain started to turn. *The president, McKaine, the FBI.* It sort of made sense—he remembered—*Camp David.*

He slid in the new pair of pants, tossed the shirt on, and focused on the buttons as McKaine arrived.

Not giving McKaine a chance, Burks whizzed in with a rehearsed excuse. "Gotta tell you—last night was god-awful. Got carried away. I didn't speak with the president, did I?"

Hands crossed behind his back, McKaine didn't buy it.

"You aren't passing judgment on me, are you, Bob? It's not like you haven't tipped the bottle before."

"I have. I wasn't the chief of staff."

"Nothing bad happened. It was a harmless night of blowing off steam."

"Are you sure of that?"

Their eyes met, and Burks stopped fixing his suit. He didn't know what to say or whether he should say anything. He stuck a hand in the coat and felt his cell there.

He glanced at McKaine, docile. "I'm not. Did you have the FBI go through my phone?"

"It crossed my mind. I had the opportunity. Your driver found your phone lodged in between the backseats. I had him bring it to me." McKaine relaxed his posture. "Spent the better part of the night debating if I should allow the FBI to go through it."

"Thank you, Robert."

"Don't thank me yet. You can't behave in this manner. You're a public servant, nominated by our president, approved by Congress. The country watches us, and if one of us screws up, then..."

Burks finished McKaine's sentence. "All of us screw up."

"That's right. All of us screw up. I won't lecture you on how your behavior was dangerous. You know that. I can see it in your eyes. The president can never know about last night."

"He won't."

"I've spoken to the people you came in contact with last night. Missy's handling your staff. We're gonna keep a lid on it."

Burks's eyes traveled to the top of the mountain. "But one."

"Which one?" McKaine's jaw tensed in defense.

"I spoke with Osmani before, you know, the drinking. The conversation might have triggered some of my desire to drink more."

"The middleman who's handling the hostage negotiations in Syria for us? What did he have to say?"

Burks was too afraid to admit he didn't remember. He grabbed his phone and scrolled through his text messages for a hint to help him.

McKaine stepped forward. "What did he say?"

He found nothing in the text messages, but he had recorded a memo to himself, close to the time of the call with Osmani, that looked promising.

"This might help."

Burks played it, after which McKaine plopped in a chair. So did Burks. McKaine rubbed his forehead, deciding what to say.

"We have to tell the president."

"I'll hand in my resignation immediately."

McKaine groaned at the suggestion. "You ain't going nowhere. This is your mess too. Withholding information of such magnitude. Handing in your resignation would be a gift to you. The president oughta fire you. But he won't do it, unfortunately. He has a soft spot for you."

"You should be the one to tell him. I can't."

McKaine checked his wristwatch. "He should be done with the jog soon. We tell him together. Do you think you spoke with someone at NSC about this?"

Burks's expression said no.

"We'll tell them too. By nightfall, we could have the SEALs prepared with an extraction plan."

They fell in silence that was interrupted by Dax.

"Mr. McKaine, you must see this."

Dax handed McKaine a tablet with a breaking news feed.

A shadow crossed McKaine's face and stayed there.

"What is it, Bob? Did something else happen?" Burks asked weakly.

"The media knows. The world knows what we've been hiding for days."

37

Waterboarding Amelia was apparently out of the question. Monroe fumed as he prepared to enter the interrogation room, where she'd been sitting on a hard chair for hours. He flipped through a typed-up report that recorded her behavior since the last time he saw her.

Monroe swiveled the other chair around and straddled it. Her face bore the expression of borderline exhaustion and sleep deprivation. Her eyes, haunted, were contoured in circles.

"You aren't looking well." Monroe toyed with her.

"What time is it?" She was fighting the fatigue of going without sleep for too long.

"Do you have anywhere to be? I don't think so. You won't have anywhere to go for the rest of your life."

With avoidance in her eyes, Amelia asked, "Why are you doing this to me? I've told you everything that I know. Please, let me call my daughter." Tears slid down her face as she sobbed quietly.

Monroe was repelled by her weakness. He saw her as a waste of space.

"Turn off the waterworks. No one cares if you cry or not." He jumped off the chair, which surprised her. He slammed a fist in the wall, proving a point. "Soundproof. This entire building—soundproofed."

"Why? Why me?"

"Poor Amelia. The world's so against her. Why me? It's simple, you dipshit." Monroe was out of control. "You have something I want. You haven't given us what we want, so we got to keep you alive. It beats me. I was ready to gun you when I saw you, but orders were clear. Bring her in. There you are—still breathing."

He walked around the table to her side. Hands grabbing the edge of the table, he leaned back, zooming in on Amelia.

"I'm sorry I made you cry. Are you ready to tell me the truth?" He unholstered his gun, released the magazine, and held a bullet in his two fingers. Monroe brought it close to Amelia's face. "You know what we call a 'silver bullet'?"

She shook her head nervously.

"A bullet that has your next kill's name on it. Can you guess whose name's on this fat boy?"

They locked eyes in a weird cat-and-mouse game as several minutes elapsed between them. A voice from an intercom in the room called out to Monroe to come to the observation room. Monroe left the bullet standing up on the table for Amelia to stare and think about while he was gone.

Post had witnessed his lackey's outburst and worried Amelia would clam up even more. He asked the room to clear, but him and Monroe.

"You losing your touch?" Post said soberly.

"You've taken away the tools I would use in the field to make her talk. No roughing her up, no dunking her head in ice-cold water, no shocking with high voltage. Then what?"

"She knows where Jets is. I told you to find out, then kill her."

"She ain't talking. Leave finding Jets to me. My men can track him. I saw that guy with my own eyes—the sniper got him good. Pavel bashed his head in the pavement. Jets couldn't have gone far."

Post flinched. "He's one of the best. Better than you—I don't know."

They heard Amelia crying and saw her bury her head in her hands.

"You promised me." Monroe nudged Post.

"You can kill her, just not now." He handed Monroe his cell phone with the FBI's Most Wanted list on it. "The Feds placed her at number one."

"They want her. We have her. What does that mean?"

"That I can't kill her yet."

Post hated the idea of bringing Amelia out of the black site and into the open. He didn't have eyes and ears on Jets, whom he considered unpredictable. Add in the fact that McKaine was forced to place Amelia on the Most Wanted list, and Post ended up with a recipe for disaster. The CIA couldn't dispose of her, because she was a hot target, too hot even for him.

Inside her holding cell, Post improvised.

"Miss Sinclair, I apologize for my associate's behavior." He placed a hot cup of coffee in front of her. He sipped from his. "He was out of line, and I'll make sure the agency reprimands him."

Fearful, Amelia wiped her face off.

Post encouraged her to drink her coffee. "It hasn't been easy for you. I'm sure the worst's over."

"How do you know that?"

He smirked. "It has to be. We know the truth now. Twenty hours ago, we were still investigating, but now we know."

"I don't understand. You found who took the four? Did you send help to get them?"

"We found out who's behind it."

"That's great. So I can go? You believe me that I'm innocent?"

Post sipped from his coffee and then calmly explained to her, "According to our CIA analyst Polina Kuchek's research, the IP address that sent you the first email belonged to Rashid Haddad."

Amelia's fingers trembled when Post mentioned that name.

"The night we suspect the four were kidnapped, Pakistan's ISI shot down a terrorist in Damascus with the same name."

Wide-eyed, Amelia listened intently.

"ISI agents included in their sitrep that they discovered on Haddad's body a number and a name of a woman in the States he'd been working with."

She opened her mouth to interrupt, but Post's finger motioned her to stop.

"That number was your business line. And there's more." He offered her his smartphone, displaying a news story.

She read the title in a hurry: "Famous US Photographer Falls Victim to Muslim Brotherhood."

Post instructed, "Watch for yourself."

In a video like the thousands she'd seen before, a victim was kneeling down on a prayer carpet, dressed in rags, with a bag over his head.

When the bag came off, dismay fastened on her face. "Bo. It's him. Bo."

As the camera pulled back, Bo's frame swayed side to side, ready to nosedive to the floor.

She shut it off, unable to stomach what she just saw.

Post had finished his coffee and played with the Styrofoam cup. "And as of this moment, the FBI has placed you on their terrorist Most Wanted list. Like I said in the beginning, we've got the right man."

"You're making a mistake. I've never conspired with a terrorist or planned on hurting others. I'm a journalist. I write. I tell stories. Please, you've got to believe me."

Like a sly fox, Post swooped in and made her an offer. "I'm a powerful man, and maybe I can put in a good word for you. But I have to ask you for something."

"You name it and I'll do it. Please. Help me."

38

The cart was gone. So was the homeless guy left in charge. Jets had to move. If he stayed in one place, he was an open target.

The developments at the post office were puzzling to him, and Mr. Rogers was at the top of the list of enigmatic figures Jets had dealt with in this business.

Jets cringed at the sound of flapping wings of crows hovering low in the dreary sky. He stepped up his speed, stopping briefly at the next dumpster he saw to trash the coat, grateful to have freed himself of it. On the main street clogged by people, hustling in a rhythm, Jets stayed with them, relying on their able bodies as a shield.

His attention was split between constantly scanning the rooftops for a sniper and reading the faces of walkers for a potential Eastern European-looking killer sent to finish off the job. It was counterproductive, and Jets decided that he wouldn't get far by doing that. He'd killed the power to his cell, preventing the CIA tracking his location. But he had to get an address for the Sour Cherry Bar, and without the web browser on his phone, he was at a loss. Jets came up with an alternative solution after a quick check of the surrounding stores. The flashing sign of a U Mobile Store toward the middle of the street gleamed in his face as he walked through the front door. The situation inside resembled outside: packed with early birds buying minutes for their phones, asking whether the employees can illegally unlock the latest model smartphone they'd bought off Craigslist.

Despite his best efforts to avoid making an eye contact with an associate, a young woman approached him with a crooked smile. "Hi, I'm Mandy—what can I help you with?"

"A new tablet for my wife." Jets lied convincingly. "How about those?" He pointed to a row of tablets connected to a wall.

"I'm sorry, these aren't the real ones." She lowered her voice. "People try to steal them. Management put dummies out to deter them from doing that. You can still look at them. If you like a particular model, I can bring one out from the back." She returned to her crooked smile.

Jets cursed Murphy's Law under his breath—a phone store with no real electronic devices. Mandy must have asked him a question, because she looked at him with expectation.

He answered, "Yeah, sure," which did the trick, and she left him alone. Free to roam without her, Jets looked through the displays, picking up random phones but putting them back down when they turned out to be cheap plastic. This had been a bust and a waste of his time. He should head out to the closest library. Then Mandy returned with an open box.

"I think you'll be happy with this one. It's a real big seller." She pushed the power button of the tablet.

"Can I get a minute to check it out?"

"I'm not supposed to do that, but you look like a solid guy. A minute."

Wasting no time, Jets typed in Sour Cherry Bar in the search bar. His expression betrayed his disappointment when the search yielded a total of 221,657 hits containing that name. The very top had an address to a local place in DC. Jets jolted it down.

Mandy showed up. "Well? What did you think?"

"I like it, but I think I'm going to look online."

The smile vanished off her face. "We have 30 percent off current products. The sale's going on until the end of February if you change your mind."

After two bus rides and several hours later, Jets set foot on Fifty-Third Street in Lincoln Heights, a neighborhood east of Anacostia. A regular on the local channels for its high drugs and guns crime, with an occasional murder investigation. At first glance, Lincoln Heights offered little to the newcomer. It was poorer than dirt, and it looked it.

He grew up in a similar place—Highland Park, Detroit—with his mother, after his dad up and left. His mom couldn't keep a job. All they had she spent on her heroin addiction. On his sixteenth birthday, a day after Christmas, he found her dead, with a needle still stuck in her arm, laying on their bathroom floor. The past couldn't be reckoned with. Jets shook his head to clear it from the clutter and marched on the asphalt, looking for the Sour Cherry Bar. He walked by a white, frail building— the local Methodist Church, according to the granite sign in the front lawn—but no bar. He resumed walking, though; the place could be the other way. He had no idea.

When Jets reached the family planning place, a one-story structure with a slanted roof, he stopped to marvel at the irony. The Sour Cherry Bar was glued directly to the family planning place, sharing the same roof.

What were the odds of that? He had to push the door in, because the handle was missing. The bar was sketchy, at best. There was no doubt about that, but he'd run out of time, friends, and options. If Polina trusted this guy Vito, then so should Jets.

A suffocating odor of stale cigarette smoke hit him the moment he walked into the bar. The lights were dim, and it made it difficult to see anything. He thought it looked small, judging by the cramped room with empty tables. On the right wall was the bar with some barstools, and on the left wall was an old TV, resting on a beat-up black desk with chipping paint around its corners. The TV played daytime soaps with the sound muted. Instead, a jukebox next to it blared Alice Cooper's *Greatest Hits* album.

"Hello?" Jets raised his voice above the din and squinted to see better.

No one returned his call. Jets walked around the bar, noticing a door with a Do Not Enter sign. Through a crack in the door, he witnessed what appeared to be a woman with her panties around her ankles having sex with someone. Not his kind of party, he took a step back.

A grip to his shoulder sent him sidestepping, pressing on his heels, coming face-to-face with a guy two heads taller than him. Distracted by a spider tattoo on the guy's buzzed-off head cost him. A right hook knocked Jets in a corner, who delivered a lower jaw sufficient punch, while feeling the wear and tear in his body.

The tattooed prick was light on his feet—quick to recover, too. He loosened breath-taking blows to Jets's stomach, then waited. When Jets got in range, the man clapped a hand over Jet's throat, squeezing. It looked like it was game over for Jets, who in between coughs yelled, "Vito!"

"Who the fuck are you?" The grip loosened.

"Let go of me." Jets wiggled out of the titan's massive arms. "Is that how you treat your customers?"

"Just the perverts like you. Getting off on watching women getting it on, huh?"

The overreaction now made sense to Jets. This must be the hooker's pimp. "Listen, I came here to find Vito, not to get jerked off. All right? Walked in at the wrong time. If you'll excuse me, I'll be out of here."

"Who are you?"

"I'm not looking to make friends, pal. I'm sure the lady behind the door is worth the twenty bucks. Just not my sort of thing. Don't get offended."

"Man, screw this shit. How do you know Vito?"

Stretching his sore neck, Jets shot back, "I don't. A friend sent me."

The woman started to moan louder, startling Jets. Her protector smirked, a sign he was warming up to Jets. They took the conversation out in an alley, keeping a safe distance between each other. With a lit cigarette hanging to the side of his mouth, the guy probed Jets with questions.

"What's the name of your friend?"

"Forget about it, buddy. But I'll appreciate it if you tell me the quickest route to the next bus stop?"

"Don't you wanna know how to get to Vito?"

"Wait. You know him? You know Vito?"

"It depends."

"Money. I get it. What's the price?" Jets fished from his pocket a measly twenty bucks.

"You trippin'. Put your money in your pocket. All I'm asking is the name of your friend. Be cool." He inhaled the cigarette smoke and held it in.

"Polina. My friend's name was Polina Kuchek."

That got a rise out of the other guy, who flicked the cigarette bud in a trash can, eyes not leaving Jets.

"I told you my friend's name. You got a number for Vito?"

"I'm Vito. Did something happen to Polina?"

Judging by his reaction, Jets concluded Polina's Mayday hadn't reached Vito. "She was killed last night. I'm here in part because I'm after the man who did this to her."

The initial shock of Vito's rough looks began to wear off. Questions swirled in Jets's mind of how precisely Polina and Vito knew each other.

Vito hadn't uttered a single word. Jets allowed him the moment to process. He didn't have a clue of who Vito was to Polina. He could be speaking to a brother or a boyfriend. Jets didn't want to come across as insensitive.

"That means you're Jets?" Vito's lips moved.

"Aha. Polina has told you about me?"

"A little. Has she told you about me?"

Jets let out a nervous laugh. *Was she supposed to?* He gave an honest answer. "I didn't know you existed till three hours ago. Mr. Rogers at the post office said to look for Vito at the Sour Cherry Bar."

"You met with Mr. Rogers?"

Jets was growing tired of Vito's one-liners. "Briefly. He also didn't say much. It seems to be a recurrent theme in this group."

"Did you bring something with you?"

"I got an envelope from a mailbox. Haven't looked at it yet. And a smaller one. Looks like a note. Haven't checked it out. Why?"

"Come with me."

The woman had left following her early-afternoon tryst. The corner room smelled of sweaty bodies and dollar-bottle perfume. Jets held the door closed with his back, Vito in a chair.

"Before anything, I wanna clear the air." Vito carried on. "Some creeps come in to spy on Cherry when she's with a client."

"Cherry? The bar's named after her?"

"She's the owner. To help pay the bills, she, you know, pays the bills by other means."

"I prefer if we don't dwell on that."

"So, you're CIA?"

"What makes you think that?"

"Come on. You CIA bastards are shifty mother-you-know-whats. Plus, you're friends with Polina."

"What difference does it make to you if I'm CIA or not?" Jets grumbled.

"Suit yourself. The envelopes—let's see them."

Jets expected the larger envelope would contain a document, pages, something else, not a flash drive. Interested, Vito took the lead and plugged it in the computer.

"Knowing Polina, this should be good."

The thought of Polina no longer among the living hurt Jets's soul. He had avoided thinking of her dying video.

Vito's eyes glossed over with dismay at the documents saved on the flash drive. He sprung to his feet and ripped the drive out of the computer.

"You sure Polina sent you?" The look of a huntsman, gearing up for a fight, had returned.

"Easy. Take it easy. Polina sent me. Mr. Rogers sent me. I need to know what's on that drive."

"You're a lying bastard." Vito jammed his finger into Jets's chest. "Polina died protecting this garbage?"

"I think so. She stole it from the DOJ server while at the CIA. Two mercenaries showed up, wanting her to go with them. She bolted." Jets took a break, collecting himself, and resumed. "Later, I was with Amelia at Amy's. We, too, got ganged up on, probably the same perps." His mind trailed off.

"I missed what you said after Polina being scared off by the two hombres. Who's Amelia?"

"It's a long story."

"I'm a bouncer at a shitty bar in the projects. All I got's time on my hands, bro."

"Amelia Sinclair is a journalist who received a video clip showing the kidnapping of US journalists in Damascus. Her boss called me that morning, asking for help. I drove to Brooklyn to meet with them. He got killed. I saved her. Polina was helping me. She stumbled on the documents after she saw a guy's face in—what did she call it?—the dead space of the video."

"Yeah. Dead space. Did she tell you the name of the guy?"

Jets thought about it. "Thomas Monroe. No hits on a SSN or DOB. She tracked him in the SEAL database. That's all I know."

"Come with me. This ain't the place to conduct our type of business. I live in the apartment building out back. Better suited for this shit."

Jets wasn't going anywhere before Vito gave him something in return. "Not so fast. Tell me about the stuff saved on the flash drive. What is it?"

Vito brought the drive close to Jets's face, really close. "This here caused the end of my career at the CIA. I helped hide it in the DOJ."

39

Delay passed through the door of the main residence, his shaggy hair matted in sweat. With a visibly interested expression, he spoke to McKaine first.

"The Secret Service radioed in. Said it's urgent. Is it the hostages?"

McKaine hadn't fully prepared how to explain to POTUS the gaffe the White House was currently facing back in Washington. "It is, and you have to see for yourself."

Delay ignored McKaine, courting Burks next, who was pale and sickly looking. "Nice of you to stop by. Are you sick?"

"Mr. President," McKaine insisted.

"All right. Show me what got you two in a tussle."

Despite being the leader of the free world, the president learned of breaking news like the rest of the people—from watching the news. And Delay didn't like what was being reported presently.

Bo Breeks was tied up, kneeling in a rat hole, and read off a demand list through clenched teeth. An absurd demand list, conjured by a terrorist with a wild imagination. The reporter on the TV was speaking directly in front of the White House, telling the world the president wasn't home. Delay muted the sound, but the room vibrated with his bravado voice.

"Goddamn it, Bob. I thought we had a lid on this? Is this the doing of that woman?"

"The FBI's checking."

"Screw the FBI and screw the NSC." He pointed a finger to McKaine and Burks. "And screw you and you."

After a tense minute, POTUS resumed, "Where is she?"

"I'll get Dax." McKaine cracked the door so Dax could join them.

"Sinclair failed to arrive at the diner last night. We spoke with the owner, who said he hadn't seen a woman matching her description." Dax laid it out in the open.

"They know. The sharks were circling in the water before this. Now they're going for the kill."

"We should try to remember that at least the kidnappers are making a move," Burks said.

Delay had to agree with him. The media and half of the country would always hate him, no matter what. It came with the job title and large house.

He sighed. "We leave for Washington in an hour. Get the helo ready."

• • • •

McKaine watched the helo loaded with the president in tow lift off the ground. The Washington establishment was melting with sinful outrage and poisonous accusations directed at the administration's lack of response to the hostage situation. The president's visibility at the White House was imperative. McKaine was the point man of mending things at Camp David. He excused Burks as he prepared to speak with Dax and Lance, tête-à-tête.

Inside the Aspen Lodge's kitchen, he turned his attention from the large frosted windows overlooking a pond to the two FBI men. He scratched behind the ear, carefully choosing his words. "The woman—the story's she didn't show up, huh?"

"The owner said she hadn't been in that night, that he can recall." Dax cemented his original statement.

"I presume you've got people watching her place?"

"Her place, cell phone, family members, coworkers. We've added extra eyes at airports, bus stops, and train stations. The whole nine yards."

It sounded good and all, but McKaine had a hard time stomaching the notion that a journalist without special training in military or intelligence evasion could lead the White House's top dogs by their noses.

"Help me out here, guys. She's, what? In her mid-thirties, a mom, hasn't been out of the country in what, four, maybe five years? Her computer history didn't turn out any meaningful evidence. How am I doing so far in profiling her?"

Lance, reticent, played devil's advocate. "The ISI report is a solid lead that she was in communication with a high-ranking terrorist. The same one the Pakistani offed in Damascus."

"She didn't come to your meeting at the diner, and her phone has been off," Dax added.

"Good points, but there could be reasonable explanations to both."

McKaine's leather bag lay flat on the kitchen counter. He picked it up in one hand, having heard plenty on the topic. "We'll continue this discussion at the office. That should be all for now."

The chief of staff made sure Burks made it into a limo, separate from his, as they embarked on a seventy-mile ride back home. He rested casually in the seat, thoughts of Amelia not giving him peace. To distract himself, he reached in his bag, looking for a report to read. But the only thing worth reading was the original FBI report he'd received on the night the administration found out about her. He spread the pages on his lap, undeterred by the setbacks.

Even the president's official vehicles got stuck in traffic on occasion, while the local cops directed traffic to let the black SUV pass. McKaine eyed a footnote he'd skipped over before. It was a sentence long, and without knowing the background, it was reasonable to dismiss it. Bookmarking the page with a finger, he flipped back to the index page, looking for the agencies who supplied the material for the report. He went down the list: Department of Homeland, Office of Intelligence and Analysis, National

Security Agency—of course the FBI was on it too—National Counterter-rorist Center, and the Central Intelligence Agency. He flipped back to the bookmarked page and, with a sharper focus, re-read the sentence.

He had a million reasons to walk away from the theory taking shape in his mind, one that pushed him to hold on to it. From the cord tele-phone in the back of the limo, he rang Burks's car. "You know how to get in touch with Post's middleman?"

"He gets in touch with me. Why?"

"That guy then controls the flow of information. He decides when to tell us, what to tell us, how much to tell us. Or at least he gives the impres-sion that he has the power. At the White House, make sure you give Dax your phone. I want to see if we can trace his phone number."

"Bob?" Burks asked for a clarification.

"I've got my finger on the smoking gun."

McKaine's first stop was the Sit Room when he arrived at the White House. The intensity of the happening events was showing on Delay's face. The men and women around the table were the brightest, plucked from each branch of the military. The think tank was standing up, a stark contrast to which option the president was leaning to.

The briefing went as McKaine expected it. Delay asked questions, angered by his people's answers. His decisions would be recorded by his-tory, not the decisions of his underlings, and Delay had to come to terms with this.

"Troops? That's what this has come down to? Troops," Delay lament-ed.

"We can hit their oil fields in the north. Take the three major ones," the secretary of defense said.

"What good would that do?"

"It sends a message to our country—number one—that we aren't playing. Two, sends a message to Syria that we don't negotiate. We're com-ing for our men."

"Do we know where the kidnapped are being held at?"

The questions cut through McKaine like a cleaver. *Should he tell Delay that Burks had a possible location? What if that were a trap?* He flicked a look in Burks's direction, who seemed to have a similar thought. McKaine slightly shook his head and then brought his attention to the table discussion.

"We don't have that at the moment. With the oil fields leveled to a parking lot status, we gain the leverage."

"Last question. Make it the million-dollar question, if you wish—can you guarantee me that the Syrian president ordered the hit on the Americans?"

McKaine slipped a word in. "Earlier in the day of their disappearance, the Syrian military forces jointly with the Russians were tangled in a gun offense with the opposition forces. It appears they wanted to push the opposition out of strategic Damascus neighborhoods."

The generals' heads moved in agreement with McKaine's assessment.

In a furry, Delay raved, "If their president isn't behind this and I send in the Marines—that's an act of war." He stood and leaned forward, fists planted on the table. "I won't agree to invade another country to save the four."

The statement fluttered in the room, over their heads, saying a lot about Delay's pacifist personality.

40

Delay was held up inside the Oval Office with his communication team, strategizing, and McKaine could hear the occasional shouting through their shared wall. Dax had come through on tracking the phone number used by Osmani to call Burks. It was up to McKaine to make his move. He stared at his phone and then back at Dax's sticky note, deciding. *What good could come from that?* Delay's lecturing voice disturbed his thoughts and gave him the necessary push to make the call.

Did Osmani recognize the number or assume he knew who was calling? He came to the phone with a hint of familiarity, as though he expected it. "You calling from inside the White House?"

McKaine grimaced. "May I speak with General Osmani?"

After a brief pause, Osmani said, "Speaking."

"My name is Robert McKaine—do you know who I am?"

"Mhm. The chief of staff."

"Did you expect my call?"

"Not in the least bit. Are you calling to verify my tip?"

"Mr. Osmani, your name came in association with a person my government is looking into. I've got advisers who're telling me I'm wasting my time. That you won't ever speak with me truthfully."

"Are those advisers working for the CIA?"

The question struck McKaine as odd. *Why would Osmani, a general in the Saudi Arabian Royal Army, worry whether the CIA was involved?* McKaine rubbed his chin, measuring how much to say. "None of them work for the CIA."

"How can you be sure?"

The foreigner was right. McKaine had no idea who worked as a CIA informant. That information was the agency's family jewels, guarded behind a wall of lies and lawyers. By the same token, McKaine had to take his inner circle at face value till evidence led him elsewhere. "As sure as I can be."

"Then go ahead, ask me your questions."

"I have an FBI report—"

"A fairy tale." Osmani cut him off.

"Excuse me?"

"My apologies. Please go on."

"Like I said, I read an FBI report and a profile on Amelia Sinclair. Your name was mentioned, vaguely. I'm concerned that an agency might have overlooked the connection between you two, because I was never notified, and given the fact that you're helping us with the Damascus crisis, I'm, well, astounded. It doesn't help that Ms. Sinclair was scheduled to meet with me and she never did. Can you help me understand?"

Osmani drew in a breath and then offered McKaine an alternate version of the chain of events in Damascus. By the end of the call, McKaine had exhausted a range of emotions. His face was depleted of color, and he was speechless, when words were mandatory.

He couldn't recollect what he'd said to Osmani to get him off the call. *Had the general completely lost his mind, suggesting what he did? And if it was true, the American people, the president, could never know. Then who could he task with this? Who?*

His office door swung wide without a knock. Delay wagged a finger in the air, barking at his communication director, Peter O'Connolly, and now McKaine.

"Bob, Pete wants me to do a round of interviews. They're slaughtering me on the talk shows." Delay's tone spoke to his exasperation.

"It's a good idea. Maybe we can find a friendly reporter, Pete?"

Pete nodded.

"What else are you thinking?" McKaine ignored Delay like a child with a tantrum and went directly to the adult, O'Connolly.

"A press briefing is a must and this evening, cut into their broadcast to deliver an address."

"Solid plan. What's your reservation, sir?"

Delay slouched in a chair. "The nation wants a victory speech. They want to hear that we triumphed over the boogeyman. America's still a superpower."

"The American people also don't want to be lied to. We'll get to the victory speech."

Down the hall from the Oval Office, the newscasters could hardly contain themselves in their seats. McKaine accompanied O'Connolly, feeling sorry for him, but thankful for once someone else had the short end of the stick rather than him.

"Dodge their questions if we're planning a military strike," McKaine ordered.

"Are we?"

"It's definitely on the table." McKaine squeezed O'Connolly's shoulder, giving him the atta-boy pat. "Pete, they know only one is kidnapped, bear that in mind."

With that, O'Connolly was sent into the lion's den. The room exploded with hands and shouting matches after he stepped behind the podium.

"I see you fine members of the media are eager. Please calm down. It's going to be brief. Okay?"

McKaine huddled with a speech writer, watching the press briefing on a monitor, in an aide's cubical. O'Connolly had gained control of the press room, and he read from prepared remarks. It looked as though they were headed for a win.

"The president is scheduled to address the nation at 1800 hours tonight. I haven't seen the speech myself, but I can tell you that the president is taking this situation very seriously and working tirelessly to bring Mr. Bo Breeks home. The White House's getting in touch with Mr. Breeks's immediate family members, and the president plans to call them personally. We're saddened by this situation but remain optimistic. We want a speedy resolution and Mr. Breeks back home to his loved ones." O'Connolly lifted his head to face the mob of cameras. "I'll take a few, and I repeat a few, questions."

The journalists circled him like jackals, a herd of vultures, hungry for fresh meat.

"Mr. Pellington, from the *Post*, you go first."

Reading off a smartphone, Pellington went for the obvious. "Is the president considering any military options at this time?"

"I can't answer that question at the moment. The president has met with his chief advisers several times today behind closed doors."

Pellington tried to wedge a word in, but O'Connolly jumped down his throat. "As I said in the beginning, short day today. Moving on. Mr. Ro, sitting in for the *Times*, go ahead."

"Has the president been in contact with Syria's president?"

"The president continues to encourage Mr. al-Azizi to listen to his people and resign peacefully. The two have not spoken on the phone or otherwise today. I'll take one last question."

O'Connolly pointed to a random face he didn't recognize immediately.

"Roger Punk, *Democratic America Daily*—we have a source telling us that Mr. Breeks isn't the only kidnapped American. Three more. Does the White House care to respond?"

The earth felt like quicksand, and McKaine was sinking in. The blows on the White House were coming from every direction.

O'Connolly snapped his spine straight and replied pointedly, "I'm not commenting on rumors. We'll leave it at that. Thank you."

This wasn't a gaffe, a stroke of bad luck—no, it was deliberate, planned, calculated, and then executed to optimize the blow. McKaine could still hear the angry reporters yelling, even as he reached the plush carpet adorning the walk up to the Oval Office. The general feeling in the waiting room was anxiousness. A particular visitor stood out to McKaine, who zoomed in on him.

"I didn't see your name in the meeting ledger," McKaine said coolly.

"My deputy said that the intel from the middleman was never discussed in the Sit Room. I brought extra materials so the president can see the urgency in the situation."

"No. The president will be preoccupied for a while. Come with me. I'm curious to see what you got."

McKaine didn't wait for Post to wiggle out. He dashed to his office, and Post followed with the same level of earnestness.

"I'm all ears." McKaine took a seat in a chair in front of his desk and pointed Post to the open seat next to him.

"Burks called me, tanked-up, last night, while Delay was at Camp David. He told me that the middleman had given him coordinates of a possible location." Post spoke with ease. "He read off to me the coordinates, and I think the CIA has a solid lead."

McKaine accepted the aerial images Post handed him. "Go on."

"You're looking at Jobar, a suburb in Damascus. It's been in the center of chemical attacks since the beginning of the civil war." Post marked down the north point of the suburb, where he wanted McKaine to pay close attention. "The northeast side has been occupied by rebels. It's our assertion that the Americans are held in this five-street radius."

With economical gestures, McKaine glanced over the images and then returned them to Post. "What makes your people sure that Jobar is the place we oughta look at?"

"Two things. We linked the background used in propaganda videos to the same used in Breeks's. The ISI intel, the one linking Sinclair to the terrorist—he lived in Jobar too."

The mention of Sinclair further rubbed McKaine the wrong way. "You know, I had a meeting with her, but she never showed up."

"Not surprised to hear it."

"I was, actually." He stood and walked around his desk, fishing for the FBI report. "I went back and read again the FBI profile on her."

"Did it help you?"

"It did." McKaine allowed silence to lapse between them. "Do you think you can arrange a call between me and the middleman?"

Post's facial muscle clinched. "I thought Burks was in charge."

"Like you said, Conrad—and this stays between us—has us worried. He's been hitting the bottle pretty hard. I want to make sure the middleman feels comfortable speaking with a new face from this administration."

"I don't see why not."

A rap on the door diverted McKaine's attention. "Yeah?"

O'Connolly's shiny bald head popped in, and he told McKaine that they were ready in the other room, meaning the Oval Office.

Post didn't wait to be asked to leave. He stood, buttoned his jacket, and left in a hurry.

McKaine crossed over to the president's office, astonished at the amount of people it could cram in. Cameras, lights, producers of some type, a makeup person applying a generous amount of face powder on Delay's forehead.

O'Connolly got closer and whispered, "He doesn't know. His speech only acknowledges one hostage."

"Why didn't you tell him?"

"I asked for a minute alone—he brushed me off."

McKaine would have to shoulder this on his own. He neared Delay and lightly leaned in. "A minute, if I may, sir, before we begin."

"Everyone, I need the room," Delay called out from his desk.

Alone, McKaine crossed arms over his chest and, in his most gentle voice, filled Delay in on the latest.

"I want a name," POTUS seethed through his teeth. "Whoever leaked this, find him."

Reading the disappointment and worry on Delay's face, McKaine nodded. He stepped away from the desk, letting POTUS speak directly to the American people.

When the camera dot blinked red, Delay, in a velvety voice, read off a teleprompter.

"Good evening, my fellow Americans. Today, we witnessed a series of videos, showing American journalists courageously standing up to tyranny. Four of our citizens were kidnapped by nameless shadows, who wish nothing more than to incite fear in us—but they have failed. They have failed because our country is strong, we are strong, and we stand united against their hatred.

"In these videos, we saw evil, we saw the desire to destroy, but we also saw four brave men standing up for what they believe in—this great nation. Their selflessness and belief in freedom was shining through the darkness, and no one will take that light away from our countrymen or from us.

"Immediately after my office became aware of the kidnapping of four Americans, I instructed my chief advisers to put together an emergency response plan. Let me make it clear to those who've tried to impose darkness: we won't stand for it. We are prepared. It's been our policy all along that we do not negotiate with terrorists.

"I've dedicated all available resources to our intelligence and law enforcement agencies to locate the people responsible for the kidnappings. Our citizens will not hide in fear.

"Much has been speculated in the hours after the video was uploaded on the internet. We have confirmed that the four Americans who were kidnapped are members of the news media. We're still in the process of notifying their family members, so I'm not at liberty to divulge their names at this time.

"Tonight, I ask you, my fellow Americans, to pray for those men and their families. As I pray tonight, too, I'm reminded of Corinthians 16:13: 'Be on your guard; stand firm in the faith; be courageous; be strong.' Tomorrow is a new day and with it, a promise of hope that our men will be safely returned to their loved ones.

"Thank you. Good night, and God bless America."

41

Vito brought Jets to his apartment, a brownstone, scrubbed from its glory days: the front door was missing, the hallways permanently inundated in weed smell. The apartment wasn't in better condition, but at least the door locked with a dead bolt. Standing in the living room, Jets worried that Polina must have missed the mark, sending him to meet Vito.

"Got some clean clothes for you." Vito flung a tee and jeans to Jets. "Too small for me, should fit you."

"You think this place's safe?"

"It's the projects—as safe as we can be."

Vito booted a bank of computers and jammed in the drive.

Jets had been patient with his new friend refusing to explain himself at the Sour Cherry; Jets started to speak, when a story on a news site made him rethink his line of questioning. "Hold on, I wanna see this."

Jets scanned the text, interested in the video more. "Play it for me."

A CWG reporter, Cooper Trapp, in a somber voice, narrated to the viewers a story of a photographer gone missing in Damascus, who worked for the network. Vito and Jets listened to the story.

"You're watching CWG with a special report. A disturbing video of an American, captured by unknown terrorists, has been leaked online. CWG identified the man in the video as one of our own, Bo Breeks, an award-winning photojournalist with over two decades of experience reporting from war zones. At this time, the network can't release any details of Mr. Breeks's assignment in the Middle East due to concerns over his safety and our country's national security.

"Bo is not only a coworker to us, but a dear friend. CWG is his family, and we're working with the appropriate agencies to get a better understanding of the situation. Out of respect for Bo's family and friends, CWG is refusing to play the video. We ask other media outlets to do the same."

Trapp briefly paused and wiped a tear from his face. *"Bo, stay strong. And to all of you who are watching, thank you for your prayers and support. For the latest updates, visit our website."*

With renewed energy, Jets called out, "Amelia."

"Is that your girl?"

"Huh?"

"You've mentioned that woman a few times. Is she your girl?"

"The protectee. She got snatched. Polina was helping me track her down." Not allowing another minute to go to waste, Jets went on. "The files on the flash drive—you said you recognize them?"

"This is fucked up. Some serious shit, bro. Unless you got a heavy hitter behind you, walk away, or you'll ended up like Polina."

It wasn't in Jets's nature to walk away from anything: not from a mission, not from a witness. He stayed put and chased the scent till the bitter end. "I'll worry about that."

"Easier said than done, son. If you're on a suicide mission, fine, but make sure there aren't any people left in your life who can get hurt."

"Is that what happened in your case? They came after your family? That's how they shut you up."

Vito looked past the computer screens, into the void.

Jets wasn't cutting him any slack. "These people should be held accountable for their actions. They killed our friend. An innocent woman's going to get blamed for heinous crimes she never committed. I'm not asking you to get involved. Tell me what you know."

"After 9/11, Bush and Congress allocated an unlimited budget to the CIA, and Post saw an opportunity." The truth had been eating at Vito every day since. It felt good to share the load.

"I remember. I was embedded with the first boots on the ground."

"Post worked the budget and invested some of the money into a dark ops military group. Seven highly trained assassins who reported only to Post and no one else. I'm talking about not even the president or even Congress knew they existed."

That dropped on Jets like a ton of bricks. Jets scowled in distrust.

"Nicknamed the Band of Seven, it has been in operation for sixteen years. Killing, kidnapping, bribing, God knows what else."

"Where do you come into play?"

"When Delay was sworn in, he was kicking a hornet's nest with the CIA—making them accountable with how the agency was running things. Post didn't like that. It spooked him. He had the Band of Seven shut down. Or at least that was presumed."

The top-secret documents peered at them from the screens.

Vito recollected more. "Almost a year ago, Post's secretary calls me late at night into a meeting and assigns me to a new unit—redacting and bleaching the CIA digital archives. Purging the systems of any mention of the Band of Seven."

Jets analyzed the information, piece by piece. "What about the identities of the seven?"

"No. Don't think so. They were coded. I'm talking about layers of codes so complex the rest of the world hasn't discovered them." Vito tilted his head to one side, his memory digging deeper into suppressed archives. It came back empty-handed. "Sorry, no name."

"Polina gave me a name. Long story short, she tracked the guy in the SEAL rosters. Thomas Monroe. Ring any bells?"

Not bells—alarms went off in Vito's head.

"You sure she said Monroe? Are you absolutely sure?"

"I'm sure. Why?"

"He's one of them. Like, Post's anointed one."

Jets dove toward Vito, a hand gripping his neck. He was pissing mad from being jerked around.

Vito thrashed in his seat, face red from the cut-off blood circulation. "Let go of me." He wheezed between breaths.

"Don't fucking lie to me again."

"Okay. Okay."

His hand gradually released Vito's neck and eventually returned to the side of his body. "How'd you ended up in Lincoln Heights?"

When Vito regained his ability to speak, his voice sounded hoarse. "Where was that strength at Cherry's? Post had me boxed. Polygraph after polygraph, I failed my yearly board review. Got canned."

"What can you tell me about the files?"

"It's what we call a throve. Basically, a spider program collected any mention of Monroe's name nested in the DOJ servers and bundled them up for Polina. The files range from low to high priority. Like here and here." Vito smudged his finger on the screens, pointing to Jets.

"How useful can they be?"

"Hard to say. Polina had done a lot of work on them, but they're still a long way's away from giving you a clear picture."

"Can you find anything she might have found on Amelia and where they took her?"

"Nothing of this sort. The documents in these files are not recent. Didn't you say Mr. Rogers gave you two envelopes?"

It had slipped Jets's mind that a second, smaller envelope was still in the back pocket of the dirty pair of pants on the living room floor. He tore the flap, but found more depressing news in it. A flimsy note, containing *"B133,"* written in black pen.

42

B 133 meant nothing to Jets. It meant he was faced with a question he didn't know the answer to. It was getting old to run around in circles, feeling doors slammed in his face.

"Is it a message from Polina?" Vito interrupted Jets's self-loathing.

"It beats me."

He left the note on the desk by the computers and put his hands on his hips, left without conviction.

"B133? It's a code."

"I can tell that much. A code to what?"

"You sure she didn't pass a key to you to make sense of the code?"

Negative, Jets's eyes said.

"Do you think you can break the code?"

"I'm an algorithm guy. Code breaking's hardly my specialty. I'll try." Vito swiveled his chair and faced the computers, stunned by the short code. "It might help to figure out in what context she was sending you a code. Like, she was dying, so what was so important to guard? We write codes to shield our secrets from the world."

Jets got nothing again. Polina was an enigma to him. Sending a Mayday, working with an underground opposition to the CIA, even befriending a washed-up agent like Vito. He was still chewing on these new discoveries; he didn't have the mental capacity to cram in her reasons to write to him in code.

"Did you two have like a hiding spot, where if things went south, either one can go to? I've heard of hook-ups between agents and their handlers."

"No. We—our relationship was never romantic. So no place where we went to bang," Jets said. "Isn't there a program you can open and type in B133?"

Vito took his fingers away from the keyboard, obviously rubbed the wrong way by Jets's plain arrogance.

"Man—" he started to say, but Jets was glued to the window, inspecting the increased traffic of onlookers.

"Shit. This isn't good." Jets stuck a hand in the back of his belt, grabbing the handle of his gun.

Vito didn't wait for a clarification. He sprung to the bedroom and returned with a loaded semi-automatic. "Your friends from before?"

"It feels like that. The building on the south's hindering the view." Jets peeled eyes off the road and locked them on Vito's weapon. "You got an extra baby for me?"

"Now we're dancing to the same music."

The wait was painstakingly long. After five minutes of hanging by the window, Vito went back to his seat, the semi-automatic resting against his desk. Jets stayed at his post, guarding.

"Walk me through the last twenty-four hours of Polina's life."

"Huh?"

"B133. It's probably connected in a way to the files she tapped, if it isn't a meaningful place for the two of you. It's not a date for sure, and it's not a code to a lockbox, like a safe."

"How'd you figure that?" Jets counted the bullets for the double barrel pump action shotgun. He planned to rain bullets on the fucking assholes.

"Too short and too short."

"Talked to P on the phone that morning. She'd traced the IP to a location, couldn't elaborate. Talked again before she left the CIA. I asked her to check the kidnapping video."

Vito interrupted, "The leaked one? What was she looking for?"

"No, Amelia received a video, completely different than this one. Shaky, amateurish, like it was shot without the people in it knowing they were being filmed."

"Did you speak with Polina after that?"

Jets paused, haunted by the visions of that night. "I warned her to leave her place. I told her holding onto the files wasn't a good idea. Damn it, P." Jets tensed, his face rigid with remorse. "I asked her if she had any idea where Amelia could've been taken. We talked a little more about Monroe, then the phone call dropped. I didn't think much of it."

"There was nothing you could've done to save her."

"I should've been there for her. Should've never involved her the way I did."

A soft knock on Vito's front door sent them both to aim their guns. Vito was closest. He pointed to his eyes with two fingers forming a V, then to the window. Jets gave an approving nod and crouched down, the barrel of the shotgun sticking out the window.

The soft knock returned. Vito, by that time, was at the door, lowering the gun, asking with gestures for Jets to do the same.

A teenage boy, face framed by thick glasses, stepped in. Vito patted him on the back and gave him a wide grin. Jets watched the two from the opposite end of the room, noticing the kid tugging on the edge of a white tee and avoiding eye contact, suspecting he was on the slower side.

"Mr. Vito, hi." Jets's suspicions were confirmed as the teen started to speak. "My mama's sick again."

"Come in, Smalls." The teen stayed in the same spot. "Your mama not doing good again? At the clinic, they couldn't help her?"

Smalls traced the plank boards of the floor with bug eyes. "Nah, her pimp paid a visit last night, and since then, she locked herself in her room and won't come out."

"That's tough, kid."

"Mr. Vito, two Humvees scouting for you."

Jets perked up at the mention of the Humvees. The mood shifted in the room urgently.

"Did you see who was in the SUVs?"

"The windows are black, like the cars. They're driving with a wad of cash, giving it to anyone with information of where you at."

"You seeing them?" Vito nodded to Jets, who was already peering out the window. Nothing had changed on the street.

"Smalls, I want you to listen to me very carefully. Go straight home. Don't stop and talk to people. Home. Lock the door and stay there for the rest of the night."

At the top of the hill, Jets spotted the first Humvee rolling slowly, with a buff-looking dude poking his head out of the sunroof.

"Got a view on the first one," Jets said over his shoulder.

The familiar sound of clacking keys made him turn around, and he threw a *what-the-fuck* look at Vito. "Checking your email?"

"B133."

"Forget the code. We've got mercenaries about to gun us."

"This will only take a minute."

"A minute we don't got."

Vito didn't hear a word of what Jets was saying. He worked at max speed, checking the larger files for a reference to B133. Jets left him alone. He heard the slamming of doors and voices talking in the distance. He couldn't quite make out what they were saying, which pissed him off.

Jets adjusted his aim when a guy slid into his view, an open target. He could take him out, but the shot would reveal their location.

"Damn it, Vito. Hurry," he howled.

"I think I got it." Vito was up and moving, shutting down his computers, when a wave of bullets hit the ceiling plaster.

Jets crouched low and let the double barrel hang off the window to return the greeting.

"Won't be long before the po-po bust all our asses." Vito slapped a clay texture on top of the desk and stuck sticks of dynamite, connected to a countdown timer.

"Tell me there's a back exit out of this building."

"Nope. The way we came is the only way out."

"Shit."

Their company had fired off a magazine of bullets into the building, hitting the couch, the walls, and windows. They had come to kill Jets and whoever was stashing him. The ghetto was the idle backdrop for this mission. The boss of the Humvee owners could sell it to the public as another turf war between gangbangers gone bad.

Vito unlocked the door, letting Jets slip out first. Jets squatted, protecting the right flank, Vito to the left. Their plan was to shoot their way out of this building and dash for the closed-down mill factory directly behind Vito's apartment.

"If by any chance you survive, brother, B133 is a code name for a CIA black site in Baltimore. I believe you'll find your girl there." His gun clicked after he reloaded and then unleashed a barrage of bullets.

The slightest chance of reuniting with Amelia was the encouragement Jets needed to hear. Keeping his head low, gun pressed hard on his shoulder blade, he made strides, successfully defending his position. When the gunfire ceased, all that was left was smoke and bullet holes. Lincoln Heights residents were holed up in their homes, but two. Jets and Vito stood over six dead bodies, scattered on the asphalt, out in the open. They were lucky to be alive, thanking God under their breath for being on their side.

"Let's bounce—we can't stay for the bomb grand finale." Vito nudged Jets in the ribcage.

They ran for a good mile after the explosion went off, taking out half of the roof with it. Vito stopped running for a short second, turning only to see the fire raging in his home, then said screw it and caught up to Jets. In an open field, overgrown with tall weeds, they figured they'd run enough.

Catching his breath and wits, Jets said, "How do we get to Baltimore?"

"I've got a stashed car past the clearing." He pointed in the distance to Jets. "Baltimore's next."

43

The Baltimore derelict factory chimneys were visible from the interstate. Vito drove. Jets was in the seat next to him, with an aching body.

"You think B133 is a black site?" Jets hummed under his breath, eyes locked on the road littered with potholes. The night had swooped down, transforming the terrain into low visibility.

The CIA used black sites in the US to test psychic meds and interrogation techniques on live subjects. These weren't just social fables, told by CIA's myth busters. They were real and protected. To his knowledge, in its sixty-year history, Jets had never heard of a person successfully gaining access to such a site without permission, who lived to tell. They were a bouquet of highly guarded secrets. If the CIA believed that the motherland could be protected by the work done in the black sites, then it was justifiable.

When the headlights illuminated a road sign that said "Military Zone Two Miles Ahead," Jets was starting to buy Vito's discovery.

"Shit's about to get real." Vito veered off 895. The tires skidded over bumps on the unpaved road.

When they reached an overgrown countryside with tall weeds and brush, he slammed on the brakes and killed the engine. The two became one with the darkness.

"What did you do that for?"

"Can't get any farther than this unless you've got a boat." Vito showed Jets the coast line. "The Masonville Cove is reachable exclusively by boat."

Jets squinted. "You think Masonville Cove's the place?"

"According to the files, the CIA has a black site here. It makes sense that she'd be brought to Baltimore. Virginia's too close to Washington to run a place like this. If you go past Baltimore, it becomes too long of a drive. Doubt they summoned a helo for her."

"B133, huh?"

"B stands for Baltimore, thirteen is the thirteenthth letter in the alphabet, same with three. Put together, you get Baltimore MC, or Baltimore Masonville Cove."

Jets was impressed. Even in death, Polina was looking out for him. He eased out of the car, leaving the door cracked. His feet stepped on the marshy, soft ground as he assessed. Running in these conditions would slow them significantly and tire them out faster. Swimming from end to end was out of the question. He was out-numbered and out-gunned. Across the water, Amelia was probably scared and confused. He didn't dare think they might have hurt her to extort information leading them to him.

Vito stood right behind him. "Best bet we've got is to watch the place. If they make a move, we make a move."

Jets hated to admit it, but Vito had a point. "We'll take shifts. I take the first few hours; you can catch some shut-eye."

"Or..." Vito cast his eyes on the horizon. "Be right back." He walked to the back of his car. His head disappeared in the trunk, and he lifted a pair of military-grade night vision binoculars. The view through them was crisp and clear. Jets was immediately transported to the battlefield of Afghanistan early on in the war.

"Check out the ridge point with the highest altitude on this side of the cove," Vito directed Jets. "From that point, we'll have a better shot seeing their movements."

"It's close to a mile hike. They'll be in the wind by the time we get back to the car."

"It's a two-man job. Go up there—I'll stay by the car. Send me a signal through the shortwave radio if you spot movements."

The first and the second hour flew as fast as it could for Jets, who was squatting low in the brush, the night bugs and mosquitos feasting on him. The main building of the black site was a textile factory with the original business name painted with red bold letters on the brick. Several smaller buildings were spread out in the yard, safeguarded by an electric fence and patrolling guards. Most likely military contractors, Jets summed up.

By the third hour, Jets grew tired from boredom of having to stare at the factory, especially considering it had minimal movement. He ran out of things to think about, imaginary conversations he could have with Amelia. His eyelids drooped; he had to slap his face to stay awake. Movement on the front woke him up, barely. An SUV sped through the gates. Jets brought the binoculars to his face and adjusted them. The face that reflected in them caused his hands to tense. So did the rest of his body. Post's spiteful eyes surveyed the area too, but Jets was too far to worry the DCI might make him.

He squeezed the handle of the shortwave radio, sending a "prepare" message to Vito, who waited down below. Post walked in the building, shielded behind a steel door, but he didn't stick around for long. According to Jets's calculations—fifteen minutes, then back in the car and he was gone.

Jets thought of running down to the car to follow him. But then came Amelia, with a bag over her head, walking out from the same door. Her feet were staggering, hands tied behind her back. A man walked after her, pointing a Barrett rifle at her head. Jets pressed the radio as he galloped down the hill.

Vito swung the door open, the car sending small rocks and dust in the air. "Get in!" He realized they had a very narrow window of opportunity to catch up with the two SUVs.

"I had eyes on Post. Came alone, left two minutes before they brought her out." Jets gave the update, window rolled down and hand holding onto the roof of the car. "They can't be too far ahead of us."

Vito gradually slowed down as they jumped back on 895, south-bound.

"What you doing, man? Gun that sucker."

"The only way out of the Cove is the road we're on. I did some map digging while you were up there. Two streets they could take: Roosevelt Avenue or Park Drive. They're perpendicular to each other, and 895 cuts through them both."

Jets began to see Vito's argument. Two black SUVs stood out on the empty streets of Baltimore. They would be able to spot them when they got closer to the mainland. If they drove too close to the SUVs, in a hot pursuit, they would tip their hand and most likely end up in a gun exchange.

They first caught sight of the SUVs when they skid on the Key Bridge. Several smaller cars were between them.

"That's a good, safe distance." Vito eased more on the gas pedal, but his hands remained locked on the wheel, ready to maneuver at any given moment.

It was true, then. Seeing Post on site reassured him of the evidence Polina had unearthed in the DOJ files. It wasn't a coincidence that Amelia was dragged and locked in a black site. Post orchestrated it. *Did he give the order to kill Polina and him too?*

The traffic had thinned out, and Vito struggled to stay far enough behind and still have eyes on the moving SUVs, but they made a sudden stop at Maryland's state line. Vito came to a full stop and waited it out till the SUVs resumed their course. They had dumped a silhouette, swaying, fighting to stay upright.

"It's Amelia!" Jets was ready to bolt out the door.

"It's a trap." Vito grabbed Jets's collar, holding him in.

"Let me go."

"Don't be stupid. It's their last ditch to get you to come out. A sniper could be anywhere, prepping to blow your head off."

"Fuck them." Jets struggled.

"Leave it for another day. Today we hide, we run, we survive. He'll get his," Vito said, brotherly.

Was that moisture Jets felt—drops wedged in the corners of his eyes? He chased them away while breathing heavy against the grief of emotions eating him up inside.

44

The phone call was a game changer for McKaine. He jotted on a scrap piece of paper a street address in Maryland. But before he had the chance to ask any follow-up questions, the caller disconnected. *You'll find Amelia Sinclair at the crossroads of Muller Avenue and Buckey, at the Maryland state line.* The caller had been explicit.

Long past the time he should have gone home, McKaine remained behind his desk, staring at the dry-erase board with the word "deception" still written and underlined at the top. Then the call came in and turned things on its head. He wasted no time in summoning Dax and Lance. They better get it right tonight and bring her in, McKaine instructed.

"We can trace the call, sir. Do you want me to call the FBI tech team?" Dax said.

"When you get back. I don't want her to vanish again. She seems pretty good at that." McKaine reclined in his chair, eyes averted away from the two agents.

"What's she doin' all the way up in Maryland?"

"Agent Lance, to be frank, I don't give a rat's ass. I want her brought in."

"To FBI Central?"

Dax's question held McKaine's attention in place. If they took her to the Hoover Building, Justice would have first dibs on where the investigation went from there. McKaine was a lawyer by trade and didn't trust his kind, especially when political careers were on the line. He scraped that idea. From his briefcase, McKaine fished out his phone, searching for a name through his address book.

"I'll meet with her at the Hilton Garden Hotel." He looked at the agents through his reading glasses.

Their expressions gave away the feeling of displeasure with the plan.

"Sir, down the road, that might be problematic with the DOJ when they prosecute." Dax approached the conversation from afar.

"I'll work it out with DOJ—you focus on bringing her in." A typical answer by a politician, prepared to cut a deal under the table.

• • • •

The chilled night air slapped Dax across the face when he stepped out of the car. He zipped up his leather jacket to keep the cold out. The crossroad in Maryland was desolate, swathed in a thin layer of fog. They had driven up the road a mile past the original address, with no trace of Amelia in sight. The lack of streetlights hindered his ability to see, so he turned on the flashlight. He swayed the light from side to side, checking the ditches along the path. About a hundred yards away, he spotted a shape slumped by the road sign they had passed by, but due to the lack of lighting, they could have easily missed it. He walked briskly, getting closer. The shape transformed into a human, wearing just a tee. When he reached her, he crouched beside her, checking for her pulse. She was alive, nearly frozen. He pulled the bag off her head and positively ID'd her.

Amelia Sinclair looked pale and miserable. A far cry from her attractive CWG headshot.

"Miss Sinclair, my name is Special Agent Dax. I'm with the FBI. Are you hurt anywhere?"

"I don't think so," she replied in labored breaths.

"I'm going to help you, okay?"

The look in her eyes worried Dax. Her eyes were round, full with fear. Her lips trembled as she tried to let out a warning. Too late, though, Dax heard the familiar sound of a gun cocking behind his head.

He raised his hands in the air, his training telling him to bargain. "Don't do this. My gun's in my belt. Talk to me."

Lance smirked at Dax's gullibility. "I actually liked working with you and honestly feel kind of bad that I have to kill you."

Dax felt like a bucket with scolding water had been dumped on him, hearing the voice of his partner.

"She doesn't look too pretty. I expected more."

"Lance, what the fuck, man? Drop the gun."

"Can't do that. Can't. Sorry, pal."

"I don't understand."

"You've always been dumb as a rock. We've got no use for her—we've got no use for you either."

"You're a federal agent."

"Correction—I'm a CIA agent working for the FBI."

Dax twisted his head just barely to catch a glimpse of Lance, rapidly moving the gun from him to Amelia and back.

"Still, we're on the same side."

"Ah, man, now you're starting to irritate me. I was gonna kill you after her, but now I'm thinking not so much." Lance bent down, close to Dax's ear. "The CIA's gonna run this motherfucker."

Lance pulled his gun slide all the way back, sealing a bullet in the chamber, and then squeezed the trigger.

Dax closed his eyes, preparing to die. Instead, he heard Amelia's hoarse voice cry out. He jumped to his feet, seeing Lance lying in the dust with a bullet hole in his forehead. He didn't see anyone near them and couldn't logically explain how Lance ended up dead. Amelia twisted in agony, petrified by the body. Dax removed her zip ties and helped her up.

"We could be next. We better move." He drew his gun, knowing it was useless in the darkness. With the right equipment, a professional gunman could kill them just the same.

Amelia was hyperventilating in the front seat while Dax sped into the night. He had no chance of processing Lance's confession, nor did he know how to explain to his superiors the dead agent in Maryland. His only salvation was Amelia's witness account that could back him up. On the same token, she was a suspected terrorist, placed on the FBI Most Wanted list.

"Shit. Shit. Shit!" he yelled in the car, slamming a fist in the roof.

Amelia sobbed uncontrollably, making no sense.

Eventually, Dax calmed down and began paying more attention to her. She looked worse in the light. Her wrists were covered in cuts, probably from being bound in zip ties for too long. She had a crescent moon bruise on her neck that at closer examination appeared to be a thumbprint. No doubt she'd been roughed up.

"Ms. Sinclair—I don't have a fucking clue what in the fucking world happened at that intersection. My guess is I would get fired over this." *What was he doing? Why was he saying that to her?* "I'm assigned to work from the White House, a special unit that works with the president and his staff."

Amelia trembled despite the heater working on max in the car. She chose not to speak, only listen.

"Robert McKaine sent me to pick you up."

To Dax, the mention of Robert McKaine made her act frightened. He reached to the backseat, feeling it with a hand, and brought back a bottle of water.

"Drink some, please. I think we should go to the ER," Dax suggested, not sure how McKaine would react. Then again, McKaine wasn't here, seeing what Dax was seeing.

"No hospital. No, please." Amelia accepted the bottled water and chugged it down, choking in the process a few times.

Hydrating helped to bring down her anxiety level, though it was impossible to say how the experience of the past week would affect her psyche in the long run.

"Why not kill me back there?" she asked between breaths.

Bewildered, Dax had no idea what to make of her question. "I assure you—we don't want to kill you."

"Just to keep my mouth shut. I promised I would."

"Again, ma'am, the opposite. We want you to tell us everything you know about the kidnapped Americans. The video of Bo Breeks shows him in dire need of medical help."

"Where are you taking me?"

"To a hotel. McKaine set it up."

His answer to her prompted him to check his phone, revealing a serious number of missed calls by the chief of staff. He pressed on McKaine's name and waited for the line to connect.

"Why didn't you call sooner?" McKaine sounded pissed.

"There was a major complication." It had come to the moment Dax had to give a statement he preferred not to.

"Amelia Sinclair?"

"She was the least of it." Dax threw a glance at the ghost-like woman in the car with him. "The tip from the caller panned out. I found her at the exact spot. Bound and gagged."

"Bound and gagged?"

"I'm afraid there's more." Dax continued to speak. "Lance tried to shoot us. Me and her. A shooter killed him before he had the chance to kill us."

McKaine had the same reaction as Dax. "FBI Agent Lance wanted you dead? Why?"

"Before he prepared to shoot us, he was rambling on that he was a CIA agent, working for the FBI as a mole. The CIA would dominate the world. Made no sense, sir. I think he was mentally disturbed."

"You said another shot him?"

"That's right. I didn't get a look at the guy. Got the woman and high-tailed out of Dodge. Didn't know if he was gonna whack us too."

There was a brief pause. McKaine then said, "The shooter couldn't save her, but he didn't want to let her get killed. Interesting."

"Still want me to take her to that hotel?"

"Absolutely. I must speak with her ASAP."

Amelia had been following the conversation up to the point Dax had retold the part of an unidentified shooter gunning Lance. Her heart told her it was Jets, but her mind rejected that idea. She closed her eyes and preferred to believe her heart.

45

It was painful. Excruciating. Soul-wrenching to watch her shiver in the cold. She must have been going out of her mind. He was going out of his, unable to save her. Vito was right. With him, she was in danger. As long as the chief of staff had a vested interest in her, Amelia would be safe with him. But still, the pain of being near was killing him slowly inside.

A car drove by her and didn't stop. It was the first vehicle in over an hour since he placed the call to McKaine. It stopped, reversed, and then drove up again. They must have been thrown off by the darkness and couldn't see her, sitting by the sign, head curled in her knees.

"Look at those idiots." Vito was entertained by the situation. "Get out of your car, you lazy bastards."

It was as if they heard him. The car came to a stop, and the driver stomped on the ground, shining a flashlight on the patch of road.

"You sure they can't see us?"

"No chance in hell."

Vito had driven their car in low land, hilly, on the opposite side of the road of where Amelia was. Fortunately, the binoculars gave them a front-seat view of the action. Jets hadn't stopped using his pair. Vito glanced from his on occasion.

"Does she know?" Vito was killing time with small talk.

Jets preferred he shut up. "Know what?"

"How you feel about her."

"You don't know what you're talking about."

"Yeah, sure. You don't think I'm buying the whole protectee bullshit story?"

"I've known her for less than a week. I don't want another dead person on my conscience."

"Ditto." Vito looked through the binoculars, interested in the movement of the FBI.

Jets zoomed in closer, freezing the frame on the agent kneeling by Amelia. "That guy." He seethed.

"Who's he to her?"

"Not to her. I saw him at Amy's. He showed up with two others right after I got ganged up on."

"One of McKaine's dogs then?" Vito moved the binoculars in the same directions as Jets. "Don't know him, and it doesn't seem very CIA to me."

Vito got distracted by a pack of hyenas hunting two miles away, when Jets punching him in the chest startled him.

"Gun. What the fuck? The second one's pointing a gun?"

That threw Vito for a loop. Supposedly, McKaine wanted Amelia alive for questioning. *What had changed?*

"This dude's crazy. Seems like he's freelancing. His partner is like bargaining with him or somethin' of that nature."

"What's the highest range rifle you've got in the trunk?" Jets asked in a hardened voice.

"Be cool."

"Either I shoot him from here or from up close."

Vito didn't have to leave the car; his favorite toy was under the seat. The long-range rifle was made of steel, black and light.

"Precision, speed, 800 yards away." He introduced the weapon to Jets as if it were his date.

Jets couldn't care less as long as the sucker packed power to smoke the dipshit waving a gun in Amelia's face. He reached for the rifle.

Vito hugged it closer. "No. I'll shoot."

"Vito—I got no time to play games."

"Then don't."

Vito pushed his door open enough to point the barrel of the rifle out. He remained seated. Talking to Jets, he instructed, "Read me the coordinates on the top right corner in the binoculars."

It looked as if the guy was ready to shoot, so Jets better play ball or he risked Amelia's life. He complied with Vito and read off the green numbers located in the corner. He'd barely finished calling out the last number as Vito tapped on the trigger, a bull's-eye in the maniac's head.

"Damn," Jets mumbled.

Vito rubbed the top of the rifle. "She never disappoints me." Then he gently slid it back in its original hiding spot.

The dead body dropped to the ground with a thud. The crouched FBI man was back on his feet, gun out of the holster, pointing in the night.

Vito cracked a wide grin, proud of the shot, proud of the kill. Jets, however, was far from amused. Amelia screamed in a worn-out voice, tears dripping from her eyes. The suit picked her up and was telling her to run. Jets winced in the seat, seeing them make a run for it.

"Going after them?" Vito stomped on the gas, jerking the wheel after the car. "You plan on bumping in McKaine with the flash drive? Stick it to Post?"

The DCI was responsible for Polina's murder. He sent killers after him and Amelia. Sending Post to jail would be a gift, and Jets was not in a giving mood.

"The flash drive, your testimony, throw in the Monroe monkey wrench, then maybe Post would get twenty. Maybe." Jets had been long in Washington and knew politicians feared his boss.

"I like you, buddy, but let's get one thing straight—I'll never testify, repeat, put pen to paper, what I told you in my house. Get that romantic idea out of your head."

"Good."

Jets's answer surprised Vito, who expected a different reaction. "Just like that, you're okay with it?"

"I'm okay with it. That means I'll have to deal with Post discreetly. Unobstructed by the law and without the constraints of the public eye."

They took turns speculating where McKaine would take Amelia. The Hoover Building was an obvious choice, but the Fed's car drove in the opposite direction of town. They toyed with the idea of Amelia being brought to the White House. To their dismay, the Fed passed 1600 Pennsylvania Avenue and navigated to the heart of DC with its Michelin-rated restaurants, modern art museums, and overpriced-to-excess hotels.

"McKaine's gonna wine and dine her before he hammers her with questions." Vito could taste the prime rib some of these places prepared. "From nearly being shot at the state line to a five-star hotel—did she make a deal with the devil?"

The sound of Vito's voice reinforced in Jets why he worked alone. Partners were a double-edged knife—a nuisance he'd been fortunate to not deal with in his career.

"You always talk so much?"

"Only when my partner's a mute." Vito winked at Jets. "You got to admit, it's odd."

"I bet Amelia doesn't know where McKaine's taking her."

"For our sake, I hope you're right."

The Crown Victoria had pulled in the Hilton Garden Hotel private parking, a concrete seven-story high monstrosity. Vito drove past the entrance, reached the next set of stoplights, and made a U-turn.

"Not good, my brother. You got a thousand bucks in your pocket to rent a fancy room for the night?"

"We can't follow them unless we've got a room number." Jets stretched his neck to look out Vito's window.

"Yeah. Security cameras and a guard too."

A street parking spot opened up as they were coming around, several cars from the stunning hotel foyer. Vito maneuvered the car, but left it running.

The Hilton Garden Hotel was an impressive modern building: glass towers and an outside elevator that offered its visitors a bird's-eye view of downtown. Vito and Jets watched as the elevator went up.

"Ain't that cool."

It was cool, cooler then cool, but gawking at it didn't get them closer to Amelia and the FBI agent. Jets's eyes came back to the main entrance, observing a mix of men in penguin suits and women in ballgowns piling into a white stretch limo, as if they had stepped out from a different area. He had to gain access to the hotel. Straightaway. It wasn't impossible to accomplish, but if Post wanted him that badly out of the picture, it presented a unique set of challenges. The DCI was most likely monitoring Jets's bank and credit card transactions, while waiting for hits from a facial recognition system. Jets wouldn't put it past Post to send a drone in the sky to hunt for him, too.

"I'm going in." Jets reached in his pants pocket and grabbed the flash drive. "Post won't let me come out alive. Make sure McKaine gets this."

Vito swatted away Jets's hand. "You aren't going anywhere. If one of us is going in, it's me. Your ugly mug's on their radar. Every damn camera in this city's pinging you."

"Post knows what you look like; he knows you're helping me."

"True. But he wants you dead more than me." Vito checked the foot traffic behind and in front of the car. "Doubt he'll send the cavalry after me, especially if McKaine's in there."

"You got a plan?"

"How much cash do you have on you?"

Jets went through his pockets, digging for every dollar he could find. It came to a total of $200 and change.

"That would work." Vito only took the money and not the change. "We'll use the shortwave radios again. Give me a warning if you see someone unusual coming in."

Jets expected that Vito would go directly for the front of the hotel, but Vito went out back and got lost in between the alleys.

Jets stared on at the consistent stream of expensive cars driving up to the hotel curb, the drivers tossing their keys to the valet boys, in a hurry to get in as strikingly attractive women in skimpy outfits hung off their arms. Jets didn't need a complicated sociology book to explain to him that the lives of the haves and have-nots played out in front of the Hilton Hotel and probably every other hotel on this block.

Eventually, the megalomaniacs ceased for the night. Jets grew worried for Vito. The radio had been dead silent next to him for hours. He'd seen no sighting of Post, his people, or McKaine. *Should he send a signal to get Vito back to the car? Had he made a tactical mistake allowing him to go in without him?*

He glided eyes to the side view mirror that car brake lights reflected in. A figure, built similar to Vito's, emerged from a side street. Jets abandoned the front, attention locked on the shadow approaching from behind.

Vito was a transformed man—black slacks, white pressed shirt, burgundy vest, with a shiny name tag buttoned on the lapel: Joel.

"How did you swindle this get-up?" Jets said, wild with questions.

"Nice, huh?" Vito dusted imaginary specks off his shoulder. "Check this out. I go out back, *Joel's* blazing one by the dumpster. High as a kite, he starts freaking out, thinking I'm management busting his ass. I told him I was a PI busting an old geezer with a hooker shacked up at the Garden. But to get paid, I needed to snap him in the act. Gave Joel the two hundred greens for his uniform and ten percent of what Mrs. Geezer paid me for the job."

"Get the fuck out. He ate it up?"

"Ate it up, right out of my hand." Vito grew quiet. The second half of his story wasn't as funny.

"Did you get far?"

Vito nodded his head, expression hardening as if preparing himself and Jets. "I was in her room," Vito said. "She looks better. Clean clothes and a shower."

"Did you speak with her?"

"Negative. The floor she's on is heavily guarded by the FBI and Secret Service. McKaine was in the room with her. Good tipper. Gave me a fifty for my trouble, when I dropped off their room service order."

Jets sat back in the seat, disappointed.

Vito thought some more, then added, "I slipped her a note. Telling her you're outside."

Words of gratitude died in Jets's throat. There was no time to spend on "thank you" and "you're welcome" between the two. Post lumbered in their view, his Secret Service detail glued to his back. From this angle, to Jets, the DCI bore no expression on his face, which played with Jets's mind. He didn't look pissed or livid: just a cold face with motionless eyes, a soulless excuse for a human being, Jets rationalized.

46

The screw-up at Camp David costed Burks, dearly. McKaine had ordered extra agents to shadow Burks, keeping a watchful eye over him, or as he perceived it—ensuring he didn't blurt government secrets to the wrong people. He felt inept in his office, reading cables and on occasion speaking with a representative from the White House, who was not the chief of staff.

Post had lost interest in him too, though Burks wasn't upset at having fallen out of favor with that despot. He successfully convinced himself the old Burks had survived a daring game, dodging a land mine. That illusion, however, fizzled out on this particular day. Burks had arrived at the usual time to the Truman Building—8:45—with a piping hot espresso in hand. He settled in for a new day of serving as a prop, when Hobbs walked through the door with a request from McKaine.

"What did he say exactly?" Burks cringed in his armchair.

"The White House requests you sit in on a presentation at Langley." She showed him the tablet with a follow-up email with the time of the presentation. "It starts in a little under an hour. You want me to gather your briefcase?" She meant well, but Burks didn't see that.

"Get out. Now."

Hobbs leapt backward, unprepared and caught off guard by his reaction. Her lips trembled with fear, and her hands shook noticeably.

Outside his door, Burks heard her whimpering. He swiped the receiver off his desk phone and punched McKaine's number as if he were punching a human face. Waiting for an answer, Burks's initial reaction of rage wore off, and he began to repent. It was hardly Hobbs's fault, and it was hardly the White House's fault. He placed the receiver back down, letting his hands, one on top of the other, rest on the desk, building courage to face his tormentor.

• • • •

Dense clouds, heavy with rain, had gathered over McLean, Virginia, home to the Central Intelligence Agency's brain—Langley. Under different circumstances, Burks would have looked forward to visiting this fortress, considering it would be his first. His body shivered despite the mild wind and wearing a raincoat. Within the walls of the CIA, the most sinister secret, from the agency's conception, was taking place. He was just a cog in the wheel.

Burks was subjected to the routine visitor check, regardless of status and job title. CIA outfits searched him and his bag, and signed off on his ID without much of a customer service touch. He chose not to pay attention to his feelings of personal space being violated. What did he expect? He was allowed to enter the CIA, a rare privilege, even for a highly regarded Washingtonian.

A tall woman, black hair outlining her round face, dressed in a suit tailored to her body, approached Burks from the stairs, but stayed behind the metal detectors, allowing the guards to finish their work.

"Mr. Secretary, what an honor." She extended her hand and warmly shook his, smiling tenderly with lips painted in ash rose.

Burks couldn't place her face. Not one of Post's regulars. His expression hinted at surprise.

"I'm head of DCI Post's administrative services." She motioned they take the bank of elevators on their right. As they stepped in, she pressed her badge to the infrared recognition camera beneath the buttons. The system displayed her name—Darby Hennesies—along with a photo of her. The word "Clear" flashed in green on a small screen.

"Have you ever been to Langley?"

"First time," Burks said. "Seventh floor?"

"Actually, no. The presentation's on the sixth—the cyber security wing. Director Post thought you might like a private tour of the CIA's most prized department." There was something robotic in the way she spoke, cult-like. Burks couldn't put his finger on it.

"If I'd known that, I'd have asked my girl to better free up my schedule."

"I promise it will be worth your while."

She led him through a corridor decorated with the ex-DCIs' official portraits on the wall. Large windows looked at the center of the campus, with a blossoming rose garden, a waterfall, and benches. It would cut the mustard for serenity.

"Never suspected the CIA grounds to be done so tastefully."

"We get that a lot. People's perception of what we do and who we are has been distorted in the media and the films." Hennesies walked ahead of him, talking. "We don't dwell on that too much." She stopped at two vaulted doors that resembled a bunker. "Behind this door—it's what really matters, Mr. Secretary."

Burks found himself in a large space, equipped with computers and monitors, sufficient to wire a medium-sized Eastern European country. He was in awe of how vast it looked. "The Cyber Security Center?" Burks asked.

"We like to call it the Hamilton facility." She curled her lip in a smile.

"As in Alexander Hamilton?"

Hennesies's eyes lingered in the facility. She explained, "Hamilton was excellent at decrypting letters, designing codes, and forming a spy ring to assist at that time General Washington."

He jolted at the mention of a spy ring. Post wasn't showing him the CSC because he was a gracious host; he was reminding Burks that he belonged to a modern-day spy ring. Unfortunately, Burks wasn't brave and articulate as Alexander Hamilton.

He exhaled, loaded with remorse. "I'm grateful for the opportunity, but I'm afraid time isn't on my side and I'll have to go back to DC pretty soon, Ms. Hennesies."

"Darby is perfectly fine." She pointed to a door off to the side.

Their conversation transitioned in a conference room with a video screen, a long table, and several chairs. Standard and in line with the fashion Burks would expect from the CIA.

"You would like a briefing on what we've found thus far, correct?" Hennesies skimmed her smartphone for the email description of the meeting. From under the head of the table, she pulled a remote and pressed a button that dimmed the lights as the projector showed its first slide.

"Director Post won't be joining us?"

"He's in DC, has been since early this morning." Darby locked her attention on the screen, prepared. "We provided the White House with a detail summary, but Mr. McKaine asked for a face-to-face update. The CIA's happy to assist, of course."

Burks swore Hobbs told him McKaine had called his office to sit in on a CIA briefing for them, implying new intel was discovered.

"Will you be presenting new information, different from what the White House already has?"

"I don't think so." Hennesies slid a copy of what she was going to talk about across the desk. "It's in the file. Better quality photos, same info. Shall we start?"

Hennesies's presentation winded down after roughly forty minutes to an hour. She was nearly to the end, when her phone vibrated and cut her off mid-sentence. Burks had sat through the masquerade, patiently taking in geo images of neighborhoods in Damascus, the long, but accurate, account of the current events inside the Middle Eastern country, and paid scant attention to the video of Bo Breeks, a bonus at the end.

"I'm afraid there's a change of plans, Mr. Burks," Hennesies said.

Burks was not in the mood for it. "Young lady," he stood, raincoat in hand, "as I've said before, my day's pretty packed."

Post had an impeccable timing, always showing up precisely and especially when he was least expected.

"Darby, you can go." Post stood at the door, his posture casually relaxed, unlike his face. "There's a place I want to take you."

"I've seen the so-called Hamilton facility. Besides, I was headed back."

Post stepped forward. "That's not how friends treat each other."

Burks wasn't sure Post knew the definition of friendship or whether he had a living being to call a friend. He was a sociopath who'd strangled his way to the top.

• • • •

Post pumped the brakes on the Humvee at a set of heavy iron gates. He'd said only a handful of words on the drive, which cause Burks to grow antsier. He didn't dare ask the CIA head whether they were still on the CIA campus. From the surroundings, they had stopped on a flat stretch of land, guarded by hills and a dense forest, a shape of a building visible in the distance.

"You feel like going for a walk?"

"If I said no, would that matter?"

"There's a walking trail outside the compound. We can use it. Leave your coat."

Burks missed his Secret Service detail on the lonely patch of rocks Post called a walking trail. He longed for the burly guys whom he'd perceived as nuisance, trained to catch a flying bullet meant for him.

"Did you speak with McKaine this morning?" Post walked in measured steps, as measured as his personality.

"The girl at State did."

"Strike you odd that he wanted you at the CIA to listen to a presentation the White House's been sitting on for a day?"

Did it strike him as odd? It did, along with this walk and questions. "I assumed since I've been in contact with the middleman, he was bringing me in the fold."

Post flicked him a look. "He insisted that I show you the material they have."

"Eugene, you don't think he's suspecting discrepancies, do you?"

"He's on a fishing expedition, but he's gonna end up drowning." Post ceased his walking, turned, and faced Burks. "Here's what I want you to say to the president at the Sit Room briefing today."

47

Water dripped from the edges of Amelia's hair. The dirty clothes lay in a pile at the foot of the hotel bed. Her mind moved at a sluggish speed. The FBI agent had reunited her with her bag—with her phone, laptop, and wallet visibly missing from the rest of the contents. She dug out a clean top to change into and sat on a firm chair facing a window, the view blocked by the massive curtains.

"For your own safety," she remembered the gumshoe explaining when he drew them and then locked her in the room.

Spending the last hellish twenty-four hours in a windowless cage drove Amelia to the brink of her mental toughness. She wanted nothing more than to sit and watch the world go by through a window.

A keycard was inserted in the door, and the door handle rattled. Amelia threw a worried gaze behind her shoulder, frightened.

A voice she vaguely recognized asked, "Ms. Sinclair, may I come in?"

She raised herself off the chair, not fully standing, when an older man, who looked like a concerned father, stepped past the entrance.

He glanced at her bag and clothes on the floor, then returned eyes on her. "Dax has given you your bag, I see. That's good."

He pointed for her to sit back down in her seat. He approached, unbuttoned his coat, and dragged a chair closer to hers. They both sat by the window with no view of the outside.

"We're meeting at quite bizarre circumstances; wouldn't you agree?" His eyes traced the quarter-sized bruise on her left cheek and scratch marks on her neck.

Amelia felt as though he were sizing her up, making calculated observations, judging her. That gave her mind a little breather to think. She had seen his face on TV during the presidential election and after. The president's chief of staff appeared shorter in person, which didn't surprise her. Cameras usually lied about a person's shape and features.

"You're Robert McKaine," she murmured.

"I don't know what's appropriate to say in this situation—nice to meet you?" His face grew in a smile, momentarily returning back to its original position.

Amelia didn't say anything back. She didn't want to be rude to him, but she also didn't want to be stuck in a room with him either.

He glanced at his watch. "It's rather early, and I'm going to order some breakfast and coffee for myself. Would you like anything?"

She was starving. In the hole where they kept her, she drank stale coffee and had a pack of peanut butter crackers. She was ready to leap in happiness at the offer of room service food. Her head bobbed in agreement.

"Fair enough. What would you like?" McKaine picked up the phone. "I like to start off my day with pancakes, coffee, and yogurt. The yogurt is just to make my doctor happy."

"I'll have what you're having."

As he placed the order, her thoughts swirled around the drain of exhaustion. She doubted even caffeine would boost her level of energy. She was willing to give it a try.

After he finished rattling off their food demands, McKaine returned to his seat, back resting, elbows pushing his sides, prepared to hear her out. A tense minute of silence between them disappeared as McKaine took the reins of the conversation.

"We can wait until after the food to have our talk if you prefer. I don't see a reason to wait. Up to you."

"What would you like to know?"

"The FBI built a time profile of where you've been. It shows me a peek into your choices, but I'm afraid it doesn't explain the motives." McKaine's mind rewound to the night Dax, Lance, and him worked in the boardroom. The two columns on the erase board swam to the surface. "I don't know if you were involved in the murder of your boss and coworker in Brooklyn, and I don't see a point in discussing this. It's a murder investigation, and the local law enforcement is handling that."

"I didn't," she said tersely.

As if he didn't hear it, McKaine continued, "I have a report by the Pakistani Secret Services that I can't explain. That bothers me. If you're innocent, then maybe you can help me. I'm afraid that report, in addition to the FBI evidence, is enough for the DOJ to take over and file charges against you."

"Then what are you waiting for? Why am I not in handcuffs and in a cell?" Amelia was in free fall, wanting to gamble with a judge and a jury, as long as she never spoke with another man who used her as a pawn.

McKaine wheezed, impressed by her gutsiness. "I've got at least ten agents outside who've asked me the same thing. I'm telling you what I've told them—a jailed innocent American weakens our country; it doesn't make us more secure."

The rest of their conversation was put on hold while the waiter brought in the cart with their order. McKaine turned his back to Amelia and the hotel employee, counting money for a tip. Amelia held her eyes on the waiter. He was dressed for the part, but looked like a Tarantino character.

Then it happened. A subtle flick of his eyes guiding hers to a spot under the coffee cup plate. *Was he trying to tell her something or had she spent too much time on the run with Jets?*

"There you go." McKaine broke their stare with his words and made a move for the cart.

Amelia sprung to her feet. "Let me," she said to McKaine, eyes steady on him, fully aware that the waiter was still in the room. "I got this," she added, letting the waiter know it was all right for him to leave.

McKaine didn't mind her eagerness. Back at his spot, he was talking as Amelia took the plates and cups, pouring coffee with a splash of milk and one sugar for him, black for her. She cautiously lifted the last plate, her back blocking McKaine from seeing her action. A little piece of paper was neatly folded, hiding underneath. She swiftly lifted it, and it disappeared into her jean pocket.

"Is that true?" McKaine had asked, though Amelia had missed the entire conversation.

She handed him his cup of coffee. Faking embarrassment, she probed for clarification. "Is what true? I'm sorry?"

The look on McKaine's face had changed from calm to inquisitive. His stunted pause made her nervous.

"The ISI report had raided a home in Damascus of a well-known to them terrorist. Shooting broke out; they took him out. On his body, they found instructions and a phone number. Your office number at the UN. I asked if that was true?"

"To a radical government, a person with ideas, a keyboard, and internet connection is perceived as a threat. When, in fact, that person only wants to bring about peace."

"So your position then is that Rashid Haddad isn't a terrorist?" He stopped short from disclosing to her that the father of her child, Khalib Osmani, had volunteered Haddad's identity and not the Pakistani government.

She could tell what McKaine wanted to hear, but she couldn't bring herself to do it. "He was a journalist. Idealistic. He was guilty of wanting to lay the foundation of *Life, Liberty, and the pursuit of Happiness* in Syria."

"Dangerous ideas, radical." McKaine gulped from his coffee.

"Rashid, to my knowledge, stayed away from the militia. He'd lost two brothers to bombs. He wasn't buying into their dogmatism."

Their Q&A had transitioned into empirical discussion. McKaine entertained it.

"When we grow emotionally too attached to something, even an ideology, we can easily talk ourselves in justifying most awful atrocity. No?"

"Absolutely. There's a false prophet on every corner."

"Correct me if I'm wrong—you're partly disputing the ISI report?"

"That's right. Rashid was our man on the ground. He helped us set up the interview, and he was supposed to get in touch with my coworkers after they checked in their hotel."

"I'm an open-minded man for my advanced age and even I find it out of the question that President al-Azizi would reach out to a journalist—if that's what you call Rashid—to help lock down an interview with an American network."

Amelia couldn't blame McKaine for his skepticism; he was examining the situation from the point of view of the government.

"Al-Azizi's regime has been choked by UN economical and humanitarian sanctions. Despite the substantial financial backing he receives from the Russians, Syria's been leveled to the ground. Al-Azizi was looking to appeal to the West and make his case to win sympathy."

"Not doing a good job by ordering the kidnapping of Americans."

Her thoughts tangled in a net: Seed's smiling face; the Beretta rifles in the video, not a first choice by kidnappers according to Jets; her own brush with death. *Should she say that to him or hold on to it until she read the note?*

She opened her mouth to let the truth dictate her fate.

Dax stormed the hotel room, addressing McKaine. "We've got a major problem in the lobby headed for this floor."

In a smooth move, McKaine stood and placed his coffee cup on the cart, freeing his hands for a handshake with Amelia. "We'll resume this conversation soon, Ms. Sinclair. I see no reason why you can't go home, and I'll be in touch with you again. Dax will give you a lift when you're ready to go."

After he left, Amelia fished the note from her pocket and read it. Her eyes traced his name on the paper, reassuring her that he'd been staying close by.

48

The crowd had grown painstakingly large to accommodate everyone in the Oval Office, so McKaine proposed they reconvene in the Roosevelt Room, gallantly called "the fish room" by staffers, which was right across from the president's office.

A steady stream of bodies piled in, taking a seat, arranged in a circle—Delay's idea of promoting equality, ala King Arthur and his knights. The White House's phones were under a constant assault from congressmen and journalists for most of the night and part of the day, threatening political retaliation if the president didn't appease them with his decision. Their wishes ran wild on the gamut: from peaceful resolution, to caving in to the terrorists' demands, sending in the Marines. Each call came with a new proposal of what Delay should, must do.

For that purpose, McKaine instructed his aides to unplug every phone and wire in the fish room; he also asked the invitees to leave their mobile devices outside the door.

Delay was not close to making a decision, but he vowed for that to change by the last stroke of midnight.

"I'm open to all possibilities. I prefer if we can minimize the casualties on the ground." Delay opened the meeting, one foot resting on top of the other. His attention skipped from face to face. "The demand list is a tall order and unfeasible. Releasing Gitmo prisoners back to their native countries will set us back and leave us vulnerable down the line." His eyes stopped at the director of counterterrorism, as if Delay were repeating his words, carefully curated.

McKaine had a finger on the pulse of the room, measuring the rest's reaction to Delay's lead. They were receptive and thus far in an agreeable mood.

"I believe by now we've all had the chance to glance over the CIA assessment plan of the situation in Damascus." Delay's eyes continued to travel and came to a full stop again on McKaine. "Bob?"

"Conrad was at Langley. Let's turn it over to him."

The bodies in the room shifted toward Burks, whose viewpoint dropped to the carpeted floor.

"It's my understanding the CIA had pinpointed the hostages' location to Jobar." Burks's voice crackled in the fish room.

McKaine watched him closely, every twitch, every nerve spasm, a telling sign of how uncomfortable his experience at the CIA had gone. But that was expected; it didn't surprise McKaine, and it wasn't the reason he sent Burks to the CIA.

"They have rock-solid intel based on eyes on the ground and our own experts, who back up that Jobar is the place we oughta be looking at."

"What's your assessment?" McKaine spoke up.

Post's diatribe played in Burks's ears. The DCI promised to let him resign with no blowback on his family if he did this.

"Al-Azizi won't help us in this situation. He's been politically wounded; I'm thinking he'll cave under protests by the Russians to defy us," Burks said genuinely. "Pakistan couldn't care less if anything happens to our kidnapped journalists. As long as they get paid, they'll feed us information." That was the first and last truthful statement he would speak throughout the discussion.

He went on. "My concern is this—the time has run out on a peace talk. The terrorists on the left are demanding, and al-Azizi with the Russians in his ears to the right would be demanding too."

Delay leaned forward and uncrossed his legs, letting his arms rest in his lap. Hearing his secretary of state leaning into a military option perplexed him.

"You're siding with the CIA report, then?" McKaine chimed in.

"I personally would back a plan where we send a team of SEALs into Jobar to extract the hostages."

Delay raised his hands in the air, an exaggerated expression painted on his face. "Come on—am I the one person in this room who thinks that the SEALs have a high probability of failing? Then what? We lose the SEALs plus the four Americans."

McKaine suspected the rest were growing tired of Delay harping on their ideas as he was. A quick stock of the mood in the circle revealed to the chief of staff that Delay risked turning people against him. Perhaps Post had forged alliances with some of them, perhaps a few were worried about their status quo after they're long gone from the White House, perhaps deception had already corroded the foundation of trust in this administration.

"General," pointing to the secretary of defense, McKaine said, "you can put together a plan, ready for us in four hours?"

Eyes glared at Delay, anticipating POTUS's reaction. He expressed none.

"I've got a team ready to go. Say the word when," the general replied.

There was work to be done and four hours before the SEAL deployment was less than desirable for McKaine. Huddled in his office, he phoned Dax but got his voice mail. More waiting, wasting time, while Post plotted God knows what in Jobar or maybe the States. He wanted to nail the son-of-a-bitch to the wall. Post had been planning the coup for months, maybe longer. McKaine was running against the clock, praying for a Hail Mary. He tried Dax again and got through.

"I was getting ready to call you," Dax said in a hurry.

"In four hours, a SEAL team will most likely leave for Syria unless you've got something for me."

"Sinclair's back at her house. A car was tailing us from the hotel to the home. Two men. Ran the plates but they were fake." Dax briefly stopped, waiting for a question, and then resumed. "She let it slip that a CIA agent helped her. He got hurt at Amy's. She got jumped by men she never saw after that."

That was interesting. Amelia didn't mention the diner or the CIA agent to McKaine. He prompted Dax, "Did she give you a name?"

"No. Caught herself and told me to forget about it."

"Where's the car now?"

"Nearby—I'm watching them."

McKaine gripped the phone tighter. The next question was important. "And what about the information I asked you to look into for me?"

"Legitimate mission trips to mostly the Asian peninsula—Bangkok, Penang, Melaka. Travel documents, plane logs check out. His first visit was in the early nineties and the last four, years before the secretary of state nomination."

To say that McKaine was relieved by the news was a lie. He didn't buy it that Burks wasn't hiding a monster-sized skeleton in his closet. Post knew it was there and was extorting Burks. McKaine, however, worried that he and Dax weren't thorough.

"You found no hookers, drugs, paying off gambling debts, wife's out-of-control spending habits?" McKaine was scraping the bottom.

"Clean as a whistle and his wife has a fat trust fund. The girls are fairly young."

McKaine had to admit that was a major setback for him.

Then Dax said, "This is far-fetched, but shortly after each mission trip, parents of young boys came forward to claim their children had been raped by a foreigner. The investigations never panned out, because somehow the families withdrew their criminal reports a few weeks later. In every case."

"In every case?"

"Hard to tell, sir. Their records aren't very pristine. What do you want to do now?"

"Hang in there. I'm going to pay Ms. Sinclair a second visit."

Inaudible sounds vibrated over the wire and into McKaine's ear. Dax was coughing, more like choking. Then McKaine heard a bump, followed by dead silence.

He stood from behind his desk, frowning. "Dax."

Another person was on the other end, McKaine could feel it, but it wasn't Dax.

49

She'd reached home, almost. Dax hadn't parked the car; while still in motion, Amelia leapt out and ran toward her front door. An elderly woman, with dust-gray hair, braided, edged to the side, clearing the path for Ava.

Amelia fell to her knees, arms stretched wide, embraced her kid, and held her in.

"You're home, Mommy," Ava whispered to Amelia, who was fighting back tears.

Her voice shook. "I'm never leaving again."

As she turned to close the door behind her, Amelia saw Dax and waved him good-bye. When he cleared her block and she couldn't see his car anymore, her eyes traveled up and down the street, watching for Jets.

Ava tugged on her mother's shirt. "Can we have some ice cream?"

Amelia scooped her in her arms and planted a messy kiss on the child's cheek. "Mint chocolate chip!"

The half-eaten ice cream was melting in bowls in the kitchen sink, while Amelia and Ava danced in the living room to corny songs that played on the kid's channel. Their bare feet were stomping on the wood floor, causing plenty of noise. Amelia didn't care who heard them. She was back and alive.

It must have been the ice cream or the exhaustion from dancing for a straight hour, but Ava was dead asleep in her mother's arms as she climbed the stairs to the toddler's bedroom. Amelia stuck around for a while, just watching Ava dozing off, arms stretched above her head, dreaming peacefully.

• • • •

Below the first floor, in the remodeled basement, hiding, Jets listened to the happy celebration with a heavy heart. Before his chance meeting with Amelia, he rarely imagined a different life from the one he'd chosen. The CIA apparatus dispatched him to corners of the earth so savaged, he couldn't put a family through this. And then the men he'd killed—there were many murders, justifiable and legal under the crest of the CIA, but murders nonetheless.

His mind rejected instantaneously Jets's romantic flirtation with alternate reality—cash in his retirement chips, after taking care of Post, then disappear in the oblivion with this pretty lady.

Amelia walked in, lights off, paying scant attention to the room. She made it impossible for him to breathe with that body of hers. She slipped out of her jeans and threw the shirt on a chair, headed for the shower. As if she suspected Jets was close by, she left the door cracked. Steam saturated the air.

Had he known all along that he loved her? That she'd be the first and only woman he'd love? What difference did it make? He wasn't fighting his urges; he was caving in to them. Because of her, Jets put his life in danger, destroyed his career, and readied to kill presumably the most powerful man he knew of. Another trepidatious moment of doubt held him back, perplexed by the possibility of rejection. Even that was not enough to stop him.

He closed his eyes and imagined Amelia's lips on his, his arms wrapped tightly around her—he wouldn't let go. As his thoughts concluded, he found himself in the bathroom doorway. A few steps separated them. He knew he was defying every rule of professional conduct, so he stepped back into the darkness, away from her. He lost her once at Amy's because he allowed his feelings for her to control the situation. He wouldn't make that mistake again.

• • • •

Amelia cut off the hot water, feeling renewed. She was moving about, her body covered with a towel, distracted by her own thoughts. When she hit the light switch, his face didn't register with her right away. She froze and let out a gust of breath.

"Amelia." Jets shortened the distance between the two. She trembled. "I'm sorry," he said to her. Then pulled her in his arms, stroking her wet hair.

"It's you. It's really you." Amelia came back, raising her head to look into his eyes.

"Will you forgive me?"

"There's nothing to forgive."

"I let you down. I should've seen them coming."

"How could you? They were going to get to me no matter what."

He took the breath out of her lips as he kissed her. She kissed him back, slowly, then passionately, savoring the moment. It felt good. It felt right.

Jets and Amelia were responsible solely for the current state of the bed—a tangled mess of sheets.

"You're a little fighter, Ms. Sinclair," Jets said. "I heard you kicking and screaming. I bet you scared them shitless."

"I thought my number was up when they tied me up in the back of that damn SUV," she replied.

"Can we talk about what happened at the black site? Are you up to it?"

"How'd you know? Actually, never mind, don't tell me. Two guys interrogated me. The first looked military. At first, he was calm, focused, but as time went on, he became a monster." She shivered.

"You can stop if it's too much."

As if she didn't hear a word, she said, "That guy wasn't with the group at Amy's. I've never seen him before. The second man—now, I've seen his face plenty. Anyone with a working TV and C-SPAN would recognize him."

Jets shoved a hand under his head, fully aware of the name she was about to give him.

"Your boss, the director of the Central Intelligence Agency, Eugene Post."

"Did he hurt you?"

"Not physically. He threatened me, and Ava too. Showed me the FBI Most Wanted list with my photo under number one. Gosh, I hate this so much." Amelia sat up in bed. "If I can't prove my innocence, then they'll lock me up and throw away the key for...for...ever."

She was back in Jets's arms, and he brushed her face with his fingers. "Nothing's going to happen to you. You hear me, Amelia—I won't let it happen."

He got up and looked for his pants. "Do you see them?"

"Try behind the couch?"

"I want you to have this." He spread out her palm and put the flash drive in it.

"What is this?"

"Ava's and your life insurance. Post is too scared of the files on this device. He won't kill you as long as he knows you have it."

"He'll kill you."

He wanted to say to her that he'd spend the rest of his life trying to kill Post. She didn't have to know that, not at the moment.

While Jets jumped in the shower, Amelia went upstairs to prepare coffee, glancing nervously at the flash drive on her kitchen counter. Jets had failed to explain to her what exactly was so important on the drive that Post wanted so dearly. The out-of-the-blue banging on the front door scared the living crap out of her. Jets must have heard it too, because he shut off the water.

McKaine was on the top step, accompanied by two guys, miked and wired. She'd seen him hours earlier, and she couldn't fathom why he was back.

"May I come in, Ms. Sinclair? I don't want to draw any more attention to your house."

She let him in, but not his detail.

"Fair enough. Your home, your rules. I can accept that," he said. "Is this coffee?" He pointed to the second cup on the table. Amelia showed him to a seat in the living room and handed him Jets's cup.

"You owe me an explanation." McKaine looked agitated to her. "Your comments to Dax—that you were picked up at Amy's Diner, someone else helping you. Amelia, I can only work with you if you're truthful."

She wasn't a liar and hated being called one. The comments she made to Dax were off-the-cuff, brought on by stress.

"I should've been more forthcoming. Please try to understand. I had spent a day under awful conditions. I was paralyzed by fear."

"There's still a chance. The president's planning to send a SEAL team to Jobar in less than three hours. I think you might be my last hope to convince him otherwise."

"Mr. McKaine, I don't know whether I should be flattered or alarmed by you."

"Neither. The SEALs would be quick, quiet, in and out."

Amelia saw no issues with the plan, so why did McKaine? "Can it work?"

"The SEALs are highly trained. The best in the world, in fact. The plan should work."

"I'm sensing you aren't on board with the decision."

"Based on preliminary evidence—nothing solid, I'm afraid—someone wants to draw our government, country into an international scandal with such magnitude that it brings the current administration down. Destabilize our society."

"Why? Who would gain anything from seeing America tearing itself from the inside?" Her voice died. Then she started back on. "Only one agency powerful enough to pull it off."

"Tell me, Amelia—which agency comes to mind?"

"The CIA."

"I think at this precise moment, you and I are about the only two people who think that."

"Three people."

"Come again?"

"You said you and I are the only people, but it's actually three."

"Who's the third one?"

"This could be a trap." Amelia was on her feet, undecided.

"I assure you—there's no trap. I demand to know who's the third person, Ms. Sinclair. Our country's national security is in jeopardy."

"Mr. McKaine, please meet CIA Agent Gabriel Jets."

McKaine broke eye contact with her and locked in on the new face. He stood and extended his hand to shake Jets's. "I bet we've got a lot to go over," McKaine said, hands still in a grip.

"I bet so too."

50

McKaine pointed to the couch. Jets rebuffed his hospitality and opted to remain on his feet.

"Can I get anyone more coffee?" Amelia said, bleakly.

They ignored her, and the three continued this weird tiptoeing, each sizing up the other.

"Did you hear what I confided to Amelia?" McKaine finally said, calm eyes transfixed on Jets. He'd broken protocol by bringing Amelia in the fold on a classified mission; Jets was a miscalculation on his part.

"Most of it."

"What do you make of it?"

"I'm not on the ground in Damascus, and assessing a SEAL op without access to the intelligence gathering tools makes me a quack." Jets crossed his arms over his chest, sculptured muscles bulging under his shirt.

He'd passed McKaine first test, measuring Jets's level of honesty. Meanwhile, Jets was conducting one of his own on the chief of staff. At first glance, Jets's memory bank didn't pull meaningful data, placing McKaine and Post together. Then again, he had very little to work with, having worked exclusively out of the country in his tenure as a CIA agent.

"Who's running intel recon on the ground at the present moment?" Jets assumed the White House had mobilized a friendly foreign intel agency like the British MI6 or the French DGSE to set up shop and feed his government intel. He didn't suspect things to be in the dire state they were.

"We don't have that in place."

Post knew the weaknesses of the young Delay administration and had led them astray from procedural must-haves. What Jets couldn't fathom was why the State Department and the NSA weren't being more forceful in handling the hostage crisis by the book.

His mouth opened halfway, caught off guard by the cracking of the one-way radio in his pocket.

"What's that?" McKaine looked at the device in Jets's hands, concerned he'd walked into a trap.

With his peripheral vision, Jets saw Amelia also staring at him with intensity.

"It's my partner sending a disturbed call," Jets said as he went for the door, fidgeting with the volume of the radio. "Does the White House know you're here?"

McKaine stood, hands in his pockets, shoulders curved to accommodate his tense posture. He nodded his head with an affirmation.

Jets squeezed the radio intercom, then rethought that and released it. His impassive expression told little of what was going on in his mind to Amelia and McKaine, who exchanged troubled glances.

"Foxtrot, do you copy?" a voice echoed in the comm.

The skin around Jets's eyes burned, hearing Vito breaking their cardinal rule of never tuning in live over the OWVL, unless your life depended on it. He pressed the intercom. "Copy, Charlie."

"Two tangos flanking the east corner of the street. Moving your way."

The CIA had been using the OWVL since the early '70s to allow secured communication between their spies. The prerecorded messages exchanged by CIA agents were encrypted and rarely captured by enemies, with a few exceptions. The OWVL was easily traced back to the users when voice scrambling wasn't employed. Jets was willing to bet his life that his enemies were listening to Vito's transmission too. He had to join his partner out there, but he was stuck with two civilians inside.

"Roger that," Jets said.

Amelia darted for the upstairs, where Ava slept. McKaine reached for his White House-issued encrypted phone to call reinforcements.

"Put that away. If the cavalry shows up—our president will be making an entirely different statement tonight."

"Then what?" McKaine answered, sober.

"You have your two men outside and a bulletproof car—take Amelia and Ava with you and leave." He had laced his boots and was securing his shoulder holster. Jets stopped and listened for Amelia upstairs, waking up Ava frantically. He would love to stick around and keep her calm, but the tangos weren't going to let him do that.

Jets flicked his head in the direction of the stairs. "Keep them safe for me."

It was dead quiet on Amelia's block, which Jets counted to his advantage. He started up to the north corner, where Vito had originally dropped him off. Their car was still parked at the same spot, minus Vito. He was nowhere in sight. To check it out up close, Jets had to leave his observation hideout, crouched behind the bumper of a red Chevy Camaro.

He eased on the concrete, left hand gripping his 9mm Glock previously secured in the shoulder holster. All hell broke loose when his feet were both planted on the street. Bullets flew in his direction. He lay flat on the ground and rolled over, a gun now in each hand, returning the fire.

A tango, camouflaged in black, head to toe, was kneeled four cars down, pushing bullets out of his Beretta. His partner was positioned directly across from him, both aiming at Jets.

He managed to drag himself to safety behind the metal of Vito's car, with minimal abrasions and no bullet wounds. His mind ran recon options and variables during the brief breather while guns were reloaded with magazines. The growling of a motorcycle in the opposite direction of Jets had apparently blocked the tangos, leaving them no room to pull back. On one side was the motorcycle; on the other, Jets. He edged his back along the trunk and leaned in to canvass the unfolding development. A speeding Kawasaki bike was laying the enemies to waste with his rifle. Jets didn't waste any time jumping on the action and double-hammering them. The body of one of the two absorbed a bullet, which killed him instantly. The one left put up a fight, pulling back away from the street and toward the houses. Jets killed the power to his guns once the guy was close to the front windows, fearing bullets would ricochet and kill innocent bystanders.

"Jump on!" Vito yelled to Jets from the Kawasaki. "We'll catch up to him on the other side."

Vito twisted the throttle, veering the bike off the street, directly on the grass in pursuit of the tango. Bent at the waist, Jets reached in his partner's belt to retrieve a spare gun. One of his had run out of ammo.

Neither one of them had a plan of action—they were simply improvising. The Kawasaki built up speed, but it made it hard to clear corners. They took a bed of flowers out as they bounced on the muddy ground.

The chase had turned into a scene, a spectacle. First, Jets had to eliminate the last tango. Then he would worry how to handle the local cops.

Behind the second row of houses, the Kawasaki grazed a fence. Jets felt Vito swerve to avoid hitting the wood posts. The bike violently jerked, and for a second, Jets thought Vito had lost control of it. By a sheer miracle, Vito straighten the handles and in the momentum, cleared the fence.

His mind returned to the game. Jets's eyes prowled for the target. It was as if he'd vanished into thin air.

"Where he'd go?" Jets had missed the muddy footprints, but Vito had not. He directed the bike back on to the asphalt. Now Jets had spotted them too. At about the halfway mark, the footsteps disappeared. Vito kept the engine going, but unclutched the foot pegs.

"Car picked him up probably, while we were back there," Vito said.

It wasn't Post's fashion to go public with a mission. He was discreet, well-organized, leaving no room for mistakes. This was sloppy. Jets tapped Vito on the shoulder and let his hand rest there. He didn't like that they were on the street, exposed.

"He's gone. We should be too." Jets summed it up.

Vito started back on the bike, when they got a glimpse of a black SUV at the top of the street, rolling their way.

"I guess he went home to get Mommy and Daddy." A tone of amusement could be felt in Vito's voice.

Vito twisted the accelerator, showing off its powers.

"Hold up. What's that?" Jets motioned to a second SUV pulling up to the first one, almost side by side.

"Damn. It's a cluster fuck." Vito liked their odds with one SUV—two, no chance in hell. "How much ammo do you have left?"

Jets didn't reply right away. The SUVs were identical, and he had a problem with that.

Vito tried to come up with a strategy for them. "We can try to draw them out, one by one, a tight street back there—pop the drivers in a blitz attack."

Jets would've said no to Vito's ridiculous suggestion, if he was even listening to him. He was trying to remember the make and model of McKaine's vehicle. It didn't look like the two SUVs were getting along. The second one rolled down a window, and an occupant was showing a badge. The other SUV didn't buy it and drove off, directly at Vito and Jets.

"Go, go, go," was all Jets had to say.

Vito took off, headed for a collision.

Jets brought a rifle out, stood up on the seat, and fired rounds into the SUV. When the gun stopped shooting, Jets leaped off to the side, hitting the pavement hard. After a few seconds, he dared to open his eyes—there was a lot of smoke and the smell of fresh gasoline in the air. He lifted himself up to check out the results of the shootout. The SUV was a wrecked pile of scrap metal, ten steps away from him. Jets continued to survey the rest of the street. Vito was getting up too, having landed in a front lawn.

He yelled at Jets. "You okay, man?"

Jets nodded and approached the SUV with hyped-up caution. The driver lay on the wheel, with a bullet in the head. The guy next to him was dead, though Jets couldn't tell whether it was from a bullet. He was covered in blood, lots of it, and shattered glass.

He heard the second SUV pulling behind and jumped back, anticipating the worst. Jets reached for his gun, but the holster was empty. He shot an asking look to Vito, who raised his arms in the air and shook his head. He was out of weapons.

The back door swung wide. McKaine, speechless, got closer to Jets. His hands rested on his hips and his lips pursed together. In a shaking voice that didn't match his collected demeanor, he said, "Agent Jets, you're just the man I've been looking for."

51

"He's dead?" Post asked. "You sure about that?"

"Milo's dead and two of his men," Monroe replied grimly.

That wasn't necessarily a bad thing. Milo was going to be killed once Post had no use for him anymore. He flicked a lighter and put the flame to Milo's mugshot. Monroe watched as the blue flame transformed it into ashes.

"Nothing ties him to us. He left a trail to the Russian mob—guns, illegal gambling, and prostitution."

Monroe had been summoned to Langley to explain the corpses left behind each time Post got near Jets. *It shouldn't be that hard to get rid of one agent. Then why couldn't Monroe hack it?*

As if reading his boss's reservations, Monroe went on. "The Feds showed up on scene. The last we heard, they're hauling the bodies to the morgue for an autopsy. It could be weeks, if not months, till the ME gets to examining them."

"We had to kill Jets early on. In Brooklyn. Tactical mistakes were allowed, and we're at the tipping point of losing it."

"The problem is—we've sent others to eliminate him. You've held me back in the wings. Next time, I should be the one who kills him."

Monroe was Post's best man and the last remaining of the Band of Seven. He couldn't risk losing him right before the SEALs were due to deploy. Jets had to be distracted, at least until Monroe was no longer tied up with the hostages in Damascus.

"It's imperative we dispose of the hostages. The man I had in charge has proved to be unreliable." Post lost focus, thinking of Osmani. His stocky body leaned back in his chair, for the first time in his life doubting himself. "Take Milo's remaining men and fly to Turkey. If you leave now, you'll be in position in Damascus before the SEALs."

Monroe had no objection at the order to kill. It would do him good to get out of the country and back in the field. He felt his skills were lacking precision, especially after Polina's murder turned into a bloodbath. The question of Jets and what to do with him was still unanswered.

"And Jets?"

"We should assume that Jets has possession of the flash drive. He'd use that as leverage against us. Going at him with guns blazing has been counterproductive—wouldn't you agree?"

The question posed to Monroe didn't require that he actually respond to it. He shuddered, unnoticed by Post.

"Jets's involvement was tricky, and we weren't well prepared for it." Monroe agreed to shoulder some of the blame. "The mercenaries we hired were mid-level, not technically trained in combat." He was referring to Milo and his Eastern European associates.

Post was highly intelligent, with a keen eye to foresee his opponents' weaknesses, and even he couldn't have predicted Jets's fierce loyalty to the female journalist. His mind cascaded back to *fierce loyalty*. Jets had been an excellent agent, devoted to the agency. He wouldn't want to see the CIA in peril and the hard work of so many brave men and women jeopardized. Post had to figure out a way to turn Jets against the Delay administration.

After some deliberation, Post finally said, "Leave Jets to me. He's my screw-up. When you get back from Syria, the road will be cleared of roadblocks and you can take care of him."

Post reached for paperwork on his desk and handed it to Monroe to view. It was a typed-up report of what Post had given the White House, with minor improvements. He'd failed to mention to McKaine, for instance, that al-Azizi was tipped off US SEALs would be violating his air space. That information, of course, was also shared with the Russians. Post hadn't notified the White House that he knew precisely where the hostages were being kept. He'd ordered Osmani to phone Burks at the last minute with this intel, leaving the White House to scramble with updated adjustments.

Not hiding his admiration of the information spelled out in the report, Monroe proclaimed, "Pretty straightforward stuff. Old school. Let the Syrians and their big brother the Russians shoot down the SEALs while still in air." Monroe clapped his hands together.

"Should be beautiful to watch. I regret not being able to be there to see."

"Lastly, we haven't discussed the FBI agent Milo killed outside Sinclair's home."

Yes, FBI Agent Dax's death was unfortunate, to a degree. He was helping McKaine, and Post had no idea how much he'd shared with the chief of staff. McKaine remained elusive and went along with what Delay said and wanted, but Post felt as though he were putting up a front.

"What happened to the body?"

"As far as I know, it was left behind. Milo was ambushed by Jets, and in the chaotic atmosphere, the Fed was left undealt with."

"Milo killed him in his car?"

"Mhmm."

Post reacted visibly to Monroe's last item on the agenda. His entire face burned with anger when he said, "Fucking third world shits." He continued, "The White House has to be diverted before and during the SEALs' hostage extraction mission. McKaine won't have the time to dig into his lapdog's death; he'll be in crisis mode."

"You've got something in mind, then?"

"The perfect someone. A little pedophile."

Monroe visibly reacted to the word *pedophile*. His face grimaced, but said nothing.

"A sicko who should never had access to kids."

"Is it someone I can take care of before I leave?"

"No. This has to be done publicly. With the most media exposure as possible."

Not waiting around for the DCI to change his mind, Monroe left his office in a heap. The job in Damascus would occupy most of his time for the next twenty-four hours; then, when he returned, he would watch Jets dance his last slow dance with life.

With a damnable obsession to see the government in power diminished, Post was failing to calculate properly the risks of the Damascus mission. He was still too preoccupied with how to revive the hostage crisis when he made a call, bound to flip things around.

52

The decript church bells of the Basilica of the National Shrine of the Immaculate Conception reverberated throughout the courtyard. Raindrops spat against Burks's car, parked in the church lot. He'd been here last twenty years ago, and twenty years ago, he smoked at this exact spot his last cigarette, till today. The clouds orbiting above Washington were as gray as the tobacco smoke he exhaled.

That burden of betrayal wasn't going away despite the whiskey and the self-encouragement. It sat on his chest like a two-hundred-pound gorilla. His demons were refusing to leave him alone, to go back deep, to allow him to continue to be the shallow man he'd been his entire life.

He took a last slow drag from his cig before he put it out, wishing he could put out his own thoughts as easily. He better get on with it and not make Father Raihkart wait. Burks walked across the stone path that led to the main chapel, steeling himself at the marble steps. He stayed there for a long time. The granite pillars obstructed his view. The familiar pull of memories rushed over him; he'd spent his youth laying on the grass, looking up to the church domes, built in a Byzantine style, a nun pointed out to him one time. He treasured those memories and had turned his back on the memories where he spent years on his knees in the priest's private chambers, accepting God's blessings.

The front doors opened, revealing Burks to Father Raihkart. A frail man with a lined face placed his arms around Burks's neck, who had bent down to accommodate for their height difference.

In a shepherd's voice, Father Raihkart greeted him. "You've come back, Conrad."

Burks brushed the moisture from his eyes and nodded in agreement.

"Sit by me." Raihkart held onto Burks's hand and led him to the wicker chairs placed by the fireplace.

Burks didn't want to sit. He didn't want to even be there. He didn't know where to go. He knelt on one knee and let his head rest in Raihkart's lap. The old man didn't object because he'd known Burks for generations.

"Forgive me, Father, for I've sinned. It's been twenty years since my last confession."

"Let God in, Conrad, and let God lead the way."

"I'm afraid, Father, that what I've done, God can't forgive."

"God can and God will. You're here now, son. It's never too late. Tell me your sins."

"I can't speak of them, Father." Tears gushed in rivers down Burks's face as he cried, inconsolable and afraid.

Raihkart didn't push the topic further. He bowed his head. In the meantime, his long, bony fingers stroked Burks's hair.

"God, the Father of mercies, through the death and resurrection of your Son, have reconciled the world to yourself and sent the Holy Spirit among us for the forgiveness of sins. Through the ministry of the Church, may God grant you pardon and peace. I absolve you of your sins, in the name of the Father, the Son, and of the Holy Spirit. Amen."

They spent another forty minutes visiting, mainly Raihkart speaking, Burks filling the gap of silence with one-word answers. When it was time to go, Burks had found the courage to ask, "Are the priests still using the old chambers?"

Raihkart's eyes glossed over, understanding what Burks really meant. Though Raihkart never partook in his underlings' sick abuse of children, undoubtedly he knew or at least suspected it.

"We demolished them awhile back. The parish built the garden of the Holy Mother instead." Raihkart continued, "If you have time, stop by—it's a really nice place, now."

Burks swallowed his anger. "On my next visit."

He had no intentions of revisiting the space that shaped the monster he'd become. He also had no intentions of ever coming back to the Basilica. He had come to say his good-byes.

Just before he climbed back in his car, a phone call came for him, and he took it with a sense of dread. The familiar voice belonging to Osmani forecasted more lies Burks would have to tell.

"Mr. Secretary." Osmani sounded different, nervous, as if he were not supposed to call. "You can help me make this right?"

"If this is Post's idea of testing me—tell him that I'm keeping my word and doing as he tells me."

"I assure you that I'm taking on a great deal of risk by calling you." A gap of silence followed. Osmani said, "You should speak with your president immediately."

"Unfortunately, my sway with the president and his advisers has been diminished."

"Al-Azizi knows that the SEALs will be invading his air space. The Russians will be prepared."

Burks perked up. "How do you know this? Who told you?"

"I can't go into details. Like I said, this is our chance to make it right."

"What changed your mind, General?"

After some thought, Osmani admitted, "A little girl."

Burks had two kids of his own, both girls. If there was a blip of hope he could redeem himself in the eyes of McKaine and at the same time undermine Post—he shouldn't pass on it.

His driver threw the key in the ignition. Burks, from the backseat, shouted, "The White House. Hurry—it's urgent."

53

Irritated, McKaine continued to ignore Burks's calls, sending them to voice mail. The secretary of state left a message after each call. What he'd said, McKaine had no time for. He was sitting in a pub, with Jets and Vito and pints of beer.

With resolve in his words, McKaine nodded to Jets and said, "You've seen it, then?"

"Many times. A good friend of mine was working on it too."

"What did it look like?" McKaine corrected, "Or better yet, where is it?"

"The quality's really bad. You can hardly make out shapes and objects. A few seconds here and there. You can see the hostages being shoved, roughed up."

Vito chugged his beer and then joined in. "We've collected a little bit of background information on the video since then." He threw a glance at Jets to see whether it was okay to trust McKaine with that information.

Jets didn't acknowledge him.

"It'd help me a great deal if I knew the backstory." McKaine worked an angle.

"First, I want you to guarantee me that all charges will be dropped against Amelia. Her name comes off the FBI Most Wanted list."

McKaine descended in a mute stare away from Jets, on a group of college students throwing darts at a bull's-eye. It wasn't as simple as picking up the phone and ordering the FBI to drop the case. Jets must have been well aware of that. McKaine had to give them a reason and evidence. Setting that aside, the FBI answered to Justice. He bet the attorney general would have an avalanche of questions.

Abruptly, McKaine asked, "Immediately?"

"Immediately."

"That can't happen. She's good for it right now in the eyes of the FBI. If I had something solid to offer them, maybe that would significantly slow down their investigation. But as it stands—there's a federal warrant issued for her arrest."

Jets wasn't buying it. McKaine was downplaying his clout, and it rubbed Jets the wrong way. "I'm afraid I can't help you then." For the first time, Jets reached for his beer. He just held his hand on the handle, not drinking it.

"Okay. Let's say that I've got you two's full cooperation and Ms. Sinclair's—written statements, the whole nine yards, then possibly we can cut a deal with the FBI. That's a big maybe."

"I'm out," Vito said.

"I'm out as well."

"What's the issue?"

Vito and Jets exchanged concentrated looks, each coming from it at a different angle. In the gap of silence, Jets was delegated with the task to explain their position to McKaine.

"Vito's ex-CIA. Post fired him because he knows too much about the Band of Seven."

"Band of Seven?"

"Just listen," Vito said.

"Presently, I'm an active CIA agent. If the DOJ learns of my identity and reveals it in court proceedings, they'll burn me. It's what we call agents who no longer can hide in the shadows and be allowed to do their jobs."

The explanation was far more reasonable and not at all sinister as McKaine had suspected.

"If it helps you—I'm convinced that Ms. Sinclair is innocent. I've suspected that much all along. I'm after the really bad guys, who've dragged you, me, Amelia, the entire country in a shit creek."

McKaine's phone buzzed again. All three flicked eyes at it.

"Someone's desperate to get a hold of you," Vito pointed out.

"It could be anyone." McKaine picked up the smartphone off the table and dropped it in his pocket to prevent further interruptions.

"What's the White House going to do with the hostages?" Jets moved on from the suspicious calls.

"We've relied on a middleman, a Saudi, to be our eyes on the ground in Syria. Pretty much what we know is based on what he's given us." McKaine purposely omitted the connection between Osmani and Sinclair. He doubted the journalist knew her former lover was the point man for the administration.

"That's unusual—can we agree on that?" Jets said. "No Brits and French to help us in a bind?"

"Every country, besides Iran and Russia, picked up and left Syria when the Muslim Brotherhood gathered traction inside the county. Al-Azizi proved helpless in stopping them. Fearing for the safety of ours and their people, we mutually agreed to withdraw from Syria."

It was rare for a CIA agent to speak with a policy maker candidly. They represented the two opposites of a swaying pendulum. And that was the root of the problem. Hearing what McKaine was saying reinforced the image of an out-of-touch politician CIA agents imagined worked on Capitol Hill. In a military conflict, especially a volatile one like Syria, his country had to double its spy efforts. Cutting the information pipeline from flowing nulled the CIA's overall mission. In the meantime, McKaine was admitting the government preferred to rely on faulty assets headed toward costly mistakes.

"The problem with trusting a middleman is that you centralize too much power in two hands. They call the shots on when, how much, and with what means to divulge the intel." Jets scanned the faces around him, not looking particularly at just one. "Have you corroborated his intel?"

The look on McKaine's face didn't spell confidence to Jets. He shook head, disapprovingly.

"From the limited digging we've been able to do, Vito and I have a pretty good idea that Americans are responsible for the hostage crisis."

"Go on," McKaine encouraged.

"My friend I told you about, she worked on the video Amelia received and found a face that belonged to an American—Thomas Monroe.

He's an ex-Navy big shot in hostage negotiation and extraction." Jets carried on. "We've got two files containing hundreds of classified data linking Monroe and other powerful men." Jets refused to say out loud Post's name to McKaine. He wanted Post for himself. Kill him, himself. No jury, no court, no deals made. Polina lay dead in the gutter; Amelia could be killed at any time—Post was Jets's.

"Out of curiosity, have you shared all of this with Director Post?"

"No." Jets left it at that.

"And why not?"

Jets felt a flare of uncertainty growing in him. McKaine didn't have a hint of surprise at what Jets just told him. *Was it remotely possible that the lawmaker and the spook were playing on the same team?* Jets shrugged aside the feelings of vulnerability.

In a whisper, he said, "DCI Post was one of the names on the redacted document we discovered."

McKaine withdrew to himself, before he went on. "Tonight at midnight, the White House will green-light a team of SEALs to parachute into Jobar, where we believe the hostages are currently being held." He raised his hand to prevent both of them from interrupting. "From what I've learned in this meeting, I would like to ask you if you're ready to help your country."

"I thought you'd never ask." Vito was like a kid who got what he wanted from his Christmas list.

Jets, not so much. "Post still wants Amelia dead."

"You have my promise, I'll personally see to it that she and the child are looked after, safe, until you return." McKaine reached over the table with a hand extended.

Jets hesitated, regretting that he'd have to leave Amelia behind. But duty called; love would have to wait. Jets firmly took McKaine's hand, forging a pact.

54

The ride to the White House flew in a haze for Burks. He'd given up on McKaine, who was obviously dodging his attempts to get him on the phone. He checked the time on his watch, calculating the SEALs' TOD. It was cutting it close. Burks cussed under his breath. McKaine was usually the man who spoke tough with the president in ways that changed his mind. Without the chief of staff's backing, Burks was going it alone. He admitted it—he felt invigorated.

Just before his car pulled inside the iron gates of 1600 Pennsylvania Avenue, his phone lit up. McKaine's name showed on the screen. Evidently he had a change of heart.

"Bob, where are you?" Burks said in a rapid manner with matching intensity he sensed in his gut.

After a slight pause, McKaine said, "Walking up to my office."

"We have to speak with Delay. It's the hostages."

"Slow down. Where are you?"

"I'm coming up to the White House." Burks stared forward as his driver maneuvered in the underground garage of the president's main residence.

"Come by my office when you get in."

"You'll get the president?"

"He's tied up at the moment with the budget committee. I don't want to rock the boat there unless it's life-or-death. Is it life-or-death?"

No. At least not yet. But the less Burks said on the phone, the better. "See you in a few." Burks disconnected.

McKaine was sitting behind his desk, face buried in paperwork as though no hostage crisis was looming over the White House. The image struck Burks as odd, but he simply wanted to get the Osmani intel off his chest and hand it over to another, someone more knowledgeable.

"Hey, there you are." McKaine's face broke in a friendly smile, a rare sight since Burks's screw-up at Camp David. "You want coffee or water?"

"No, thank you."

McKaine pointed to the couch, then asked, "Mind if I do?" Not waiting for an answer, he dialed the girl working in the front office and asked for his afternoon coffee.

Burks gathered his wits about him, before approaching the topic of why he was coming to the White House. "Thanks for seeing me, Bob. I really appreciate it."

"Don't mention it. What's on your mind? On the phone, you said the hostages."

"I tried calling you." Burks wasn't sure why he said that. The chief of staff wasn't obligated to call him back.

"You did." McKaine broke off eye contact. His arms rested on his knees; his back was hunched over, relaxed. "I was stuck at the budget meeting with POTUS. Boring stuff. The president loves it."

"Of course. I didn't mean to be rude."

"Silly talk." McKaine waved his hand in the air. "Tell me what you got."

"Osmani called. I got the sense he wasn't supposed to."

"What he'd say?"

"He believes al-Azizi knows of our SEAL plan. When our boys enter Syria's air space, the Russians are gonna shoot them down. Calling it an act of war."

"Horse shit."

To Burks, McKaine's reaction was genuine for the first time since he walked in his office.

"That's what I said when I heard it."

"An act of war? Have them call it that—by morning time, we'd flatten what's left of them if they dare shoot that plane."

McKaine's eyes darted for the door. The knock on the other side disturbed his thoughts.

"Not now, goddamn it!" he shouted, stopping the knocking instantaneously.

"We bring that to the president, right?"

"You know how I asked if this was a life-or-death?"

Burks nodded, while McKaine reached his desk and swiped the phone in hand. "It's life-or-death."

• • • •

Delay didn't hide his dissatisfaction of being dragged away from crunching numbers, talking debt ceiling and tax breaks. His right-hand man had been nothing short of being vague with his message. Delay was in the Oval Office with McKaine and Burks, and for some ungodly reason, they were expecting Post to show up.

"ETA four minutes, sir." McKaine updated Delay on Post's arrival, as if he cared. He couldn't care less where Post was at any given time, as long as he didn't tatter the nation.

Delay winced at the news and continued his small talk with Burks. "And the kids? Going back to Aspen, I presume."

"They love Aspen. Can't get enough of the mountains."

"You planning on involving them with your missionary work?"

The question took the breath right out of Burks's lungs. "Not at the moment. They're too young."

Burks couldn't have been more relieved when Post finally arrived and interrupted them. His thoughts scrambled to block Luciano's little body, with no success. He was permanently engraved in Burks's membranes.

Delay clasped his hands together. "Come on then—I've got a budget to fix."

Without so much as an easing into it, McKaine shot out, "We got a word from the middleman, who believes al-Azizi and the Russians have been tipped off about our covert mission tonight."

POTUS hardened his posture upon hearing the setback. "Jesus Christ."

He said more, but Post wasn't paying attention. He visibly twitched to Osmani's backstabbing, a sign McKaine picked up on. Delay was shouting, and it looked as if he were shouting at Post.

Post winced and then blurted out, interrupting the president abruptly, "I can't offer any military maneuvers around the Russians' impending air strike. My agency has the exact location where the hostages are being held."

That brought a short order to the Oval Office.

McKaine zeroed on Post, probing the latest lie. "You do?"

You could hear a pin drop. Post drew in a breath. What he'd tasked his foot soldier to do for him, he had to deliver himself.

"A three-story house on Dohar Street in Jobar. Well-guarded by insurgents." He continued. "We can pay off al-Azizi; in return, he holds back the Russians. The SEAL team goes in and out tonight."

"The international community is watching, sir." Burks opened his mouth. "If it comes out that we've paid off a dictator, then it'll be hell to pay."

Post took Burks chiming in as a play against him. *Not good.* He slid in, with a last-ditch effort to resuscitate the SEAL takeoff. "This country—this administration—can't afford more beheading videos of Americans to be played out on the internet."

"For clarification—we've locked down the exact location of the hostages. Our new obstacle is the president, himself? Am I following this?" McKaine was on his feet, separated by the rest, back turned against them.

"You've got it right," Post fumed. He checked his phone. No missed calls or urgent message. Still, he said, "Sir," addressing Delay, "I was overseeing a clandestine operation when the White House urgent message came through. If there's nothing else?" He let the last part hang in the air.

Delay nodded in approval. He didn't know to begin with why Post was in the room. His presence had been less than satisfactory.

McKaine turned to face Post and walked him to the door like a gracious host. He had summoned the DCI to the White House, the same way he'd summoned Burks to Langley for a brief, putting them both on notice. "Thanks for coming." He leaned in closer to Post. In a whisper, he kept going. "Between us, I think there's room to persuade the president to go on with the original plan."

Post had a dull expression, tangled with confusion plastered on his face. A flash of hatred sparked in the wedges of his eyes upon hearing McKaine's load of crap. When he sobered up, Post rejected that illusion wholeheartedly.

"I'll be waiting for your call," was all Post could reply.

Delay's voice at the other end of the room cut short the two's stares. "Bob, we should call in the general."

Post grimaced. "Don't make the president wait."

McKaine stood at the threshold of the door, watching Post's linebacker back stomp out. This meeting had poked the bear, angered the beast, unleashed the monster. McKaine better brace himself for an equal offense.

"Bob, you comin'?" Delay was calling his name again. "I'm waiting for the general to come to the phone."

Post was soon a distant memory to the men in the most powerful room in the world. The secretary of defense commanded their attention, salvaging what was left of the SEAL plan.

"It might just work," he declared definitively on the phone.

Hunched over, the other three exchanged agreeable looks.

Delay went first. "Legal would sign off on that?"

After a brief lapse of silence, the general said, "You're the president, sir—it's within your powers."

"And Congress can be stalled?" McKaine didn't pretend he understood the complex mumbo-jumbo when it boiled down to invading the sovereignty of another country.

"The commander-in-chief has last say."

Burks's phone buzzed repeatedly in his pocket, interrupting him. He'd put it off long enough; he better deal with the caller. His eyes dilated, not with fear or fright, but with something far darker. His skin lost its color. It resembled the one of a dead man.

"I should go," Burks said, aware that he had stood.

Eyes were on him, but no more words left his throat.

"Is it family, Conrad?" Delay was asking.

Yes and no. Family. His. Ruined forever. A sick feeling kicked him in his gut; he couldn't swallow. "I'm sorry. For everything."

It sounded like a call for forgiveness; though, Delay didn't get that, and McKaine was unable to prevent the inevitable. They let the secretary of state go.

"What do you think that was about?" Delay asked, when the general disconnected.

"Burks?" McKaine winced in direction of the office door. "Who knows." His shoulders rose then quickly fell down.

"Isn't it wild what the military can do?"

"Sir, I've been waiting to speak with you in private," McKaine said. "There's another way."

"Okay, but I got to say, the general got me pumped up."

"CWG sent in their men with fake papers. They were on the cusp of securing the highest profile interview of—I don't know—the decade? Regardless, al-Azizi will be waiting for us to come in either through air or land under the crest of our military. He won't suspect if we smuggle the SEALs under the cover of foreign journalists."

The idea was out there. Delay tensed up, then replied. "Bob, if this could be done, the CIA would've suggested it."

Wrong. McKaine didn't say it. He seethed through his teeth. "The agency hasn't been effective. They missed the mark on it."

"Post. When can I fire him?"

"The SEALs could travel commercial; we'll plant a legit journalist in their group to solidify their cover."

"Who in their right mind would agree to that?"

"Amelia Sinclair."

A name Delay preferred not to hear, let alone trust her with a top-secret mission. His adviser was out of his mind. "She's a suspect. A terrorist. You don't actually suggest we hand her the blueprints to our mission?"

"I personally questioned her, and the FBI is clearing her name. It's been a mix-up," McKaine explained weakly.

A mix-up? Delay fixed his eyes on McKaine, certain he'd gone haywire. The president thrust himself to buy the spelled reasoning. He couldn't.

"Bring her in. I want to look her in the eye and see for myself. If she's who you say she is—then I'll give it more thought."

POTUS didn't commit, but to McKaine it was just as good. He crossed over to his office, dreading the next conversation.

55

Burks was aware his body was in motion. His feet were crossing the passage leading to his office; his right hand waved to a friendly face. His heart was the issue. It had stopped beating in his chest when he read the alert on his phone. *Game over.* He had no tool powerful to fight this.

He remembered he'd closed and locked the door behind him, while Hobbs updated him on the media requests coming in at a rapid speed. *No comment. He would never comment.*

His eyes shifted around the office, looking for that item. Hobbs began to knock on his door, persistently. Burks chose to ignore her. His phone vibrated lightly in his pocket, sending chills down his spine. He glanced at it, one more time for good measure. Maybe he'd misread it. *Nope.* The journalist had cobbled several compromising images of younger Burks, naked torso pressing against a half-undressed little boy. The email was a one-liner:

"Care to comment on this, Mr. Secretary?"

Burks dragged himself to his chair, and his body dropped on its own. He pulled out a bottom drawer of his desk, where he kept the good liquor. He didn't bother with a glass, tilted the bottle to his mouth and drank straight out of it. A desperate man's drink.

Hobbs's knocking morphed into pleading. "Mr. Burks—are you all right? Can I call someone for you?"

Should he call his wife? was the first logical thought that entered his deranged mind. *Absolutely not.* He was not man enough to tell her himself. He swung the bottle again, holding it upward as a generous amount spilled down his chin, dripping from his neck and soaking his shirt.

In a moment of desperation—or a moment of clarity—Burks reached for the bundle of keys in his pocket. He didn't touch his house key, his bank deposit key, but went directly for a small key that unlocked a square metal box he hid from the world in another desk drawer. He brought the box to the hard surface and stared at it as if it held the answers to all his problems. Another gulp from the bottle to boost his bravery. His eyes broke off from the box, traveling to the framed pictures of his family and stopped there.

He should call his wife; she didn't have to find out this way. Burks picked up the receiver, delicately pressing each number, prolonging his time. The line rang for a while, but eventually the answering machine, not his wife, picked up.

"You have reached the Burks family residence. We are currently not home. Please leave us a brief message along with your name and telephone number, and we'll call you as soon as we can. Beep."

He hung up.

It was his wife's voice. Hearing her choked him. Then, the first tear came rolling down. He brushed it off his face with the back of his thumb. *What good would it do him to cry?*

In a fit of rage, he swiped the mountain of paperwork on his desk to the ground. It made a dull thud; he was sure at least Hobbs heard it.

From his stationery, Burks pulled a blank sheet of paper and grabbed his fountain pen, a present from his family when Congress cleared his nomination for secretary of state. He put the pen to paper and wrote a farewell note to his wife and their daughters.

"My Dear Margo, Jennie, and Ottie, I love you very much and that love for you has kept me going through the years.

"Margo, our wedding day was by far the happiest in my life. I remember us dancing, even after all of our guests left. The DJ was gone, as was the music, and the light was turned off. But we kept dancing. You have danced with me now for the past thirty years. This letter can't express how grateful I am for that dance and for the life you blessed me with. But I was not worthy of your love and the gift you were in my life. Inside of me was a monster I tried to control, but I failed. My sins can't be excused, and I hope you never forgive me. I don't deserve any tears or grief.

"Jennie and Ottie, be good to each other. Be good and kind to your mother. She'll need your strength now more than ever. Don't allow the darkness of this world to consume you. Instead, when the time is right, go out and make a change for the better. I'm so proud to be your father and to have watched you grow. No doubt you're destined for greatness. I love you now and forever."

The bottom, he signed with "Love, Conrad." When he added the last period, he felt as if he added a period to his existence. He better hurry. Hobbs wobbled the doorknob, hitting the door panel with an open palm.

Inside the box was a .22 caliber revolver with a box of bullets. He took two from the box and loaded the chamber. The gun felt cold, heavy. It had a sense of finality to it. He stroked the photos with a finger, the closest he'd get to hugging them.

He lifted the gun and pressed it against his left temple. His thumb was on the trigger, but he didn't have the strength to pull it off. He relaxed his arm; the gun relaxed with it too. Burks was afraid of dying. He was afraid of dying in this office, under the heavy flag adoring the wall behind his desk.

Hobbs called to Burks. By the sound of it, she was in near hysterics. "Mr. Burks, please, Mr. McKaine's on line one."

Damn it. How did McKaine find out about this so fast? Burks ground his teeth. He tore a piece of paper, scribbled a few lines on it, then folded it and placed the note in his inner coat pocket.

Without allowing himself to cave in to any other distractions, Burks picked up the revolver and sank his teeth into the metal as his finger tapped the trigger. The .22 fired a single round in Burks's mouth. His body jerked, and his head flipped backward.

56

Amelia didn't reply to McKaine right away, forcing him to repeat his question.

"Amelia, do you understand what I'm asking of you?"

"You're asking for my cooperation in a cover op." She exhaled and added, "In one of the deadliest countries in the world." Her voice pitched, void of emotions.

"Will you?"

She refocused her view on McKaine, who sat at the edge of his chair, grabbing the rest in one hand, the other folded on his leg.

"Robert, that life's behind me." She stood up, with nowhere in particular to go. "I'm all my kid's got. It's best if you find a person better suited for this than me."

"There's a lot to be considered in a short time span. You're our only chance at getting this right." He thought for a brisk pause and continued. "Four people, you know them better than us, are fighting like hell to stay alive. They've got families. They've got lives ahead of them." He was tugging on her heartstrings. "Think of the SEALs who could be killed if al-Azizi goes through with his threat to shoot their plane down."

Amelia sighed, arms crossed in front of her and eyebrows hunched downward. "How much time do I have before deployment?"

"We're still working out a few logistics, but it's wheels up tonight, 2300 hours."

"And Jets? What's going to happen to Jets?"

"He's cooperating with us."

Amelia didn't fully understand what that meant. "Can I see him before I leave?"

McKaine stood and walked to the cart with refreshments to fetch himself a cup of coffee, stalling. Jets didn't have a clue that McKaine was asking Amelia to serve as a cover to the SEALs. The CIA spook would go apeshit on McKaine if he found out. He had to be delicate.

"I'll try to arrange it. Time might be a bit of an issue." He'd have to back down if Amelia pushed for it. To his relief, she looked aloof.

"You don't give me much of a choice here."

He walked back to her and placed his hands on the sides of her arms. "You'll do it, then?"

"I will."

His chest swelled with pride of his work as a delegator. He prepared to thank her on behalf of a grateful president, when commotion broke out in the corridor. Voices shouted at each other; doors were slammed. He inched to check on the situation.

A staffer beat him to it and walked in, a satellite phone in hand, pointed to McKaine. "I'm sorry, sir. You need to take this call. It's the head of the Secret Service."

McKaine put the phone to his ear and waited.

"Special Agent Toby Stew. I'm calling from the State Department," the agent said urgently.

"What happened?"

"The secretary of state is dead."

McKaine didn't reply, just stood there with the phone pressed to his ear, receiving the news, but allowing it to sink in would take awhile. A group of suits gained access to McKaine's office, immediately surrounding their protectee and the woman he was with. Additional men stepped in, taking cover by the windows.

"Sir, please step away from your desk. The White House is in DEFCON 3, under a complete lockdown."

McKaine pushed to remember the DEFCON chart—three was not good; it was yellow, which if his memory served him well, meant the Air Force prepared for attack in fifteen minutes, followed by the military rapid response shortly thereafter.

He called out, "Give me an update on POTUS."

An agent pressed his hand to the wire in his ear, being briefed. "Roger. POTUS secured in the Sit Room."

Amelia was past the point of panic. She pitched forward to her purse hanging on a chair. A move the agents didn't approve. She was staring at a barrel of a Glock, pointed at the center of her head. She raised her hands up, catching her breath.

"I was checking my phone," she managed to spit out.

"Stand down." A man gave an order to the rest.

A new agent showed up in McKaine's office and pulled the chief of staff to the side.

"We spoke on the phone, sir. Agent Stew. We're lifting the DEFCON. POTUS is on his way up for a briefing." McKaine heard Amelia speak up from behind and turned to face her. Two agents were helping her gather her things. She didn't have the clearance to stay in this part of the White House during the DEFCON assessment procedures.

"It's all right, Amelia. This is classified. These agents will drive you back home." He rubbed her arm to reassure her that her safety was a top priority for him.

With her out of his way, McKaine pressed on his heels, focused on Stew. "Tell me what you know."

Stew cleared the room with a head nod. "We found the secretary of state's dead body."

"What in God's name are you talking about? This must be a mistake. Burks was in a meeting with me and the president an hour ago or so."

"It appears that he shot himself."

"Are you sure? You don't suspect foul play?"

Stew shook his head. "We're currently investigating all possibilities. His assistant discovered him first, after she heard the shot. Less than fifty seconds, my agents were on scene, checking for vital signs. They proceeded to try to resuscitate Mr. Burks."

McKaine felt like the wind got knocked out of his chest. "He had no reason to kill himself," he said, not fully believing in that.

"We're still working on a motive. But right now, all avenues point to suicide." Stew paused for the transmission to be over in the wire. "The president's back in the office."

The news of Burks's suicide hit Delay hard. He was in a stage of grief, hating the fact that he was the president.

"You can wait a little before you call her," McKaine said softly.

"I want her to hear it from me." Delay let his head drop low, wincing at the task of telling a personal and dear friend that her husband bit a bullet.

McKaine locked their shared door, convinced this was just a bad dream, expecting to wake up drenched in cold sweat. Still running the facts of what he knew from Stew, his assistant asked whether he could have a minute with Burks's staffer. He motioned for the staffer to be let in. A young woman, with red eyes, approached him, tugging on a well-used napkin.

"Thank you for meeting with me." She spoke through tears.

"Come in, please."

She didn't move. Instead, she glanced behind her back, making sure no one else could hear them speak. "I found something." She tried to fight her tears, but they overpowered her.

"Did you find him first?" McKaine handed her a tissue.

"Yes. I'm Missy Hobbs, Mr. Burks's secretary. He came back from the White House looking...I don't know, like he was sick."

McKaine recalled Burks's final moments at the meeting. He fidgeted with his phone, looking pale. "Go on," he encouraged her.

"A reporter had called for Mr. Burks. He asked if the secretary had a comment on a set of photos he'd emailed him. Mr. Burks didn't mention anything about any photos, before or after he visited the White House."

He probably received the photos while in their meeting, McKaine concluded, consumed by sadness. "Do you remember the name of the reporter, by chance?"

"I've got it written down on my desk. I can go back and get it for you."

"That's not necessary."

"He worked for the WaPo, I believe."

"You said you found something?" McKaine changed topics.

"I'm probably breaking the law by doing this, Mr. McKaine. I don't want to go to jail." She spoke in whispers. "Mr. Burks was always nice to me. He helped me a lot. We've worked together for seven years. He was a great person."

"He was. No question about that. Why do you think you're breaking the law?"

"You see, sir—I was the first to see him. His head was stretched all the way back. The gun was on the ground by his chair, and then, there was the blood. So much of it, too. Splattered on the wall, a pool of blood on the floor." She recalled a scene that would be with her till the end of her own breathing days. "I reached over to check for a pulse. Nothing. I don't know what possessed me, but I checked his pockets. I guess I was hoping to find a suicide note, but I found this instead."

She unclutched her hand, where she'd kept safe a flimsy note. McKaine picked it up while she retrieved back her hand, thankful she didn't have to worry about it anymore.

Hobbs, sobbing a little less, reported to McKaine, "Lately, he wasn't himself. I took the note on a whim. Didn't know if I could trust the agents. Mr. Burks always liked you, so I knew I could trust you."

"Did you read it?"

Her face said no, and to McKaine, that was good as receiving an answer.

"You did the right thing. Conrad was lucky to have you. Take as much time as you need. When and if you're ready to come back, see me again."

The note held a clue and a warning. McKaine read it slowly, word by word.

"Robert, find it in your heart to take my advice—look no further than the bald eagle watching you from a compass."

57

The street in front of Ankara Esenboga Airport was packed with people. Monroe swept the field of the view from corner to corner, expecting Post's man to be waiting for him. He wasn't and probably wouldn't show up.

"Dude's late." One of Monroe's two muscles stated the obvious.

"Better call the boss, Tommy," the second one barked in a heavy Slavic accent.

Monroe lifted his head toward the sun, slightly grimacing at the humidity and Turkey's orange haze. The cool, dreary skies of Washington were thousands of miles away.

He brought his attention back to the streets of Turkey, a fractured country with a solid reputation of supporting terrorists. He was unfazed that their pick-up was nowhere to be found.

"We're gonna walk." Monroe bent down and picked up his carry-on.

He heard grunting from behind him as the two obeyed his order. They set north, up with the traffic, which looked as if it had a life of its own. No driver seemed concerned with following traffic laws. Cars swarmed in and out of lanes at speeds surely to impress a NASCAR racer.

Turkey had grown increasingly sympathetic to Syrian refugees who were invading the land by the thousands daily. The EU was paying the host government handsomely for its hospitality, but failed to hold them accountable of their money-laundering schemes with terror groups like Hamas.

Money was flooding the country to offset the skyrocketing cost associated with caring for a dispersed foreign population. Undoubtedly that money skipped the refugees' pockets and went straight into the bank accounts of those responsible for their plague. Even for Monroe, who was usually blind to the human suffering, it was hard to ignore the sheer devastation of misery littering the first neighborhood they reached, after leaving the industrial part of town behind them.

He'd been to Turkey less than three years ago. The place had transformed into a slum haven rivaling Jalalabad, Pakistan. Humans had built structures directly on piles of trash. They were defecating on the choked-up asphalt. Kids picked scraps of food from the garbage.

Ordinarily, Monroe would never travel unarmed. This mission required extra precautions. His guns were on board a boat docked on the other side of Ankara. The present situation spelled trouble, with potential high risk for Monroe and his men. The slum occupants began to leave their huts, gawking at the three foreigners. The news of their arrival would reach the lords in charge of this settlement. Monroe suspected they wouldn't want to hear his explanation. They'd shoot him out of spite or in a robbery attempt.

Monroe raised his hand. His guys were tightly packed to his back, each watching sections in the slums, anticipating the first shots to ring momentarily.

"Call the boss, Tommy," the Slav prompted.

More bodies stepped outside and started to descend toward Monroe. It would be a nightmare for Monroe to run and, frankly, impossible. He would be surrounded shortly, with no room left for maneuvers. Gun-wielding maniacs could be seen trotting behind their people, coming to defend and deal with the strangers.

Monroe reached inside his vest, fishing out a satellite phone. It rang. Post came to the line in no time. "You with my guy?"

"I'm surrounded by unfriendlies. Cincin. Make a call to the locals."

"The local suggested that route," Post said, underestimating the dire scenario Monroe faced.

"Make the call, now." Monroe clicked off the satellite. A ring of refugees formed around him.

He glanced behind him. His men had clenched fists in a fighting position, ready to strike if a refugee made another step. He'd been in worse-off positions in his career, but Monroe hoped to not have to make a spectacle right smack in the middle of Turkey's capital. It would complicate things for the mission down the road. He still had to cross over to Syria, and that would be a nightmare if the local police were searching for him.

A group of rounds reverberated in the sky above Monroe's head. By habit, he spaced his feet, prepared to fight. The human ring got a little bit tighter. Just before a fight broke out, car honking stopped the refugees from gaining momentum.

A white Fiat, navigating through the pile of bodies, dodging them, parked a foot away from Monroe. He could feel the heat from the engine pushing against him. Monroe made an educated guess that the Fiat, given it was the only car around, belonged to the slum patron.

A dark-skinned, burly man, with unruly eyebrows and a thick black beard, eased out of the car. Pointing to Monroe, he said, "Get in." His English was peppered with an Arabic dialect.

Keeping a close eye on the hostiles, Monroe edged forward. His men were a step behind. Sitting at the wheel, their unofficial driver and tour guide scuffed off after letting out a series of threatening honks for good measure, in case the crowd was not in a mood to listen.

"You fuckers would've been dead if I wasn't around," he said.

Monroe was in an agreeable mood and didn't object. "What's your name?"

"Emir. Remember the name."

No. Monroe was not planning to remember. He was contemplating shooting Emir when he dropped them off at their destination.

"Why you walk alone? Don't you know how dangerous Ankara could be?" Emir was dead set on conversing with his passengers.

"We got lost." Eyes on the rearview mirror, Monroe was watching another car.

"You Americans have fancy navigation gadgets, no? No bring with you?"

"Do me a favor and take the next right, over there." Monroe showed him the turn he wanted Emir to take.

"Bad traffic there. We stay on the highway, much faster."

Monroe didn't take pleasure in people who disobeyed him. Emir was dancing on his last ounce of good grace. Ready to snap, the Slav reached for the wheel from the backseat, gaining control of the vehicle.

"What you doing, pig? Stop." Emir's protests were left unanswered.

The Fiat skidded, and the back tire jumped a curb. Emir's hands were once again in control, correcting the car.

"A tail?"

Monroe nodded in agreement to his man asking. "It looks like it."

"Boss sent extra help?"

"Most definitely not. We've got company." Speaking to Emir, Monroe said, "Stay on course on this road. Every traffic law you could think of, follow it."

Emir's face froze in a confused stare at the strange request. He was in no position to argue. The white man on the seat next to him called the shots.

"Who do you think that could be?"

"Let me know when we lose 'em," Monroe said to the occupants out back, choosing to speak less with Emir in tow.

The traffic ahead thickened. They spent more time in one place then actually driving.

Monroe growled at Emir. "Roadblocks?"

"Who knows. It could be anything. Police checks, roadblocks. It'll get worse around your stop."

Monroe had anticipated and accounted for setbacks. Again, he was in a far better position than he'd been in millions of times. He couldn't buy back lost time, which he had little reserve left of in the tank. Monroe glanced at his watch—indicating that the last bus for Syria for the night would leave in less than two hours. If he missed it, he was looking at carjacking a car, an unnecessary complication Monroe preferred to avoid.

"We shook off our tail."

News Monroe welcomed. They could go back on the highway, where traffic was significantly faster moving. "Get us back on the main road."

Emir didn't respond verbally. He twisted the wheel. Their ride joined the long line of cars crossing the Ankara Bridge. Below them, the waters of the Black Sea rippled against the rocks, leaving foam markings on the smooth surface.

By the time Monroe arrived at his last stop, another precious hour had gone by. He stepped out of the car, with the sun sinking low in the horizon, and motioned to Emir to stay in.

This neighborhood didn't resemble the slums. The homes were older buildings; generations of Turks shared roofs. In a place like this, your neighbor's son was your son; his daughter was your daughter. No secret had a nook to hide.

"Why are we still in Ankara, Tommy?" the Slav said.

Eyes transfixed on the last frontier between the west and the east, Monroe replied with his signature cool-headedness. "We can't leave Turkey without a cup of Turkish coffee."

The Slav pretended he understood the comment, left his boss to his vices, and went back to the trunk of the car to retrieve the bags. Under the hiking bags, the Slav spotted a loaded AK. Emir had been holding out on them.

"You pay me now?" The Turk had made a tactical error in speaking, sealing his fate.

"Pay the good man." Monroe zipped an order to his muscles.

Two rounds flashed. The one in Emir's head splattered his brain; the other hit him in the neck. An overkill by every stretch of imagination.

• • • •

The café was a shack, outfitted with old-fashioned TVs. Antenna ears stuck out, not helping the spotty broadcast. A soccer match was getting the men rowdy and verbally abusive. Monroe's presence added to their anger. His only saving grace was that Mehmet, the owner, waved him in.

"You've come back!" Mehmet's lips pulled away from the hookah, then returned back to it.

"Got something for me?" Monroe said.

"Did you bring me a present?"

Monroe tossed a package to Mehmet, who, upon inspection, approved of the amount and led the way to his office.

"Why the fuck you want to go to Syria? Nothing but stray dogs and goons with guns." Mehmet handed Monroe his purchase, stealing a glance at the two extras.

"Work. Always work."

The passports and the photos matched Monroe and his men. The forgery was a perfect job, rivaling that of the CIA con artists.

"I presume transportation was arranged?" Monroe knew the answer. It didn't hurt to ask.

"A group's leaving at dusk. Your new identities are on the list." He stopped there. A big question mark hung over Mehmet's head.

"Spit it out."

"Not much left in Syria. The land's flattened. I got no help to get you out of there if it gets dicey."

Monroe received Mehmet's concerned look. He didn't get it, as if during conception, his empathy chip was wiped out or never put in.

"My associates and I would like coffee. Can you get us that?" His answer was mechanical, lacking a dose of human emotions.

58

The helo's nose dipped, shortening the altitude. The pilot in the control peeked out back to his passengers, who grabbed on to the net for extra support. The pilot leveled the chopper while the cargo felt the sharp change in course.

He should've called Amelia before departure. She should've heard it from him. She would have questions; he wouldn't have answers. Together, they'd figure it out with time. That was a white lie. He winced at the admission. His current mission could possibly, most likely, be his last. Jets knew it since he'd boarded the chopper. Again, he grabbed the satellite phone and again, put it back in his pocket. Nothing good would come if she heard his voice. McKaine had a point. Amelia might back down from going into witness protection if Jets got involved.

"Prepare for landing," the pilot said in Jets's headset.

He threw a look at Vito, who was stretched out on the seat across from him, hands folded behind his head, not a worry in this world.

"Sleeping Beauty, wake up," Jets barked in the mike.

Vito opened one eye. "Called your girl yet?"

There Vito went, hitting Jets in his sore spot. He hesitated. "McKaine thinks it's best—if I keep my distance."

Vito swung his boots off the bench and onto the ground, legs spread out, shoulders forward, preparing to drop pearls of wisdom on his partner. "And you gonna let another man dictate how, when, and what to say to your old lady? Pfff...you don't deserve her and the kid."

That comment stung. Jets wasn't letting McKaine dictate, but he didn't really put up a fight either. He was more concerned with Amelia's safety, preoccupied with his guilt of leaving her.

Before he replied, the chopper dove harder. The containers tipped to the right, then to the left, then slid forward. A couple of grenades got loose from their compartment and rolled on the floor.

Vito spotted them and jumped off his seat. "Dipshit!" he yelled to the pilot. "You want us dead?" He turned his head to Jets. "Can you believe this guy?"

Jets said to the pilot, "What's the deal?"

The former Air Force didn't say a word, watching his beeping control. The system wasn't responding.

Jets noticed the issue, though he didn't fully understand what was causing it. He poked his head inside the cockpit, his pilot wrangling the throttle. His general impression was that the pilot was losing control of the helo.

"The chopper is spewing oil. Lots of it. Fast." The pilot had taken off the headset, spoke directly to Jets.

"How far is the base?"

"Right below us, but we can't land." He was flipping knobs with no response. The helo jolted forcefully. The vibration unbalanced Jets, who grabbed onto the sides of the cockpit door for support. "It'll get worse."

He didn't need to be a pilot to know that their ride was going to crash. That's why the parachutes were on the helo. Their altitude presented a problem. Too close to the ground—the parachutes wouldn't open. Jets doubted the pilot could get the chopper to fly higher.

"Can we make it—if we jumped?" Jets said.

"If you do it now." There was brassness to the guy's voice.

Plans changed, especially for a CIA clandestine agent. Jets operated well when that was the case. He didn't hesitate when he went back to his seat and pulled out the chute bag.

"Put yours on," he said in the mike.

Vito wasn't moving.

Why? Jets yelled to stress the seriousness of the situation to his partner. "Do it! Now!"

At the side door, Jets yanked the latch, about to open it, when Vito made a confession.

"Bro, I've never done this." His hands clutched the chute.

"Boys, better go for it. I've lost power to my controls. We're in a free fall." The pilot gave them a final update.

Jets's arms stretched out, placing them on Vito's shoulders, who felt their strength. He secured the chute around Vito's arms. The side door was pulled all the way back, and the wind whipped their faces.

"Don't look down," Jets cautioned, like that was meant to reassure Vito.

In a fitful moment, Jets clamped a metal hook onto Vito's harness, linking them together. The wind absorbed their weight; gravity drew them down. The fall normalized when Jets released the chute in the air. The nylon seemed to be working properly. It expanded, slowing their speed.

The landing was far from smooth or by the book. Moments into their jump, the chopper exploded, disseminating in the air. A piece of shrapnel had nicked the nylon, ripping a baseball-sized hole in it. Jets tugged on the risers to clear tree branches, but the raisers had stopped performing their main function—guiding the nylon. A gust of wind aided him, thrusting them toward the water. Vito was yelling inaudibly to Jets since their mikes in the headsets were rendered useless.

Right before the Black Sea consumed them, the wind wound down to nothing more than a breeze. They slammed into a reef. If given the opportunity, Jets would have picked the waters. Vito landed first, taking a hard tumble. Jets, on top of him, heard a crack. He couldn't be sure whether it came from his partner or something else entirely different.

Jets rolled over instantaneously, tangled in the raisers. A part of the nylon had wrapped them like a burrito. Vito wasn't moving or making sounds. That worried Jets—a hunk of a man like Vito didn't just faint. The issue had to be more complicated. Jets couldn't rationally explain it. With a hand on Vito's shoulder, he squeezed without reaction from the other guy. Then he felt the ground vibrate under the tires of an approaching truck.

"Over there. Help them." A man was yelling orders.

The nylon began to move, quickly being pulled from them. A hand reached in. Jets took it and was pulled out.

"My man—he's still lying under it," Jets said, trying to catch his breath. He hadn't realized how much pressure the chute had put on them.

An extra set of hands got involved. The nylon was fully unwrapped; underneath it, Vito lay still. Jets could see it now. A film of blood had formed a puddle, Vito's hair caked in it. He leaped forward, but didn't get too close. A man clenched his grip around Jets's waist, grounding him in one place.

"Stay back, son. He could have a broken neck. We've got to stabilize it before we move him," a voice from behind him said.

A team of uniformed men worked on Vito. Their backs blocked off Jets's view. He caught a glimpse of a neck brace secured on Vito's neck. Then they turned him over, checking for pulse and other vital signs. Examining from the front, the reason for the blood was discovered expeditiously. It was from a wound on his left side of the skull, indented in that spot.

Jets had seen men in worse conditions, but it hit him hard when it was one of his men. The scene reinforced the feeling of working alone was best. No strings attached.

"The colonel wants to see you ASAP." Jets heard that same voice. He glanced back and saw a clean-shaved, blue-eyed soldier. By the uniform he wore, Jets knew he was addressing a first lieutenant.

"Where you taking him?" He meant Vito.

"Triage on our base. Please, this way." The lieutenant pointed to a Humvee.

The colonel was less than pleased with Jets and dropped the hospitality act as soon as the lieutenant left them alone. The name tag on the colonel's lapel read Bradocks. Jets imagined Bradocks came from a family line of servicemen. It was all he'd ever known.

"What the hell are you doing on my base?" Bradocks said from behind an oak desk. His eyes never left Jets's.

"Our chopper was dispatched to this location. Before landing, it experienced mechanical issues, forcing me and my crew to abort the flight."

"What were you transporting? The flight manifest was the worst forge job I've seen come out of your employer in decades."

"My employer?" Jets was losing his cool with the colonel. He wouldn't be dicked around. Monroe had probably crossed into Syria while Jets was jumping out of a burning chopper.

"You listen to me, son." Bradocks sucked in air. His finger pointed at Jets. "I won't be dragged in whatever cover mission you pricks are running on my turf. I've got orders."

So did Jets. He was following orders, McKaine's orders, who wouldn't be pleased to hear of Bradocks's uncooperative behavior. The colonel's saving grace was Vito. He was in a triage on Bradocks's base, with an undiagnosed trauma. Jets would play nice, for his sake.

From a group of photos arranged on a wall behind the colonel, Jets concluded he catered to the big players in Washington. Bradocks was snapped with President Delay at what looked like a black tie gala. He squinted on the faces captured without their knowledge in the still— McKaine drinking from a champagne glass, chitchatting with another, whose face was obscured by Delay.

Jets picked up the conversation. "I don't mean to step on anyone's toes. I'm on a mission authorized by my employer."

Bradocks reached for the phone, fingers blazing on the numbers.

Jets placed his hand over his. "Before you do that—I think you should speak with Robert McKaine."

A flinch of anger danced in Bradocks's eyes when Jets namedropped the chief of staff. "I'm not buying it. Move your hand, or I'll have you arrested."

Jets moved back. This guy was playing hard ball, forcing him to take drastic measures. While the colonel was explaining to the CIA switchboard who he was, Jets had reached McKaine.

"You want to speak with him?" Jets paused, listening to McKaine. "Yeah, that's what he said." Followed by more pausing.

Bradocks's finger tapped the mute button on his phone set, expecting an explanation. He didn't get one, and the operator was calling out to him to come back.

"I'll call back later. Thank you." He got off the phone, rethinking his treatment of Jets.

"The chief of staff would like a word." Jets tilted his head to one side and handed him the satellite phone. "I'm gonna step outside to grab a drink. I'm parched. You got this, right?"

There was no response from Bradocks, who sheepishly stared at the phone, concerned about the consequences of his faux pas.

In the corridor outside Bradocks's office, Jets followed the signs that led him to the hospital wing. He approached the nurse's desk, looking for an update on Vito.

"Excuse me, your rapid response team brought in my friend." He chuckled at the word friend, having spent most of his career as a lone wolf.

She glared at him from thick-framed glasses. "You caused a lot of ruckus, you know that, right?"

He would be causing a lot more of that, once he caught up to Monroe, who at this moment had manifested in an afterthought. "I'm looking to find out how he's doing."

"Just fine. The doctor's finishing up with him."

Did she say "just fine"? The comment threw him for a loop and the nurse could tell.

"He's not good with heights. When you guys fell down, he lost consciousness. He hit his head pretty good on the rocks, but nothing that will require hospitalization." She was reading from his chart. "In a few hours, he'll be good as new."

Jets let out a long breath. Then his mind switched gears. The purpose of this trip materialized in his mind. Two hours to stick around for Vito wouldn't do. If Monroe was still in Turkey, he could catch up to him. He hated the thought of leaving Vito behind, but Monroe was the biggest threat for the SEALs, who were hours away from descending into Syria.

"Here's your phone back." Bradocks's voice boomed from behind Jets.

"All squared away?" Jets didn't want to add more insult to the colonel's egg-shell hard ego.

"You've got my full cooperation."

The two turned to go back to his office, with Jets thanking the nurse.

"Mr. McKaine asked me to pass along a message. He said Baker has landed and is on foot."

Understanding what the message meant, Jets shot a look at the colonel. He might just be able to pull this off with a little extra help. "What type of civilian cars do you got on base?"

In less than fifteen, Jets was behind a gray Honda, racing out of the military base. When he distanced himself farther, the base no longer in his view, he dialed McKaine. The line rang about six times. When McKaine answered, he sounded groggy.

"I take it you know that Baker's in Turkey," McKaine said.

"Happen to know where he's headed to?"

"Thought you were the spy?!"

Jets didn't say a word back.

McKaine moved on. "As a matter of fact, I do—he's on foot. Last known whereabouts, north from the Esenboga Airport."

A glance at the Honda GPS showed that Jets was not too far from the airport. With marginal traffic, he could catch up to Monroe. "Got to give it to you, McKaine."

"Stick to the plan, agent. No freelancing in Turkey. That would cause a fiasco with huge potential to embarrass the president, and I won't have it." He clicked off after that.

As he suspected, the traffic to the airport was moving at a fairly reasonable speed. The problem started when he passed the airport, precisely, the arriving terminal. Lines of cars were stretched out for a good mile and a half. He scanned the side roads in his line of sight for walkers. There were a ton of people who'd opted to brave Ankara's unforgiving heat rather than be stuck in the hellish traffic.

It was stop-and-go for a while, but Jets didn't give up. His car was creeping on a group of pedestrians lugging suitcases—all but three of them. *Hell yes.* Monroe and two others crossed the overpass, completely unaware Jets had eyes on them.

He lost the trio as fast as he'd found them. The traffic was at a gridlock, not allowing him to exit. He considered leaving the Honda parked on the side of the highway, then chose against it. *What good would it do him to be without a vehicle in a city he barely knew?* In the midst of indecision, his attention went straight to the road sign on the overpass directing that way of traffic toward "Cincin." Monroe was headed there, but why? It was not in the direction toward the Syrian border. He must be making a final stop before he crossed. Jets's phone buzzed in the cup holder; he checked the caller ID, not recognizing the number showing.

He swiped the screen and picked up the call, not saying a word.

"Yo, bro—left me at the ER? No flowers, no chocolate—bad manners," Vito said, jokingly.

His face relaxed in genuine satisfaction, recognizing that voice. "I see that you're back with us. Good. I didn't want to mess around transporting a body bag back home."

"I had a strange convo with a very stuck-up colonel." Jets heard static on the line. Vito returned to the wire, his voice clearer. "He said you asked for a car then hightailed out of his base. And I repeat, 'his base.'"

"McKaine said Baker had landed. Gave me a general idea of where I could track him down." Jets cast a disappointed look at the merging lanes of traffic.

"Well, did you?"

"For a little bit. Lost him and his men. They're gone for good. We'll have to pick up their trail in Damascus, if you're up to it."

"If I'm up to it?" Vito said in an exaggerated tone. "How long before you get back?"

"Beats me. Are you near a computer?"

"Not right now. Though, I think I can figure something out. What do you need?"

Jets concentrated for a long pause, bothered by not knowing why Monroe was going to Cincin. "Can you search for Cincin online?"

Vito didn't return to the line right away. By the time he was ready to brief Jets, he was edging an exit that would get him off the highway.

"It's the slums. Pretty bad."

"How bad we talking?"

"The local cops won't even go there. They've left the lords to run the place."

"Monroe was headed in that direction. I might just follow them, then."

Vito sighed, irritated. "Don't be so fucking stupid. One man, one gun, against Monroe and whoever he's meeting there." He abruptly stopped talking and then returned to their conversation, speaking rapidly. "On Google maps, Cincin is a shortcut to the last neighborhood at the Syrian border. And since Monroe is on foot, it makes sense that he would go for the quickest route. He knows the city well enough."

It was a solid point; Jets couldn't deny that. Monroe was smart, a worthy adversary, who shouldn't be underestimated. Jets placed himself in Monroe's shoes, and he agreed silently with his enemy's course of action.

As he prepared to reply, a white Fiat ramped its way on the road he was on, causing another car to veer off to the side. From his peripheral view, Jets spotted Monroe's arm holding on to the roof through a rolled-down window. He floored the gas, darting behind them, while the rest of the cars pulled over, wanting to avoid a collision. Jets was well aware that he was blowing his cover by tracking the Fiat closely. Monroe had slipped through once; Jets hated to see him vanish again.

The Fiat zigzagged between cars, forcing Jets to do the same. He was sure Monroe had made him and was planning a defense strategy.

It was a miracle the Fiat cleared the sharp right turn, without tailgating in the storefronts along the road. It must have been a surprise for Monroe how backed up that exit was. Jets eased on the speed, letting cars get in front of him, while he came up with a maneuver. If he continued with the surveillance, that would place his Honda directly behind Monroe's. In a split moment, Jets allowed Monroe to get away from him.

He spun the car around, going in the direction of the military base. From the road, he dialed McKaine's private line, prepared to cash in his chips for a major favor. When the chief of staff accepted the call, he sounded none too happy.

"You've got to ask Bradocks to send a bird in the sky to watch Monroe. The traffic presented a problem with no workable solution."

"A drone? You're out of your mind. Can't authorize that without sounding off alarms." McKaine lost it.

"Either do that or I can't guarantee you that Vito and I can trace Monroe in Damascus before the SEALs' extraction op tonight."

McKaine was silent, hesitant, which stirred a gut feeling in Jets that he didn't know the full story.

"You there?" Jets prompted.

He heard McKaine sigh loudly, exhaustively. The conversation transformed into a blur after McKaine mentioned Amelia and Turkey in the same sentence. Jets heard himself yell back to McKaine, "You son-of-a..."

59

"Gabriel." Her voice took his breath away. He veered off the road and threw the car in park. "Are you still there?" The connection was static.

"Don't." His heart sank low into his chest. They were an ocean apart. "Don't do it. It's not worth it."

She exhaled, perhaps agreeing with him, never daring to say it. "Of course it is. To save a life—it's always worth it."

"Whatever he promised you, he's lying." If McKaine was in front of Jets, he swore he would tear the chief of staff's head right off his body. "Give me twelve hours to come back."

"Stop." Her voice hardened a little bit. "This will all be over in a day."

"In a day, you could be dead." He choked on his emotions.

"In a day, you could be dead. It makes no difference."

"Where are they going?"

"A hotel in Ankara. I don't know the name of it."

Muffled voices in the background interrupted their call. Amelia put her hand on the cell phone to prevent Jets from listening. McKaine was pointing to his watch, saying time to go. She returned to say her good-bye, prolonging it for a moment more.

"He tell you to hang up?" Jets asked, calculating whether he could swing a private jet back to the States. His contacts in this part of the world were strong, but he also had made a substantial amount of enemies who would gladly see him dead if the word got out he was back in town.

"It's fine. We're boarding in a few."

With the phone pressed to his ear, Jets finally asked, "Would you consider going on a date with me when this is over?"

Amelia, with a wide smile and her stomach tied in a knot, played it cool. "It took you long enough to ask."

"Can I take that as a yes?"

"You can take that as I'm going to tell you my answer in person."

• • • •

The phone was out of her hand. McKaine looked as if he were fed up with their loved-up exchanges. His hand on her elbow guided her to the tarmac. She swallowed her agitation with McKaine, attention locked on the runway. A luggage crew was supervising the loading of suitcases on the Boeing, her mind obsessed with the details of the mission. The stakes were high. A failure could lead to loss of human life. She wasn't prepared, nor did she think she'd ever be.

"They're calling your flight." McKaine glanced at the corridor, leading her out to the plane. "Stick to what we talked about. Everything will be fine."

Confusion written on her face, Amelia had to know. "The SEALs? Where are they?"

"They've boarded. It's better off if you don't sit together. Try to blend in the best you can. It's a plane full of civilians."

He sounded sterile to Amelia, projecting unlikable qualities. This flight could be her last; she might never see Ava again. She instantly frowned at the notion that McKaine had to be the one shaking her hand good-bye.

As if he'd read her mind, the chief of staff's face relaxed, nearly welcoming. "Nothing's going to happen to you. The SEALs will do their job. You stick to yours."

As the plane climbed in the sky, Amelia studied the faces in the cabin with her, figuring out who could fit her description of a SEAL and who could not. Right off the bat, she rejected the elderly and children, plus anyone who had a dog with them. That would be the two guys occupying the seats in front of her. First class and business passengers were blocked off from her field of view by bulky blue curtains, which still left her with a pretty good number of people seated in the general cabin.

"Nervous on planes?" the guy next to her said. He was a black man in his mid-thirties, she presumed, with wide shoulders and smooth skin. The ice cubes in his club soda sloshed at the bottom of his glass when he tipped it to his mouth.

"It depends." Amelia sat back in her seat, anxious she'd blown her cover.

"The weather app said calm skies on this trip. I wouldn't worry too much." He briefly broke eyes off the *SkyMall* magazine that sold pricey junk to drunk people spread out on his lap. There was a twinkle in his stare. Amelia picked up on it as a clue to take it down a notch and chill.

The thoughts in her mind didn't ease up. She closed her eyes anyways, blocking the nightmarish scenarios forming inside her. With a lot of convincing and self-talk, Amelia allowed herself to drift off to her happy place. At home. At dinner time, sitting around the table with Ava. Then, out of nowhere, it was pitch black in her head. She had fallen asleep.

The plane jerked from the turbulence. Amelia bounced awake, disoriented of what time it was or how long she'd been asleep.

"The plane's descending." The guy gave her an update.

"Thank God," Amelia said under her breath. If he heard her, he didn't say a word.

They spent close to forty minutes stuck on the runway. Supposedly a chopper had exploded in the air the day before, causing a backlog in traffic control—or at least, that was the gossip in the cabin. Amelia poked her head to the window, noticing the sun sliding away, dragging the sunrays with it.

She stepped in the line of people with their bags, the black guy behind her, one by one exiting the Boeing. She wouldn't see much of Ankara, a city she'd been to a handful of times before.

Her passport cleared customs without a hitch, and she didn't notice issues with the rest of the passengers on her flight. She walked toward the transportation terminal, somewhat surprised that she hadn't run into a SEAL or the entire team. From the escalator, she zoomed in on a driver holding a cardboard sign with "AJA" scribbled across. For a brief moment, she thought there was a legit media conference going on. McKaine had taken care of minor details to appear convincing that gave her a little bit of comfort.

"Ankara welcomes you!" The driver clasped his hands, searching for her suitcase.

"No. Just my travel bag. Not here for too long," Amelia said, looking through him. Still no SEALs.

"We wait for four more." The driver showed her four fingers.

Amelia nodded politely, but reserved. She didn't know whether he was a McKaine plant or an ordinary Turk with a job to do. The deception was driving her bonkers, but if it kept her alive, she'd roll with it.

The driver opened arms, gesturing to a person behind Amelia. She threw a look over her shoulder and then froze.

"And there were two." The same black guy was joining her. Confusion cascaded on her face. She couldn't hide it. "You?"

"The other three are coming too. Bathroom before the drive." He spoke to their driver, avoiding Amelia completely.

She had to give it to him—he was confident, polite. Not a twitch in his face said he was a US trained killing machine.

"Is this the American Journalism Association ride to the hotel?" A deep baritone announced the arrival of the last three.

The same guys whom she'd rejected on the grounds of their pets were SEALs too, plus another guy she hadn't spotted on the plane. *But where were their dogs?* She bit her lips to prevent words leaving her mouth. It was none of her business.

"This is all of us," the black man said to the driver, effectively asserting his status of their group leader.

The casual talk faded in a moment's notice when the driver took off. The SEALs' demeanor switched from a professional on a business trip to a combat soldier. She could see it now—their faces shared similar sharpness to them that was controlled, measured. Her body sank deeper into her seat, flabbergasted by her own insignificance.

"This way," their leader said.

Amelia guessed he felt he was her boss too. She saw no point in convincing him otherwise, considering they wouldn't be spending a significant period of time together.

At the reception desk, he stepped forward. Amelia cut him off instead.

"Welcome to Ramada. How was your flight?" A female receptionist wanted to know.

"It was long. We're from AJA for the conference," she said matter-of-factly.

The receptionist bent her head down, checking her computer and confirming the hotel guests. "Right, three suites on the six floor. Unfortunately, all of our ocean-view rooms were booked. I hope the main street view would be sufficient?"

"Perfectly fine."

In the elevator with their keycards in hand, Amelia had to say something, confront the elephant in the room. Without looking at them, in a hushed voice, she sneered. "Suites? Not obvious at all." Her comment, however, didn't get a rise out of them.

That hotel room would serve as her prison cell for the next sixteen hours, give or take. She tossed her bag on the floor, no essentials to unpack. The walls were dreadful, wallpaper adorned with gold leaves. She closed her eyes, transformed to her basement, lying still in Jets's arms. *Could their attraction survive the turbulence of this mission? Would she even have the chance to see him again?* Amelia wrapped her arms around her shoulders as if she were in his arms.

The assertive knocks outside her suite forced her back to reality.

"Who is it?" She didn't bother getting up.

"Suite 1609 in five minutes. Be there," the SEAL ordered.

She was the last to join the rest, who were dressed in desert colors camo. The arsenal of guns, bullets, and other equipment she didn't recognize grabbed her attention.

"Gee, you're prepared," Amelia said weakly. "Were these on the plane with us?" She was curious.

"Amelia, I'm T.J." The black guy had finally decided that it was time to share names. He extended a hand for shake; she accepted it.

"Why did you want me on your meeting?"

"We've got a minor issue."

Amelia's forehead frowned, not fully following.

"It's this map. Can you look at it and see if you can make sense of it?" T.J. showed her a large map of Damascus, spread out on a queen-sized bed.

She skimmed it over, understanding their predicament. "This map won't do you any good." She quietly studied their faces.

"Yeah? How so?" a guy inventorying the guns asked.

"It's old. Pre-insurgent days. Things have changed significantly." She used her finger to show them pockets of the city that were a no-go zone. "Rival terrorist cells have claimed neighborhoods as their territory. They've renamed several, of what I know."

"You know this how?" The guy by the guns wasn't warming up to her.

T.J. shut him down with a stern look and then spoke to Amelia. "I'm afraid our backup doesn't have an updated map. Washington is asking us to abort."

Amelia wrinkled her nose. Going back home without Bo was not an option. She snapped, "There's a workaround."

"Not according to Washington," T.J. challenged.

"In the past year, Syrian freedom bloggers have created shadow websites on the dark web with maps outlining the worst areas in Syria and showing who holds the cities and neighborhoods. These maps are constantly updated. Some of them show Damascus, too."

"You know how to access that intel?"

"I can try. Get me a laptop and net connection, and I'll get to work."

Her fingers clacked on the keys, too preoccupied to see that T.J. had slipped out of the suite.

• • • •

In the hallway, T.J. punched in a memorized number, then waited to be connected. When the other side answered, he explained, "It's me." He briefly paused. "Amelia's helping. The team's leaving on time. She'll be alone." More waiting for the other end to finish talking. "Another team will pick her up in the morning. You got it. Take care." T.J. ended the call after that. He dropped the cell on the ground and smashed it with his heavy boot.

In the suite, Amelia had recalled a digital version of a map, looking as if she were lecturing them. "This is what Damascus currently looks like. Nothing to do with your map, huh?" She was greedy. "The areas marked with black dots are the areas occupied by militia."

"By the look of it, the nearest wacko is two kilometers east of the house with the hostages." T.J. said.

"It appears that way, yes."

"It's not adding up. Why keep the hostages far from your backup? By looking the map, it's like they're hiding the hostages from their bros?"

Amelia saw the pattern of logic at play, before the SEALS. She said, "It's actually pretty clever. Our government could never establish if the four journalists were kidnapped by the Syrian government or the insurgents. So, whoever stashed them away wanted to keep a low profile." She drew in a breath and continued with the cartography lesson. "Most people have already left, which means you have to deal with a lot of abandoned buildings in the surrounding area."

"Not good. Snipers could have the advantage point on us," the last of the SEALs said.

"If anyone is taking aim at us, our backup will know," T.J. reassured them. "The government has a drone circling the neighborhood for hours." He put his hands on his hips and carried on. "Time to start packing, boys. We'll be leaving shortly."

He then turned to face Amelia. "May I have a word with you in your room?" It wasn't so much of a question—more like a statement. The meeting had concluded; she was to go back to her prison.

• • • •

Watching him surveying her room sent chills down her spine. She froze like a statue. Her lungs dried up with fear of what he could possibly want to talk to her about.

"I know Mr. McKaine has gone over your part in painstaking detail. Another team will be here to collect you at 0600. Don't leave the room. Don't answer your phone. Stick to these rules, and you'll be on the next flight homebound." His confidence should've reassured her but had a reverse effect on her.

He reached for the doorknob. "Ma'am—I am out of place for saying this. You're not alone. The CIA's watching the place, all right? If something or someone tries any funny business..." His voice trailed off.

Did he say the CIA? She was dead. Done. Her lips shivered, and her eyes grew wild with fear.

T.J. came closer to her, patting her shoulder. "You okay?"

"The CIA?" Words left her mouth.

"That's what I've been told."

"By whom?"

"Mr. McKaine." T.J. studied her battered expression. The time was pressing him to wrap this up. "Are you sure you're okay?"

"I'm fine, T.J. Jetlagged. Gonna turn in for the night."

He was out the door, when she called behind him, "Bring my friends home alive."

"That's a promise."

It was hard to breathe despite the AC churning cold air. She lay wide awake, fully dressed in the bed, her mind turning "the CIA's watching" on a loop, like a scratched record. The electronic clock on the side table displayed "12:30" in neo-green lights when she checked the time, with maniacal obsession.

At 12:31, the corded phone by the clock came to life, ringing in a high-pitched tone. She rose to her feet, feeling a stabbing pain in her chest. The phone stopped after a few more rings. Wrong number, she assumed. Then the ringing returned. Against better judgment and a promise to McKaine, she picked up the receiver.

Breathing with labor, Amelia said, "Hello?"

60

Delay looked on from the window of his private residence, emotionally drained from being on the phone, consoling Burks's hysterical wife. She sobbed. She asked questions, then repeated them. Delay had little to offer in terms of compassion. He took a slug from the glass of scotch, aware it was early afternoon. Outside, it started to snow, slowly at first, hitting the ground and melting, creating a slush.

"You plan on staying by the door for the rest of the day?" He took his eyes from the view, refocused them on McKaine's.

"Didn't want to disturb you. You looked like you were having a moment."

Delay combed his fingers through his graying hair. "I'm gonna have another one. You?"

"I don't think that's a good idea, sir. The interview is starting shortly."

"Watch it." His tone rose an octave, hardened.

"You're the president of the United States of America." McKaine walked forward. "Drinking won't help."

They were locked in a prolonged stare, before Delay caved. "You're right, of course." He dropped his head low, finger on his lips, a question burning on the tip of his tongue. "Is it real?"

"Is it what real, sir?" McKaine asked in confusion.

"The photo of Burks with the little boy circulating in the media?"

Burks was sadistic, torturous, and reckless. To POTUS, the deceased was a close friend. McKaine doubted those feelings of loyalty would evaporate, even if he told Delay that Burks was a traitor to his country on top of a child molester.

"Yeah, I'm afraid the photo's authentic. The FBI believes there are videos and more photos. It wasn't Burks's only victim."

"I think Conrad was a good man, a just man, and a fair man. His indiscretions, as awful as they are, are his indiscretions. And for a little bit, I think we need to remember the man he was striving to be."

That was a complete waste of their time. Media vans were swarming the White House, sharping their teeth to sink in this administration's flesh. The president's sentimental wallowing would only hurt him politically. McKaine understood that. Delay was blind to it.

He searched for ways to carry on to the touchy subject, finally abandoning diplomacy, adopting a straightforward approach.

"The communications department thinks Alison will ask if you knew about Burks's side gig during your decade-long friendship."

Delay's face twisted in agony. A vein on his forehead bulged, near explosion. "The nerve of these people. A man shot himself across the street from this building. He was the secretary of state. Where's human decency?"

Human decency? There was none. Burks was a pedophile, and the fact that both the CIA and the FBI failed to unearth his criminal past was preposterous. McKaine brushed off his president's meltdown, pushed the topic harder.

"The country, the media—they've got the right to know. We're on the cusp of solidifying the Delay administration as the greatest in the last decade. Playing as sympathizers to Burks, however, will bury us." He'd thrown the gauntlet at Delay's feet.

Delay sighed. Bags under his eyes had manifested, and to McKaine, he resembled a shell of a man.

"In this room, you and I are taking this moment to grieve the death of a friend." He shifted his body weight to the double doors. "For the cameras, we disavow the pervert."

That was the best McKaine would get from the president; he could live with it. They lapsed into silence, long and uncomfortable for both. McKaine went for the knob, then glanced behind him. Delay hadn't moved from the spot by the window. He searched for encouraging words to lift the president's spirit. None came to mind, so he left to check on the preparations for the interview.

Alison Devenport was tall and willowy, with the personality of a shark. No makeup artist could give her what God didn't intend for her— beauty. To McKaine, she looked especially shrew under the harsh fluorescent lights, expecting to nail the biggest interview of her lifetime.

The White House communication team had arranged for the interview to be set up at the Roosevelt Room; it had plenty of windows, providing ample natural light, and it wasn't as official as the Oval Office. They banked that the atmosphere would ease the viewers into thinking Burks's death was a tragic event, and leave it at that.

McKaine had to agree the Roosevelt Room was a suitable choice. If only now their main player pulled it through, they might have a shot at re-electing Delay, two years from today.

There was an undisguised commotion happening at the front doors. People clamped around it; a few worked their phone cameras, snapping stills of the president, who was making his way toward Alison Devenport. Amused, McKaine watched Delay's charm kick up to a boiling notch. His phone vibrated in his pants. McKaine winced at the number. It belonged to the military base in Turkey, which meant Jets had intel for him. He squeezed through people, preferring to take the call in the Oval Office.

"Jets?" He groaned.

After a brief stunned silence, the other party went ahead. "Not exactly." Vito sounded concerned.

McKaine bit right in, "Where's he?"

"Can't find him. He never returned to base."

"What about the satellite link?"

"It's off. No tracking device. Thought he might have checked in with you."

He hadn't. Last time they spoke, Jets had referred to him as a son-of-you-know-what. He was kicking himself for allowing Amelia to call him. It was a total mistake, one that would cost him dearly.

"Haven't spoken to him since you two left." He lied for two reasons. The conversation had to wrap up; the interview was about to begin, and Delay would have a cow if McKaine wasn't in there. Two, if Vito knew Jets was in touch with Amelia, he might go searching for him. It was bad enough that he'd misplaced one CIA agent; two would be a world-class circus.

"I think I should go in town, look for Jets."

"No, Vito. Hook up the equipment and work from the base. Stick to the plan." With chin retreated in, he signed off. "I'll deal with Jets."

As he'd suspected, Alison sat across Delay, cross-legged, leaning in to him and speaking in a whisper. "Are you ready, Mr. President? It'll be an emotional one."

Delay tilted his head and wet his lips. "Aren't they all, Alison? Fire away."

McKaine paid scant attention to the unfolding interview considering Delay handled it with poise and grace. *Where could Jets be? He didn't know which hotel Amelia was stashed in.* McKaine didn't like the odds of an unaccounted-for spook meddling right smack in the middle of a SEAL extract op on a foreign land.

Alison's high-pitched voice broke the rhythm of his thoughts. It seemed as though she was digging in her heels to crack open Delay's politician persona.

"Mr. President, in the last few weeks, this administration has had to deal with a number of complex situations."

Delay didn't bite. He shrugged off the question with the cliché, "This is the White House—all situations are complex."

Their icy laughs were a telling sign that one of them would walk away from this wounded.

"That might be so, Mr. President, but let's look at the facts. You're working on resolving a hostage crisis when your secretary of state kills himself. That would be tough for any president. Now, I think the nation wants to know, did Conrad Burks ever share information with anyone about that salacious trip?"

McKaine imagined he was wringing her neck; Delay's façade didn't crack.

"Alison, the death of Mr. Burks is still under investigation, so I can't reveal any details on that. The Burks family is grieving the death of their husband and father, so we should keep in mind that even if it turns out that the allegations are true, his family deserves some respect and privacy."

"How do you think Burks's indiscretions that led to his ultimate demise will affect this office?"

McKaine was gesturing to O'Connolly to get in there and kill the interview. He didn't care whether the communication director wacked Alison with a camera on her head; he wanted it shut down. POTUS wouldn't hang in there on the slippery slope. Alison was about to score a precious victory.

"You know, it's too early to say and especially since there is still an ongoing investigation. We have two more years in this term, and we're looking forward to leading the country for four more."

O'Connolly had cornered a producer. The two were in a heated exchange, which didn't help McKaine. Delay should have shut his mouth and not say another word. POTUS, however, pressed on.

"To end this interview, I must use Ronald Reagan's words: '*I know in my heart that man is good, that what is right will always eventually triumph, and there is purpose and worth to each and every life.*'"

McKaine moaned—*shit*. Delay had gone overboard, lost at sea and not even his chief of staff could have thrown him a lifejacket. From here on, the only hope to save this was a successful retrieval of the hostages.

61

"**A**me?" The voice that haunted her for years rang in her ears. She prepared to hang up. Clearly she was hallucinating from the stress. Then the voice called out to her louder.

"Ame. Please...this might be our last chance to speak."

"Khalib?" She said his name as though it were a ghost from the past.

"Yes. Ame. It's me."

"How do you know that I'm in Turkey?"

"I know that and more. I need to see you."

"I can't."

T.J. was explicit: nothing would happen to her if she stayed in the room, if she didn't answer the phone. *Was he warning her then?*

"Please. Trust me, *habibi*."

She'd heard those words before from that same person, and each time, she was left with a fractured heart. This was her chance to show him she'd learned a lesson. *Then what was stopping her from disconnecting the call?*

"Look out your window, right now."

Hesitant, Amelia inched to the curtains and drew the left panel back. The view revealed a hectic traffic scene with people jumping in front of the cars, unbothered by the sound of slamming brakes. Under a streetlight, a man in light-brown khaki pants and a dark shirt was talking on his cell. Casually, he lifted his head toward the hotel—her room, as if it wasn't planned.

"Give me twenty minutes. For old time's sake. After that I'll leave you alone. Forever." His words were pleading.

"You got five." For the first time since she arrived, she reached for her carry-on.

On the streets of the Old City, Osmani noticed when Amelia exited the hotel and motioned to a cab. She dashed in his direction, the black headscarf on her head serving as her decoy.

In the backseat, his fingers brushed against her cheek, pulling the burqa away slightly from her face. She winced at his touch. She preferred they maintained a reasonable physical distance.

"Where to?" Amelia said.

"Kahveci Efendi." He'd pulled his hand back. "It's a liberal place where no one would care that we're there."

She could hardly breathe under the heavy fabric covering her face. She was sweating, though she didn't know whether it was the humidity or the pressure of Osmani's presence.

Their ride pulled beside a curb. The driver didn't dare turn back and get a better look at the white woman out back.

"Keep the meter going." Osmani stuck a roll of cash in the window.

Gallantly, he escorted Amelia out and to the front door of the café. In the years they'd spent together, not once did he act that attentively. It weirded her out.

A hostess greeted them both, more Osmani than Amelia, with a certain degree of familiarity. Amelia felt the knots in her gut tighten up.

"Your usual table's ready." She directed them to the second floor.

Amelia found herself in a private room with candlelight pumping the mood to romantic. A few years ago, maybe this cheesy get-up would have worked on her for a night; then, in the morning, she'd sober up and remember who was asleep in her bed. Today, she interpreted Osmani's swagger as pathetic. Amelia planned to stick around to figure out how her former lover knew where to find her and then bolt.

She swiped the headscarf off her head, and her weight dropped in a chair. Osmani watched her, but she didn't like how that made her feel.

"You always hated wearing one of these." He glanced at the scarf draped on the table.

"I still do." She studied the surroundings, then went for it. "What's all of this?"

Osmani tensed, explained the basics. "The café is safe. The owner's a good friend of mine."

That didn't provoke a response from Amelia. She told him he had five. *Get on with it.*

"Tonight is extra special," he said.

She rolled her eyes. Clearly she'd made a mistake. Maybe it was a huge coincidence that they happened to be in the same city at the same time. Amelia rose to leave.

Osmani placed his hand on hers, begging her not to go. "Don't go. Indulge me for a moment so I can try to rectify the years of wrong I've done."

"How did you know that I was in Turkey?"

"I did some favors. Pulled some strings. The logistics are not why I asked you to join me." He averted his eyes. "There is a possibility that you could hate me more after tonight is over."

"I never hated you."

"Then tonight you will."

Their waitress returned to the room with coffee, lokum, and halva and placed the tray on the table between the candles. She smiled to them, but they were intensely staring at each other.

"Go on. Tell me. Why am I going to hate you?' The skin around her eyes was tight.

"Do you believe in redemption?"

"Is that what tonight is, Khalib, redemption?"

"In a way. And in a way, a confession."

From his coat pocket, he retrieved the photo of Ava in her Easter dress, the same one Post had given him. He let Amelia have it.

Seeing Ava's beaming smile, Amelia snapped, "Where did you get this?"

"An American gave it to me." Osmani's voice shook. He looked scared.

"What does that mean?"

Docile, Osmani told her the truth. "For years, I've been working for the CIA. Helping them with affairs in the Middle East. Keep the world safe." The last was a stroke to his damaged ego.

"You're failing then—on the safety part."

"My Amelia, always blunt. One of the many qualities I love about you."

It made her skin crawl when he called her "my Amelia." For the record, she was never his. She wasn't a prized possession, though she allowed him to treat her that way at times.

"Is Ava in danger?"

His avoidance to answer the question reset her panic button. She was too far from home to protect her. McKaine might be able to help, but she lacked details.

"Both of you are in danger. I'm sorry." He broke down.

"I've been accused of plotting a terrorist attack against my country. The FBI placed me on their Most Wanted list. I was kidnapped, and I'm pretty sure the CIA locked me up in a black site—do you see where I'm going with this?" Amelia was livid and her words flew. "Did you know what they'd do to me?"

He nodded.

Amelia was choking on emotions; her tears were too angry to roll down her face. Her lower lip trembled. At least he was right that she would hate him.

"I tried to warn your government. You've got to believe me, Amelia. I've been speaking with the president's chief of staff. I told him what I knew."

Did he say McKaine? Robert McKaine knew she had nothing to do with anything. *He knew who'd been behind this, and he played her. He was probably playing Jets too.* Her thoughts were no longer cascading in a fluid motion; they crashed into each other, hijacking her senses of reason and logic.

They heard the screams on the first floor at the same time. Osmani leaped to his feet, and Amelia did the same. He ran for the staircase; she stayed behind. He couldn't be sure, the cement pillars were in his view, but a man and a woman were reciting a passage from the Quran. In a flash, he caught a glimpse of a suicide vest strapped on the male.

"Get close to the wall." He ran back to Amelia. His body blocked hers from what followed.

In a fraction of a second, Kahveci Efendi turned into another terrorist site. The blast threw her against the wall. Her skull slammed into the plaster, and her body instantly went numb.

Amelia opened her eyes. She couldn't breathe. Debris from the explosion lay on top of her as she tried to move, causing her pain. The ringing in her ears made her disoriented as she gasped for air.

"Khalib?" she whispered before losing consciousness.

Somewhere in the distance, she thought she heard a man talking to her. His arms pulled at her body, making the pain more unbearable. She moaned and tried to open her eyes again, but she found it hard to focus. Hands stroked her face, and their touch felt familiar. The agony of her injury pushed her to shut down. The identity of her savior would be a mystery.

"Help is on the way. Hold on. Don't leave me." She heard a voice and recognized it. It belonged to Jets. She smiled vaguely, fighting to stay awake—for him, for Ava, for them.

"Jets? Stay with me. I'm scared," Amelia wheezed as she closed her eyes and started to drift away.

Was he talking to her? She couldn't tell. The high-pitched ringing in her head blocked any audible sounds.

Then it stopped. "I love you," Amelia whispered as blackness smothered her.

62

Right now, tracking Amelia in Ankara looked like the easy part. He'd picked up on two CIA in an unmarked car, plus a street watcher, the signal man, scouting a two-block radius. Four agents, plucked to resemble the native population, served as signal men. Most likely loaners from the Turkish Secret Services, working for Post. Two men and two women, they switched their positions randomly, which Jets reluctantly admitted complicated his job by a lot.

Slipping past them wouldn't be child's play. He didn't have a disguise bag with him and he didn't have a distraction team. He was flying solo.

He'd been sitting at the same damn market store, keeping a close eye on the street front, figuring out a hole in the CIA's surveillance. They were tight, organized, and if he had to bet his life on it, the trunk of their car was jam-packed with weapons. The store clerk had begun to chime out, singling out Jets, pestering him into buying. He planned to stick around for another five, and then step out on the pavement where Post's huntsmen had marching orders to kill.

If he killed the signal men, one by one, then he would have to worry about the agents in the car. In theory, that would be the best maneuver. But since the news of Amelia's arrival caught him unprepared, he had to rely on the Glock holstered under his jacket. All in all, he was somehow to neutralize four people with fewer than his seventeen rounds, while not arousing suspicion.

Jets gazed at the clerk, who was eyeing him back.

"That's it?" The clerk glanced down at the pocketknife he tossed in a plastic bag.

"Keep the change." Jets swiped his purchase from the guy's hand and dashed for the door.

Signal man number one was just turning into an alley that, from canvassing the block radius on his own, Jets knew was a dark passage with parked cars along the curb, almost no foot traffic. He eased onto the street, being careful to avoid the other three. In the alley, Jets dropped his weight on his left knee behind a car and swept his field of view, locating the target. Predictably, number one was taking a cigarette break at a huge oak tree, his back turned against the main road, where Jets was preparing to attack. That was the problem with hiring non-CIA to do CIA work. A mistake for Post was going to turn into gain for him.

Normally, he would drop the target with a round. Tonight's circumstances, however, pushed him to improvise. The blade of the pocketknife popped when he released the latch, switching its position to face upward in his hand. Jets gained ground, staying low with the shadows as number one was sucking on the cigarette filter, unfazed by the strain of the night shift.

Focused entirely on his target's back and paying no attention to the ground in front of him, Jets's boots cracked fallen tree branches that made distinct noises, costing him. The non-CIA dropped the bud and swiveled around, interested in the sounds. The night was thick, and the lack of streetlights were Jets's only salvation at this moment. The target got off balance when he came face-to-face with Jets. His first instincts were to warn the others; Jets predicted that. In a flash, he dragged the blade over the number one's neck, hitting the carotid. Blood gushed from the cut in a fountain; the body began to feel the loss instantaneously. Jets hadn't realized the severity of the assault, until the target slouched on the dirt path by the oak tree, the head practically severed from the rest. He didn't plan on it being as gruesome, but he didn't have time to feel sentimental about it either. In a brush area the locals were using as a leaf dump site, Jets discarded the body and buried it, the best that he could, under a pile of dead leaves.

A woman's voice crackled in the target's still active earpiece. "What's taking you so long?" A short pause, then she added, "Coming to check."

Jets had to make it quick. She would alert the others that their man was missing, causing the passage to flood with more of them. He'd be overpowered. Jets dashed for the fire escape on a building. In the darkness, it looked empty—or at least, he prayed that it was. He barely made it to the last step and crossed to the roof, before he heard the sound of incoming footsteps.

He was at a better advantage shooting point, though number two was guarded by the same oak tree's hundred-years-old claw-like branches where seconds ago, he'd killed a man. She had to step sideways to get in his frame of fire. His visibility was less than stellar with no streetlights; the sound of her feet was the sole indicator of her location.

"Mo," she said.

Though, Jets didn't have to hear her in the earpiece he'd stolen from her partner. She was right below him.

"Mo, you there?"

Her feet shifted to the side. She was exactly where he wanted her to be. The first round he sent out hit her torso; she moaned. A miscalculation on his part he wouldn't repeat again. Number two fired three quick ones in response to his one in no particular direction, considering the darkness was a key factor for them both. His second round pierced her heart; she choked, the same choking he'd heard hundreds of times when one of his bullets lodged in his enemies' heart chambers.

Number three and four rushed in the alley together, double-teaming Jets. *So much for keeping this job quiet.* Their shootout was going to raise hell, drawing local reinforcements.

It didn't take long before they shot at him first. He doubted they could see him; he simply assumed they were making an educated guess. He'd be doing the same if he were in their shoes.

Jets rolled himself over to the other end of the roof, checking on the CIA plant in front of Amelia's hotel. They were still there; he took that as a good sign. The CIA didn't suspect him, so they'd allowed the hire guns to handle the situation on their own.

More bullets echoed in the night. A few managed to hit the concrete close to him. He was going to end them and get off this roof.

"The top of the building," one of them said in the earpiece. "Take the outside stairs."

With a warning of their coordinated attack, Jets stationed himself behind a plywood structure, fashioned as a getaway between the roof and whatever was underneath it. His back felt the flimsy wall, calculating that it wouldn't slow down a bullet, but had no time to recalibrate his offense.

One had gained access to the roof; Jets allowed it. He had rounds in the magazine but more men to go through before it was over. The gunman, banking on the element of surprise, shot a round, a warning he was coming for Jets.

"You won't get out of this alive. Unless you come out with your hands over your head." Jets heard the voice clear, as though it were right behind the same wall Jets used as a shield.

He slid from left to right where the moon was brighter, partly improving his visibility. From that angle, Jets saw the shape of the guy, before he made out Jets. His finger squeezed the trigger. A well-placed bullet bit the enemy in the lungs. It was an excellent shot. He collapsed and never moved again.

Onto number four, who was hiding somewhere in the brush area of the passage, waiting for Jets to come down. And he would have. Then the earpiece woke up with voices—the CIA saying Amelia was on the move, getting in a taxi with an unidentified male.

He sprinted in the opposite direction on the roof, with a bird's-eye view of the main street. By the time he got there, the CIA officers were chasing Amelia. No way Jets could shoot his way out with number four.

The jump to the next building was steep. His back absorbed the fall mostly. Sharp pain radiated up his left arm—he'd pinned it down under his legs during the landing. Paying little attention to his injuries, Jets sprinted toward the edge of that building and leaped down. His feet planted on the ground with a distinct thud. Several onlookers stopped to watch him as he gained momentum, darting in the direct line of traffic.

Jets could see the CIA's unmarked car, but was about to lose them if he didn't jack a set of wheels on his own. The Glock was in full display.

He gripped the handle with his right hand that extended in a hectic second, smashing it against a face. Out of desperation, Jets was forced to act in a manner that violated his own code of ethics. He didn't have the time to bribe a car driver; he didn't have the time to explain to the guy with a bleeding upper lip why a total stranger was stealing his car. He couldn't see the CIA car on the horizon any longer.

With nothing else left but an instinct, Jets stomped on the gas. A woman screamed at him from the backseat. She threw in a weak punch, but the sight of his loaded weapon shut her up, or at least brought her to low weeping.

"Please, my baby," she cried out.

Did she say a baby? Jets threw in the rearview mirror a *you've-got-to-be-shitting-me* look, spotting the car seat with a strapped infant in it. He winced when the mother's tortured eyes begged silently.

"I'm not going to hurt you." Jets gripped the wheel, avoiding a head-on collision with the car in front. "At the lights, get your kid and get out." That's when he noticed the nasty open gash on his hand. The flesh was raw and exposed.

He kept his word and stopped the car, long enough for the woman to leave, cradling the baby in her arms. Free from his passengers, he resumed his pursuit, though the CIA car was not ahead.

Fuck. Jets slammed his injured hand on the dashboard. They could have taken a side street or parked the car, following Amelia on foot. He didn't have a clue how many men were hired by Post to finish off Amelia. The earpiece transmitted, *Kahveci Efendi* and nothing else; in a broken-down mood, Jets suspected because it was out of range.

Kahveci Efendi happened to occupy one of the busiest streets in the Old City. Flashy cars were paraded by the offsprings of Ankara's absurdly rich.

Whoever the unidentified male was with Amelia factored in that the CIA wouldn't shoot up this venue out of fear that it would spark a diplomatic war. He'd lost track of the unmarked car, so Jets ditched his ride. The wire in his ear was junk too, he guessed. Before he had the chance to make any significant movement toward the café, gunfire erupted. The shots fired were rapid, missing him by inches. He dropped to the ground, aware of the close call situation he found himself in. His every attempt to separate from the corner he was boxed in was met with rounds. A last transmission came over the wire, and it mentioned something about suicide bombers on scene. He discarded that information, then returned to it, not putting it past Post to be capable of detonating this place to get revenge. *Where were the bombers headed to?* Extra bullets flew by him as he eyed a possible location—Kahveci Efendi looked like the only explanation.

Jets pushed forward while a bullet hissed past him. This time he returned the fire. Between the cars across the street from him, relying on his peripheral vision, Jets spotted a running body with an assault rifle.

Amelia was in grave danger; no point in arguing that. A gas station was the last structure before the café. Jets couldn't let the runner past that point. In full sprint, Jets made it to the gas station first, kneeled by a steel light post, and calculated the trajectory of his bullets. Their rounds carried more impact than his handgun, judging by the bullet holes left behind. The Glock wasn't a match for theirs, plus he had only four rounds in the magazine. He aimed at the gas barrels and let every bullet out he had in them, creating a pattern. The sparks discharged from his gun flared but not with the effect he'd suspected.

The explosion was massive. The blast swung his body in the air then dropped him on the ground like a bag of rocks. By instinct, Jets checked the result of his work. He didn't get it—the gas tanks were intact, with the minor difference that they were spilling oil freely. At least the CIA jerks had pulled back.

Then it registered with him. Women were yelling in gut-wrenching hollers, gathering around where Kahveci Efendi once stood. He barely made it up. His injured hand was limp; his feet dragged. *Amelia was buried under ashed concrete. He couldn't save her.*

63

Damascus looked haunting at dawn. This part of the city was especially desolate. Buildings stood empty, abandoned, with dust and broken glass covering the stone streets. The heat could drain a human of his will to live; Monroe was unfazed. He adjusted his scope and focused on blood spatter caked on a decaying structure two hundred yards from him. He lay flat on the ground, shielded from what was left of a stone conclave, with a direct view of where the hostages were held.

He cleared the rest of the buildings with his scope, not expecting to discover a sniper. The SEALs were due to descend in a couple of hours; until then, Monroe expected a relatively quiet night.

The screams of a young child diverted his attention from his target. They were coming, not too far from him. He directed the scope in the direction of the noises. A girl, no older than twelve or thirteen, was being pushed around by men, old enough to be her father or uncles. They didn't appear related. She cried out for help as they slapped her across the face. The louder the kid yelled, the more they seemed to be aroused.

One bullet; that's what it would take to end the uproar. If he fired, though, he risked giving up his location. Then he'd have to kill all five men; otherwise, they'd come back with reinforcements.

His body tensed. He moved his finger off the trigger, but watched the despicable acts they did to this child, one after the other. When they finished, the men got up and left her on the street to die from the injuries her body had sustained. She was curled in a ball, and for the longest time, Monroe couldn't tell whether she was dead or alive.

The haze of the sun settling low on the horizon brought sweet relief from the heat. A gust of wind danced by Monroe's hideout, and he felt the coolness. The girl was still prone on the broken asphalt, with the exception that a woman had come to her aid. She tried to stand the kid up, who couldn't manage the task. She let her lie back down, ran off to where Monroe couldn't see—the buildings were in his way—then returned with a second woman. He'd lost interest in their sad existence; in fact, he'd been too involved by his own accord.

"Delta 1." Monroe's earpiece crackled. "I'm seeing movements in the house on the east corner. Do you copy?"

Monroe reacquired the target with the scope, seeing nothing out of the ordinary. He pressed on his throat mike. "Copy Delta 3. Nothing on my end. Delta 2—what's your status?"

Delta 2 didn't come to the line. Monroe remained calm. He repeated his command. "Delta 2, do you copy?" Nothing again. Monroe sighed, like any other professionally trained assassin of his caliber would do when he had to work with mercenaries. "Hey dipshit, you alive?"

"Delta 2 copy," the Slav's voice boomed. "No movements on my end. Sorry about that, boys. Had to take a leak."

As if Delta 1 and Delta 3 asked to hear the reason for leaving his post unattended. He was better off keeping his mouth shut. Monroe was already planning to kill the Slav first after they ambushed the SEALs.

"Don't do that," Monroe barked.

At 2300 hours, the SEALs were supposed to make their grand entrance, or according to Monroe's wristwatch, three minutes and forty-one seconds from now. He re-adjusted his body one last time. He wouldn't have that chance again when automatic rifle fire erupted.

"Get in position. Going dark in three."

The humming of the propellers announced the arrival of the SEALs. Monroe and his men switched off their radio communications, an extra precaution to prevent tipping off America's most elite rescue squad.

Monroe estimated by the gust of wind created by the low-flying chopper that the pilot was hovering directly over the hostage stash house.

Two SEALs were reeled down with a rope, their shadows the only indications of impending attack. Once they hit the roof, they split fast. They reminded Monroe of roaches.

Post's right-hand man held his rifle trained on the house, expecting Delta 2 to unleash automatic assault fire first. Delta 3 was in charge of the RPG that would destroy the chopper. Monroe had tasked himself with gunning down every soul who walked out of that house. He guesstimated the mission should take no more than thirty; he'd preferred if they were in and out in twenty.

As suspected, the two SEALs gained access to the house by breaking the windows on the second floor. Unsurprisingly to Monroe, they shot up insurgents in the home, not giving them the opportunity to lay their weapons down and surrender. Precisely what he would have done. Six flashes meant six shots fired on the second floor. By now, the two SEALs had overpowered whoever was left to guard the hostages.

Delta 2 wasn't shooting. It became crystal-clear to Monroe that the jerk with the automatic weapon had run into a jam. Delta 3 wasn't shooting either.

Monroe slowed down his thinking, and each detail, minor or not, fell into focus. The number of SEALs who actually got out from the chopper troubled him the most. *Two was too low. Where was their backup? They needed two more; best if they came with four more.* Monroe hugged his rifle closer to his body, eyes steady on the front, when he should have looked behind.

When he heard the hiss of a bullet, it was just too late to do anything about it. It lodged in his spine, severing vertebrates. It left him paralyzed on the spot. With immediate medical intervention, he could have survived the hit. But his attacker wasn't here to disarm Monroe; his attacker was here to neutralize him for good.

In this profession, there was always the chance that the current mission could be your last. Monroe dropped on the ground, the floor smelling faintly of dead meat. He'd picked a meat packing plant as a hideout. The irony was not lost on him, even in his dying minutes.

Involuntarily, his hand reached for his back. A finger plugged the bullet hole. The second round splattered his brains on the stones. He didn't even have the chance to blink, it happened that quick.

Thomas Monroe died with eyes wide open, staring into the yellow Syrian moon, under a foreign sky.

• • • •

T.J. kneeled and checked Monroe for a pulse, but found none. He searched the body, rolling it over, taking his weapons, wire, radio, and phone before removing his clothes, too, and putting them in a bag. He stripped everything that might associate him with the American government, in case someone ever discovered him. When the SEAL finished with the body, he covered it with dirty burlap.

"It's done. Monroe's dead. He was hiding just like you said he would," T.J. said on a satellite phone. He shut the phone and crossed the street to the house, where the rest of his team had secured the hostages.

64

The long-distance call for McKaine lasted seconds. He was off it when Delay barged in his office with that face that said, "let's kill some terrorists." A face McKaine could get used to.

"Sit Room's waiting." Delay draped his suit jacket over his arm and gestured toward the door.

"Phase one's concluded, then?"

Delay didn't acknowledge the questions, asked a question of his own. "Champagne or whiskey?"

"I'm sorry, sir?"

"To celebrate our victory, victories perhaps, tonight."

McKaine stopped himself short from telling the president he was celebrating prematurely. It was true that the SEALs had invaded Syrian's air space without al-Azizi and the Russians shooting it down, but the mission was still a long shot.

Knowing that, McKaine took the news in the Sit Room better than Delay, who lashed out collectively at every member of the Joint Chiefs of Staff.

"Are you telling me that you don't know where they are? You don't have the slightest clue? The SEALs and their bulletproof chopper just happened to drop out?" Delay's eyes trailed to the flat-screen showing a GPS map marked with the last known location for the SEALs.

The chairman was visibly upset with POTUS and mostly with his out-of-line tone. Nonetheless, he shoved those feelings aside and leveled with the president and anyone else in the Sit Room who didn't have combat training.

"Eight minutes ago, the SEALs entered Syria. We lost audio communication with the team for reasons we can't confirm right away." The chairman, too, glanced at the flat-screen. "The Sit Room tracked the chopper movements via the GPS, but again, due to unknown reasons—we're working on resolving that connection, which also went down."

"Do you have a reason to believe they've been ambushed?"

"No, sir." The secretary of defense, who was part politician and part military, joined in. "Our boys have the ability to shut off audio communication if they think it will be best for the mission."

"How come?" Delay pushed back.

"If they believe there's imminent danger, they would go dark, which would prevent the enemy of tampering with their communication transmitters."

It sounded worse than it was, but Delay was falling in a tunnel vision. A faulty commander-in-chief would significantly hamper the military op. McKaine slipped into the conversation with a solid reason.

"This won't be by the books. Let's sit back for a while and see where this goes. The explanation could be simple. If we insist on pulling them back, we might do more harm to them than we can foresee," he was saying to Delay, when they overheard the chairman.

"Is the CIA on the phone, now?"

"Post? Are you speaking with Post? What is he saying?" Delay stopped listening to McKaine.

The chief of staff suspected Post might already know that Monroe was out of the picture for good. He couldn't be sure of it, but either way, Post's involvement in the op could further complicate the situation in the Sit Room.

"DCI explained that a Black Hawk, a backup for the SEALs, is four minutes out." The chairman glared at the secretary of defense, deciding how to advise. "Sir," his voice was stern, "I wasn't a fan of this mission from the get-go and under this circumstance."

"Cool your jets off," the secretary of defense said, reading a just transmitted cable. He tossed it on the table. It made a dull sound, catching the rest's attention. "We've got a confirmation. The team has reached their checkpoint."

The tension in the Sit Room came down to a simmer. Just like McKaine had said, the reason for the SEALs going dark could be simple. McKaine personally was feeling more confident in moving ahead with the rescue mission, since T.J. had sacked Post's top dog, Monroe. For the first time in a while, he thought of Jets. Despite losing the CIA spook's tracks, McKaine had significantly lowered Post's chances of scoring against this administration and this president.

Delay leaned forward, interested in their odds. "What's next?"

"The house is located outside the insurgents' territory, but the team will still face a threat of being captured. If our intel is correct, the house is guarded at any given time by four to six men. The hostages are being held in separate rooms, scattered throughout the house," the chairman explained.

"We're now in phase two of the extraction," the secretary of defense said.

With a minimal gap, Delay said, "How many phases are we looking at?"

"If all goes by the plan, only three, four if we count debriefing," the SecDef pointed out.

At this point, the Sit Room attendees broke in small conversations among one another until they had new intel on the SEALs.

Delay turned to McKaine, probing, "So, champagne or whiskey? Last chance or you're out."

There was a certain lightness to him McKaine hadn't seen in weeks. He indulged POTUS. "Two old farts like us drink whiskey."

"I preferred to be called a gentleman." Delay winked.

A phone ringing in the background shifted the room's attention to unrelated news as to why they were meeting in one of the most secured rooms in the White House. A staffer read from a note, with scribbled information.

"There's been an explosion in Ankara. No survivors. The Turkish government believes it was the act of suicide bombers."

McKaine immediately suspected Post in meddling. *Why would he hit Ankara?* He checked his phone—no news from Vito, no sign of Jets. *Had the CIA's DCI figured out a way to sabotage the rescue op?* McKaine shuddered at the possibility.

"How is that going to affect our plans, Mr. Chairman?" McKaine was the first to ask.

"If at any point our SEALs get ambushed and we need extra help, the Turks will be too busy with their own mess on the ground. Or, in other words, Mr. President, we're now officially on our own."

"Is it too late to bring them back?" Delay tossed his question out in the open.

It had a chilling effect in the room. The staff expected their president to be decisive, rarely exploring the option of backing down. In their eyes, it was a call of defeat; McKaine interpreted it as fear.

"The Black Hawk has plenty of gunpower to defend the SEALs if they get stuck in the mud." McKaine was addressing Delay, his words shutting down the doubts of the few extra skeptics. "The SecDef can confirm that, even without direct help from the Turkish forces, we've got other means, which could be explored when that time comes."

The SecDef nodded his head, definitively.

McKaine's bold decisiveness had paid off, since Delay had regained his presidential composure as the commander-in-chief. In the meantime, McKaine's phone sounded in his pocket, alerting him to a text.

"Amelia was hurt in the bombing. Barely breathing. Send help. Jets."

65

The chopper lowered two of them to the roof, a headlight spotting their descent down. When their boots touched the metal sheeting, the SEALs went to work. T.J. slid the rope securing his harness to gravel, outback the building, and released the hilt. His backup man did the same.

"Go on." T.J. motioned with his rifle to the side door. His partner sprinted forward; T.J. placed his hand on the SEAL's back and held it there. There were moving in unison.

The side door wasn't a match for the C4. It popped out of its hinges on explosion, allowing them to proceed forward. The noise it created could have been written off by the locals as gunfire. The SEALs expected no interference this early on in the extraction.

"I'll take the front," T.J. said in his mike.

If there was an objection on the other end of T.J.'s obvious deviation from protocol, he didn't hear it. His partner slipped inside, rifle trained on the still walls.

Up on the second floor, the rest of the SEALs had smashed the top windows and were handing death sentences on the insurgents without the right of a judge and a jury—just the way they preferred it.

"Where are the hostages?" a SEAL whispered to the sole surviving ISIS sympathizer.

He chose to ignore the question, which was about to be the worst decision in his life. The SEAL pointed his assault weapon to the center of his prisoner's head, then asked the question in Arabic, slowly. He'd understood him now, the SEAL guessed, considering the dude pointed to downstairs.

"How many of you?"

The unfriendly showed two fingers.

The two SEALs had neutralized three upstairs and were facing two downstairs. Judging by the weapons discovered on the bodies upstairs, one AK-47 and two M-16, downstairs shouldn't be a complication.

While the ISIS soldier was questioned by a fellow SEAL, the other one went into the two bedrooms on the upper floor to triple check for survivors. Nothing caught his eye as out of the ordinary and alerting him to danger. The SEAL turned to walk back to his buddy. His headlight spotted a makeshift crate with hand grenades. He kneeled to it and pressed the mike on his throat.

"Alpha—you copy?"

"Copy, Lima—what is it?" T.J. said.

"We've got a crate with grenades. Second floor, west bedroom, unrestrained."

"Secure the premises from the insurgents first, then we worry about the grenades."

The SEAL got his marching orders, stood up, rifle hanging off his shoulder, and rejoined his partner.

"Ready to do this?" he asked the other American.

"I'm missing a warm meal and my wife's smoking-hot body—hell yeah—I'm ready to get out of this hellhole."

With night vision goggles on, they embarked down the stairs, the ISIS soldier between them with the barrel of the rifle pressed against his back. One wrong move, he was a dead man walking.

An outline of a man darted in the hallway. They saw him and unleashed their gunpower jointly. A barrage of bullets impacted the walls and windows, total annihilation. The fire ceased, but the ISIS soldier had crumbled on the stairs, whimpering, his hands covering his head protectively.

"Get up, dirt bag." A SEAL raised him on his feet and gripped the insurgent's neck. "How about you and I go outside, on the street. I'm gonna shake your hand and make sure everyone hears how much you've helped us kill the rest of these retards."

The foreigner shook his head. "No. No. They kill me."

"Wait, what? You speak English, asshole?" The SEAL dropped his hand to his side. Momentarily, the shock wore off. "Where are the hostages?" The Barrett M82 reloaded.

"I show."

"Lima—what did he say?" asked the SEAL on the first floor, holed up behind the only wall to be spared from the bullets.

"He's going to help us find them."

"I'll be damned."

The SEALs, with the insurgent in tow, cleared the last few steps and found themselves on the first floor. He pointed to a darkened corridor, same direction they saw an insurgent run off into. *It had to be a trap— what else could it be?*

"Alpha—what's your location?"

"Coming in."

T.J. pressed on the front doorknob and stepped in, checking his left flank first, then his right. Through his infrared goggles, he paused on an image of three figures. A fourth approached, hanging around the back of the house, close to their entry point.

"You ladies wanna explain why you're just chitchatting?" His bravado voice was easily recognized by the three SEALs.

"The hostages might be in the basement. Before that, we need to clear the hallway. According to our new friend, there are only two more of his friends left. The bodies upstairs had AK-47 and M-16." Lima fired off a sitrep.

"Roger that," T.J. said. "Deploy a smoke bomb. Even with the windows shot up, the ventilation is at a minimum."

The SEALs donned their breathing masks and rolled the smoke bomb on the floor. It made a funny fizzle, before it fogged the space. The insurgent choked on the smoke, and the smell suffocated him as he tried to draw in a breath. The SEALs stayed put, waiting for the bomb to have a similar effect on the still alive unfriendlies. At the sound of the first blunt bang, they made a move.

Team one had reached the bottom of the basement first, with no issues. However, they had a zero illusion that their upper hand couldn't be switched.

"Alpha, hostages located." The Lima team transmitted back to T.J. "One's badly hurt."

"Can he walk?"

"Negative. He's barely breathing." The brief was shut down for a moment. Lima team said, "The other three are also in rough shape. They're moving on their own, though." The transmission died.

"Roger that, Lima. Get them up. Time to go home."

It took the Black Hawk six minutes to reach the house, but it couldn't land. That meant the hostages were lifted on board with a winch. The sickest one of them presented a number of challenges. For one, he was a dead weight, heavy and limp. Two, the SEALs couldn't tell whether he would live long enough before they arrived to their base. He couldn't sit in a harness on his own. T.J. and his men would have to improvise. That was far from ideal, given their location.

The pilot came in with bad news. "Insurgents headed our way, two minutes out."

T.J. was stuck on the damn roof with nearly a dead man he couldn't leave behind, because the president of the United States expected four men to be rescued. "Lima, did you find anything we can use?"

"The harness is about all we've got."

T.J. squatted beside the motionless body and stuffed the feet in the harness, then pulled it all the way up. He stopped at the waist where he secured the device, best he could. He would feel better if they were using a carabiner to secure the hostage to his body, but rope was all he had.

As the SEALs began to reel them in, shots rang out.

"Go. Go. Go!" T.J. yelled back to his team.

The Black Hawk veered off the building to avoid the bullets. T.J. was still suspended in the air. He felt the rope jerk and drop slightly; he thought they surpassed the rope's weight limit. He was wrong. The chopper banked to the right. A machine gun burst into fire, sending copious amounts of bullets toward their unwelcomed company. The action was taking place directly behind him, but T.J. focused his strength on getting that last American onto the plane. Then he would join in on shooting the little bastards on the road. As they got to the Hawk's door, T.J. had to immobilize the hostage's head since the neck looked to be in a fragile state. He was worried that the lift was going to finish off the old guy in his arms.

Catching his breath on the steel floor of their ride, T.J. winced. "Get us home."

During the flight, T.J. examined the hurt American. He pulled a wallet-sized photo from his side pocket and stared at it for some time.

The man moaned at first, but for the most part, he showed minimal signs of life on transport. He attempted to open his eyes when he asked, "Why did Americans kidnap us?"

T.J. bent down closer. "Sir?"

"American military stormed our hotel room in Damascus when we arrived."

"Can you look at a photo for me?" T.J. roused him. He held the photo real close to his face, then asked, "Do you recognize this man?"

He nodded in affirmation, then succumbed back to his injuries, never regaining any meaningful consciousness after that.

In thirty minutes, the chopper lowered its altitude and began to prepare for landing. A collective sigh of relief was felt among the SEALs. The pilot, though, reset their course.

"You gotta hang on a little longer, boys."

T.J. barked in the mike hanging from his headset, "What's the word?"

"Two suicide bombers took a café in Ankara. We've been rerouted."

"Where to?"

"Incirlik Base. Headquarters signed off on the plan," the pilot said.

"What's our new ETA?" T.J. threw a nervous look at the hostage, who was looking blue around the mouth.

"Twelve minutes."

"Make that ten. We'll need a medic team on the runway. My guy's blue."

The lights lining the airstrip were visible from the chopper even from the sky. As they got closer to touching down, T.J. saw the shape of a truck parked and waiting. His team and the three hostages got off. T.J. waved in the medical team, showing them the lifeless body.

"We found them in the basement area. That one's in the worst shape. He woke up for a moment, then not a peep."

A man in a white coat quickly scanned and assessed the injured. There was no question this hostage survivor was on the verge of death.

"Bring in the stretcher. Can you help us move him onto it?"

They slid the stretcher off the chopper. The medic placed his hands on his patient's torso, applying light pressure.

"Broken ribs. He's bleeding internally. Better get him to surgery STAT." Looking at T.J., the medic asked for some basic information. "Which one's this one? Did he tell you his name?"

"No. We just got them out. At the end, we fought off an ambush."

"We'll figure it out. Great work over there, by the way. The commander suggested that the president's personally going to call and congratulate you."

T.J. watched the stretcher being wheeled away. With some reservation in his gut, he asked, "Is he going to make it, you think, Doc?"

"Hard to say. Unlikely."

Alone on the tarmac, T.J. felt a level of guilt for wishing Bo Breeks wouldn't make it. He had recognized Thomas Monroe off the photo T.J. showed him. Down the road, Breeks could be a witness. Questions would be raised about what had happened to Monroe—worse if his body was ever discovered. Holding on to that, he dialed the White House.

66

The Sit Room had reestablished video and telecommunication with teams Alpha and Lima. They watched as the Black Hawk was reeling in one by one the SEALs and the hostages. It was a painfully slow process. A SEAL was still on the roof, waving his hand, gesturing down to a person lying stiffly at his feet.

"What's the holdup?" Delay asked, concern detectable in his voice.

The SecDef had left his seat at the table and resumed control of the phones, personally answering the incoming calls.

"Apparently the man on the ground, one of the hostages, is in rough shape." He returned to the phone, then said again with new intel, "The team on Black One is searching for ways to lift him up."

A bank of phones lit up instantaneously, as if predicting the exact time shots would be fired toward the SEALs. McKaine stood up; so did Delay, who rolled up the sleeves of his shirt. The flashes of gun exchange rattled his cage.

"What's that?" Speaking to his SecDef, Delay scoffed. "Mac, talk to us, God damn it."

"The intel's suggesting that a truck with ISIS foot soldiers was tipped off. They know our boys are cornered on that roof and comin', guns blazing."

"Jesus—Mac." McKaine ran fingers through his hair and held it there. "Do they have a plan B?"

"We can send another aircraft, but by the time they reach Black One, I'm afraid it'll be too late."

"Then tell them to get on that helicopter now," Delay ordered.

By now, the team on Black One was sliding a harness down; the SEAL hovered over the body, but the Sit Room couldn't tell what he was exactly doing. The audio was broadcasting every other word, which only added to the building anticipation that the chopper and its cargo were doomed.

Delay audibly reacted when he saw the Hawk veer sharply, as the SEALs and the hostage were hanging in the air. Things came in perspective when a SEAL seized control of a machine gun and spared no bullets to defend the team.

"Come on. Come on. You're the SEALs," Delay said under his breath. His words summarized how every person in the room was feeling.

Despite the fancy American satellites orbiting the Earth and the advances of modern technology, again the Sit Room lost video feed with the SEALs. In the tense seconds that followed, the general impression was ISIS had scored a victory, shooting down their chopper.

"What happened? Can we get them back online?" McKaine was the first to speak.

"We're trying to reconnect. Even our back-ups are down. That's unusual," SecDef Mac said.

"Can we at least confirm if they shot down the bird?" Delay pointed to the obvious.

The SecDef resumed working the phones. For a stretch of time, he didn't come back with an update. If ISIS captured the SEALs and the hostages, Delay rationalized, then he wouldn't just send in the Marines: he would send in the Marines, Navy, and Air Force, unleashing the mighty fury of the most powerful country in the world.

The incoming audio line beeped, and the SecDef patched it through directly. A voice crackled in the speakers.

"Black One, all on board. I repeat. All on board. Moving to phase three."

The room stood still, then erupted in cheers in a chain reaction. The suits and the uniforms hugged it out with congratulations on a job well done, as if they were in the trenches, piloting the chopper. It had been Delay's first major dark op of his presidency, and it was a homerun. For a short time, the media would love him again. He would be their beacon of hope again. The golden boy, the path to a brighter future. His chief of staff extended his hand for a shake. Delay swatted it away, instead embracing him.

"You did it, Bob. All you."

McKaine hadn't expected Delay's reaction. *Would he say that if he knew McKaine had ordered the murder of a traitor? Would he say that if he knew that the CIA's DCI was next in line to receive the same type of justice?*

"Where are they going next?" McKaine broke away from Delay to speak with the SecDef.

"Incirlik Air Base."

"I want to personally speak with the team right when they land," Delay said.

Catching a private moment in his office, McKaine dialed a number that went straight to voice mail. He re-dialed—same message. In the Oval Office, POTUS wasn't running into any problems getting foreign dignitaries on the line to announce that he wouldn't be invading Syria, at least not today.

The front desk girl slipped her head in to tell McKaine he had a call on line four. The caller was persistent that he had to speak directly with the chief of staff and wouldn't give her his name.

"It's fine. I'll deal with it." McKaine picked up his desk phone. The blinking line turned to a solid color.

"Sir." T.J.'s voice echoed in the receiver.

"Got the photo. Did you encounter any problems?"

"Not really. He didn't see it coming—the bullet, I mean—but we have another problem."

"What?"

"Bo Breeks asked me, and I quote 'Why did Americans kidnap us?' end of quote."

"Are you saying...?"

"Yes. He recognized Monroe, too."

"Where is Bo Breeks now?"

"He's in surgery. The doc isn't sure if he'll make it or not."

"Do nothing. Make sure that no one goes into his room until I get there. Do you understand?"

"Roger that. See you when you get here."

He couldn't kill an innocent man. He could, but he wouldn't do it. That was the difference between him and Post. A life was better saved than taken. Though, it was undeniable, if in the event Breeks woke up from surgery and decided to tell his side of the story, it would leave McKaine vulnerable. He just had to wait it out. Breeks was a sickly man, with a shaky memory.

Delay was receptive to the idea of McKaine leaving for Turkey. He could get things sorted out on the ground; then, when the hostages arrived at Dover, the president would visit with them—accompanied, of course, by cameras to capture it on film.

"Let's see, we're looking at tonight's and tomorrow's news cycle, for sure," Delay said.

"The communication department will be in charge in the meantime. O'Connolly will capitalize on this with max exposure."

"You really have to go?"

"It's for the best. A visible face from this administration would show the nation that people matter."

"You're right. I know that." A fleeting thought entered Delay's mind, flashing across his face. "I was reading the CIA sitrep on the bomb explosion in Anraka. Guess two Americans were among the dead. Post had left for Turkey hours ago, didn't even bother to ask for permission." His eyes hardened, and he shot a look to McKaine. "I should fire him."

Post was running, and if McKaine didn't get to Turkey soon, then he risked the murderous lunatic going deep. McKaine wouldn't ever find him again.

"That's a solid reason for his termination, Mr. President."

67

Kahveci Efendi's two-story building was burned to a crisp; its only remains were the exposed steel beams. The firefighters had battled the fire for an hour, before first responders could gain access and the search for survivors could begin. It smelled like seared flesh as first responders entered the café.

On the second floor, Jets flinched at the sight of his mangled arm. He tried to move it, but it laid there, stiff and unresponsive. Next to him, Amelia was buried under debris; he couldn't see her body, just her head, and he was alarmed because he didn't remember the last time she moved. He dragged himself even closer to her and bent down, his ear to her mouth to check her breathing. It was shallow and irregular.

"Ame?" He stroked her hair to arouse her. "Ame, wake up. Please."

No response and no reaction to his touch. He sat up and cradled his injured arm in his lap. The fallen plaster from the blast had blocked them in the private room. The entry was demolished, concealing their location. He turned his head toward the slow waft coming from the gaping holes of where the windows were before the bomb went off. There was light outside, bright, fluorescent. It reminded him of the lights used during football games. If he was correct, then it meant the Turkish military had their bearings together, looking for survivors.

"Help. We're here," he called out, but his voice was drowned out by a helicopter hovering over.

There was a good chance that Amelia was already dead. He didn't want to leave her alone, but to get help, he had to. Jets's lips touched her forehead. It felt cool and clammy.

"Hang on, Ame. I'm getting us out of here."

Jets pulled himself up on the bricks surrounding them and slipped through a small opening. There was still plenty of smoke, which obscured his view. He was relying on his memory of the café's layout to guide him through. His back brushed against what he thought was a wall, and he stepped down on the few existing stairs.

"Help!" Jets was yelling, sounding hoarse from the smoke inhalation. He coughed right after, his lungs dried from the gas and dust.

Outside, people were screaming and sirens were blaring. *Then what was holding up the first responders?* He was about to find out. Suddenly, the temperature dropped significantly. He extended his working arm out to feel out his surroundings, swatting just air.

"Up here. We need help." He waved his hands, not knowing whether he could be seen by others. Maybe he should get closer.

A set of hands grabbed him by the shoulders. He moaned at the pain from his injuries. They pulled him back in and pinned him to the ground. Without asking, the same hands donned a breathing mask over his mouth. He was hit by a wave of flowing oxygen in his nostrils. His eyes slowly discerned the shapes of men in rescue suits lifting crumbled walls to look for people underneath it.

From the corner of his eyes, Jets saw Amelia being lifted from the pile. They laid her flat on the ground and began to perform CPR. The fire-fighters were speaking Turkish, a language Jets knew a handful of words of. His mask came down. His words dragged, fighting fatigue. He wanted to know her status. "Is she alive?"

His English must have surprised them but didn't prevent them from continuing with their job. From where Jets was sitting, Amelia looked pal-er than when he left her, with deep-purple circles under her eyes. Seeing her like that just about killed him.

"One more survivor," a responder called out in English, for which Jets would be eternally grateful for the rest of his life.

They brought a man out from the same room where he had found Amelia. Jets hadn't seen him, nor did he know to look for this man. After the blast, his only objective was to get to her. Then, when he discovered her, the dire shape she was in scared him.

Amelia and the man she was found with were carried out on rescue boards. Jets walked with the aid of a rescuer. Outside, the bomb site was cut off by yellow tape. A crowd of people had materialized, many more of them since the blast happened. Ambulances were ready to whisk them away, but Amelia's unstable condition delayed them. Paramedics lost her heartbeat and were pumping her chest to get her back. *What would he do if she died?* Jets wasn't used to having deep emotions; he'd always operated on auto control when it came to matters of the heart.

"Is she okay?" He knew his question was stupid. He couldn't blame the medics when they ignored him. He was a grieving victim, forced by fate to watch his loved one die.

"Got something." A medic showed a shaking line, jumping erratically on the monitor of the cardiac machine. "Now or never, guys. Best we'll get."

Amelia was loaded in an ambulance, secured with red restraints, and the back doors of the vehicles were about to be slammed in Jets's face. He latched on to them and refused to let go.

"I'm going with you." He meant it.

"Buddy, one patient per ambulance. You two are going to the same trauma hospital," the medic said.

"Not gonna happen. Coming with you."

The cardiac machine beeped, and the monitor showed a flat line, which drew the medic back to his patient. Jets wasn't waiting for an official invitation; he jumped in the back and shut the doors with anger.

At the ER bay, a team of nurses and a doctor took over caring for Amelia as soon as the ambulance arrived. On the trip, her status was touchy. They'd get a pulse, then lose it again a minute later. She had a large hematoma covering a large portion of her face, and by the time they got to the hospital, the hematoma had darkened in color. The medic speculated a chunk of plaster from the ceiling must have wacked her there and she was bleeding internally.

Jets wanted to go after her, but a police officer told him this entrance was for critical patients only, and because he was able to walk on his own,

Jets should go through the main doors, where a triage nurse would examine him.

His energy was drained, and his right arm was practically garbage. Jets didn't have it in him to fight with one more person, so he cooperated.

"Excuse me, got a lighter on you?" A guy with an unlit cigarette hanging to the side of his mouth called out to Jets in front of the hospital.

Jets held his eyes on him, glancing at him and his light-gray suit twice over. He looked out of place, and Jets didn't like that. The two CIA he chased down had run off after the explosion. *Were they already back?* That would be pretty ballsy of them.

"I don't smoke," Jets said, not continuing in.

"Good. I don't either." The guy tossed the cigarette in a trashcan. "Never have."

"Do I know you?"

"Of course not. A mutual friend sent me." The guy reached under his coat in his back belt.

Jets reacted by going for his Glock that was usually holstered on his shoulder. It was empty.

"Wow. Let's take it easy, cowboy." He drew out a wallet and flashed military credentials at Jets. He did it so quick and efficient that Jets couldn't read them.

"Your name is?"

"It makes no difference to you what my name is. You should know that I'm going to get the female transferred to the American base."

"Which one?" Jets wasn't letting up.

"Incirlik Air Base." The guy stepped in front of Jets and walked through the sliding doors and then turned back. "You coming in?"

A mass of people had shown up at the little waiting room. The news of the explosion had sent a shock wave through the capital. Any relative with a car had descended to the trauma center, searching for news whether their loved ones had made it out alive. The hospital was still not releasing any names, since the number of patients had significantly overwhelmed them.

When he first got in, Jets was repeatedly offered a checkup by a nurse. He refused repeatedly; however, he accepted the offer of aspirin for the pain, which was now wearing off. His adrenaline level must have been through the roof considering he barely felt anything at the café. Sitting on a bench, squeezed by a thousand people, the pain was agonizing.

A short guy in a medical coat and round glasses walked out from the surgical wing, and every person in that room hoped he was coming to get them. He called out to Jets and his new associate.

"Come with me." The doctor swiped his medical credentials and let them beyond the waiting room.

Jets cradled his arm, fighting to stay balanced on his feet. The doc hadn't told them they could pick up Amelia's body. Jets took that as she had a shot at recovery. They stepped into the elevator.

"We had to put the lady on a ventilator," the doctor told them.

A ventilator. It meant Amelia wasn't breathing on her own, because she couldn't. At another hospital, from his childhood, his own mother was also put on a vent, when she overdosed. Eight hours later, she was pronounced dead.

In that moment, Jets was overwhelmed with the strong odor of saline he'd remembered from the last place he saw his mom. *Déjà vu.*

"The blast had done extensive and I'm afraid severe internal damages to her," he said. "Do I understand correctly that it's your wish to move her to another location?"

The guy went ahead. "You would be correct."

"I advise against the transfer. But judging by the look in your eyes, you'll proceed forward with it."

They reached the ICU floor and the door opened. Jets and the so-called friend got off; the doctor stayed on. He cleared his throat, perhaps wondering whether he should warn Jets of Amelia's dire condition.

"Room 431. Last one on the right. My team is packing her to go." The doctor, his hands in the pockets of his medical coat, said grimly, "I wish you the best of luck. The young lady in that room sure could use it."

Jets drew in a breath. The image of Amelia in this hospital bed wouldn't fade away easily. A group of military American medics had asserted their control of the patient. They moved with efficiency and precision. Their razor-sharp focus gave him a sense of security that she'd be safe in their hands.

"You family?" A nurse in dark-green camo approached Jets with a pen and a clipboard.

"No. A friend."

"The flight is less than ten minutes, and we don't have an extra seat for you. I'm sorry."

"He can catch a ride with me." The guy stood somewhere behind Jets.

Suddenly, others were making decisions for Amelia and Jets, whose emotions were clogging his mind. As her hospital bed started to roll down the corridor, Jets asked himself again—*was his life worth living without Amelia in it?*

The guy in the gray suit cleared the checkpoints at Incirlik Air Base with a flash of his badge. Under different circumstances, Jets would have loved to figure out additional details surrounding this mysterious character, who dropped him off at the military hospital.

"Take care of yourself, son," he said to Jets before he sped off.

At the ICU nurse's station, Jets looked at a nurse, who read his expression.

"I was told you'd show up at some point. Have you seen a doctor?" Her Southern drawl was music to his ears.

"I'm fine," Jets lied. "Can you tell me how my friend is doing?"

"She's done with surgery. Beyond that, you'd have to speak with the girl's physician."

"Is it all right if I see her?"

"Briefly. Then I want you in a hospital gown so you can see a doctor too. That arm looks like it's about to fall off. Deal?"

Jets nodded acceptingly.

Amelia was moved to a new hospital bed, bigger than the one at the Turkish hospital. IV bags dripped copious amounts of narcotics into her system and then there was again the vent. Just the sight of it made Jets shudder. He pulled up a chair beside her and sat there, his eyes on the verge of crying.

"You must be the man who found her."

He looked up and saw a tall woman get closer. "I'm Dr. Desiree Walsh."

"How is she?"

"Critical, but stable. It was touch and go for a while, but she's a fighter, I can tell. Right now, she's in a medically induced coma to help her body heal. We won't know if there's any damage to her brain until we start weaning her off."

"Do you think...?"

"I think we need to wait and see. Her scans look promising. Has anyone looked at your shoulder, Agent?"

"I'm fine."

The doctor gave him a stern look. "No, you're not. I'll send a nurse in."

"I don't need anything."

"Agent, Amelia is receiving excellent care here. You saved her by finding her. Now let someone else help you."

She stormed out of the room. Her authority wouldn't be undermined by the special guest.

Night turned to day. Jets sat on that same chair by Amelia's side, leaving for only an hour to have his dislocated arm fixed and immobilized by a sling.

Her heart improved slightly, evident by the squiggly lines on the monitor; they were arriving at normal intervals, which the doctors believed was a sign of her body recovering. They were cautiously optimistic.

Jets turned his neck away from her bed to the shadow cast at the door. The face of the black soldier in a muscle shirt and cargo pants didn't ring a sliver of recognition in Jets's mind.

"Sir, I'm here to escort you to the conference room." He eyed Jets and Jets only. His eyes never shifted to Amelia, and that angered Jets.

"The fuck you are." He mouthed off.

"I have orders. I don't want to use force, but if I have to, I will."

That sounded like a threat, and Jets took it that way. He rose to his feet, shoving the chair with just the right amount of attitude. "Who sent you?"

"I'm not at liberty to discuss that with you, sir. Please come with me."

Dr. Walsh's high ponytail was barely visible behind the soldier's broad shoulders. That snapped Jets back to his settings. Reluctantly, he went along with the black guy, who led him to a conference room and left him there.

Jets's ass hadn't completely hit the hard seat of the chair, when a visitor walked in and slammed the door.

"What are you doing here?" Jets needed a second to comprehend that the chief of staff to the president of the United States stood in front of him and was not looking pleased.

"Post's in Turkey. Maybe for not too long."

"Amelia nearly died in that explosion. I got held up by two of my own. You know where she'd have been safe? Back in the States, in witness protection."

McKaine sighed, backtracking. "I'm sorry about Amelia. She was instructed not to go outside her hotel room." McKaine grabbed a chair and brought it closer to Jets. "She's in excellent hands."

"Why did she leave the hotel? Amelia knows better. She'd never put herself in harm's way, for Ava's sake."

The chief of staff knew the real reason Amelia had left. He also knew that telling Jets might be the last straw.

Jets wasn't letting it go. "I know you want Post dead. So do I. But before I do it, I want to know the truth of why Amelia was on the streets of Ankara."

With a measured dose of reservation, McKaine caved. "She was meeting with a man. Khalib Osmani. He's Ava's biological father."

The words actually hurt Jets more than McKaine had intended. He tried to warn him, but like a bull, Jets wasn't letting that one off the hook.

"If it means anything—Osmani wanted to warn Amelia that Post was dangerous. He had threatened their lives."

"That bastard that they saved from the rubble, is he Osmani?" Jets was fighting the grief inside his chest.

McKaine confirmed it with a nod.

"He cost her life. You telling me that fuck didn't know Post's boys were in town?"

"Osmani is a scumbag and he knows it, Agent. Do you really want to be the one who kills Ava's father? Do you really want to be the one who tells Amelia that?" McKaine put a hand on Jets's shoulder and let it rest there. "He deserves to die. Not from your gun."

Jets let his head hang low, fingers crossed between each other. He was done with it. It was obvious Amelia had dealt with a jerk in the past; he would be a complication she shouldn't worry about.

"Amelia would never be safe for as long as Post continues to breathe. He was strong running the CIA. In the underground world, he would be God." McKaine again, of course, was telling the truth.

"You know where he's at?"

"I do, and I have a plan." McKaine lapsed into a short pause. "You won't like it, Agent Jets."

68

McKaine was right. Jets didn't like the plan. His brow furrowed as he rationalized it in mind. He hated Post plenty—how couldn't he? But what McKaine was asking would make him a marked man for the rest of his life.

"There has to be another way." Jets pushed back. "With the redacted documents on the flash drive and Amelia's collaboration—Post could be prosecuted. When in jail, we can get to him."

"No." McKaine shook his head firmly. "You're the man for the job, and it has to be done the way I laid it out for you."

"And if I do this, take care of Post, then what? I can just walk away from it?"

"You'll never be able to walk away."

"I'd never be able to see Amelia? Ever again?"

"It's for the best. You have to stay away from her. Even without Post, your job has made you a big target. Do you see yourself with a family and being an active CIA agent?" McKaine said.

"It's doable."

"You can't be selfish, Gabriel. This is for your country. For Amelia." McKaine chuckled. "Some men just don't have a choice when duty calls them."

Jets grunted, wanting McKaine to spare him the lecture. He was painfully aware of the fact he had little say in the matter. His number was up, and duty called upon him one last time.

"I want to tell her good-bye," with a hardened expression, hiding his sorrows away, Jets demanded.

"Of course. I'll arrange that."

Dr. Walsh was expecting Jets when he walked in Amelia's room. To him, Amelia looked about the same; Walsh offered a kernel of good news.

"Her strength is returning. Really, what a transformation. This girl turned the corner around, and she did it fast," Walsh said.

"I don't follow. She's better?"

"Well, yes and no. She's in a stable condition where we can try to pull out the vent. It will give us a better idea if she can handle breathing on her own."

"And if she couldn't?"

"There are other options after that. You should remain positive. Ms. Sinclair might surprise you." Walsh tapped Amelia gently on the foot and left.

He wouldn't be by her side when they shut down the vent. He wouldn't be back tomorrow or the day after that. The thought of never seeing her was crushing and overwhelming. He leaned in, kissed the top of her head, and touched her skin with the tip of his fingers. Then he whispered words meant just for her.

"Please don't hate me for this," he uttered in her ear. "You've given me a reason to live, but to protect you—you need to believe that I'm dead." He'd imagined a different ending for them. "Amelia Sinclair, I've loved you since the moment I met you, hiding in that bathroom. Holding you in my arms was the best thing that has ever happened to me. You have to be strong for me and Ava. When the doctors come in, I need you to breathe. I need you to get healthy again. Can you do this much for me?"

Amelia lay still. Instead of her voice, he heard the beeping on the cardiac machine. He'd take it, as long as it meant she was alive.

McKaine escorted Jets out of the hospital to an idle car. He recognized the black soldier behind the wheel, staring at him with an even look.

"Who's that guy?"

"T.J. A SEAL—and by the way, he killed Monroe when you deserted your true target."

Jets had nothing to say back. If given the chance, he'd do it again; this time, however, he'd get to Amelia sooner. McKaine probably suspected that much; he didn't force the conversation further.

As the car sped off, McKaine in the back, Jets in the front passenger seat, T.J. ran the specs of the op with them.

"Post's hiding in the Lebanese embassy. Intel is he's planning on going underground. Egypt or Pakistan—he has ties in both places." T.J. glanced at Jets to see whether he was paying attention. "A team's in place, waiting for you in the embassy. You won't have problems getting to Post. When you finish the job, the team will extract you."

"Any questions?" McKaine was growing concerned with Jets's aloofness.

"Fair enough." T.J. had taken Jets's silence as an indicator he was mentally prepared. "Check the glove box."

Jets grabbed the Glock, checked the magazine, and pulled the top half of the gun toward him till he heard the familiar click, sealing a bullet in the chamber.

"The serial number has been shaved off. Not even a forensic tech with chemical testing can tell where this gun came from. Did the same with the bullets. You're all set," T.J. said, proud of his work.

T.J. parked the car at the bottom of a hill when they got to Ankara. The Lebanese embassy was nestled in a business section of a modern neighborhood with moderate traffic. Jets stuffed the gun in the back of his pants and covered it with a jacket. He had a few seconds to live as a man with a free will. Once he set foot out of this car, he'd spend his life running.

"This is good-bye then." Jets exited the car.

The other two stuck around for several more minutes after he had disappeared over the hill.

"You think he can pull it off?" T.J. said, twisting the wheel.

"Who—Jets or Osmani?"

"Osmani."

"Yeah, I do. He hates Post equally as Jets."

"What made you think it's a good idea to fess up to Jets that the woman was meeting with Osmani?"

"His love for her got Jets in the car, his jealousy of Osmani made him get out of the car, and his hate for Post will drive him to fire off that bullet."

"How you want to handle the female?"

"When it comes to Amelia, we leave it alone. She's been through hell, and when she wakes up, she still has a long road ahead of her."

They grew quiet for half a mile, before McKaine asked, "The Lebanese?"

"It was expensive getting them on board, and you'll have to come up with a lot more, once the news breaks that the CIA director was killed in their embassy—but they're willing to do it."

McKaine threw a nervous look at the clock on the dashboard. The next hour would be crucial for them.

69

Amelia woke up in a bed that wasn't hers and in a room that wasn't her bedroom. She felt tired, despite just waking, and groggy. She pushed her mind to recall a memory that could explain the current situation, but came back empty-handed. As she opened her mouth to call out, a stabbing pain in her throat slashed her, as if rupturing her vocal cords.

"Amelia, don't try to talk." A shadow of a man, whom she couldn't see well because the room was void of natural light, handed her ice chips. She gladly accepted. "Your doctor said your throat will be sore for a few extra days."

"Where...where?" She was permanently silenced by the fit of coughing that followed.

"You're still in Turkey. The Incirlik Air Base Hospital, precisely. You probably don't remember. The doc mentioned you might experience memory lapses. Do you know who I am?"

The shadow bent down closer to the beams of light on her hospital bed so she could see him clearer. Her eyes didn't hide the disappointment in them when she connected his face to a name. She had hoped to find another man by her bedside.

"Get some rest, child. I'll get the doctor," McKaine said.

As if her body knew she couldn't handle the stress at this point in her recovery, her left thumb pressed on a pump in her hand. The morphine drip dispensed a dose, which her body readily took. It drowned out her thoughts. Jets transformed into nothing more than a dream.

Out in the hallway by Amelia's room, McKaine received an update on Amelia's recovery from Dr. Walsh.

"Her vitals are getting stronger every day. I don't see a lot of miracles, but her recovery is one of them, McKaine," Walsh said, reassuring. "I can sign off on a hospital transfer back to the States as early as tomorrow. In my opinion, she'll be able to endure the ride."

"Her family would like that," McKaine told her, not taking his eyes off Amelia.

"One last thing, sir. A patient here, Bo Breeks, insists on visiting with Ms. Sinclair. He says they are close friends? On my end, that's not a problem. How would you like to go about it?"

"A visit with a loved one could be helpful to her. She'd need all the love they could give her."

When the doctor left, McKaine scurried to the TV screens in the visitors' lounge, playing the latest development in last night's breaking news. A body of a man was discovered in the Lebanese embassy in Ankara, and the person was finally identified. A US passport had been recovered from his personal belongings; the name matched to CIA's DCI Eugene Post. He'd died from an apparent gunshot to the head. Investigators were not ruling foul play yet. Of course the Lebanese officials were denying any connection or knowledge of the tragic event.

The cell in his pocket buzzed. He fished it out and answered it, alarmed. "Mr. President—I just watched the news." A short pause as PO-TUS spoke. "It looks that way. I agree, sir, O'Connolly has to bury this story." Another pause, then he resumed. "I'll be leaving tonight or tomorrow morning. According to the doctor, the female can be discharged to a US hospital. Certainly."

The line went dead, and McKaine held in his breath, having lied to the president. He'd broken an oath to his country, to the flag, and the US Constitution. It had to be done. *Then why did he feel this much guilt?*

• • • •

In the middle of the night, Amelia woke up, haunted by her dreams. She whimpered. A hand reached out and grabbed hers, letting her know all would be all right, eventually.

"Ame?"

Tears rolled down her face when she heard the familiar voice of her mentor, Bo Breeks. *The SEALs had saved them; did she know that?* Her memory was scrambled, chopped up in bits and pieces without a clear indication of days and weeks.

"Bo, I'm sorry." She scanned the room for the other man who'd been watching over her, though his presence was not as welcomed. "Did McKaine leave?"

"He's still around. Outside. Making calls."

"And Jets?" Her voice was peppered with undisguised despair.

"Who?"

"Gabriel Jets. Where is he?"

"Hold on. McKaine said you might ask for Jets if you woke up. I'll go get him."

He pushed himself off her bed, his lower body prisoner of a wheelchair, rolled to the door, and called McKaine in. She saw their shadow glow at the doorframe, wishing she'd never asked. McKaine's absent expression wasn't giving her any explanation of Jets's whereabouts. It had to be serious, though, by the way he stepped, then sat down on the edge of her bed.

"Do you want me to leave?" Bo asked McKaine.

"You better stay."

Even in her deep state of confusion, brain fogged by the drugs dripping in her blood stream by the IV bags, Amelia felt McKaine held back not telling her something important. He looked reluctant to her, contemplating ways to avoid this conversation. He went on. "It's with deep sadness that I have to be the bearer of bad news," he opened his rehearsed statement. "Jets was killed in the bomb blast in the same café they found you."

He had more to tell her, but nothing prepared him and Breeks for the gut-wrenching wail that she let out. It shattered their souls. No human should go through that much pain in a lifetime. It looked as if she were having a hard time breathing. Her face lost its color, and the cardiac machine hooked up to her heart went crazy with weird sounds.

"Breathe...breathe..." McKaine heard himself coach her, which made it worse.

The night nurse barged in, placing an oxygen mask over Amelia's face, who grew combative.

"Leave now," the nurse barked. "Code red. Get a cart in, STAT. She's going into V-tach."

Through the window in the hallway, McKaine witnessed the doctors shocking Amelia's heart to get it to beat again. Unable to stomach it, he turned his back on what was happening in that room.

Breeks was still watching, when he said, "I've never heard of Gabriel Jets. Who's he?"

• • • •

It took the doctors two more days to stabilize Amelia. On day three, against their medical wishes, she'd insisted on boarding the Boeing C-17, bound for Dover Air Force Base, transporting Jets's body. She sat by the flag-draped coffin, staring at it the entire flight.

Amelia had scanned through the closed investigation file of Jets's death. The photos showed a badly burned human. A part of her rejected that it was him. McKaine let her have the DNA test confirming with 81 percent certainty that Jets's blood was on that body.

What the file, the evidence, and the tests couldn't explain was her memory of Jets being in the hospital with her. She could hear his voice calling out to her in the night; she could feel his touch, laying alone in bed. Despite the doctors telling her that her brain had gone through a traumatic experience and it could play tricks on her, her heart told her those memories were real. She leaned in and kissed the top of his coffin.

"They're telling me you've died; then how come I feel you're alive? Will this feeling ever go away?"

McKaine called her personally at her home several days later. A tape had leaked to the media of DCI Post discussing a plot to blow up buildings in capitals across Europe. McKaine wanted to assure her—he was keeping her name away from the press. She waited for him to ask about Jets; his refusal to do so enraged her.

"You coming tomorrow?" she probed.

"Where?"

"To his funeral. It's tomorrow at 10 o'clock."

McKaine was silent, then reluctantly reminded her of the constraints associated with his attendance. "Jets was a CIA agent. The government can't acknowledge him publicly. His identity must be shrouded in secrecy. It's how his world operates."

• • • •

It was an ugly morning for a burial. Wet and bone-cold, miserable, like the handful of people who bothered to show up. Amelia held tight onto Ava's little hand. Although mourning a man she knew not that well, she loved him wholeheartedly.

Toward the last rows of the cemetery, Jets watched her through long-range binoculars, a shell of a man. Getting out of Ankara had been a sticky situation. First, he entered Serbia by bus with a fake ID, then crossed the Black Sea by boat to Russia. He made it to the States in the trunk of a car, operated by a man he'd met shortly before that at the Canadian border.

The sound of skidding tires in the mud alarmed him; Jets went for his gun. The back window of a town car rolled down, showing the face of a man he wished to never see again.

"Not a good day for a funeral, huh?"

"I thought you told her you wouldn't come?" Jets said.

McKaine flicked a look back at Jets. "I was in the neighborhood and thought I might find you here."

"What do you want?"

"Take a ride with me. It's starting to snow."

He didn't have a better place to be, and despite his anger toward the chief of staff, he'd kept his word to Jets and cared for Amelia. Jets climbed in the backseat with McKaine, stealing an eyeful of Amelia before he shut the door.

"You did well with Post," McKaine said. "I've had some time to think, and I've got a proposition for you."

"Let's hear it."

"Post had the right idea when he created the Band of Seven. I like the idea of a highly trained team of men who take care of business outside politically correct lines. The problem is that Post used the team for his own personal gain, which, of course, in the end, cost him. I think we can do it better." McKaine leaned in closer to Jets. "I want you to put together a new team and lead it. Your team will work on missions that the SEALs can't handle because of the politics on the Hill."

Jets chuckled. "Post isn't even cold in the ground, and yet, there's another ready to take his place and run the world with his own personal army of killers."

"We're the good guys, Gabriel. We're not like Post. We'll only use the team to benefit the country," McKaine insisted.

"Aren't you forgetting something?"

"What?"

"I'm already a dead man," Jets said, his tone sarcastic.

"That makes you the ideal candidate."

The town car dropped them off at an undisclosed location, when the snow started to fall hard outside. They walked in an empty lot resembling a hangar, where T.J. waited for them.

"Does this mean the spook's officially my boss?" T.J. busted their chops.

He extended his hand to Jets, who shook it, forging an agreement to sign on to McKaine's team. The moral lines for Jets had blurred, since Amelia was no longer his compass. Maybe if he killed all the men like Post, then he'd fill that void in his chest where his heart was once beating.

ABOUT THE AUTHOR

Jolene Grace grew up in Eastern Europe and has witnessed firsthand theregion's geopolitical makeover as well as the economical struggles of poverty faced by all, which is a prevalent theme in her writing.

She holds a Bachelor's Degree in Journalism and Broadcasting, which fueled her interest in politics. Jolene interned for CBS Evening News, working on the foreign desk at night time and has covered many wars, including the American/Iraq War.

A member of Mystery Writers of America and Sisters in Crime, Jolene makes her home in Massachusetts with her husband and children, where she writes full-time. *Going Dark* is her debut novel in her Gabriel Jets spy series.

CPSIA information can be obtained
at www.ICGtesting.com
Printed in the USA
BVHW072135210120
570028BV00002B/17/J

9 781643 970486